Readers love
E E MONTGOMERY

The Planet Whisperer

"If you're looking for a good science fiction novel, I highly recommend this one."

—The Novel Approach

Just the Way You Are

"In short, if you want a sweet love story and see that love is stronger than everything, then go ahead and get yourself your copy. You won't regret it."

—Chris McHart Reviews

"It is very emotional and poignant."

—MM Good Book Reviews

Ordinary People

"Much like Vinnie and James, I am convinced that my feelings (about the book, at least…) must be love. I recommend that you read this delightfully different and charming story!"

—Prism Book Alliance

"The book is well written, and it was a very quick read…"

—My Fiction Nook

By E E Montgomery

Between Love and Honor • The Courage to Love
Ordinary People
The Planet Whisperer
Warrior Pledge
What About Him

JUST LIFE
Just His Type
Just Like a Date
Just in Time
Just the Way You Are

Published by Dreamspinner Press
www.dreamspinnerpress.com

WARRIOR PLEDGE

E E MONTGOMERY

Published by
DREAMSPINNER PRESS

5032 Capital Circle SW, Suite 2, PMB# 279, Tallahassee, FL 32305-7886 USA
www.dreamspinnerpress.com

ISBN: 978-1-63477-760-5
Digital ISBN: 978-1-63477-761-2
Library of Congress Control Number: 2016913025
Published October 2016
v. 1.0

Printed in the United States of America
∞
This paper meets the requirements of
ANSI/NISO Z39.48-1992 (Permanence of Paper).

This one is for Lois. She loves cats.

Acknowledgments

I DO the imagining and the writing, but as with all my books, publication wouldn't be possible without the help and support of a lot of people.

The Belles have been working with me on this project for a long time, never giving up on encouraging me to imagine better, show better, write better. Thank you, ladies.

Kristen, with her uncanny ability to see exactly what's missing and how it needs to be fixed, helped me enormously with the last major rewrite of this work. Without you, I'd probably still be sitting there chewing my nails and whining that it wasn't working.

The editing team at Dreamspinner, with their unfailing patience and professionalism, show me how my work can be lifted from finished to publishable. I can't express my gratitude enough.

THALAZAR

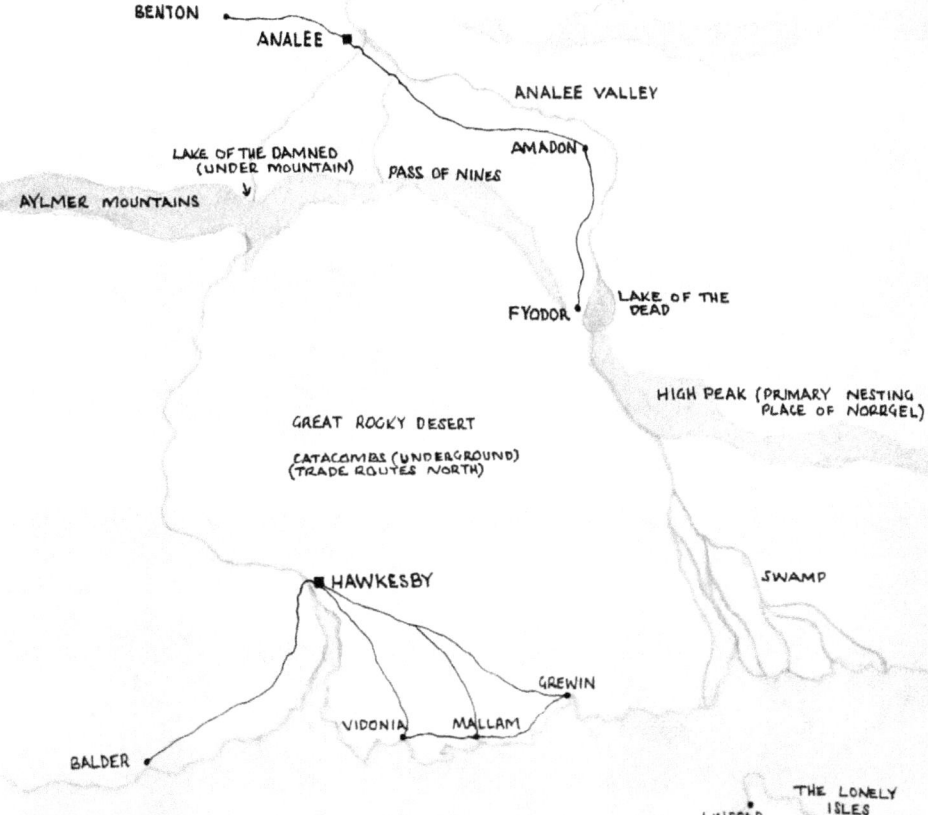

THE ICY WASTES

THE SEVEN MOUNTAINS   ■ BARTHES

BENTON •
    ANALEE ■
                        ANALEE VALLEY

LAKE OF THE DAMNED   AMADON •
(UNDER MOUNTAIN)   PASS OF NINES
    ↓
AYLMER MOUNTAINS

                        FYODOR •   LAKE OF THE
                                    DEAD

                                HIGH PEAK (PRIMARY NESTING
                                    PLACE OF NORRGEL)

GREAT ROCKY DESERT

CATACOMBS (UNDERGROUND)
(TRADE ROUTES NORTH)

                                            SWAMP
■ HAWKESBY

                        • GREWIN
        VIDONIA   MALLAM
BALDER •
                                        THE LONELY
                                            ISLES
GREAT SOUTHERN OCEAN   LINSPAR •

ECM

THE WARRIOR PLEDGE

At the end, the world will fail
Threads consuming the land
Brittle band, cracking hand
   Nothing left in the pail

With the key they will come
Ruby red in bright of day
Warriors four show the way
   To split the stone in one

Loss follows silver search
Born of death and tragedy
Alone yet strong he will be
To destroy much of worth

One Pure, prophecy revoked
One Great Heart Farseeing
One Changeling fooling wing
One Shining Silver from Rock

Dangers untold test the damned
Farseeing falls, life released
Water brings eternal peace
For only then will evil calm

And trusting only his own
Hold to reason's hard edge
Man must await the Pledge
To find the way home alone

Together traitor and thin man
Bring a sorrow true
Course found, the four break through
Dead man and kin unplanned

Joined in peace and battle they merge
Linking ever hearts and minds
Four become one; two moons rebind
And as one will lead the purge

Silver brings them all again
In loyalty comes trials unknown
Four blended, a choice to own
Silver Bonds under ice and rain

Myths alive, legends return
Raining gold upon the land
Hundreds follow adventures grand
Dragons clasp amber's dark burn

Deep in the Pass of Nines
In dark of night, hand on right
Against all odds feeling might
Silver strength and black arise

Anguished grief defeats entire
Crumbling tablet forms of stone
Amidst melted walls of bone
In the sky fly reborn fire

Ally, enemy, colleague, friend
Charged protection overhead
Loss and laughter make your bed
Support and help always lend

At the end, the world will fail
Threads consuming the land
Brittle band, cracking hand
Nothing left in the pail

—extract from the Warrior Pledge, prophecy of the Mafdeti, natural inhabitants of the planet Thalazar.

1.
WARRIOR PLEDGE

THE BREEZE dropped as the sun peeped between the mountain peaks on the other side of the valley. A shiver ran across Checa's shoulders, and with a thought he deepened his slide from human to were and thickened the fur at his ruff. To the north the trees that followed the river were dry and brittle, more than half of them already dead. Radiating out from that line were patches of darkness and light, a camo pattern of toxic sludge and severe drought. Even this high up, he could smell the rot that had taken over the valley. The farms provided a patchwork of gray and brown, sliced unevenly by the sludge emanating from the river systems. Smoke curled from a few farmhouse chimneys, but most lay abandoned, their inhabitants having long given up trying to eke a living from the dying land.

To the east the sky grew dark as the norrgel took flight and headed south. Checa blinked to enhance his sight and watched the wings rise and fall, the deadly threads trailing from wings and tail, waving gracefully in the movement. Far below the first horn blew, its familiar sound picked up and echoed by other watchers throughout the valley.

Wings up. Time to find shelter or die.

Checa had never known a time when a norrgel watch wasn't needed.

A parrot squawked. He closed his eyes against the growing light, and deep in his soul, the two moons, Makai and Nayeli, moved inexorably closer in their ages-old battle for supremacy. Another sign the prophecy was coming true.

Checa refused to be part of it. No matter what, he wasn't going to be the hero who would save the world. He wouldn't let his star rise on the back of another's death.

His be-damned eyes had turned bright silver when he was sixteen, the moment he'd killed the Bastard. The judge had found out, proclaimed Checa the Silver Shining from Rock, overturned his conviction, taken him to the palace, and put him with the guards for training. None of his fellow trainees had believed he was the one. Checa was a gutter rat from the slums, a murderer. He knew how to fight, though, so that's what he did. Every time another guard challenged him.

In the ravine below, a flock of parrots took flight. Checa shook his head and huffed in irritation. Even with fifteen years training behind him, Heath could never move anywhere quietly. Checa checked the norrgel, but they were still flying south, their screeches rising every time they found something to hunt.

Checa had killed for the second time when he was eighteen. It was an accident while training in the field, but his eyes had changed to silver again. No one challenged him to a fight after that, except when forced to for training. For a long time, no one spoke to him. Except Heath.

"Checa!"

His name carried in the still air, and an involuntary smile overtook him at the joy in Heath's voice. Checa's muscles twitched, wanting to move, to go down and meet him, see the morning light grow as it reached Heath's features. Just that one sight would be enough to make Checa's day complete, even if it hadn't yet really begun.

He returned to his human form and counted his breaths to ensure he remained in place, sitting cross-legged on the platform. There'd been an unusual vibration in the air during the night, an unsteadiness growing louder the closer the moons moved, and even though he wasn't a Seer, he had to determine what it meant. As Captain of the Guard, it was his duty to keep his people safe. Whether they liked or trusted him made no difference.

"Checa!"

Heath was closer now, the sound of him crashing through the brush a rhythmic counterpoint to his steady footfalls on the leaf-strewn ground. Checa allowed his posture to relax and straightened his legs. He shifted forward so his balance would be stronger, wiped the new smile from his face, and waited.

Heath burst into the clearing like a new spring bloom and launched himself at Checa. Checa braced his legs against the edge of the platform, opened his arms, and caught the younger man as he flew to him. They landed flat on the platform, the bare skin of their chests fusing, Heath's sweat soaking into Checa's chest hair and becoming his own. Checa *oomph*ed as his head hit the stone and Heath's landing knocked the air from his lungs, but he didn't release his hold, and his smile broke free again.

Some days this was all he had. This was the best of everything he had.

He wrapped his arms around Heath more securely.

"Sorry," whispered Heath as he snuggled his head under Checa's collarbone.

Checa ran his fingers through Heath's long, tangled hair, relishing the touch of smooth skin at the back of his neck. "You've been running," he said as he loosened another knot. He lifted the now-smooth strand and released it. It fell like a waterfall of gold and bronze, copper and chocolate in the strengthening light.

"I had to." Heath pressed his lips against Checa's chest and inhaled before relaxing in a boneless heap. "It's faster."

"And you just had to race up here to snuggle?"

Heath nodded, then chuckled. "I don't think I'll get any more time alone today. And snuggling with you is always worth racing for."

"So what had you in such a tearing rush?" Checa continued gently smoothing Heath's hair, not in any hurry to break the contact he craved, but Heath bounced up to sit squarely over Checa's groin. Checa groaned at the change in pressure and punched his hips up. Their loincloths prevented direct contact, but Heath's every ridge and bulge pressed against Checa and raised his interest.

Heath grinned. "Yeah, that too, but you've got to hear this. It's happening, Checa! It's finally happening." Heath bounced in his excitement.

Checa grabbed Heath's hips and lifted him off, ignoring the pouting scowl he got in return. Once they were seated on the platform, with dawn washing its gentle light over them and the soft breeze returning, he raised an eyebrow and waited.

"Stop it." Heath slapped Checa's arm. "I'm not some test animal. You don't have to experiment to see how long I stay silent."

"Clearly not long. So tell me what's happening."

Heath leaned forward and pressed his lips to Checa's neck. Checa groaned at the light suction. Unable to resist he dragged Heath back on top of him and gripped his asscheeks, pulling him tight against him. Heath groaned. They wouldn't be doing any more talking for a while.

Times like this, when they were alone with little likelihood of anyone discovering them together, were rare. Checa slipped his hand between them and pushed their loincloths out of the way. Heath's solid, hot cock pressed against his stomach. As Checa wriggled his hand, Heath lifted just enough to align their cocks, then pressed down again.

Checa wrapped his arms around Heath, not letting him slip or slide just yet. "Let me feel you," he whispered.

"If I could, I'd brand you."

Checa stilled.

Heath huffed an irritated sigh. "I know you won't bond with me, Checa. I know my mother would never give her approval. But none of that changes the fact that I would do so in a minute. I'd have you wear my brand so everyone would know you're mine."

As Heath spoke, Checa writhed, unable to remain still at the possessive note in Heath's voice or the picture he painted of the two of them bound forever. He slipped his hand between them again and grasped their cocks together, squeezing before setting up a rhythm that would bring them both to the brink.

Heath lifted up until he was sitting on Checa's thighs again, his hands between them, slipping in the precome as he fisted Checa's cock hand over hand. They stroked together, in tandem, their gasping breaths loud in the quiet of the early morning.

"Come for me, Checa. Let me see your eyes when you come," rasped Heath.

The words were enough to set Checa off. With effort he forced his eyes to stay open as he shot stream after stream of milky liquid on his chest and stomach.

"Yes," hissed Heath as he leaned forward, his gaze locked on Checa's as he convulsed in the throes of pleasure. After a few frozen seconds, Heath collapsed, boneless, on top of Checa and snuggled his face in the crook of his neck.

"I think this is your favorite position," said Checa once his breathing began to even out.

"Any way I get to touch you is my favorite." Heath huffed, relaxation slowing his words. "I love the way your eyes change when you come. They're so bright and beautiful."

Checa resumed rifling through Heath's hair, sifting the soft strands over his shoulders and back. Only Heath thought his very ordinary green-gray was beautiful. "Tell me why you came tearing up here."

Heath jumped off, fixed his loincloth, and bounced around the clearing. "You've been summoned by the Matriarch."

Fuck. They'd been found out. Heath's mother had made it clear that Checa wasn't good enough for her only son. He was going to be banished, or worse. The roaring red pain flashed through him and he hunched his shoulders and allowed the Change to take him.

As fur grew across his shoulders and his muscles bulged underneath, his incisors lengthened and his hips and knees articulated. He could run on all fours like this, in his were form, or he could continue to full cat mode. He could run faster like that. Faster and longer.

Checa jumped off the platform and flexed his arms to prepare for the full shift, only to find Heath in front of him. Scowling. Angry.

"What the fuck are you doing?" Heath shoved hard at Checa's chest, making him stumble backward. "Change back right now."

Heath. *His* Heath. Checa deflated. As his breath left him in surrender, so too did his muscles reduce and his fur diminish. The sting of it popping back beneath his skin made him shiver. Heath was right. A leader, especially a military leader, couldn't run when something went wrong. A good leader would stay and listen. A good soldier would stay and fight.

He crossed his arms across his chest and gifted Heath with a scowl of his own. "Why does your mother want to see me?"

Heath huffed out a frustrated breath and looked over the valley, his jaw tight. Finally he closed his eyes in a long blink and breathed deeply. When he opened them again, his temper was restored even if his eyes didn't hold the same joy they had a few minutes before.

"The summons is from the Matriarch. If my mother found out about us, she wouldn't hide behind her job. She'd scoop my balls out with a spoon and send you to the norrgel nests."

Checa sighed. "You're right. I'm sorry. I'm just—"

Scared.

"I know. Me too. But, Checa—" Heath's eyes glowed with renewed excitement. "—it's coming. The signs are all there. It's time for the Warrior Pledge! The Matriarch has called the Seer to the city."

That's what that vibration was.

Checa jammed his fists onto his hips and looked out over the Analee Valley. The Descendants lived there now, those born of the aliens that had landed a millennium ago and taken what they wanted—but once it had been the hunting grounds for the Mafdeti. If the Warrior Pledge worked, it would be again, but Checa wouldn't live to see it. The breeze dropped along with his hopes. If Heath was right and it truly was time for the Warrior Pledge, then he had to say good-bye. He'd studied the legends and knew only one of the four would survive. As Silver Shining from Rock, it probably wouldn't be him.

"Checa, do you know what this means?" Heath was so close behind him, Checa could feel him vibrating with anticipation. He turned to look at the only man he would ever love. "You're Silver Shining from Rock. You're the only one who has the eyes, and now that it's time, that means it's you." Heath reached up and cradled Checa's face. "It's you!"

Checa had endured the fascination with his eyes since he was sixteen. He preferred disbelief. No one else had silver eyes. Everyone else in every pride throughout the mountain ranges both north and south of the Analee Valley had yellow or green or, in the case of the ruling families, brown. Like Heath's. Checa's were a common green, as pale as sun-dried grass, except when he killed.

"Checa?"

Checa ignored Heath as much as he could with him standing so close, his warmth seeping into his back. He continued to look out over the valley. "What signs have you seen?"

Heath sighed, a contented sound that let Checa know he'd been waiting to be asked. "The Chronicles detail a series of events that lead up to the Pledge. The norrgel are nesting earlier this year. Their numbers are double what they were five years ago. The Crystal River has dried up, releasing only a toxic sludge that's threatening every life in the valley." He grabbed Checa's elbow and turned him away from a wisp of smoke at the far end of the valley. "I had a dream," Heath said significantly. "Last night, I had a dream."

"You've dreamed before. What was special about this one?"

"There were four in the dream, just as the Pledge describes." He crossed his arms and lifted his chin smugly. "And when I woke, I was standing by the window."

"The window?"

Heath nodded. "The one that looks over the valley." He grasped Checa's hands and squeezed them. "I was in Pledge stance, Checa. Pledge stance. You know what that means, don't you?"

If it was anyone else, Checa could ignore them. Not Heath. Heath came from a long line of rulers and Seers. If he told you he had a dream, you'd damn well better listen. He looked down the valley again. "So… the Warrior Pledge."

"Yes! And I'm one of them." Heath bounced on the balls of his feet in his excitement. "And so are you."

"No, you're not." Checa gestured to his eyes. "I have to be, but you're not going to be involved."

The Farseeing dies.

"Bullshit. I've known since I met you that I'm the Great Heart Farseeing."

"You were eight. You couldn't know anything that young." Checa increased the derisive tone in his voice. He had to get Heath to accept he couldn't be part of this. He needed to speak to the Matriarch and get her to forbid Heath to go. "And why would you think you're the Farseeing? Because you had a dream?"

Heath's face changed so rapidly Checa couldn't keep up with the emotions flitting across his features. Hurt, certainly—again—but also anger. He saw that one clearly a split second before Heath hauled back and let fly, his fist hitting squarely on Checa's jaw. Blood flooded Checa's mouth as he bit his tongue, and he staggered back several steps before he found his footing again.

"Fuck you, Checa," panted Heath, his eyes glowing wetly in the bright morning light. "Fuck you," he whispered.

Heath turned and trudged back down the mountain. Checa waited just long enough to acknowledge he was a bastard, then ran after him.

"Heath! Wait!" He stumbled over tree roots on his dash down the hill. Heath must have shifted as soon as he was out of sight to be so far ahead already. Checa crashed between some trees, back onto the rugged path they used to reach the top. In front of him was a large, growling cat, his tawny fur ruffled aggressively. "I'm sorry," Checa panted. "I shouldn't have said that. It's not true."

The air wavered and the cat's features blurred and shortened as his body rose. Checa sighed in relief as Heath allowed his body to flow through the stages from cat to were to man. He smiled at the graceful Change. "I love watching you do that."

Heath strode toward him, fists clenched. "Why do you always do that?"

The smile evaporated, and Checa took a step backward.

Heath shoved at Checa's chest. "You're my m—my best friend. Friends are supposed to support each other, not lie."

"Heath—"

"Shut up! What is it? It's okay to spend every day with me but it's not okay to acknowledge I might have a future outside this claustrophobic warren of caves? It's okay to fuck me, but only if you make me feel worthless at every opportunity?"

"You're not worthless."

"Then why do you always tell me I am?"

"Heath." Checa tried reason. "The Warrior Pledge is for warriors, not Seers."

"I *am* a fucking warrior, Checa. You trained me yourself. Remember? There's not one fucking soldier I can't flatten if I want to, except maybe you. Don't you dare try to tell me I'm not a fucking warrior."

"You're a Seer."

"Yes, I'm a Seer. What the fuck do you think being a Seer means? It means I'm farseeing. I'm a fucking farseeing fucking warrior! How long since you recited the fucking Warrior Pledge, Checa? Or are you just going to ignore that because you don't think I'm capable of being the Farseeing one?" He punched Checa's shoulder. Checa rolled with it. "You think being a Seer is easy? I've worked fifteen years to get where I am: a Warrior Seer. All you had to do was kill the bastard who murdered your brother for your fucking silver eyes to come out, but *I'm* the one not good enough?" Heath's voice wavered and tears welled in his eyes. "Fuck you, Checa." He angrily brushed the tears away and reached to shove Checa again, but he didn't make contact. The fight went out of him: his shoulders dropped, his hands unclenched, the breath left him in a rush. "Fuck you," he whispered again.

Then he turned and ran down the path.

"Heath," Checa whispered. "It's not you who isn't good enough." The gusty sigh that left him as Heath disappeared into the forest took most of the joy he'd been feeling just a few minutes before. Killing Warden wasn't the only thing the Bastard had done. It wasn't the only reason Checa had spilled the man's guts over the basement floor. After what the Bastard had done to Checa, Checa would never be good enough for Heath. But he'd do whatever it took to protect him, both from the knowledge of what Checa had done and from the dangers inherent in the Warrior Pledge.

He followed Heath down the mountain, slowly, no longer interested in watching the new day's light awaken the lands.

A few months before

JUN PUSHED farther back between the rocks as the men in the tan uniforms walked by. Imperial soldiers on patrol. That wasn't unusual, but this was the fourth patrol in this area this week. At least Fan was with them. He grinned at the thought of what he'd do to his lover when he finally got him away from his unit.

The soldiers clung to the thin shadows around the rocky outcropping. Like twists of dust, they slipped between the tall columns of stone into the only shelter from the unforgiving sun.

As the heel of the last soldier disappeared around the outcropping of boulders, a shadow caught Jun's attention. He moved his head slightly, not enough to let the hidden man know he'd noticed him. An Exile, the detritus of the land, criminals and madmen the lot of them. When the man stopped and slipped between two nearby boulders, Jun edged closer, glad he was in were form. A thick black wedge of fur ran from the back of his neck to the crack between his buttocks, thinned and faded to gray as it wrapped around to his stomach. The fur darkened and thickened again on forearms and shins before thinning to nothing over his large square hands and feet. It helped him blend with the landscape. With luck, Jun would be able to move past the man's hiding place and follow the soldiers without being seen.

Then the fool moved and Jun knew the man had spotted him. There was nothing for it now but to engage and see if he could get some answers as to why he was there, following an Imperial patrol.

Jun sidled up against the rock, keeping to the slim midday shadows, his focus partly on the soldiers ahead and partly on the sky, watching for norrgel.

As he approached the crevice where the Exile was hiding, the man grabbed his arm and dragged him into the gap between the boulders. Jun reacted, swinging the Exile around and pressing his forearm hard against the man's throat. The Exile gripped Jun's arm, his breathing harsh in the confined space.

"What the fuck are you doing? Imperial soldiers kill people like you," the Exile croaked through the pressure against his throat.

Jun tensed. Why would the Exile be concerned about a Mafdeti? At least he was smart enough not to try to fight. Jun, like most Mafdeti, was a massive, heavyset man, his body rippling muscle and strength. He fought to win or die, and he fought dirty. The Exile didn't stand a chance.

Jun relaxed his muscles so that all the Exile would feel under his fingertips was warm, soft fur. He waited while the man sucked in a tight, relieved breath.

"The patrol has been here since dawn." The man tilted his head so he could see around the edge of the rock and out to the desert beyond. Jun knew there wasn't much to see, just white and charcoal on black, the dark shapes shimmering in the heat, the landscape stripped of color in the noonday sun.

"That's not a regular patrol," Jun murmured as he crowded behind the Exile.

"I know. They're searching for something. Or someone."

Jun cursed and released the man, stepping farther back into the shadows. Had they found out about his visits? It was the only explanation he could think of, though he always approached the city from a different direction and never stayed in one spot long enough to be detected.

"Shit. How could they have found out?" the Exile cursed.

Every molecule in Jun's body jumped to high alert. "They're after *you*?"

"It's possible."

"Because you're an Exile or…?" He left the question hanging. He couldn't think of any reason a lone Exile would be in this area, unless…. "Are there others out there?" Drett. Was he going to have to spend the entire day rescuing careless bloody Exiles?

"No." The man offered no further explanation.

Jun pushed farther back between the rocks. It would be relatively easy for the soldiers to find them. It wasn't as if there were a lot of hiding places out there in the desert. Not on the surface anyway, but Jun had another agenda. Something more urgent. "Are you going to stay squashed in here all day?" His voice rumbled through the black hair hanging down the Exile's neck.

The man shivered and took a small step forward, putting space between their bodies. He turned his head and whispered, "If we're going to be that intimate, you'd better know my name. I'm Fisher."

Jun looked closely at Fisher. At first he thought the man wore camouflage makeup but then realized it was the pigmentation of his skin that made him look mottled with patches of smooth ivory and darkest chocolate.

Fisher moved forward a little more to look out at the desert, then back to Jun. "I'd rather be stuck here all day than dead."

Jun smiled, just the corners of his lips lifting, and leaned back against the wedge of rock behind him. "So, what are we going to do to pass the time?"

Fisher scowled and slid down the rock to squat in the sand. There was something not quite right about the Exile, but Jun couldn't work it out.

Why would he be this close to the city and alone, unless he was looking for something… or someone? Fisher had been following the patrol, not trying to avoid it. Jun didn't need to know. He had an appointment to keep, and he needed to warn Fan they were being followed. He just had to make sure that he and his lover weren't caught in the cross fire, whatever it was.

Fisher looked up at him and smiled a smile that would fool Jun's mother. "I don't know what you have planned, but I'm going to sleep for a while, then leave." He lowered his buttocks onto the sand but kept his feet under him, like a soldier, ready to rise quickly. Then he closed his eyes and ignored Jun.

After several minutes, Fisher's breathing slowed and the muscles in his neck and back relaxed. His head dropped forward, cheeks landing on his knees. The pressure forced his mouth open and saliva dribbled out. Time passed and Fisher settled more comfortably into position. Jun wasn't fooled Fisher was asleep, but he was almost impossible to track once he was out of sight, so he moved past slowly, barely brushing Fisher's hair, thanking the Elders he could move so quickly and silently.

Within seconds he was back in the scorching sun, following the patrol. He kept his steps deliberate and silent as he closed the distance between himself and the last man in the Imperial patrol.

The slip and crunch of a sandy body sliding against rock was the only warning Jun had before a tan-clothed arm shot out between boulders and dragged him into a small area. As Jun scented his mate, he swiftly changed to fully human form.

"Thank the Elders you managed to get away. I've been waiting all day." Jun grabbed Fan's sandy brown hair and kissed him roughly.

"We're on extended patrol." Fan was panting, whether from his flight to Jun or from arousal, Jun didn't care. He was there and that was all that mattered. "There've been intruders spotted." Jun fumbled at Fan's belt; the buckle clinked as it released. A low groan from Fan covered the sounds. "We can't…. The others."

"I'm so desperate for you it'll be over before they notice you're not right behind them." Jun dropped to his knees, nuzzling Fan's groin as he tugged his clothing out of the way. Within seconds his mouth closed around the warm, silky skin of Fan's cock. Jun sucked in a deep breath as he tasted him. It was like coming home. There was no fragrance, no taste that brought more peace to him or that he craved more.

Fan groaned, the sound muffled as he shoved his hand over his mouth. Jun sucked harder, fondled Fan's balls, and tugged gently.

"Jun, wait, it's too much. I'm going to…."

Jun moved his fingers behind Fan's balls to the delicate skin beyond. Frantic thrusts jammed against the back of his throat as warm liquid flooded his mouth. Above him, Fan keened like an animal in pain.

"Yes," Jun hissed around Fan's cock.

"Jun!"

Behind the cry sand slid against sand. Jun stilled, listening closely, his own need to come forgotten at the threat of discovery.

"What is it?"

He rose to his feet and drew his mate into a quick hug. "Nothing. It's fine. You'd better get back before they miss you."

"Two days?" Fan's smooth tenor sounded gravelly and breathless.

"I'll be here." Jun dragged him into his arms, relishing any time he could get with him, wishing things were different and they could be together all the time. He pressed closer, letting his gentle kisses tell Fan what he needed to know. "Watch out for a tail."

Fan's eyes narrowed, but he nodded his understanding. He righted his clothing and walked away, sand crunching against rock as he headed through the maze of boulders and back to his unit. Jun watched him go, leaning back against the rock, waiting to make sure they hadn't been discovered by Fan's teammates and listening for the man on the other side of the boulder.

2.
THE CALL TO ADVENTURE

THE ECHO of the last of the horns tracking norrgel movements faded with the light. Checa made sure the night guards were in position around the village, then began the long climb to the Matriarch's palace, relishing the flex and burn in his muscles.

Jun, Checa's second-in-command, joined him as he left the central quad. Checa scrunched the piece of paper confirming Jun was also summoned and continued his climb. Jun had made his opinion of having a commoner such as Checa in command very clear. Checa had worried the nobleman would actively work against him, but he hadn't seen any overt signs of it recently. Jun's recalcitrance bordered on insubordination but never crossed the line. Checa decided within a few months of being appointed Captain of the Guard that Jun preferred to be close to him; whether to query all his commands or to ensure he didn't contaminate any of the other noble soldiers, Checa wasn't sure. It made for a tension-filled day. Every day.

The one time Checa attempted to demote Jun, the Seer had stepped in and overruled him. Having an obviously hostile soldier under his command had divided Checa's force from the first day. The men had only accepted him once they'd seen his eyes change to silver. It had taken a couple more years after that for them to trust Checa as their leader. Even Jun had come around eventually, professionally, at least.

"When do you think you'll leave?" asked Jun.

Checa missed a step at the unexpected question. The tension behind his eyes had built during the day; Checa knew the Matriarch would feel it too. It was time for the Warrior Pledge, and Checa could do nothing about it. He needed to speak to Heath, to get him to understand that neither of them could be a part of it. It was the only way to keep Heath alive.

"I'm going to wash," he said to Jun. "I'll see you at the meeting." He morphed to full cat form, left the village and Jun behind, and ran to the water hole where he and Heath met to end their day. He changed back to man form as his paws touched the first of the soft sand, but the pool was empty, the sand pristine, and the waterfall fell undisturbed. Heath wasn't there.

With a pained roar, Checa ran into the water and dove. He stayed under until he was light-headed, then pushed off the sandy bottom and broke the surface with a gasp. Their cache of cleansing sand was in its place behind the waterfall, so he washed and brushed the grime off his loincloth before continuing on to the palace.

One of Checa's men, on guard rotation at the palace, met him at the door. The entry hall was empty of the usual retinue of guards and servants, the silence heavy. "Whatever they're expecting, sir, it's big." Talon leaned forward conspiratorially. "The Matriarch is wearing a hat and offered the Seer a drink."

Fuck. Not a hat. "Make sure someone's available to get the Seer home safely afterward and water his drinks down if you can arrange it." It was the only way to make sure the old man didn't end up in the infirmary with alcohol poisoning again.

The palace entry shone with glossy petrified-wood floors and polished granite walls. Its golden gleam was a permanent reminder of where he'd come from. His childhood home had been mud bricks set atop a sandstone foundation, and most of the rooms had a packed dirt floor. Around him hung portraits of the matriarchal family. Heath's sisters' lives were recorded in yearly portraits, up to and including their Bondings and the births of their children. The most recent image of Heath was from when he was eight, shortly before Checa had met him. There'd be no more portraits of Heath until he bonded, and that would only be to record the perpetuation of the matriarchy.

"You're cutting it fine, Checa." Heath leaned against the wall outside the throne room, looking relaxed and at ease.

Checa looked past Heath's studied nonchalance to his reddened eyes, firm lips, and tight jaw. Fuck. He'd really hurt him. Before he had a chance to fix what was wrong between them, the doors to the Matriarchal Court opened.

"I don't need to meet with the Seer. There's nothing he can say that would convince me to be a part of this." If Checa refused to be part of it, Heath couldn't be either, and he'd be safe. He turned to leave, but Heath pulled him back.

"Stop being a stubborn idiot, Checa. The Seer has called the meeting. The Matriarch has ordered you to attend. What are you going to say?"

Fuck. "I'm not changing my mind, Heath. I'm not going to be involved and neither are you." The only way Checa could keep Heath alive was to make sure they both stayed well clear of the whole thing.

Heath rolled his eyes and dragged Checa into the large throne room. The Matriarch sat on her throne of white granite, the seat and back padded in sunshiny yellow brocade. Her clothing, tan knee-high boots, butter-yellow leather trousers, and a mandarin-colored thigh-length overcoat worn over a high-necked ivory shirt, made her blend with the furniture. She wore a vibrant red satin top hat, perched precariously on her flowing blonde curls. Unlike most of the Mafdeti, who lost all clothing except for loincloths woven from their own fur, the Matriarch's clothing changed with her when she took her cat form. Most of it anyway. If there was a need for her to go full cat, her hat would be left behind because the colors didn't match. Checa had spent a number of his early training years searching for hats left behind when the Matriarch changed forms. He couldn't blame her for wanting to wear something that wasn't yellow, and he supposed a hat was the best choice if she didn't want to change back to human missing half her outfit.

She glared at Checa as he entered the white and gold room and bowed to her.

The tapestries adorning the walls along both sides of the long room wavered as the door snapped closed. Jun and Talon walked purposefully to a cluster of chairs ranged along the wall to the Matriarch's left.

Silently the Matriarch flicked her fingers toward Seer Pretto, indicating this was his audience.

Seer Pretto was an impressive figure, albeit a slightly ridiculous one. His nearly seven feet tall, rail-thin person stood regally next to a sofa to the right of the Matriarch. Checa remembered a time when Pretto wore only the traditional loincloth of the Mafdeti, but in recent years he'd taken to wearing a long, beaded caftan of deep purple velvet. Beneath the heavy fabric peeped glossy magenta shoes. A glass filled with red liquid stood on a low table beside him, and Checa breathed a sigh of relief.

Juice, not alcohol.

It was Pretto's eyes that drew Checa in. They were a rich walnut, at once bottomless and impervious, and saw everything. Checa had avoided speaking to Seer Pretto as much as he could since the old man announced Checa was the Silver Shining from Rock and overturned his conviction. Since that first time, when Checa's eyes still glowed silver after killing the Bastard, he rarely looked directly at Pretto. The Seer probably expected to see silver, but Checa's eyes were green-gray… most of the time.

If it was Pretto's eyes that drew Checa in, it was his hair that kept his attention. The old man had a bald swathe from his forehead to the crown of his head. Most of his remaining hair remained long and luxurious, vibrant red threaded with silver—except for the ring around the bald spot. That had been cropped and gelled to stand up in an arching curve over his smooth scalp until it looked like he had a fiery red heart sitting atop his head.

"Matriarch," said Pretto without so much as glancing in her direction, "if I might have a few moments with our captain?"

Heath's mother nodded, her hat wobbling precariously with the motion, then settled deeper into her seat.

Pretto motioned for Checa to accompany him to the other end of the throne room. Heath kept his position one step behind and to Checa's left.

Checa's hair prickled at his nape. *No!* He wanted to scream his denial, refuse to be the focus of the old man's attention, but he didn't. Pretto would get nothing from him if Checa willed it so.

"You're refusing the call?" Pretto asked when they stood in front of the large windows overlooking the Matriarch's private garden.

"He's an idiot," said Heath, who was still at Checa's side. "This is the only chance there'll be. He can't refuse."

Sweat beaded Checa's upper lip as he battled the urge to blurt out every emotion he'd ever felt.

This is why you never look at the man. Why did you look at him this time?

"Heath, please don't interrupt again," Pretto said. Checa realized Heath had stepped away from him. A small part of him wanted to grab Heath's hand and keep him near, as if Checa needed his protection. But that was ridiculous. Checa was the Captain of the Guard, the primary warrior of the Mafdeti. He didn't need the protection of a man eight years his junior.

Before Checa could tell Heath to leave, Heath gripped his biceps and turned him.

"Just to be clear," Heath said, sternness warring with exasperated humor on his face, "we all know I'm the Farseeing part of this group, so I'll be coming too." He strode to the window seat and sat.

Checa opened his mouth to argue. They weren't going anywhere. He was going to keep Heath safe.

Pretto spent a few seconds fluffing his gown around his feet until he was satisfied with the drape of the fabric, and then he addressed Checa.

"So, now we know there won't be any interruptions—" He glared at Heath who'd opened his mouth to speak. When he once again subsided, Pretto continued. "Why don't you tell me what you're thinking, Captain." Pretto clasped his hands together at his waist and tilted his head so the light caught his bouffant locks, setting the red threads aflame.

"I'm not the Silver Shining from Rock, and Heath isn't going on any quest that will get him killed." That should be clear enough.

After a lengthy pause that had Checa fighting not to fill the void with more words and Heath fidgeting on the sofa, Pretto spoke again. Instead of the commanding baritone he usually issued orders with, the old man's voice was soft and persuasive. "Why aren't you the Silver?"

Checa paced, needing the physical activity to keep his anger and anxiety in check. "I wasn't born with silver eyes. My eyes aren't silver— they're green. They only changed to silver after—" Shit, he'd have to be honest, even though the Seer already knew. "—after I killed a man."

"Do you regret that?"

"Fuck no! Not the first one. The Bastard killed my brother. He'd done worse to him and to others. He deserved to die." The response burst from him before he had time to wonder why Pretto suddenly wanted to talk about ancient history. "He won't hurt another child." He took a deep breath, settling the anger and fear and sorrow that always erupted when he thought of what the Bastard had done to him.

"So you avenged them and protected others."

Checa stayed silent. He'd spent months explaining why he'd done what he'd done when it had happened. He didn't need to go through it again.

"What about the second one?"

"The second was an accident. The idiot came at me from behind after he'd gone down." The Bastard always hit him from behind when he intended to hurt him badly. Checa had reacted instinctively, even though he'd killed the Bastard years before. "That one I regret." The guard had ignored training rules and wouldn't accept that he'd lost, but he hadn't deserved to die.

Pretto nodded and pursed his lips. The light caught the pink gloss, making his lips appear fuller. Checa looked away. "Have your eyes changed to silver since?"

"Only once," Checa responded grudgingly, then stood tall, defying what Pretto called his *destiny*. "I'm not going to keep killing people just so my eyes stay silver."

"But—" Heath began but subsided when Pretto glared at him.

Pretto turned back to Checa and smiled. "Those are exactly the qualities we need in the Silver Shining from Rock. Makai and Nayeli chose well." Pretto glided over to a sofa positioned just out of the direct sunlight streaming in through the window; he sat and arranged his garments neatly. "Now why don't you tell me why you really don't want to be the Silver."

The silence grew heavy and thick. Checa sweated as Pretto's gaze bore into his soul.

"I know you can resist my compulsion, Checa. I'm not trying to break you. I think you really want to tell someone, though, and I'm as good as anyone. What is stopping you from accepting the challenge?"

Checa sighed and nodded. "If I go, Heath will too. He insists he's the Farseeing to my Silver." He paced some more. "I've read the prophecy. Silver is the damned and the Farseeing falls." He glared at Pretto. "I'm not going to be responsible for Heath dying. He's not going to be part of this."

Pretto grinned. "Why haven't you two bonded yet?"

Checa flapped his hands in irritation, shooting a trepidatious glare at the Matriarch. "You know where I came from and what I've done. This isn't about us bonding. This is about keeping him safe."

"Exactly." Pretto rose to his feet. With the lift of his chin and the firming of his lips, the affable old man was gone, and in his place was the most powerful Seer in the land. "You are the Silver Shining from Rock, chosen in the moment of greatest trauma when you came of age. You are the only one who can protect the Farseeing from the dangers he'll encounter."

"Heath's not going."

"Don't be obtuse, Checa. You know as well as I do that Heath is the Farseeing, and he'll go whether you do or not. You have a far better chance of protecting him if you're there than you ever would have if you stayed here when he leaves."

"Fuck."

"Probably," Pretto responded cheerfully as he stood. He shook the wrinkles from his caftan and patted his stiff-as-a-board hair. "Is there anything else you need to discuss?"

Heath can't go.

Checa couldn't allow him to risk his life. There had to be another way to keep him out of it. His chest tight, Checa grasped at his last option. "The Pledge calls for four people. We only have two."

"We've identified the other two," said Pretto. "We've sent emissaries to each of them, but they haven't returned. Either they're being held at their destinations or the norrgel took them. The birds are getting bolder and, with their larger numbers, are managing to kill Mafdeti as well." He waved a hand as if to dismiss that topic for another time. "You'll need to take a band of men and collect them." He handed Checa a sheaf of papers. "The details of your companions are here, as well as the Warrior Pledge with specific stanzas noted and explained." He patted Checa's shoulder. "We wouldn't want you veering from your task. Time is short, you know."

Checa grasped the papers automatically. Pretto's touch on his shoulder came through the thickness of denial. He didn't want to be involved in this. Not if Heath was going to be in danger. "I won't be responsible for Heath's death."

Pretto smiled, reminding Checa of the first time they met. Checa was on trial for murder and Seer Pretto was still Council Pretto, the judge at Checa's trial. Pretto spoke quietly. "You're the only one who can keep him safe, Checa. You need to remember that."

"I didn't keep Warden safe."

"Your brother's death wasn't your fault. You did everything you could to keep him away from that man. The Silver Shining from Rock is the protector, Checa. You'll protect Heath and the other two." Pretto leaned closer still, his breath astringent, like wine vinegar. "She won't be able to deny a Bond between you once you've saved the world." He stepped back and smiled again. "Good luck to you, Checa." He nodded at Heath. "And Heath. I'll watch the signs for your progress."

The Matriarch stood suddenly, Checa's men following suit immediately. She strode forward, every inch a warrior, regardless of the ridiculous hat. "The Warrior Pledge must be performed at the moment Makai and Nayeli cross, not a second before nor after. We've determined the prophecies indicate the Lake of the Damned as the point of contact for the Pledge. You'll take a minimal band of warriors with you, enlist the aid of the companions identified, however you need to do so, and return home a hero." She regarded her son briefly before returning her gaze to Checa. "A hero worthy of bonding… someone suitable."

She'd bitten out the words.

Checa's heart stopped. He was sure it did even though he could feel it thumping throughout his body. He gaped at her, then snapped his jaw closed, nodded smartly, and turned to leave.

As he turned, the Matriarch spoke briefly to his men before dismissing them too.

"Checa," the Matriarch called after his departing figure.

He turned back as Jun and Talon walked by. They didn't look at him as they went.

"About my son—" she began.

"Mother."

"Stop interrupting, Heath." She glared at him before turning back to Checa. "My son is to return safely."

Checa's contact with Heath's mother had been fraught with tension and distrust, but Heath's safety was the one thing they always agreed on. "Of course, Mater." Checa would die before he'd allow Heath to be in any real danger. His heart still pounded, unbelieving that Checa could be trapped so neatly.

Pretto spoke again. "Have another look at the prophecy. I think you'll find a way to save the world and your man at the same time." He bowed to the Matriarch, nodded at Checa, then smoothly exited the room, his gown rippling sensuously as it dragged along the floor.

Checa and Heath followed suit. The doors closed softly behind them, and Checa groaned and pulled at his hair. Every muscle was tense with the need to fight. His claws snicked out as he looked around for something to slash. As he turned, he found Heath standing uncertainly in front of him.

"So," Heath said quietly. "We're going, then?"

3.
GOING

CHECA WOULD have to be honest. "Will you listen first?"

Heath's mouth twitched, almost a smile, at the reminder that he would talk over the chatterbox bird if he had the opportunity.

At Heath's nod, Checa sucked in a fortifying breath and began. "The Warrior Pledge is dangerous." He held a hand up as Heath opened his mouth to speak. "I know you're a warrior, a good one, but…." He ran his hands up his face and back through his hair, then shook his head at Heath's alarmed expression.

Right. The truth.

"When I met you, when you came to sit with me when you were eight, you saved me then. You showed me that my life didn't always have to be like that. You showed me I could do more, *be* more." He stepped forward and placed his hands on Heath's shoulders, the smooth, warm skin calming him. "You saved me, even though you were just a kid being friendly. I need everything you offered me then to be worth something. I need to keep you safe, Heath. I need to know that you'll live a long and happy life. That's why you can't be the Farseeing one. The Farseeing one dies, and it's the Silver Shining from Rock who causes it." There. He'd done it. Told Heath the truth. Not everything, but the truth. He could go to his death, knowing Heath knew how much he—

"You're a fucking idiot. You know that, don't you?"

Wait. What?

"Have you been talking to your mother?"

"You're damned right he has!" The call came from the court beyond the wall, making Checa jump. He hadn't seen the Matriarch behave as Heath's mother in many years.

Heath ignored her, so Checa did too. "You can't change the Warrior Pledge. You can't decide to take someone who isn't the right one just because you don't want me involved. Close your eyes."

Checa frowned at the random instruction but did as he was told.

"Now breathe the way you do when you're readying yourself for battle. Count your breaths."

Checa breathed, finding his center, and allowed the universe to speak to him, just as he did when he prepared for battle. This time, though, he wasn't looking for enemy weaknesses. In the palm of his hand lay a new-blooming flower, a lily that grew high in the mountain and bloomed only once every fifty years but remained fresh for longer than any other flower he knew. That was Heath, and he knew the significance of the flower. If Checa didn't bond with Heath, he'd lose any chance at true happiness. It was a sacrifice he was willing to make to ensure Heath stayed alive.

"Focus, Checa. Search for the Warrior Pledge."

The Pledge came in many forms. Traditionally passed orally through the Seers, but Heath's mentor, and now Heath himself, had been writing the Mafdeti history so more could learn their tenets. Only Seers could share the Pledge through Bond-Links, but it was a delicate operation fraught with—*No, Heath, don't*—danger… possibilities….

Too late. Warmth rushed through Checa like good whiskey on a cold night. The moons hovered above them, creeping closer and closer together. Once in a millennium, their orbits would intersect and they would cross paths. For one glorious, terrifying minute, Makai and Nayeli would share one light. It signified great change coming upon the land: renewal and rebirth. He could make out the marks upon each. Legend had it that every person saw different marks—their own Bonding mark and that of their fated Bond-Mate. Checa saw his own mark, revealed to him during his coming-of-age ceremony. It was an eye, black with a silver pupil. The other moon held another mark—three lines radiating both east and west from a center point. The mark of a Seer. Heath's mark.

Through space and water, Heath's voice came again.

"Look farther, Checa. What do you see?"

"I see a battle between the Descendants and others who are like them but not. I see a man with black hair, but he's not a man. I see a warrior, skilled but pure of heart. A Seer. I see—"

Water filled his vision, filled his mouth, his nose, his throat. His eyes popped open as he gasped for breath.

Heath was inches away, their chests almost touching, his hand on Checa's cheek, his eyes glowing with approval. And love. Checa had to get him to understand he couldn't risk Heath's life. He lowered his head and pressed their lips together. Checa drew Heath close, deepening the kiss, unable to do anything but show him how important he was. He closed his eyes again and allowed Heath to see him, and he sank into the kiss, dove in from a great height, knowing he would never surface again. He'd be plunged into Heath's essence for eternity, each cell of his body forever fused with each cell of Heath's. They'd be as one for as long as they lived.

"Captain?"

Checa jerked upright at the voice behind them. Heath's dazed face was inches away.

Fuck. What have I done?

Frantically Checa searched Heath's neck and collarbone, shoulders and arms. No Bonding mark. Nothing. The hum of Heath's personality tickled the back of Checa's mind, but that had been there since Heath turned eighteen. They were still separate people. They hadn't bonded, but it had been a damned close thing. Checa's breath whooshed from him as he stared into Heath's devastated eyes. "I'm sorry," he whispered, but he wasn't sure if he was apologizing for beginning, or for stopping.

"Which of the guard will be going with us?" Jun asked from behind them.

Heath stepped back, the scowl on his face bringing heat to Checa's face.

Checa couldn't give Heath what he wanted. Under a broken Bond, one of them would die, and the other would go feral and then die. He turned to Jun, who had followed Checa in and was regarding them curiously. Checa straightened his shoulders and glared his best parade-ground glare. "I'll let you know in the morning, Jun."

Heath said, "Pretto said the Changeling is in the Analee Valley, but we have to go to Hawkesby to visit the Queen. She'll know about the Pure."

They had a treaty with the Descendants, also called the Warrior Pledge, but it had little to do with their prophecies. The Queen had never had time for the Mafdeti and made it clear she thought they were little more than animals. Putting Heath in her path wasn't something Checa wanted to do.

Fur sprouted at his nape.

"Stop it, Checa." Heath gripped his forearms. "You know I can do this. There's no one better equipped for this kind of quest, except us. You know we work seamlessly together. Stop fighting it."

"But…."

"*Stop fighting it.*"

Checa growled and glowered at his lover. "You stay with me the whole time. Do you understand? With me."

Heath grinned. "Always."

4.
HAWKESBY

THEY TRAVELED overland in the early hours of the morning, able to take a more direct route. Even when the sun rose, they kept going, eager to put as many miles behind them as they could before the norrgel reached them.

Heath skipped a small double step to catch up to Checa's longer stride. "Do you think it odd that one of our ancient stories has links to the Descendants? I mean, it must, mustn't it? Sure, one of us could be the Changeling, but how would we tell? We can *all* change. We *all* have three forms."

They'd run as cats all night. Now, in the hours before dawn, they walked as men. Heath enjoyed stretching those muscles and chatting as they went. Not that Checa did much of the chatting. Heath grinned at the small muscle jumping in Checa's jaw. That only happened when Heath had been particularly annoying. Pretto kept telling him he had to stop irritating Checa. Perhaps, one day, Checa would round on Heath and knock him flat.

That would never happen. Checa adored him—even when Heath was at his most annoying.

He might have doubted that two days ago, but not after that kiss. Checa had been so close to bonding with him Heath had felt the tension rising. He didn't want to bond without Checa's agreement, but he was more determined than ever to wear Checa down and get him to admit they were perfect together.

Heath continued his one-sided conversation. "For the Pledge to have singled out someone who can change, it would have to be something unusual. What do you suppose they can change to? Do you know of any other animals that can change like we can? I've never heard of any. There are some obscure texts that indicate something with the Descendants, but I've never been able to work out exactly what it is. Do you think they can change to dragons? The dragons are supposed to return with the Warrior Pledge."

"By all the ancestors, Checa, will you shut him up?" called Jun from his position toward the back, with the other five soldiers between him and Heath. "We came down the mountain two hours ago and he hasn't drawn breath."

Checa growled.

"Dragons are extinct." As always, Talon paced beside Jun. "They won't be back."

"It's always good to have refresher courses," called another man. "But I don't want to learn about how the norrgel dissolve their prey when we're under threat of that happening, and I certainly don't want to speculate what animal the Descendants might be."

Heath spun around and jogged backward, keeping pace with Checa. "Ingrates!" he called back. "Riordal, it was you who asked how norrgel-strike could be treated."

Another man behind him coughed to cover retching. "I didn't need a blow-by-blow description of how my muscles would spasm so hard they'd crush the bone before the poison liquefied it all."

Before Heath could retort, Checa stopped walking and crouched. Eight sets of claws snicked out, as they all responded to his actions. All the men spread out, instantly alert to danger.

In the distance a dozen men walked into the desert and fanned out, on alert.

"They're taking an overland route? Why would they do that when the norrgel are in flight?"

Checa thought it was a good thing Heath had such a pleasant voice or he'd have stuffed his loincloth into his mouth ages ago. He cleared his throat. Thoughts of his loincloth anywhere near Heath's mouth weren't what he needed right now. "They're from the valley. The only time they venture out is during trading season."

"They probably don't know the catacombs the way we do, but they do have underground routes to use."

Checa shrugged. "There's been increased activity with the Exiles lately. Maybe those routes aren't safe anymore."

"They'd have to be safer than being on the surface with hunting norrgel," said Jun as he joined them. He twisted a lock of hair around his fist, the black stark against his pale skin, and chewed his lip as his gaze darted fitfully over the landscape.

Jumpiness was usually a sign that a Mafdeti would soon go feral, but Checa didn't know of anything in Jun's life that would cause that. He'd have to watch the man more closely, though.

A shrill cry rose on the air. To the east the sky darkened, a mottled, moving cloud.

"Norrgel are up and heading our way," Checa said. "We go underground from here. Heath, find us an entrance."

Heath froze and stared at the sand in front of him. Jun immediately fidgeted and moved farther away. He stopped when Checa glared at him. Heath didn't need everyone to be still while he did his thing, but Checa wasn't going to allow Jun or anyone else to disrespect his talent. When he was sure all his men were once again alert and surveying their area, he returned his attention to Heath.

"Do you know, I think this is the only time I ever see a serious expression on your face," he said quietly so only Heath would hear.

"Fuck you. Let me concentrate so I don't drop us into a hole with no way out." Heath took a small step forward and turned so he faced just west of south.

"What do you see?"

Heath didn't scoff or ignore him. He never had in all the time they'd known each other.

"It's a river with tributaries running like veins under the sand. Some of them are thick and solid, others narrow and fractured." He paused and frowned before he strode forward a dozen steps. "Or ready to." He looked up at Checa and grinned. "You want to see which one of us can jump the highest?" He bounced on his toes.

"There?"

In response, Heath jumped and thudded down. He coughed as the sand billowed up around him. "Close your nostrils. This is going to get dusty."

"Jun," Checa called. "Keep a lookout. Once this dust rises, the norrgel will be upon us."

"At least they'll leave that group of Descendants alone for a while longer." Heath landed again.

The other men joined them, and soon they were all bouncing up and down discordantly.

"Try jumping together," yelled Heath. "Bring all our weight down together."

A screech rent the air.

"We've been spotted," called Jun needlessly. "You've got less than three minutes before they get here."

They all jumped faster and in time.

Heath stumbled as the rock cracked. "I hate this part," he spat as the ground beneath him gave way and he plummeted through the newly formed hole.

One by one the men dropped down onto the rubble surrounding Heath. He stayed where he was as they ranged around the cave, checking for exits and tunnels. His back hurt when he landed and he'd hit his head. Again.

"Your brains still intact?" Checa asked as he dropped last of all. After a brief look at his men, he came and helped Heath to his feet.

Heath groaned as he was pulled up, then rubbed gingerly at a divot pressed into his buttock by a particularly pointy shard of stone.

"This place is pocked with narrow tunnels. Which one do we take?" asked Jun from the other side of the cave. He scowled at Heath.

Heath responded with his own scowl when he realized Jun was standing at the one opening that would lead them directly to Hawkesby. Before climbing in, Heath let his senses range. "I can't smell much more than rocks and sand." He stepped back and motioned to Checa. "Can you sense anyone through there?"

Checa frowned at Heath as he walked past, as he always did when Heath asked him to check scent, but Heath was never sure if it was because Checa wanted him to do it himself or if he was disappointed that Heath couldn't. When they bonded it wouldn't be a problem; Heath would gradually develop Checa's unique senses, and Checa would develop his. He sighed as Checa stepped back and gestured to him.

Bonding obviously wasn't going to happen right then. Heath bent and threaded his arms into the narrow opening, then slithered the rest of his body ungracefully after them.

"It's going to get dark quickly, so use cat's eyes." The only reason Heath didn't change to cat form to traverse the tunnels was because Checa's cat was too big to fit into the narrow openings. It was going to be a squeeze to get the larger man through them as it was. This had better be worth it. It would suck norrgel balls if the Queen decided they were a hostile force and had them executed before they could complete the Warrior Pledge and become heroes.

Checa's warm breath washed over Heath's feet as they wriggled through the narrow space.

And bond. Heath wanted them to bond once this was over.

5.
AUDIENCE WITH THE QUEEN

THE BREATH huffed out of Checa's lungs as he stood on the rise and surveyed the city below them. They'd made it. There had been places Heath couldn't find safe passage underground and they'd had to travel on the surface, risking norrgel attack. Even their cat forms couldn't save them from the vicious whippings of the poisonous threads. They were lucky to get there alive. His men gathered around him like early-morning campfire smoke.

Except they stank more. None of them had bathed since leaving the mountains. Checa grinned. He knew he smelled as bad as everyone else. Even his hair was matted, something it took particular neglect to achieve.

No one would assume he was the Captain of the Mafdeti Guard. The Imperials would be more likely to think he was a rogue breaking into the city.

Together they looked down on the field below them. Spaced a man's height apart, silver-domed grilles sparkled like scattered diamonds in the verdant grass as the early-morning sunlight peeped over the hills in the east. Thin streams of steam wafted through the raised grilles covering each vent and hung in the still air, the only outward sign a huge city lay belowground. Most of the openings were for ventilation, but every fifteenth one opened to one of the many corridors running through the underground city.

They needed to find one close to the city center, where the royal apartments were. Checa sobered. The danger wasn't past yet. It was impossible to drop into the heavily patrolled upper echelons of Hawkesby without triggering alarms, but there was no time to follow protocol. They needed to see the Queen and couldn't wait for court appearances to be scheduled.

Hopefully they would find the Pure quickly, and then they'd have to make the whole terrifying journey back again or lose everything.

"The sun's rising, Checa. We need to get to shelter," Heath said beside him.

Sunrise. Checa gazed at the grilles, attempting to count them. He glanced at the lightening sky, noting the position of the crescent moons before they sank beneath the horizon, one hanging below the other like a twisted comma. Time was running out. If they didn't find the Changeling and the Pure soon, it would be too late. The Queen was their best hope.

An eerie screech split the chill air, echoing across the sparkling plain. The hair rose on the back of Checa's neck as a rolling metallic *clang* traveled toward them, the rise and fall of the locking grilles chased by fine ribbons of black that darkened the eastern sky. His heart pounded as row by row the grilles closed, cutting off the thin trail of steam, each *clang* echoing and blending with the cry of the norrgel. In the eastern sky, more black threads lifted over the horizon.

Hell, they were too late. The wings were upon them.

"Wings are up" came a terrified whisper behind him.

The sweat on Checa's skin chilled and his breath caught in his throat as panic clawed his chest. They'd all grown up under the shadow of the wings, had seen what they could do, but two weeks traveling partially aboveground had brought new images to their nightmares. They'd nearly lost Talon when he'd been caught in the open shortly after the zenith, and Jun had been trapped under a rock overhang with all the medical supplies. Conway hadn't been so lucky. Checa never wanted to hear screams like that again.

They tumbled down the slope to the city. Checa ran west, searching for an access point. He slid to his knees next to a grille sitting higher than the others. It was an entrance, not a vent, and they didn't have time to find another closer to the center.

"Here!" he called to his companions and scrambled for the catch at the edge of the grille.

The others slid down beside him, dragging the heavy grate up from the hole.

"Down. Now." Checa looked at the sky, darkening with the progress of the black threads flapping closer, even though he knew the norrgel were too far away to see their group clearly. The clanging of the closing grilles grew closer, echoing the thudding of his heart.

One after another his team dropped into the hole while Checa held the grille up. "Drop straight down. Watch your shoulders." He kept an eye on the eastern sky, swallowing the bile that ebbed and flowed with each row of grilles clanging closed. The wings grew larger as they chased the ringing noise. "*Hurry.*"

As they moved closer, the wings became discernible as thin, long-beaked birds. They were so close now Checa could see the threads that hung from the trailing edge of the wings and the tail. "Talon, you're next."

The threads swirled and fluttered with every rise and fall. Checa swallowed thickly, forcing his hands to remain steady as he held the grille open. "Don't hesitate."

His dreams still echoed with the screams of friends caught without their fur by those threads.

Heath was the last man to drop, and then Checa swung his legs into the hole just as the grilles in the next row locked closed. Checa slid fully into the hole and released his hold on the grille just as it slammed closed. A black shadow passed overhead, and then the vents slid into place, sealing the underground city from the world above.

Air whistled past Checa's ears and whipped his hair around as he fell, his shoulders and elbows bumping against the smooth wall of the shaft, his hands flailing uselessly above his head. The floor hit him hard, buckling his knees, twisting his ankle, and rolling him heavily onto his side. The breath rushed from him and his head thumped onto the ground. He brought his arms in close, flexing his bruised fingers in an effort to gain control of his winded body.

"Come on, Checa. We need to move." Heath's strong hands hauled him to his feet.

Checa stumbled a few steps, then sucked in the pain from his ankle. It wasn't bad. A few dozen steps and he wouldn't feel it at all. He turned and loped south along the corridor.

"Heath, I'll take point. Jun, tail end." By the time he'd positioned himself in front of Heath, everyone was in place.

The corridors in this section of the city were at right angles from all the others and painted a dark charcoal. They were in the outer reaches.

"Double guard." His quiet voice carried in the silence of a deserted hall.

If they were going to have trouble, it would be here where the misfits and unemployed lived. Three of his men moved silently, taking position to protect them from attack. Heath stepped ahead of Checa, taking over point position.

Checa hissed, "Heath."

Heath grinned and whispered back, "You wanted me to stay close. Working with you is as close as I can be."

The men moved in concert. Heath signaled *clear*, and half the group moved forward while the rest covered against attack and moved under cover of the first group. It was a routine so well practiced none of them needed to think of it, but Checa still mentally reviewed his men.

They traversed three corridors, seeing no one else, hearing nothing, and then Heath stopped and signaled for silence. Everyone froze, Jun facing backward as he watched for anyone from behind. Heath's fingers stretched out behind his thigh, counting hostiles. Four. There was nowhere to retreat to; no way to hide their presence. They'd have to take them down and move on. Heath's fingers counted down to contact.

Three. Two. One.

Even with their wild eyes and handmade weapons held ready, the hostiles were still four amateurs against experienced warriors with retractable claws. It was swift and silent, and the group moved forward again, leaving the ragged men unconscious. When the walls were deep forest green, they encountered several more groups, but none posed any real threat. The city was awakening and going about its day, so Checa found an alcove to hide in and waited until they'd all passed. Then the Mafdeti continued their journey silently.

The closer they came to the center of the city, the brighter the colors and the fewer the right angles. More people began moving about. By the time they'd reached aqua corridors, it was impossible to move undetected. Checa signaled formation and they straightened their shoulders, hoping that if they marched purposefully through the city, everyone would think the group of Mafdeti warriors was there with permission.

Tension crawled through them. Checa watched Heath closely and brought Jun up from the rear. After being on high alert since they left the Matriarch, the team would take time to come down. They moved silently.

Several hours later, Heath stopped where the walls changed to pale gold. Behind him was an almost-invisible panel that indicated an opening to the vents carrying fresh air throughout the city. One by one, Checa's men sidled behind him and Heath, and they wriggled into the air vents. Heath indicated for Checa to go next and rolled his eyes as Checa glared at him.

"Stop wasting time. Get in there," Checa growled.

Heath scowled but obeyed.

From there, Checa and his team crawled to a ceiling vent in the Queen's private chambers. By the time Checa dropped through, Imperial soldiers held his men at sword point.

Three soldiers rushed at Checa as the Queen was hustled from the room between two of her guard.

"I invoke the Warrior Pledge, Your Majesty," called Checa as she reached the door.

The Queen turned slowly, gesturing to her personal guard to hold their positions. "I hardly think invading my personal quarters like this gives you any right to demand anything—" She scanned Checa's body slowly. "—cat."

Checa straightened his shoulders and stood taller, although he was sure she expected him to prostrate himself before her and beg forgiveness. "The Warrior Pledge supersedes all other treaties and protocols. Failure to honor the Warrior Pledge will result in immediate cessation of all other treaties and place the survival of the Descendants and the planet at risk."

The Queen strode over to where Checa stood, an angry flush rising on her cheeks. "The Warrior Pledge was a piece of fiction formulated at the time we settled this backwater, to appease the primitive race of animals living in the mountains. It means absolutely nothing." She hissed the words. Then, seeming to realize she'd lost control, she stepped back and spoke normally. "As you were misinformed and you meant no harm, I'll have my men escort you from the city."

"Your Majesty, you don't seem to realize—"

"No, you're the one who doesn't realize. The treaty was useful when we were struggling to survive as a people, but we no longer have need of your Warrior Pledge."

"May I clarify that you're refusing to invoke the Warrior Pledge and will accept full responsibility of any consequences arising from that refusal?"

"Are you threatening me?"

"Of course not, Your Majesty. The Warrior Pledge speaks for itself."

"Leave now, or you'll be confined."

Checa inclined his head, showing deference even though his claws pricked at his fingertips. "Of course, Your Majesty. My apologies for any inconvenience caused."

The Queen turned and strode from the sitting room, flicking a hand at two of her guards. The guards gestured to the group of Mafdeti.

"Checa—" began Heath as they left the room.

"Not now, Heath."

Checa thought it was perhaps only the third time since he'd met Heath that he remained silent in his company, but he could tell Heath's head was whirling with questions.

With the key they will come
Ruby red in bright of day
Warriors four show the way
To split the stone in one

    —extract from the Warrior Pledge, prophecy of the Mafdeti, natural inhabitants of the planet Thalazar.

6.
THE ENCLAVE

IN THE last row of seats in the Enclave, deep in the shadows, Checa leaned toward Heath. "I still can't work out why the Imperials incarcerated them. They'd know Rim is the Protector of the Fourth Line. He's managed the Analee Valley for the last seven years."

"That's not the King or the Queen down there." Heath nodded toward the man. "He's alone. Do you think they locked them up and this one has released them?"

"That child? He's just a boy. What authority would he have to release prisoners?"

"They say your eyesight is the first thing that goes when you age. Look again, Checa."

"There's nothing wrong with my eyes." Checa puffed his chest out as he glared at Heath to emphasize the fact he wasn't getting old.

"Of course there isn't. Keep your voice down or they'll notice we're here, and being found inside the city after being thrown out by the Queen isn't something I want to happen."

They both slunk down in their seats as the Imperial guards separated and ranged themselves around the room. The Enclave was in the center of the city, deep underground, but the ceiling reached to the uppermost parts of the city. Like the Enclave in Analee, it was a pentagon with seventeen doorways, three on each angled side, one at the northern juncture and a fourth one on the southern edge. Each wall was clad in a different color: hot red, brilliant yellow, lime green, cobalt, royal purple. The arena was tiered with carved stone seating and aisles between, all overlooking the glossy round table in the center.

Checa and Heath had settled at the top of the purple sector. The purple was the darkest color and would hide them better, and there was less chance of any of the guards coming up there. Purple was only for royalty or Protectors. When Rim entered, he moved to the purple, northern end, front row, as was his right as Protector. The boy frowned at Rim and stood in the aisle, waiting for something, but Checa couldn't decide what.

Checa didn't know what Heath expected him to see. He couldn't see anything odd about the boy except his behavior. Eventually the boy moved and sat in the seat behind Rim.

So the boy thought he should sit where Rim was now. First row, First Line. But that seat was the seat of the royal family, a trusted advisor, or the Protector of the Line, as Rim was. The Imperial guards gained their seats, scattered around the Enclave, different colors, different levels, different Lines. None ventured into the purple, so Checa relaxed a little. The guards kept their hands on their weapons, so Rim's still watchfulness was understandable.

They waited.

The sun was directly above, a sharp beam in the center of the table, when the boy behind Rim made his way forward, casually pulled out the King's chair, and sat. He turned his head and stared at Rim. The boy's profile seemed familiar, but Checa couldn't place who he was.

"You may join me." A small hand gestured to the chair directly in front of Rim, to the right of where the boy sat.

Rim rose but hesitated. "Sitting in the seat of power without right means death." He hadn't raised his voice, but the acoustics of the Enclave were so good a whisper would carry to the topmost levels.

The boy inclined his head and gestured to the seat again. Checa's heart began to pound. This boy wasn't the King. Only direct descendants had the right to assume the throne if the King wasn't available, and he had no sons of this age. They were all much younger.

"I seek an audience with the King," Rim said again, the demand clear in his voice.

Checa nodded, agreeing with the obvious rejection in Rim's stiff body.

"The King is unavailable," said the boy. "I will hear you."

Checa flashed a look around the Enclave. The guards were alert but not alarmed at the boy's presence in the seat of power. In a seat in front of each of the guards were Rim's men.

Checa turned back to the boy. His mind buzzed, but he couldn't think of one male descendant of the right age in the King's Line. The King's heir was female, his daughter Ardelle.

Suddenly the soft features made sense. Checa sank deeper into his seat and glared at Heath's superior smirk.

"Forgive me, Your Highness." Rim said as he bowed.

Checa could kick himself for not recognizing the Princess Royal. Of course she was nothing special to look at and she was dressed as a warrior, but still, Checa should at least have realized she was a woman.

"Tell me what's so important you couldn't use appropriate channels to meet with us," she asked, her voice deep and regal.

Rim leaned over to the side, reaching for his boot, and paused as her guards drew their knives. Checa leaned forward, trying to see what he held. After an interminable second, Ardelle signaled a stand-down and Rim completed his movement, bringing a small object to the table. He dropped it in front of her.

The tiny bloodred, tear-shaped gem was the size of Checa's thumbnail. He enhanced his sight to see it more clearly. Intricately engraved with words of ages long forgotten, it was the symbol of dire need between one realm and another, the invocation of the Warrior Pledge, a call to arms that every warrior dreamed of and aspired to.

And it exactly matched the one Checa carried.

Ardelle raised her gaze to Rim, her hands twitching as if to reach out and touch the small stone, but instead she clasped them in front of her. "You are invoking the Warrior Pledge." Her voice trembled.

Rim relaxed against the back of his seat. "There are foreigners in the land. We captured a group of Yeudan who had attacked a village in the northwestern sector of the Analee Valley."

"Why didn't you bring them here for questioning?"

"The language they speak has similarities to the Yeudan tongue I've learned, but there are marked and significant differences. So many differences that I can't understand them." He held his hand up, signaling silence as she opened her mouth to speak. "My father was Rimandon the Scholar. I would recognize every language in our world. This one is too changed for immediate translation. The Professor, my father's protégé, is currently working on cracking the code of the language used in the papers they brought with them."

Heath grabbed Checa's forearm.

Rimandon's son.

Checa nodded and released a sigh of relief. They'd found the Changeling.

Ardelle continued speaking. "You said it was based on the old Yeudan language. I know it's been a hundred years since our last contact, but surely there's enough in the language for you to begin translations immediately."

"The Yeudan didn't have a written language. What's in the papers they brought isn't familiar at all. It's only the rhythm of the repetitions that tell me it's a complete language and not some child's pretty squiggles."

Ardelle nodded slowly. "You understand I can't mobilize the entire army on such little information. There's the conflict with the Lonely Isles and the Exiles, as well as the unrest in the west, all demanding our attention. We need to investigate this situation further."

"With respect, Highness, there isn't time to investigate. The papers clearly show a deadline of the moons eclipsing each other. The invasion will begin then. We need to be prepared."

"We'll be as prepared as we need to be based on the information my team discovers." The Princess's voice took on a haughty tone that brooked no argument. "My team will leave at the end of the week." She reached for the gem but Rim scooped it from the table and dropped it back into his boot.

After a silence that stretched under the harsh light, he spoke, his voice slow and deliberate. "My duty in this situation is clear, Your Highness. My valley, my *people* are at risk." He gazed steadily at her, leaving no doubt that he had his own agenda. Her jaw clenched as he continued. "I give you my word I will complete the mission successfully or die." He shifted in his seat as if he wanted to leave immediately. "My men and I will be ready to leave tonight. We mean to travel overland."

"Tonight? Overland?" The exclamation burst forth.

"There is little time, Highness. We traveled here on the surface and will need to return the same way if we're to be prepared for battle before the moons become one."

Ardelle frowned at him. "I think you're wrong about the urgency, but I will give orders for readiness, Protector." She used Rim's title for the first time. "My men and I will accompany you on your quest." She stood, signaling the end of the meeting. Rim stood as well. "One of my men will collect you and your team an hour before sunset. The northern exits will be the most useful to us." She nodded, then climbed the steps to the door of the First Line.

Before she slipped through the door, she turned. "Her Majesty informed me there's a band of rogue Mafdeti in the catacombs. Make sure your men are prepared."

Rim swore. He stormed up the steps, signaling his men to follow as he went.

"Rogue Mafdeti?" whispered Heath as the door shut softly behind the last soldier.

"I think that's us," said Checa as he stood. "We can't approach them now. We'll intercept and separate the Protector and the Princess from the others."

"Do you think she's the Pure? I can't work out what makes Rim the Changeling."

"I don't know of any others who are bald. I expect we'll find out what's so special about Rim soon enough. Seer Pretto was convinced it was him. She has to be the Pure." Checa regarded his men. "I'm going to follow Rim and see what I can find. I'll meet you outside the north exit at dusk."

JUN LIFTED away from Fan and watched as his mate righted his clothing. A smile tugged at his lips. He liked watching his lover move, the muscles rippling over his hairless skin. "I didn't expect to see you so soon," he said as he watched Fan do up his belt. "Why are you so far afield?"

Fan looked around, but Jun knew he wouldn't see anything. The shadows of the desert hid everything. As long as they kept their voices low, they were safe here. "There's some sort of threat in the Analee Valley. The Princess is going to take a look."

The Princess. Jun knew she was acting for the King while he was ill. After months watching Fisher try to gain access to the royal family, Jun knew there'd be no better opportunity—as long as the Queen didn't arrange for Ardelle to meet an untimely death the next time she refused one of her mother's rulings. If Jun could orchestrate the royal family's downfall, the stupid restrictions on fraternization between races would be removed and he and Fan could be together instead of having to sneak around in the dark. Fisher was the only one who'd offered to help them toward that goal. "Have you thought about what Fisher said last time we met with him?"

Fan sighed. "Yes, I have." His mate looked up at Jun and gripped his arm as if he needed the strength. "It still feels like treason, but it's the only way to ensure the royal family survives. When the Yeudan invade, the King has to surrender." He shook his head. "I can't arrange a meeting for Fisher, though. I don't have that authority."

"He can talk to the Princess. Where are you headed?"

Fan was silent for a long time. "No harm will come to her?"

"You have my word."

Fan's next sigh brushed the hair at Jun's neck, and then he rested his head on Jun's shoulder. Jun pulled him closer, savoring his warmth, breathing deeply of the man he loved.

"They're heading to the Lake of the Damned, planning to go through the Pass of Nines."

Jun nodded. "We'll intercept, and I'll make sure the Princess and Fisher meet." He pulled back and cradled Fan's face in his hands. "I'll meet up with you as we travel. Look for me." He pressed a gentle kiss to his soldier's lips, then faded into the darkness, a smile on his face as he thought of all the opportunities he and Fan would have on the way to the Lake of the Damned.

Loss follows silver search
Born of death and tragedy
Alone yet strong he will be
To destroy much of worth

—extract from the Warrior Pledge, prophecy of the Mafdeti, natural inhabitants of the planet Thalazar.

7.
NORRGEL ATTACK

DYING LIGHT washed the rocky landscape red and black. The wings' last eerie cries echoed across the barren vista. Rim hitched his pack higher on his back and walked through the cave exit into the night. He watched as the blackness swallowed his best friend, Spook, knowing he would warn them of any danger ahead.

Behind him, Ardelle and the small band of warriors fanned out, Ardelle's personal guard staying within sight of her. His own warriors ranged farther afield, leaving Charl far enough behind to watch for danger. If anyone could recognize a rogue band of Mafdeti, it was Charl. They were twelve in total, a small group but large enough to meet any danger they might face on the surface. They'd be absolutely useless in the face of the invasion Rim was sure was coming from the Yeudan in the north. He needed to get home quickly to ensure his army was mobilized and to make sure his people were as protected as they could be with his limited resources.

A soft huff sounded from Ardelle beside him, the soles of her ranger boots silent. He hoped she would keep quiet. She wasn't happy about traveling on the surface and had argued heatedly all the way from the center of the city that they take another course, but going through the passes south the Lake of the Damned was the fastest route. All other avenues were watched by the Mafdeti. Their activity had increased since the Yeudan had burned the western reaches of the Analee Valley, and Rim could only assume they were aware of the situation, at least to some extent. The Exiles had increased their ambushes as well, so all the usual tunnels between cities were closed.

They had to reach the Lake before the two moons became one, or none of it would matter. The Yeudan invasion would begin with or without them. They'd need to go through the Pass of Nines and along the northern escarpment below the Lake of the Damned, where they'd set up their line of defense.

Rim hoped the Mafdeti were so focused on the tunnels they hadn't thought anyone would travel on top. If the Mafdeti caught them in the open, they were dead.

"You're heading north," Ardelle accused.

"The Pass of Nines is to the north, yes." Rim kept his tone reasonable. What other direction did she expect him to go? He needed to get back quickly.

A soft rumble sounded beside him and Rim started. He stared at the Princess. Had she just growled at him?

"You can't go through the Pass of Nines! You need to go east, around the Aylmer Mountains, then turn north after you cross the Torrent." Ardelle turned to the east and took several steps before she returned to hiss at him. "You need to go east first."

Rim continued north. "I don't have time for a detour. We go directly north, over the Pass of Nines, and then to the Lake of the Damned and the headwaters of the Crystal River."

The Princess's soft footsteps ceased. Whether she was stunned immobile by his pronouncement of his intended route or by the fact he didn't automatically obey her, he didn't know.

He huffed at the delay. "I told you our mission is urgent. We must return before the moons' eclipse." He flicked a look at the moons, two thick commas in the velvet sky. The tail of one was almost close enough to touch the top of the other. According to the documents they'd taken from the Yeudan, when they waxed full and formed a single circle, his time would be up. "There is no other way to take." He turned and continued northward.

The Princess grabbed his elbow and yanked him around to face her. "Are you mad? The Pass of Nines is the home of the Mafdeti. There's a rogue band roaming around. What if the whole race has gone feral? You can't just walk into their territory and expect to come out alive. You're dooming this mission before you begin." Her fingers dug into the soft flesh above his elbow. "You have to go east, around the mountains."

Rim stared at the darker shadow that was his Princess. He owed her courtesy and, in most cases, obedience. The Valley of Analee relied on trade with Hawkesby for a significant portion of their prosperity and particularly now, with the land failing. He couldn't afford to alienate her, but with the survival of his people at stake, Rim didn't care what she thought. She'd chosen only lip service in honor of the Warrior Pledge, a small part of the treaty never before invoked. He wanted battalions of soldiers on this mission, not just the Princess and her personal guard, but she had insisted. Perhaps with the Princess involved, the King might eventually send the support he needed, although *eventually* might be too late.

Rim clamped his teeth together in an attempt not to rail at her. She'd refused to allow anyone else access to the King. In fact, she refused to even tell him exactly where the King was. She knew the danger, he was sure, and she'd agreed to the immediate departure without argument. Her quick response worried him, and he was even more certain his people had little time left. The Princess was the only one who could call in more troops, so he had to play her game.

But he wasn't going east.

"There are paths that the Mafdeti don't patrol. We used them to get here." It wasn't quite a lie. They hadn't *seen* any Mafdeti, only a couple of groups of the large cats they often had with them.

Rim walked on, ignoring the pounding of his heart as he waited for a sign she was following. He couldn't leave her to go another way. Now that she was with him and his team, it was his responsibility to keep her safe. If she turned east, he would have to follow.

Behind him the ruined voice of Ardelle's guard wafted in the air. "He's right, Princess. This is the quickest way. It's also why Fan is with us. He often patrols that area."

Whispered curses wafted on the still air behind him, keeping pace, and Rim grinned. Good. They steadily picked their way across the landscape toward the mountains. The air chilled as the night deepened, and silence fell over their troop.

The first light of morning brought the norrgel. Their cries raised the hair on the back of Rim's neck and echoed from the rocks around them. Sweat dried crusty on his back, and he shivered as the sound of the birds grew closer, the eastern edge of the sky stained by their flight. He cursed softly, the same reaction he'd had every time in the last five years. The terror ate at him, becoming more difficult to hide each time. He forced his focus to their surroundings.

The wings were too close. Rim needed to find shelter now. Where was Spook? He should have found them already and led them to their shelter for the day. Rim scanned the landscape, desperately searching for an outcropping that looked large enough to shelter them all.

A hoarse cry filled the air behind them. Charl had found Spook. Rim spun around, glimpsing Spook's gloved hand waving darkly between the ochre rocks. He took off at a run, gravel crunching underfoot and around him as the others joined the race.

Was Spook signaling a hiding place or was he hurt? Rim's gaze darted around. And where was Charl? Was it a trap?

Ardelle ran to his side. "Is it safe?" Rim signaled his men to fan out and approach more cautiously. "I don't know. Did you see where Charl went?"

Spook's hand disappeared, dropping below the rocks into the cave he'd found. Rim kept focused on that spot so he wouldn't overrun it.

A loud screech floated on the air.

"Wings up!" came the cry behind him.

"We need to get to shelter." Ardelle half turned away.

Rim knew she wouldn't find anything large enough to shelter them. He reached out blindly and grabbed her arm. "Spook is our best option for shelter. He might have found something." He hoped so.

"Over here!" Ardelle pulled against his grip.

"It's not big enough for all of us."

The Princess's arm jerked under his hand. Had she forgotten there were twelve of them?

"We should check it. It's closer," she insisted.

"You might be on this mission, Highness, but it is *my* mission." He glared at her. "We go with Spook's decision."

The cries of the birds grew frenzied.

"We've been spotted," he yelled. "Run!"

He tightened his grip on Ardelle's arm and dragged her with him, his long strides making her stumble to keep up. Flapping wings sounded loud in the still morning air, and Rim risked a look behind him. At least a dozen of the black birds dotted the gray sky, streaking closer. More darkened the eastern horizon, dimming the rising sun.

Rim increased his pace, his lungs burning. Around him the warriors converged onto the place Spook had last been seen. One of Ardelle's guards fell back toward the east. Another angled his run directly for her, scooping her under his arm like a sack and continuing to the rocks where once again they could see Spook's waving hand.

One by one the soldiers dropped from sight. Rim's heart pounded and his breath rasped in his throat, so dry and hot his lungs hurt. Yet he slowed his run to the hole in the ground. He was always last down. The tighter the terror gripped him, the more important that became.

His skin crawled at the thought of Ardelle's man dropping behind to draw the wings away from the Princess. He turned to see how far away he was, thinking they could both make it yet. They couldn't lose men at this rate; they had too far to go. Rim continued his run to the hole. He wouldn't wait more than a few moments to see if the man could reach them. Risking both their lives was foolish.

Already he could see the growing shadows of the birds on the ground. Dust lifted and spun as long wings pounded the air. Their screeches were deafening, high-pitched and piercing, directly behind him. He stumbled, almost falling over, his fingertips scraping in the dusty gravel, as a scream rent the air.

It was deep and human, but the sound quickly rose to one of pain and terror. The wings had made their first pass and whipped the soldier from behind. Already the welts would be raising and bursting open. The venom would work its way into his body. It would happen so fast that in a few hours what was once a man would be nothing more than a jumbled mass, his skin burst open to expose liquidized flesh and bone. Rim's eyes burned and he swallowed the bile rising in his throat. He refused to look. He couldn't help and didn't need to see. The imagined images were added to the ones already fracturing his dreams.

The frenzy rose as the birds converged on their prey. The air thundered with the sound of their wings, the threads from the trailing wing edges cracking the air as they whipped the man behind again and again. Their exhilarated screeches slapped a painful counterpoint along Rim's nerves. Beneath it the screams of the man continued unabated. Rim dropped into the hole in the ground a few steps later, but the screams continued, reverberating with the pounding of his heart. It could so easily have been him. It could be his body up there, writhing and bubbling as the birds sucked off his liquefied flesh while he was still alive. Bile boiled in his throat.

"It's Fan! We need to help him," cried Ardelle.

He picked himself up from where he'd landed and turned to stare at her, noticing everyone else did too. Without a word they bent and crab-walked into the narrow tunnel Spook had found.

"We have to help him," Ardelle repeated.

One of Ardelle's men dragged her through with him. The cavern beyond breathed with the sighs of every warrior as the rock muffled the terror-inducing screams of their comrade.

Rim looked around. None of them met his gaze. None of them was prepared to go back any more than he was.

The man was dead. He breathed and screamed, but there was nothing anyone could do. Going back would only get more of them killed.

The screams turned hoarse.

Two hours later even the noise from the feeding birds had faded to nothing.

When the silence became oppressive, Rim moved to sit beside the Princess against the rock wall. "We might run into Mafdeti before we get over the mountains."

She looked at him, eyebrows raised. "You haven't won any points yet, Rim. We're going north, directly through their territory, so that's a given."

Rim grimaced. "I know, but going through the Pass of Nines is the quickest way." He took a deep breath and gestured to where his men lounged around the edges of the cavern. "The Exiles are becoming more aggressive, but we've noticed that all-male groups have less trouble from them. Sometimes only the women are taken, the men left unharmed."

Her jaw dropped. "You're kidding. They're kidnapping women?"

He nodded. "Seems that way." He cleared his throat. "We have to find a way to protect you." His gaze darted from her to the fire.

"I'm a warrior. I can take care of myself. I'm used to being the center of any arrangement for protection, but I wish you'd just let me do my job."

Apart from a raised eyebrow and a pointed look at her, Rim ignored the comment. "I have a way of"—Rim waved his hand in a small circle—"ensuring that, if you're taken by the Exiles, you won't be taken alone. I'll be with you."

"That's ridiculous. If only women are taken, it'll be me and no one else. You aren't a woman."

"Not yet." Rim rose and walked toward the fire. He stared into the flames, trying to still the turmoil within him. Becoming female wasn't easy. He wasn't sure if there was an easier way to become female, and there was no one he could ask. He'd discovered the ability by accident, and this was only the fourth time he'd controlled it. It still scared him shitless.

The flames danced in front of him, helping him empty his mind. Rim stared deep into the blue right at the center, watching the skip and slither, the way the flames separated and joined, separated and spiraled around each other. Eventually he closed his eyes, holding the image inside him, bringing it to a place deep within, the helix of fire eventually overlapping a similar shape inside him. He watched the flames and his helix, finding similarities and differences, then focused only on his own spiraling shapes.

There, at the bottom, a wobbly X kissed a small Y. That was the essence of him. Floating close by was a small tail, like one-quarter of the X. As he watched, the tail floated closer to the Y, soon joining it at the center. It wavered a little, then settled into place, creating another trembling X that slithered and slid beside the other one until it mirrored it exactly.

Rim panted, unable to keep his breathing even as his skin stretched, his bones shrank, and his abdomen folded in on itself, hollowing a place deep inside. He gritted his teeth against the pain. It wasn't bad, really. An arrow in the chest was certainly worse. He huffed a pained laugh. *Zar!* His jaw tensed as his skin rippled, rising and falling as it accommodated the changes in his body. Sweat beaded his forehead as he focused on remaining upright and quiet.

Harsh gasps escaped him, though, as his muscles cramped. He opened his eyes, staring heatedly at the flames, using them to center himself and keep himself connected to this world while his body rebuilt itself.

His shirt loosened around his chest as his ribs shrank, then tightened again as his burgeoning breasts stretched the fabric. A groan escaped him as his penis and testicles shrank and his trousers shifted, suddenly fitting loosely at the groin. Rim's heart pounded, his breath burned his throat, and he forced his mind clear again, focusing on the trembling second X spinning in his helix.

No distractions. Distractions made it slower, more painful. He'd found that out the last time. So he held his body rigid against the shuddering beneath his skin.

Finally it stopped.

Sweat ran down his spine and dripped from his nose and chin. His breathing was heavy, as if he'd spent the day running uphill. He lifted his head, looking away from the fire. Nine pairs of eyes swiftly looked away. Three of the men surreptitiously shifted their trousers. Ardelle's clear green gaze held his, a mixture of excited horror and awe coloring her features.

Rim had never performed the Change with an audience before. Now ten people had witnessed his body slide from male to female and— he remembered the hurried adjustments—some of them had liked it. It had never seemed like a sexual act before. It was just something that happened. Would it change his command? How would those three men who'd become aroused view him after this? Would he have to reassert his leadership just because he could be both a man and a woman?

Rim glanced around the cavern. He'd already proven he was their leader. As well, he had the ability to do something mentioned in only the oldest histories. They would respect that. He narrowed his eyes as one of Ardelle's men looked at him boldly. The lust was still there. That could be a problem.

He took a deep breath, noting how his body felt different, smelled different. He began to walk toward Ardelle, his legs trembling at the effort. He went slowly, every muscle protesting each movement. Rim resisted the urge to smash his new breasts flat. The weight of them seemed to pull him forward and his stumble became an ungainly lurching trot. He'd changed now so he could stay with Ardelle if she was kidnapped and fight beside her. They were moving into Exile territory, so an attack was likely. If he waited, any fight would be over before he completed the Change and he would be too weak to be of any help. Rim hoped he'd have time to recover his strength before that happened.

He slid down the wall beside Ardelle, automatically reaching to adjust himself and cringing when his hand came up empty. Nothing but loose trousers and… fuck… *nothing*. He wrapped his arms around his waist, but even that was different, smaller with a flaring at the hips. When he flung his head back and tried to breathe evenly, the rock behind him cracked against his skull.

What the fuck have I done to myself?

One Pure, prophecy revoked
One Great Heart Farseeing
One Changeling fooling wing
One Shining Silver from Rock

  —extract from the Warrior Pledge, prophecy of the Mafdeti, natural inhabitants of the planet Thalazar.

8.
MAFDETI

CHECA PROWLED down a narrow tunnel, looking for Jun. The bloody cat had gone AWOL again, and Checa was done with it. When Checa found him, Jun would realize how easy Checa had been on him in the past.

As he passed an alcove, a tawny arm reached out and grabbed him, dragging him off-balance and into the alcove.

Checa twisted out of Heath's grasp and shoved him against the rock wall even though he didn't need to be so rough. Heath never resisted him.

"That sort of thing could get you killed," hissed Checa as Heath lifted his head and grabbed Checa's face between his hands.

"You knew it was me. You always know." Heath pulled Checa's head lower.

The kiss was no more gentle than their hands had been. It had been days since they'd touched each other, and with the thought of what was to come, of Heath in danger, Checa was frantic with need. He plunged his tongue deep into Heath's mouth, mimicking what he wanted his dick to do lower down.

Heath tore himself away. "Gods, yes, do it now." He pushed at Checa's shoulders until Checa moved back so Heath had room to turn to face the wall.

Checa fumbled at his loincloth, lifting it to expose his dick. His hair rippled down his back as the cool air hit the warm, moist skin of his cock. "We don't have time for this."

"We never have time on a mission. When has that ever stopped us?" Heath groaned.

Checa stepped forward again and leaned against Heath's back. He could never say no to his lover, and he didn't know what he was going to do if Heath died. Checa would have to make sure it didn't happen. Not to Heath.

"Now, Checa."

"Not so fast, lover." Checa gripped his own cock, bringing it back to full hardness, then wiped the thick, sticky fluid from around the head. He pushed the lubricant around and into Heath's exposed opening.

"Yes," hissed Heath as Checa positioned his cock and slowly penetrated. "Faster."

"Patience." Checa's heart pounded with need and laughter bubbled inside him. The combination still amazed him, even after all these years with Heath.

Then he was all the way in, snug inside Heath's tight channel. He closed his eyes and savored the feeling. Belonging. Rightness. No one else gave him this.

"Checa," whined Heath. "I need it now."

Checa huffed a laugh as he reached a hand around Heath, finding his prick already exposed and leaking precome. "You always need it, Heath, and I always give it to you."

Their future might be a short one, but Checa would never stop giving Heath exactly what he wanted. He pulled out slowly, smiling at the shiver that rippled the dark hair hanging down Heath's spine.

"Checa. Now."

Checa slammed into his lover, the force knocking the breath out of Heath as he thumped against the rock. Heath's cock slid deliciously through the snug hold of Checa's fingers.

Fast and rough, and Checa came first, his orgasm flooding through him like warmth returning to frostbitten fingers. He leaned into Heath, soaking up the acceptance as his body pulsed and sparked. Finally his consciousness rose to the surface again to find Heath's fingers gripping his around Heath's cock, sliding them roughly up and down. Heath's breath rasped hot and moist over the cool rock, and it was Heath surrounding him, grasping him spasmodically as warm stickiness flooded over their fingers.

When Heath's breathing slowed, Checa lifted off him and gently withdrew. Heath turned to face him. Checa looked deep into the gaze of the only man he had ever loved. Again the laughter threatened to escape, but Checa held it in. That kind of joy was for people who deserved it.

Heath did laugh, quietly, joyfully, as he tucked his cock away. "Never stop looking at me like that."

"Like what?"

Heath cupped Checa's cheek. "I love your eyes."

Checa ducked his head and tucked himself back into his loincloth as he stepped away. There was nothing to love about his eyes. All his eyes ever told anyone was that he'd killed a man—two.

"Do you think she's the Pure? And I still can't work out how that dark-haired man's the Changeling." Heath threaded his hands through Checa's hair as he spoke, smoothing out the long waves.

The joy remained glowing inside as Checa leaned in and brushed a quick kiss across Heath's lips, but it was time to get back to business. "You check the cavern again. I'll round the others up and make sure we're ready to leave." Heath nodded, obedient but not subservient. With him, Checa wasn't just the leader. They were a team.

"Ten male, one female, far wall" came the report as Checa moved to the viewing hole, his feet padding silently on the sandy rock. His nose twitched and he frowned. The scents were distinctive.

"*Two* female." He turned away. They never looked for long.

Heath frowned and checked the group in the cave again. "I don't understand," he breathed. "There was only one fifteen minutes ago."

Checa stared through the hole, sniffing. The Princess, small and bald, looked up, and he backed away. "The Princess senses us."

"That was quick."

Checa shook his head. "Her eyes are reflective in the low light."

The faces around him settled into comic combinations of fear and anticipation. Fear of being caught or of failing to engage her. Anticipation at finding the woman they'd been seeking.

"It must be her, Checa. What about the other one?"

Checa shook his head. "I don't know where she came from, and I can't see Rim of Analee anywhere. We'll take both of them and find Rim as well." He motioned to two of his men. "Make sure they're all in the cave. There might be more in the tunnels." He looked around before returning his attention to Heath. "Where's Jun?"

Heath surveyed the cave, a puzzled frown on his face.

Just as Checa was about to resume his search for the other Mafdeti, Jun crawled out of a tunnel that led back toward Hawkesby, his lips held in a tight line, his brow furrowed. He saw Checa and Heath and came over to them.

Checa frowned at the man. "We're on a mission, Jun. Stay with the team. This is your last warning. You'll be facing disciplinary procedures once we return if you don't stay with the group." He waited long enough for the cat to nod submissively, then turned to Heath.

"You and Jun keep watch here. I'll go to the other side. The quicker and quieter we can remove those women, the better. Heath, follow me when the others report back. I'll need help getting the two women into the vent." Checa slipped his slim pack off and handed it to Jun.

"Can't we just go straight through? It's been a while since we've had a real fight." Heath bounced on his toes, his powerful thigh muscles flexing.

"It's been a while since one of us died too, and I want to keep it that way. Remember our mission and don't get distracted." His gaze slid from Heath's unruly tortoiseshell hair right down to his broad feet, and back. "Not too much anyway," he murmured, a shimmer of desire rippling down his spine as he remembered their recent interlude.

Heath chuckled. Checa winked at him, knowing what his lover was thinking. He turned and began to crawl through the naturally formed vents that fed fresh air to the caverns. He made his way to an opening in a fissure just behind the women.

The second woman was a mystery. Checa was sure Heath was right and she hadn't been there just minutes before, and no one had come into the cave. Where had she come from? They couldn't have missed her on their first inspection. Her scent was unusual. Checa would have noticed that. He imagined he could smell her still, even as thick rock walls separated them. It was spicy and earthy and seemed familiar somehow.

It would overwhelm him if he let it. He could feel the tug toward the women even now, when it was only him in a tunnel and rock separated him from the alluring aroma. He had to keep tight control on his emotions or he'd forget his reason for being here. Was this what Heath meant when he'd told Checa they'd know the other two of the Pledge team when they met them?

Fuck, he hoped Heath didn't feel the same pull to that scent. Heath could be easily distracted, and they all needed to stay focused on their goal. Checa could feel the movement of Makai and Nayeli behind his eyes, and he knew time was running out.

He slid into place behind the Princess just as Ardelle said, "You can complete the Warrior Pledge yourself. Why do you need me?"

Checa's heart pounded so hard it vibrated through his body. A tremor shivered down his arms to his hands. These women must be the Changeling and the Pure. Both of them. But Rim was carrying the other half of the key. Checa frowned into the shadowed silence. Legend had it that only a Changeling could control the key, so where was Rim, and where did this new Changeling come from?

The Princess wasn't a Changeling, for all her lack of hair. Checa could smell the permanence of her form with an underlying feline muskiness. She had to be the Pure, the one with the ability to heal others. He wasn't sure about the other woman. He sidled closer to the gap in the rocks and inhaled deeply. All woman… yet there was something else. He moved a little closer, closing his eyes to focus on separating the various odors from the cavern.

That was it—an undertone he'd only smelled once before, when he was small. His mother had staggered into the camp, beaten and bloody, sobbing "He couldn't stop!" over and over. Checa's younger brother had been born afterward. On his mother's skin had been a remnant of that same scent. His brother's sire had been a Changeling in rut.

Checa had never found out what he changed into.

The tall woman in the cavern was the same species as the man who'd raped his mother. The strength of the genes was there. She could wield the key and control the consequences. Did those women realize they wouldn't be able to trigger the ritual without him and Heath? Were they searching for him even as he was searching for them?

The tall one's voice was thick and husky when she spoke. "I don't know what you're talking about. I need you to fulfill the terms of the Warrior Pledge as it's laid down in the treaty."

Checa hissed softly. *Fuck.* It was Rim.

Rim was the Changeling, and Heath would shit himself when he found out what Rim turned into.

Then Rim's words sank in. Rim thought the Warrior Pledge was a treaty and nothing else. He and Ardelle didn't know what they were doing. Neither of them. Checa ran a frustrated hand down his face, swearing under his breath.

This was going to be worse than he thought.

9.
SILVER SHINING FROM ROCK

CHECA BACKED up along the tunnel when Ardelle headed in his direction. He needed to grab her and Rim, but he'd prefer to do it without being spotted. Ardelle stopped next to a gash in the cave wall, the opening to the tunnel Checa hid in. He wondered if she knew exactly what she was capable of. Being the Pure, she'd not only be able to heal, but she'd also have the ability to sense the planet. Like Heath could, perhaps more so.

He'd have to ask Heath more about the Pledge. All he really knew was what was taught in kindergarten and in warrior training. As a Seer, Heath would know more and be able to recognize and interpret all the signs. Meanwhile, they might have to contend with at least half of the warriors in the Pledge not knowing anything about it beyond what their weak treaty specified.

Ardelle stopped and turned back to the opening, and Checa saw his chance. As she took a step toward freedom, he grabbed her from behind, one hand over her mouth, the other wrapped around her waist to lift her off her feet. Between one breath and the next, he had her inside the fissure and backing down the tunnel, away from her people. Her breathing was all he could hear, and he hoped her men hadn't noticed her disappearance yet.

She went stiff with shock, and that allowed Checa to carry her to the turn where the tunnel ended and another arm branched off, narrower and more difficult to maneuver in. He kept a tight hold on her; she'd begin to struggle soon enough. Only a slim sliver of light crept into the narrow space now, fading to gray the deeper they went.

Checa could hear her heart thudding, an echo of her isolation. No one would hear her if she cried out. Hopefully no one even knew she was gone. They would look for her once they noticed she'd disappeared, but for now Checa was in the clear. He had to move her quickly to where Heath would be waiting.

Kidnapping. This was totally different to enticing females into the pride. This was something that Checa could lose his position over, his freedom. He'd be locked in a dank, dark cell with no way out, and the Bastard would make him… make him….

The girl lifted her feet and slammed them back into his shins. He grunted and struggled to hold her, squeezed her ribs to make sure she didn't slither away. Her hot breath washed over his hand and her jaw worked, so he pressed harder against her teeth so that she couldn't open her mouth and bite him. She'd probably have bruises later. Small sounds squealed in her throat and every beat of her heart betrayed her fear.

Beneath Checa's hand her stomach clenched, and she brought her legs up, trying to get purchase on the rock walls on either side. One foot caught a protruding rock but the forward movement continued, pulling her leg at the hip, wrenching a cry from her. She might be tiny, but she knew how to fight.

"Stop it. You'll hurt yourself." Checa shifted so her foot released from the rock and fell. "That's going to hurt when the pain catches up to you."

She writhed, kicking again, scratching at his hand, but his hold was secure. As he rounded the corner to the slim space where Heath waited, she stopped fighting against him and started scrabbling at his hand over her mouth.

"Ease up. She can't breathe," said Heath from above her.

"Fuck!" Checa stopped, and in one movement he let her go, then spun her around to face him, releasing his hold on her mouth and pushing her forehead back, his arm around her back crushing her body close to his. She was a shadow, black on black, her gasping breaths warm on his chilled skin. "Stop fighting, you idiot. I'm not going to hurt you."

The girl froze as she stared at him, the fight draining from her as fast as a waterfall. Her face was shadow upon shadow, no features visible in the darkness of the narrow tunnel, as if she were part of the rock surrounding them. He must look the same to her.

"Silver Shining from Rock," she whispered.

"Good. You recognize me. You know what this means?" Fuck. His eyes were silver? He wasn't going to kill her. He dropped her to the ground and stepped back.

She nodded. Her breath huffed from her and her eyes glistened in the dim light.

"Hand her up to me," Heath commanded.

Checa hesitated, then leaned close to her again. "Make no sound, or you will die." The words grated from him, the lie tearing at his soul because he knew he could do it even if he had no intention of harming her. He waited a breath. "Nod if you understand."

She nodded, her stiff body showing she had no doubt she would die as quickly as he suggested.

Checa spanned her lower ribs and lifted her high, bringing her closer to him. Instinctively he sniffed her, wanting to know her better. She kicked her feet, hitting his thigh. He grunted.

Heath gripped under her arms and lifted her from Checa as he dragged her through the hole in the ceiling of the tunnel. Rock scraped the backs of her hands as she passed through.

"Move back to the area. I'll get the other and meet you there." Checa was more convinced than ever that the two women were the other couple in the Warrior Pledge.

They'd better be.

"You can put me down. I'll come quietly," she said to Heath, her voice quiet and calm.

Heath chuckled as he leaned toward her and sniffed behind her ear. She threw her head back away from him and cuffed the back of his head. Heath laughed but muffled the sound immediately. "It's no problem. You're only little. No trouble at all."

She huffed.

"It's not often I get to hold a woman in my arms." He juggled her closer to him, sliding her against his body. "I think I'll enjoy it while I can. We'll have to crawl soon."

"You touch me any more than you are right now and you're dead," she hissed at him.

Heath chuckled again. "Yes, ma'am," he responded happily.

Good, thought Checa. She'd handle herself in their all-male company.

"Heath, stop fucking around and get moving." Heath moved away with the girl, leaving Checa staring at a gaping black hole. Checa rubbed the sudden ache in his stomach. He knew Heath would eventually find someone else, but he hadn't thought it would be a woman.

After a few awkward seconds of reminding himself he wasn't dying, Checa retraced his steps. He needed to find a way to get the other woman—Rim—into the fissure too. As he rounded the corner and the light from the cave spilled in, he realized he didn't need to. Rim had noticed the girl was missing and had followed.

Checa stepped back and waited as Rim took a few steps farther, the opening to the cavern now hidden from sight. No sound came from her, and Checa hoped she didn't hear his breathing. This kidnapping business was more stressful than he'd thought it would be. Was his breathing echoing from the rock?

Rim's boots crunched on the loose gravel underfoot as she edged her way around the curve. As she reached a patch of full dark, Checa lunged at her. The breath swooshed out of her lungs as he slammed her into the rock wall. Checa pressed his forearm against her collarbone, forcing her chin up, disrupting her breathing. Her heart beat fast, ready to fuel her response, and Checa pressed harder.

"Not a sound," he hissed. Then he pressed his nose behind the woman's ear and inhaled, suddenly understanding why Heath had done the same to Ardelle. Their scents complimented his and Heath's perfectly. Rim lifted her hands and shoved at Checa's broad shoulders, fumbling as she tried to find a pressure point, but Checa pressed closer still, trying to gauge how fragile her bones were, not wanting to cause lasting harm. He shoved his knee between her legs to hold her immobile and keep himself safe from any attack to the groin.

Rim pressed back into the wall, her breath coming in hard gasps. Checa followed, his breathing matching hers, hoarse and fast. Rim twisted and fought, but her movements were strangely jerky and uncoordinated. Useless against Checa's larger, stronger body.

"Checa." Heath's whisper above them brought Checa back from the need to attack, subdue, and win, and he stilled.

So did Rim.

"We need to hurry. Zenith is approaching."

Checa lifted away from Rim.

"Mafdeti!" Her voice was low and husky.

"We have the Princess," Checa rumbled through the air, barely audible. "Will you come peacefully?"

"Ardelle? Is she unharmed?" The woman shoved against Checa's shoulders again but Checa held his position. "Why are you doing this?"

Checa stepped back a little. "You won't be harmed."

"Your eyes," she whispered.

Fuck, were they silver again? How? He wasn't going to kill her. "You know of the Warrior Pledge?"

Rim stood straighter. "I've invoked the Warrior Pledge."

"Good. We need to hurry if we're to beat the zenith."

Warily, Rim nodded.

Checa sighed, a little purr deep in his throat, then bent to grasp her around her ribs. "Raise your arms," he whispered. He lifted as Rim raised her arms but didn't get far before her scent stopped him cold. Her scent assailed him, reminding him that *she* was *him*. They were the same person. "The Changeling."

"Checa, stop it. Pass her up."

Checa growled but lifted her high. Heath pulled her through the hole in the ceiling, then turned to give Checa a hand up. Checa landed softly beside them in a comfortable crouch. "Situation?" He stared intently at Rim but didn't speak to her.

"They've noticed the women are missing." Heath dragged a stone over the hole they'd just come through. "We have less than two minutes before they reach this end of the tunnel. It's only a matter of time before they find this shaft."

"The Princess?"

"With the others." White teeth flashed in the darkness. "Complaining and demanding."

"You sound like that's a good thing."

"It's entertaining, at least," replied Heath.

Checa huffed, then grabbed Rim's arm. "On my back, left arm over my shoulder, right under my right arm." He tugged her closer. "*Quickly*. We don't have much time if you want to find your friend." He dropped to all fours, allowed a partial Change to take him to were form, then tugged Rim's arm until she climbed aboard and wrapped herself around him as instructed. In the darkness she probably wouldn't see the strange way his legs folded under him or the soft pads on his palms. That shock would come later. He looped a hand behind one of Rim's knees and pulled it up, a rumbled purr vibrated under his belly when she complied without complaint. "Keep your head down," he said, and loped off into the darkness. Rim tightened her grip but kept her head up. "Put your fucking head down, you fool. The shaft narrows here."

She dropped her head to Checa's neck just in time. The rock ceiling scraped against her back. She tightened her grip further, obviously realizing her head could have been knocked off at the speed they were traveling.

Checa grinned. He loved running blind, trusting only his instincts to keep him safe. It was something he and Heath did whenever they had the opportunity.

After a few short minutes, they reached the cave, dimly lit through small holes in the wall from the fire in the large cavern where the other soldiers now searched for them. The Princess crouched under a low overhang at the farthest point of the cave, warily eyeing Checa's men gathered a few feet away from her. The six of them regarded her with equal amounts of wariness and awe. Checa wondered what she'd said to bring about that reaction in six seasoned soldiers.

The Princess still had her knives strapped to her body. Next to her was a body-sized hole just tall enough to carry them as they'd been traveling—on all fours with the women on their backs.

Heath ruffled the hair behind Checa's ear before he went to Ardelle and spoke softly to her, reaching a hand to her arm. Checa heard Heath's soft chuckle when Ardelle hissed at him, but he backed off and waited patiently while she rose beside him. He gave her instructions, then bent down. From beside Checa a soft gasp escaped Rim as she watched Heath's body fold in on itself as he changed to were form.

"It's how we travel so quickly," Checa said quietly, not revealing they had yet another form that could travel greater distances more comfortably.

Within seconds, Heath went from a tall, upright man, with long, flowing, tortoiseshell hair and soft brown eyes to a man who looked a bit like a cat, crouched on all fours, his heavy thighs primed and ready to run. The Princess crawled onto Heath's back, then eyed them warily.

"Where are you taking us?" Rim inspected Checa's men and the cave they were in. She turned her glare to Checa and gasped.

Had she not realized she was still sitting on his back? Or was her surprise because Checa was in were form?

"We need to…." Her voice was breathless, struggling to remain calm.

"I know. We're heading to the Lake of the Damned now. You'll be there in time." Checa growled low in his throat and all eight Mafdeti moved, ready to evacuate.

"My men—"

"Aren't needed for the Warrior Pledge. We'll move much faster without them." He turned to Jun. "Make sure there are enough signs they can follow. I expect these two will want their team around them once the Warrior Pledge is completed."

"You know about the Warrior Pledge?" the Princess asked.

"Of course. We're part of it."

"Analee hasn't signed a treaty with you," she said.

"There was no need to." Surely the people from the valley knew the Warrior Pledge was more than their treaty with the Imperials.

Checa's men shifted to were form and moved toward the opening they would take, their legs folded in impossible positions, allowing their torsos to be parallel to the ground. In this position they could fit into small tunnels and still move quickly, their broad, padded feet and hands barely stirring dust, hiding their passage.

One by one they entered the opening. The run through the tunnels became a blur of scraping sandstone and the occasional dripping of moisture over limestone. In complete darkness. It was exhilarating to run like this. Behind him, Checa heard Heath's steady breaths, the soft padding of his hands and feet on the sandy rock. On Checa's back, Rim pressed her cheek into the soft fur that sprouted on his nape. Her warm breath seeped into his senses. Every lope rubbed her against his back and she gripped him firmly to stop the slip and slide as they moved.

Checa's stomach grumbled for the tenth time, the sensation hollow inside him, and he slowed. Light pierced the tunnel and Rim lifted her head. Checa helped her slip off his back and find her feet again. Within seconds his entire team had stopped and gathered at a surface exit, once again in human form.

"Just stretch," Checa commanded. "Don't go far. We'll be leaving soon." The sun was nearly directly overhead, and the air shimmered like fog above the surface of the baked red rock.

Heath came over and stood beside Checa. He looped his arm with his and grinned at the Princess and the Changeling. "I'm Heath, and this is Checa. You know about the Warrior Pledge?"

"Of course," said the Princess again, haughtily.

"This is the Princess Ardelle, and I'm Rim of Analee," said Rim. "I invoked the Warrior Pledge when I was in Hawkesby. That's why we're traveling back to the Analee Valley."

Checa nodded. "The Crystal River. You need to go to the Lake of the Damned."

Confusion filled both Ardelle's and Rim's faces. "It's the Yeudan that are the threat to us," said Rim. "Yeudan. There've been sightings at the headwaters of the Crystal River."

"Checa, it's getting close," called Jun.

"Okay." Invaders weren't one of the signs of the Pledge. He wanted to ask Rim what she was talking about, but they needed to move quickly. "Shift," he ordered.

All around him his men morphed into full cat form, except for Jun who stood guard at the wedge of light leading to the surface. Checa smiled at the twin gasps from Rim and Ardelle.

"Heath, you take the Princess again," he instructed. When Heath gestured to the Princess and began giving her instructions, Checa turned to Rim. "We're going to run now. Take the same hold you had on me before and keep your head down. We'll be running fast, and the closer you stay to my back, the less wind resistance there'll be. If you slow us down, we might not make it."

"Make what?" asked Rim.

"The next tunnel."

"You're going on the surface? You can't do that. It's the middle of the day." Rim looked horrified.

It was a reasonable response, considering what the norrgel did to anyone they targeted, but Rim's response seemed more than the usual horror. Her eyes were wide, verging on panicked.

"Climb on my back now." Checa shifted to were form only because he couldn't speak in full cat form, even if it was faster.

"The norrgel!" Rim didn't move as Checa instructed.

"We move fast." Checa tried to inject a soothing quality into his voice. Heath was so much better at this stuff than he was, but he was busy getting the Princess settled on his back. Checa looked back at Rim. "We've done this before, Rim. As long as you stay low and hold on, we'll be fine. Okay?"

Rim took a long breath, then nodded.

Quickly, Checa lowered to all fours. Once Rim was settled, Checa shook himself slightly to make sure she was holding on properly. Satisfied, he moved to the entrance.

"Jun?" Checa bit out the single word.

Jun jerked and frowned before moving back to the entrance and peering outside. Near his thigh he held his hand with fingers straight out, a clear sign for them to hold their positions. Then one finger disappeared into the palm of his hand. A few seconds later another finger was folded in. Then a third and a fourth. Checa tensed, ready to run.

When the fifth finger folded into the fist, the Mafdeti moved. Checa motioned for his team to leave first. He and Heath would bring up the rear so they didn't slow the others down.

Rim sat up straight. "Do you really mean to go out there? The wings are up."

"Lie down you idiot. The norrgel rest during the zenith but not for long." Checa slid quickly through the low opening, forcing Rim to duck or lose her head. "Now hold on."

He barely gave her time to lie flat and grasp a handful of fur before he took off running.

If Rim had thought the previous ride was precarious, she was wrong. This time the Mafdeti galloped flat out, the hot air streaking over them, burning Checa's lungs as he struggled to breathe against the erratic pounding of his adrenaline-fueled heart.

10.
SURFACE RUN

HEATH'S STRIDE faltered when Ardelle lifted her head.

"Zar, we're going fast." Her voice whipped away in the wind. The landscape slid by in a rusty blur and she laughed out loud.

Heath flicked a look back at her, grinning. It was the best way to travel. "Enjoying yourself, Princess?"

Ardelle sat up straighter, using her thighs to keep balanced. "This is brilliant!"

Heath chuckled, his broad shoulders rolling as he galloped across the burning earth, the black lumps of sleeping birds flitting past in a kaleidoscope of shadows. "Glad you like it, but you'd better lie down again and be quiet."

Instead of listening to him, Ardelle raised her arms above her head, swinging them out in a wide V. The scorching wind rushed past them even as her position slowed them. Heath pushed harder, trying to keep their speed. Red gravel and round black rocks flew past beneath them, blurring in the heat and the speed.

"*Yah!*" she yelled.

Heath's stride slowed further with her movements. Fuck, she was going to get them killed. "Lie down now," he growled. "You'll wake the norrgel."

Ardelle flopped back to her prone position. "What?"

He growled again, his heart stuttering as her movement caused him to knock against a sleeping bird. "Those black rocks around us aren't rocks." His speed picked up now their silhouette was once again streamlined.

Ardelle moved so she could see to the front, then moved again to look to the side. If she kept moving, all the corrections he had to make to his stride to keep them balanced would slow them down again. As it was, Heath wasn't sure they'd make the next caves in time.

Ahead and all around them, matt black mounds dotted the landscape, staining the red-and-ochre earth like pox. Chills skittered down his spine as one of the birds moved, raising its head before settling again.

Ardelle pulled herself tighter to Heath's silhouette. "Go faster, cat," she whispered in his ear.

Too late. They were stirring now. All Heath could do was continue. He forced a ripple down his spine to ruffle his fur so it lay over her exposed limbs. Ardelle kept her hold steady, but they'd lost too much time. Heath's gaze rested on each sleeping bird as they ran. Only one had moved. The rest were as still as rocks, but Heath watched them. Once one was awake, they'd all wake. He still had nightmares from listening to one of the Descendants after they'd been wing-struck. He never wanted to hear that sound again.

The sun crept across the sky, sliding from the zenith. Heath's breathing was audible now, but he hoped he didn't show any other sign of strain as he galloped across the open ground. The other Mafdeti in his team drew ahead. Even Checa, larger and slower than Heath, was in front of them.

Gravel crunched as Heath's feet missed the careful placement from earlier in their mad run. It might have been a stray breeze riffling the feathers of the birds around them, except there was no breeze. The air was hot and heavy and utterly still, but the threads fluttered along the red earth.

The norrgel were awakening.

"Heath." Ardelle stretched even flatter along his back, her heart pounding against his spine, in time with the rhythm of his gait.

A low growl rumbled through his chest as his muscles stretched and bunched as he ran.

A few steps.

Feathers raised and fluttered.

A few more steps.

A head lifted, glossy onyx eyes blinking slowly in the harsh light. The norrgel were rising.

They were going to die.

Ardelle squeaked as a norrgel looked directly at them. Heath huffed and thought of saying something about the stupid little noise, but by now his breathing was so labored he didn't think he could get the words out.

He didn't want to admit it but she was too heavy for him and had slowed him too much when she thought it was fun. They wouldn't make it.

A whimper escaped her, and she buried her face into the hot, dusty fur at the back of Heath's neck. At least she finally realized the danger they were in.

An eerie cry exploded beside them, quickly fading behind. A norrgel had woken. Heath's heart pounded in his throat, and he swallowed down the panicked cries trying to escape. Another bird screeched on the other side. A third screech accompanied the flutter and rustle of wings as the birds prepared for flight.

In the distance, Heath's team was disappearing, dropping one by one down a shaft to the catacombs below.

The flutter of wings grew louder, merging with alarmed shrieks as more birds woke and found trespassers among them.

Five Mafdeti had disappeared, leaving only Checa and Rim ahead of them. The screeches and flapping rose above. Dust swirled and stung Heath's eyes, caught in his lungs. He sneezed, stumbling. He paused, regained his feet, ran again, but he couldn't regain his former speed. His breath rasped in harsh grunts.

The wings were up.

Screeches and the flapping of wings were above and around them as the birds found the warm updrafts and rose, preparing to dive and swoop.

Ahead, Checa lifted an arm and ran three-legged, while Rim slid around underneath his body. Only her forearms and shins remained visible. Checa shivered as he ran and within seconds the exposed limbs were covered by the cat's thick fur.

Heath slowed more, taking the risk with the norrgel to keep the Princess safe. "Ready?" he rasped. "Slide around on my command." One beat. A deep breath. Another stride. "Now!"

Ardelle slid over the side a second later. Her knee brushed the fine gravel under them, slowing them further, but she quickly lifted her leg closer to his body. She clasped her feet around his hips, her arms around his neck and across his upper back. Her body fell into place with a jolt, her spine scraping on the ground. As Heath ran, she lifted her body closer to his and buried her face in his neck. He swallowed against her lips, ruffled his fur so it covered her arms and legs completely, and then picked up the pace again.

The norrgel screeched, raucous against their trespassers. The flapping was coming closer. A siren sound grew closer: *Eeeee… whop…. Oooo* as it receded again. Heath grunted at a stinging pain, stumbled, continued running.

He'd been hit. Fuck, a norrgel had stung him. He wanted to stop and inspect the wound, see how bad it was, but if he did that, they'd be on him. He panted against the stinging pain.

Oh fucking ancestors, that was a bad one.

If it wasn't for Ardelle, Heath would be down the shaft by now. Instead he was going to die, and her with him. But he kept running and didn't scream the way he wanted to. Tears blurred his vision. A sob rose inside as the burn sank into his skin, deeper and deeper until it felt like he was breathing fire and running on coals.

"Don't die, don't die," Ardelle whispered.

Then the ground fell away and they tumbled into darkness.

THEY LANDED with a thud, Heath twisting at the last minute so he took the brunt of the fall. Ardelle landed on top of him, shooting flames of agony through his body. His breath whooshed from him and he groaned as soon as he had enough air to do so. He wasn't sure which one hurt worst, the wing-strike or the landing. He needed space to breathe, but she didn't move off him.

As the impact of the landing settled into identifiable pains, Heath knew with certainty he'd been hit hard. Scalding tendrils coursed through his body, making him twitch, tiny spasms beginning that would grow as the welts burst and the poison entered his body. Finally, Ardelle took a deep breath. They lay in a shaft of light from above, all around them deepest black, her arms still locked around him. He pushed feebly at her shoulders.

"Move, now," he said in a soft voice that rumbled with suppressed pain.

She bolted upright, gaining leverage by an elbow in his stomach.

"*Oof.*" He pushed her off him before she could bring her knees up.

"B-b-b—but you were hit! I know you were."

He scowled at her. "I know that. Hurts like the devil too." There was no point mentioning the pain was getting worse by the second. They had a mission to complete and an uncompromising deadline.

Heath rolled to his side and pushed himself shakily to his feet, the muscles in his arms and thighs twitching from overuse. His panting breath filled the cavern as he twisted his body to look at his back. The welt ran from below his left shoulder blade to the top of his right hip. He could see the bottom part of the slice and the top, but not the middle. The skin exposed beneath his tortoiseshell fur was ivory pale and gleamed in the light.

Fuck, that was bad.

"You're not going to die?" Ardelle asked.

"Not so far, but who can tell with these things. Is there any fur left on the welt?" If there was some fur left, even a little, it wouldn't be so bad. He arched his back. "Fuck I hate being scalped," he said, as if things like that happened every day. No point in panicking the girl.

Ardelle reached a tentative hand out and dragged the tip of a finger along the welt. Heath hissed, his skin cringing at the contact. Even air was too much for it right now. She snatched her hand back. "I'm sorry," she whispered. "Does it hurt?"

An exasperated huff filled the air between them. "I've just had a swathe of fur ripped from my skin. Of course it fucking hurts." He retracted the were form, gritting his teeth through the pain radiating from the strip of scalped skin. In his human form again, he took deep breaths through the stinging pain. Sand scraped on rock and his gaze flicked down the tunnel to where the others would be. A shadow separated from the darkness.

"Heath." Checa moved into the circle of light. "It's time to move."

Heath nodded and opened his mouth to tell Checa he'd been struck. He closed it with a snap. It might not be as bad as he thought it was. He didn't want to delay the team. They had the four they needed for the Pledge, so they could move quickly and get to the Lake of the Damned before Makai and Nayeli became one. That wouldn't happen if Heath started complaining about a little lost hair.

"Come on, Princess. Let's keep moving." He nodded at Checa.

Checa returned to the others, and Heath and the Princess followed.

Ardelle trotted along beside Heath. "Don't you want them to look at your wound?"

"We don't have time. The moons get closer every day." He increased his pace, calling over his shoulder. "Now move it."

Ardelle's footsteps sped up and she pushed past him roughly, jogging to catch up with the others. Heath stumbled; the push against him had triggered a cascade of spasms down his arm and through his chest. Gravel scrunched under his faltering steps and his arm thudded into rock wall. He let out a cry before sliding face-first down the uneven rock and crumpling to the ground. The dim light faded completely, and he knew he was going to pass out.

"Heath!"

CHECA FROZE at Ardelle's cry, spun on his heel, and ran. He dropped to his knees beside Heath and rolled him to his back. A fine film of perspiration sheened Heath's face and his breathing was shallow and rapid. Checa touched his cheek but snatched his hand away. Ancestors, he was hot. Heath's skin rippled, shivers racking his body.

"What happened?" The question was directed at Ardelle, but his gaze remained on Heath.

"I don't know what's wrong. He fell over. I turned and he was like this. If it was the norrgel-strike, his flesh would be bubbling out in a soggy mass by now, wouldn't it?" she asked.

Bubbles formed at Heath's lips. Checa's breath caught.

Norrgel-strike.

"Is it the norrgel-strike after all?" She pressed a hand to her stomach. "Is he going to die?" she whispered.

"Fuck," hissed Checa. Heath had been struck? Why the fuck didn't he mention it? "Jun!" he bellowed. Heath needed immediate treatment, but first they had to see how bad it was.

Jun scowled from his position with the other men, but moved quickly when he saw Heath down. Together they rolled Heath onto his stomach, hissing in unison when they saw the mottled red welt across his back.

"This is going to be a bad one." Checa tried to ignore the sick feeling in his stomach but couldn't get his hands to stop trembling. "Jun, prepare for a long one and bring the medical bag. We need the salves and grips." He forced himself into first-responder mode, then shifted one of Heath's legs until it was bent at hip and knee. He wrapped one of Heath's arms behind his knee so it held the two limbs in place.

"Princess," he demanded, "press here." He indicated the hollow behind Heath's raised knee.

Ardelle placed her small fingers on Heath's skin.

"*Press.* Hard. It helps keep the muscles stretched and minimizes the spasms."

She'd better not make this harder. Heath's life depended on them all doing the right thing.

Ardelle dug her fingers into the flesh, cringing when Heath groaned.

"Keep pressing. Don't release pressure for a second." Checa lifted his head to shout over her. "Jun, hurry up."

"Is he going to die?" The words fluttered from Ardelle, having no impact on the denial screaming through Checa's mind.

Checa looked hard into her eyes, pushing down the need to scream at her, to blame her for his mate… his *friend* being injured. "We'll soon find out," he growled and turned his attention back to Heath.

11.
NORRGEL-STRIKE

FUCK, IT was dark.

Even when he augmented his sight, Heath couldn't see through the thick blackness. His fur shivered on his right shoulder with a change in air currents. He was back in were form, and someone was about ten feet away and moving closer. He sniffed: Checa. His fur rippled again.

"You're alive, at least."

A laugh huffed from Heath, but quickly turned into a gasp.

Fuck, it hurts.

Somewhere deep inside Heath felt like he'd been beaten bloody. He lifted a shaking hand to brush his mouth. A dried, crackly substance fell away. Blood. Double fuck. That was bad. Unless...

"How long?"

"One and a half days. Jun says it's going to take time."

Double fuck and damn the wings. And then fuck it all.

Nearly two days already. He'd be as weak as a kitten for days. He dropped his hand limply to his side. That was it, then. He breathed through the tightness forming in his chest. It was the end of the mission for him, and he squeezed his eyes shut on the disappointment. Heath had been so sure he was one of the four, so sure he was meant to be there, that his presence was needed for it to succeed. But if this had happened, he must have been wrong. There must be another Seer with warrior abilities.

He sucked in air, cleared his mind of what he had wanted, and focused on what still had to be done. They'd wasted nearly two days waiting for him. They had to leave now and travel fast or they would be too late. Heath would slow them down if he tried to go with them....

Sleep took him again.

When Heath opened his eyes, the darkness had diminished. Torchlight bobbed toward him. The shadows of two women flowed behind it.

"Oh good, Checa said you'd wake again soon." Rim crouched beside him, shining the torch into his eyes.

Heath pulled away, squinting against the light.

"We brought soup." Rim gestured behind her and Ardelle moved forward with a bowl. "As soon as you've eaten, we'll move on."

Heath drew in another deep breath, his voice cracking as he did what had to be done. "Leave the soup here. I'll follow later."

Checa snorted. Heath jumped. He hadn't realized Checa stood behind the women. "You know the Pledge better than I do, Heath, so stop talking and eat. We need you to finish this mission."

Heath glared at his lover and took a sip of soup. "Are you planning to carry me the whole way, Checa? You know there are other ways to get me close." He tried to smile as he said it, but his body hurt too much and it fell flat. He reached out a hand and placed it on Checa's forearm. "Another will have to do the Warrior Pledge with you." He shook his head at the denial he could see rising to Checa's lips. "I'll slow you down too much, and you know it."

Rim cut Checa's growl short. "But the Warrior Pledge is just a treaty. It has nothing to do with the Mafdeti." Her voice, a warm contralto, was reminiscent of the hot springs on the Icy Wastes side of the Seven Mountains.

Heath and Checa froze at the implications of that statement. Checa's silver gaze mirrored the horror Heath was sure was clear in his own eyes. "Fuck," they gasped simultaneously.

Rim crossed her arms and lifted her chin.

Heath wasn't going to like what she said.

"The Warrior Pledge is part of the treaty between us and the Imperials." Her voice was clear and certain.

"Is that it? Is that all you think it is?" Checa's voice was cold. Angry. His tone called them seven kinds of fools even if his honor held the insult silent.

Heath gripped Checa's forearm for a second before easing his hold. He left his hand on Checa's arm, mostly because it felt good to touch him. Checa didn't move away as he often did when they were on a mission, so Heath took advantage and tilted his head against Checa's shoulder. He relaxed against his lover's warm flesh, absently noting that Checa was in human form again while Heath was still in his were form. Heath didn't shift. It would take too much energy, and with the pain from the norrgel-strike still pulsing through him, he wasn't sure he'd be able to do it again. He turned his attention back to Rim.

"It's a pledge between warrior nations to offer aid in time of need." Rim stood straight and proud. "There are invaders in the valley and I've invoked the Warrior Pledge to gain assistance from the Imperial forces before the foreigners arrive in force when the moons eclipse each other. We traveled to Hawkesby with the Ruby of Authority to appeal to the King for assistance. Princess Ardelle formed an investigative team and joined us." She glanced at the Princess.

"You think the Warrior Pledge is a treaty that relies on a tiny ruby to get a small bald woman to solve your problems?" Checa glared at Rim, his eyes silver, hard, and unyielding, the skin on his face granite smooth. Every muscle in his body was solid and still, waiting to react to more bad news. Heath loved it when Checa was in Commander mode.

A muscle jumped in Rim's jaw. Heath waited for her to say they knew what they were doing, that every aspect of this quest had been planned to the last detail, but she didn't. "The invaders brought papers with them. We've only managed to translate a small part, but they seem to indicate something big happening at the Lake of the Damned when the two moons eclipse. I need to protect my people." Her voice trembled.

Checa's lips moved, just a little, softening slightly around the edges. Just enough to tell Heath he wasn't happy but could understand Rim's actions. Heath could too. A small breath left him, a sigh of relief that Checa would continue with the mission.

"And you, Highness?" Checa's voice rumbled through the air, wilting the stiffness in Heath's spine with nothing more than a breath. "What can you add?"

Heath pushed the smile down; he loved how Checa always gathered all the facts before he made a decision.

"One will bring the key to a Pure who will wield it. One Shining Silver from Rock will save them." Ardelle recited the passages as if she were quoting poorly rhymed children's poetry.

Rim turned to Checa. "Your eyes shone silver against the darkness in the cave." Then she spoke to Ardelle, anger stiffening her features. "Tell me you haven't come all this way based on some childish rhyme. What about the treaty?"

Ardelle continued, lifting her chin as she pointedly ignored Rim. "The key will unleash the healing waters of the Lake of the Damned, and mankind will be saved."

Heath breathed words into the silence. "One Pure, prophecy revoked, one Great Heart Farseeing, one Changeling fooling wing, one

Shining Silver from Rock to open the door of the damned. There are four warriors of the Pledge, not two." He gestured weakly to Rim. "You are the Changeling. The only one in a thousand years."

Checa took over the explanation. "The Princess is the Pure, with the necessary mental capacity to trigger the key. I am the Silver Shining from Rock, the protector, and the one who will open the doorway and, it seems, save you from folly." He gestured to his eyes. "Again, the only one for a millennium."

"What about the Heart, then? What does that mean?"

Heath could feel time slipping away. They had to move quickly if they were to be ready for the eclipse, but he doubted he could even stand on his own feet after the norrgel-strike. Checa looked at him, a soft smile in his bright eyes. "There must be one among us who can see what will happen and show us the way. Heath is the only one who can do that."

"What do you mean 'see what will happen'?" asked Rim.

"It was Heath's instincts that led us to the cavern where we found you. It will be his talents that show us the way to the lake in time to fulfill the prophecy."

"But he's ill. He can't travel like that." Ardelle planted her hands on her hips. "I know the way to the lake. I can lead as well as he can." She flicked an impatient look at Heath. "He said to leave him here with food. When he's recovered, he'll follow."

Checa chuckled, although Heath could find nothing amusing. The others had spent nearly two days waiting for Heath to regain consciousness. At least Ardelle was seeing sense even if her callousness sat sharply on his soul.

"You don't get it even yet. The Pledge says there are four travelers, and four there must be. Without him we will fail." Checa bent to grab Heath by the arm and swung him over his back, piggyback style. "You're right when you say we're running out of time. In fact, there's no time to take the usual routes to the Lake of the Damned."

Checa walked into the blackness with Heath draped over him. Heath gasped at the pain the sudden movement caused but bit down on it as quickly as he could. Checa knew he hurt; there was no point in reminding him every time Heath moved.

Rim hurried after them, Ardelle at her heels. They moved swiftly down the tunnel, past the rest of the Mafdeti who scrambled to follow.

Rim broke into a jog beside them. "What do you mean 'the usual routes'? There's only one route from this direction, and that's through the Pass of Nines and around the northern edge of the Aylmer Mountains. It's a Mafdeti stronghold, but you'll be able to get us through."

Checa began shaking his head before Rim finished. "No time. We have to go directly to the lake from this side of the mountains, and we can't go overland all the way. I thought we'd make it, but the norrgel breeding season has begun early this year. They're too aggressive and their sleep times are unreliable. We have to find a way through the catacombs."

Heath dropped his head onto Checa's shoulder, partly because it felt too heavy to keep up, but also because he knew what the catacombs would mean. He'd be spending time counting grains of sand and smashing his way through weak points. All those times Checa insisted he accept his talents and practice them suddenly made sense. Heath had always thought it was because Checa loved him just as he was and wanted him to be exactly who he was meant to be, but perhaps that wasn't it at all. Maybe Checa had been training him because he knew Heath would be needed now. Perhaps Checa had been using him all along.

Heath's heart ached at the thought and rejected it, but his brain still spun with the possibility.

Ardelle jogged beside them, her short legs taking two steps to one of Checa's, but she still breathed easily. "There is no way through the catacombs from here to the mountains. It's been surveyed. There are collapsed tunnels and dead ends, but no passage through."

Checa's face split into a grin and he winked at Rim, causing her to trip over air. Heath couldn't help grinning as well. He knew exactly how Rim felt. Checa had that effect on him too.

"And that's exactly why we need Heath," Checa said. "He will find even the smallest opening for us."

They stopped, dead center of an intersection. Three pathways opened before them, one a large open tunnel curving into the blackness. The second was the height of a man's hips, a round hole at head height. The last path was little more than a dark horizontal slash about a foot above ground level, several meters wide but barely high enough to fit a man's chest through.

Checa slid Heath off his back, spinning and grabbing him around his chest when he would have fallen. Heath stared into Checa's familiar face. He wouldn't believe his lover had been using him all this time. They'd been friends for years before they discovered Heath's talents, and years more before they became lovers.

His face flooded with heat when Checa fondled the fur on the back of his neck, then gripped it and pulled to look at Heath's face. Heath shivered, imagining those hands on the rest of him, sliding over smooth skin, dipping between—

He blinked the fantasy away when Checa spoke.

"Which one, Heath?" The gentle tone washed over the small group. Checa bent his head toward Heath's and rubbed his cheek against Heath's face.

Heath breathed in the familiar warm spice of him and relaxed. Checa matched his breathing, and Heath closed his eyes, allowing himself to sink further into the meditation. They were perfect together like this. With Checa everything was effortless.

Within seconds he could feel the world permeate his being. The cavern ceased being a hole under the rock. Instead it became billions of molecules, the gases they breathed, compounds that fused together to create the rocks around them. Grains of sand, stuck together and compressed.

Heath lifted his chin and sniffed, searching for the pathway through the rock to the Aylmer Mountains where the Lake of the Damned had its roots. Inside him he could feel the pressure that held the grains of sand together. Without opening his eyes, he turned his head to the passage on the left. It looked promising, so he spun through it, ephemeral and ghostly, until he reached an impasse where the grains were so densely compacted they would never break through. The next passage yielded the same result, only much faster. Beads of sweat trickled down his face, the effort of reading the rock tiring him more than it had since he was fourteen and discovered it for the first time.

The third passage, small and narrow, showed immediate promise. It would be a tight fit, but they could do it. They'd have to be full cat or human; their were forms would never fit in the space. There was a dead end, a blockage, but it felt malleable. Then after that, nothing, a great, gaping pocket of air that led to the surface and the mountains. Heath gasped as he let the meditation go and opened his eyes.

"They're so beautiful together." Ardelle's voice was small and wistful.

Heath watched, half-asleep, as Rim looked at her closely. The self-assured Princess looked little more than a young girl unsure of her place in life. And she was very young—not yet twenty.

Rim shuffled a little closer to her. "They are," she said.

Ardelle lifted a startled face to Rim, drawing a reluctant smile from the tall woman. Rim looked again at Checa and Heath and sighed. So did Ardelle.

"I don't know what comes next," Ardelle said. "The original Pledge says something about tablets of stone. They must be at the lake and contain instructions."

Frustration and anger warred deep within Heath, but he couldn't give in to negative feelings now. They'd barely begun, and his people were relying on him, but he hated not having a plan of action. And he hated being so weak. He'd never been dependent on others, but in the last few days since the strike, all control had been wrest from him.

Heath turned to look at the team again, sliding his gaze over Jun. The slim, dark Mafdeti glared at him and Checa with a hatred that was palpable. Jun noticed Heath looking at him and turned away. Heath opened his mouth to warn Checa that Jun might cause trouble, but Rim spoke first.

"We have to trust the Mafdeti to get us to the lake. And we have to trust that by then we'll have a plan of action."

Heath agreed; he'd worry about Jun later. He could handle any trouble Jun caused. Time to get this group back on the road and complete the Pledge.

"WHEN WILL you take the Princess?" Jun leaned close to Fisher to reduce the risk of their voices carrying in the quiet tunnel.

"Where are you heading?" Fisher was just as quiet.

"The Lake of the Damned."

"The rest of the soldiers?"

"They were left behind. I think they're heading to the lake by another route." Jun grimaced. He'd hoped to be able to spend time with Fan since they were both heading in the same direction, but he'd had to leave when Checa gave the order. His stomach squirmed, tight and uncomfortable since they'd found the women. Hopefully he'd see his lover before they got to the lake. Maybe they could even spend a whole night together.

Fisher nodded. "That'll make it easier. I'll organize an ambush and take the women then."

Jun stared at the Exile. "Both of them? Why?"

"The other's a Changeling. She'll be valuable to the Yeudan. I can use her to bargain for better treatment for the Mafdeti."

"Better treatment? What are you talking about? We're just overthrowing the Imperial command so we can take control of our own lives again. We're not giving that up to anyone else."

Fisher sighed. "You know as well as I do that an invasion is an invasion. The winners will have control."

Jun seethed at this turn of events. "Then we have to make damned sure *we* win."

Fisher didn't respond, and Jun eyed him suspiciously, wondering if he'd been wrong to trust the man with the odd patchwork skin. He put his suspicions aside and focused on keeping his men safe. They all had to survive so he could find Fan again. He must be worried about Jun; it had been so long.

"You'll give a signal before the ambush? And my men will be unharmed?"

Fisher looked at Jun for a long time before nodding and turning away. Jun clenched his fists, wishing he'd been able to capture Fan along with the women, even though he hadn't seen him in the cavern they had taken the women from. Jun needed his mate with him now to talk to about this. Had they made the wrong decision trusting Fisher? Jun turned away from the direction the Exile had gone and jogged back to his own people.

12.
THROUGH THE ROCK

THEY'D BEEN crawling for hours. The narrow tunnel went up and down and around like a summer sea squall. Checa barely knew which direction was up after so long.

The Change from were to human so he could fit into the tunnels meant he had no protection on his hands or knees. Heath slept fitfully, draped over Checa's back. Checa loved the feel of his lover so close, but the added weight meant the sharp edges of rocks dug deeper into his palms and knees with each step. His stomach growled again, letting him know it was hours past his usual mealtime. And still they crawled in the pitch black, the torches long since doused.

The only thing that anchored him to reality and stopped blackness swamping him completely was the occasional scrape on rock by some carelessly placed knee or the soft grunts that accompanied someone's head banging on rock protruding from the low ceiling. That happened often enough for the sharp scent of fresh blood to mix with the dusty muskiness of the still air around them.

They continued to crawl. Checa kept his head down and put one hand in front of the other. His shoulders burned, his wrists ached, and his palms were raw from the sharp stones and coarse sand. He breathed in time with the stones stabbing each knee, each step a mindless exercise in accepting pain, in keeping going, because if he didn't, he'd fail. Knee and hand down, suck in a breath, smell the blood and the dust, other knee and hand down, suck in a breath…. Checa closed his eyes. It made no difference. Hand and knee forward again—

"Here," whispered Heath. "There's a tunnel."

Checa surged back onto his haunches when he realized he hadn't stopped when Heath told him to. Domino-like the line behind him came to a halt. Light flared in the tunnel as Jun lit a torch and he squinted, blinking. The numbing dark monotony had become his world; it took long seconds before he realized he was looking at people.

And he knew who they were.

Checa slowly lowered Heath to the floor so he lay on his side along the opposite wall of the tunnel. Heath's chest heaved as if he'd been the one carrying a man for half the day. Checa turned to check on Rim and Ardelle. They sat in a puppy heap, panting and trembling as much as Checa was from carrying Heath.

After checking that Heath was as comfortable as he could be, Checa lowered himself next to Rim. "We'll rest here for a while. Heath says there's a branch tunnel nearby."

Rim's head listed sideways onto Checa's shoulder. Checa rotated his hands and feet to relieve some of his pain, then lifted Rim's hand and rubbed her wrist as well. Rim sniffed tears away and pulled her hand weakly, but Checa didn't let go.

"I can do it," she said.

Checa released Rim's hand and looked down the tunnel. "Of course."

Jun came along the line from the back with Talon behind him. As Jun reached each person, he tended any injuries they had, then left Talon to issue food and water. Checa watched as Jun tended Ardelle opposite him, making sure every scrape and bruise was treated. Jun started at a low growl from Heath, then carefully moved away from Ardelle.

Checa didn't know why Heath was suddenly anti-Jun, but he trusted his lover's instincts. He'd keep a closer eye on Jun and his activities from now on.

"I'll do it," said Checa as Jun reached for Rim's hands.

Rim and Ardelle were part of the Pledge and were Checa's to care for until it was complete. He reached for the medical supplies and removed salve and bandages before handing the bag back to Jun. "Heath needs water." He waited until Jun moved away, then turned to Rim. "What's worst?"

"My shoulders and neck feel like I've been lifting twice my weight for the last week. And my wrists hurt from being bent for so long." She shrugged. "Apart from that, it's just scrapes and bruises, like everyone else has."

Checa tended the grazes first, applying a soothing salve. Then he bandaged Rim's wrists and hands and knees. "That should stop the worst of it," he murmured, his head bent low over Rim's legs as he worked. Rim hissed in pain and jerked her knee up, making Checa realize how close he was to her body.

Checa sat back and grinned at her to cover his embarrassment. He never got that close to anyone. Only Heath. Yet he felt almost as comfortable around Rim and the Princess. He shrugged and assumed it must have something to do with the Pledge. It made sense that the four of them would have to be comfortable enough to work closely together to complete the Pledge—however that was to be accomplished.

He followed Rim's glance to Heath, who was still lying on the ground, although his breathing had evened a little.

"Turn around," growled Checa, scowling at Rim. Heath was his. He had to get Rim's focus off his lover. "I'll massage those shoulders. If you don't loosen them now, you'll end up with a screaming headache by evening."

Rim turned as Checa had instructed, and Checa began kneading her tight muscles. They still had to get through the rest of the day, probably crawling just as they had all afternoon, depending on what kind of passage Heath found for them.

And then there was the next day.

And the next.

Checa sighed and pressed harder into Rim's shoulders. A small moan whispered through Rim's lips as the heat built. Checa hesitated, then continued. He dug the soft pads of his fingers in just above her collarbone and squeezed the heels of his hands toward them, lifting the muscle high, stretching it. Rim hissed at the pain, but leaned into it, so Checa kept going.

The massage continued, slow and deep, and Checa began to lose all sense of place and time. His world became no more than his hands and the body beneath them. The heat and solidity surrounded him. He struggled against sinking into it totally.

The body became soft and pliant, breathing deeply, so Checa stopped, and rested his hands quietly on Heath's—*Rim's* shoulders.

Rim heaved a sigh and lifted her head.

Checa lifted his hands off Rim and looked over at Heath.

Heath hadn't moved, but he was glaring at Checa, his brown eyes hard and full of pain. "Checa." Heath's call was barely a drop of steam in the heat shimmering in the tunnel, but Checa realized the call had the sound of repetition to it. Fuck. How often had Heath called?

Checa immediately crawled over to him. "How're you doing, babe?"

Heath's eyes widened at the endearment, the anger draining out of them. "Did you do that deliberately?"

"Do what?"

"Spend so much time touching that woman. Don't be fucking obtuse, Checa. Is that what you want?" Heath struggled to sit up, so Checa slid in beside him and levered him up to rest against his arm.

"Heath—"

"That'll make your mother happy, although after how she neglected you your entire childhood, I don't know why you still bother with her."

"Heath—"

"I know, Checa. I know." Heath slid lower, finally settling with his head on Checa's lap.

Checa wasn't sure what Heath thought he knew, but he wished he did himself because whatever it was made Heath sad. Checa ran a hand down Heath's back, then up again, and ran his other hand through Heath's thick, soft tortoiseshell hair. Heath sighed into the caress and settled into a light doze. And as Heath slept, Checa watched Rim and Ardelle.

They seemed at once comfortable with each other and yet not, almost as if they were strangers. It was a good time now to ask questions, while Jun and Talon went down the line of his warriors doling out food, water, and treatment as necessary.

"How long have you been able to change?" he asked Rim.

Rim regarded him silently for a long while before answering. "Not long, really. It happened first when my wife died." A rueful smile tugged at her lips. "She'd just melted in front of me, after a norrgel attack, and suddenly I was a woman." She shrugged. "It terrified me so badly I've suppressed it since then."

"Why did you change now?"

"All the reports indicated Exiles abducted women but left the men alone."

Ardelle spoke from beside Rim. "I've never heard of any people swapping from one sex to another before. How did it happen?"

Rim shook her head. "I don't know. One minute I was male, next I was female. I've only practiced enough to make sure I can control it."

"Do Mafdeti swap around like that?" Ardelle asked Checa.

He swallowed thickly and shifted his gaze. "I don't know of any Mafdeti who can change gender. I don't think it makes any difference anyway." He sighed at her look of confusion. "A leader has to be strong, to have no doubts about who and what they are. Can you imagine what would happen if I spontaneously changed gender in the middle of a battle?"

Ardelle gasped out a surprised laugh that tugged a reluctant smile from Rim's lips and had Checa smiling too. "I imagine your enemy would be so surprised you'd have plenty of opportunity to defeat them," she said.

"What do your men think of it, Rim?" asked Checa.

Rim froze, and then a tear slid down her cheek. She scrubbed it away angrily with the bandages at her wrists. "I don't know. But it doesn't matter either way. I have responsibilities to my people. I'll do my duty regardless."

Yet still she stared hard as Checa continued to card his fingers through Heath's hair.

HALF AN hour later, Heath woke, pointing to the rock wall as Checa leaned over him, peering at the place Heath indicated.

"It's weak here. Two feet," murmured Heath. "Four would be better."

"Two feet?" Ardelle asked. "The wall is farther away than that."

"Jun," called Checa.

When Jun joined them, Heath shuffled closer to Ardelle so Jun and Checa could lie side by side, their shoulders pressed up against one wall of the tunnel, heads bent at uncomfortable right angles, knees bent, feet placed flat against the opposite wall, exactly where Heath had pointed.

"Oh," said Ardelle. "Four feet. Against the wall."

Checa and Jun rammed their feet against the rock. A loud crack shot into the air around them, startling Ardelle so much she jumped and slammed her head against the rock wall. Before she had time to settle, Checa and Jun struck again and again. Dust filled the air.

Heath pressed his hands to his ears and buried his face against Checa's hip. Checa curled his hand over Heath's back and held him close. The gap between his hip and the wall of the tunnel formed a protected pocket that muted the sound and filtered the dust. Heath felt safe, protected.

Each time Checa and Jun struck at the rock, the tone changed, until at last, in a haze of choking dust, the rock crumbled, allowing their feet to push right through the wall.

Coughing through the settling dust, Heath lifted his head and stared at the newly formed hole in the wall. Beyond it glistening stalactites dripped from the ceiling, fading into blackness where the light of their torches no longer reached. Cool damp air wafted through the dust, settling it in clumps on his scalp and matting it into the fur of his chest. Checa breathed deeply of the clean scent, coughing slightly as dust clogged his throat. Jun slid through the hole to begin reconnaissance.

Beside them, Rim and Ardelle peered through the hole in the wall as well.

Somewhere nearby water trickled, tightening Heath's throat faster than their race through the waking norrgel had. He swallowed thickly. To have cool, clean water to drink instead of the stale water from their canteens…. Checa scrambled forward to peer through the hole into the cavern beyond.

"I'll show you where you can drink straight from the stream," Heath rumbled softly. "If we four are really quiet, we may even be able to bathe without being found by the others."

Dangers untold test the damned
Farseeing falls, life released
Water brings eternal peace
For only then will evil calm

—extract from the Warrior Pledge, prophecy of the Mafdeti, natural inhabitants of Thalazar.

13.
GOLDEN CHAMBER

"THIS PLACE wasn't formed naturally." Checa stood in the center of the huge cavern, the lightly furred muscles of his chest glistening in the light bouncing off the shining limestone.

Heath smiled at the way Ardelle glared at Checa, then grinned as he noticed Rim's erratic breathing. Checa had that effect on people.

Heath looked back at Checa, enjoying the way his hands rested on his slim hips, fingers pointing toward his groin. A shiver rippled down his spine as he remembered being loved by Checa, the way Checa's ginger fur blended with Heath's own dark grays and creams when they were in cat form, the slight coarseness in Checa's pelt gripping Heath's softer, finer fur, a symbol of the protection Checa offered, the blending of their love.

Heath sucked in a breath, shaking the memories from him, and looked around the cavern. His hair rippled gently in the occasional currents of cool air drifting between the doorways on opposite sides. The area was roughly rectangular, fifty feet long and twenty wide. The walls had huge irregular chunks gouged out, but the doorways were neatly formed squares. All over the ceiling and the floor, stalactites and stalagmites grew, the sound of dripping water creating a musical cacophony. Heath closed his eyes and let the rock speak to him. Water dripped and dribbled down the sturdy columns and meandered over the uneven stone until it flowed into other caves and gathered into clear pools. The largest pool would be cold but perfect for bathing.

"It's a mine." Heath straightened his trembling legs and pressed back into the rock, hoping it looked like he was lounging. This was as close to upright as his battered body could manage right then. He closed his eyes against the dizziness that threatened every time he looked up, and focused his mind on the mine cavern so he wouldn't fall over.

Sensation flooded him, almost toppled him, and he gritted his teeth until he could control it. Words burst out in a rush as though they needed to get out quickly. He frowned as he spoke them, not sure if the words were panicked because he might fall soon, or if it was the weird cavern doing it. "The stone is old, formed deep under the surface before the planet became what we know now. Lava currents pushed the cooled rock upwards, and the harsh northerly winds wore away the protective coating above. Eventually people found the stone and began taking what they needed." He pushed his palms into the gritty rock behind him, wincing as his hands slid slightly, his skin catching and tearing before pressure stopped his downward slide. Perspiration beaded his brow and matted his hair surrounding his face. It was no use. He didn't have the strength to stay upright.

Heath slid to the ground and leaned his head against the monolith. He'd skip bathing. Maybe by the time the others were finished and ready to leave, he'd be able to stand.

"The mining ceased abruptly. No one has been here since," he said to cover the fact he'd practically collapsed as soon as he stood up.

"There's still plenty of rock to mine. Why did they leave so quickly?" asked Checa.

Even though he knew he wouldn't learn anything new, Heath closed his eyes and focused again on the rock beneath him. He felt every grain press against him as if it fought his presence, but there was something else too, a low rumbling in the back of his brain. "I don't know why the mining stopped, but we can't stay here."

He looked up at Checa, now squatting in front of him, and held still under his scrutiny. Checa's look was intense, almost as if he could find the answers he wanted carved into Heath's forehead if he only looked hard enough.

Finally Checa nodded. "We'll bathe and eat, then move on. We can rest at the next stop." He looked around the cavern. "You said there's a stream nearby?"

Heath gestured to one of the rectangular doorways. "Down there. It's a large pool, big enough for everyone, and there's a secluded cove for some privacy."

Checa waited, but Heath had no more to say. Exhaustion lay upon him like a cloak, protecting him from the needs of others. He could feel that Checa wanted something more from him even though he wasn't sure what that was. Heath just couldn't speak now. The feelings surging through him were too nebulous for him to identify, let alone share with his lover.

"I'll help you to the pool." Checa's deep voice was a soft rumble in the open space.

Heath shook his head. Where Checa went, the others would follow, and Heath didn't want them to see how weak he was still, not right then.

It would be bad enough when they had to move on again. He didn't know why he was still so weak. Usually if the Mafdeti survived a norrgel-strike, once they regained consciousness, full healing came fast. If given the correct combination of spices and herbs immediately after the strike, their metabolism pushed the poison from their system very quickly. Heath distinctly remembered Jun shoving something grassy and piquant down his throat before he passed out completely. He should be better than he was.

"Ardelle will help me later." Heath couldn't see her but felt the air ripple as she startled and turned to stare at him. Beside him, Checa's brow lifted and he turned a speculative gaze on the Princess before staring again at Heath. Realization of what he'd just intimated inched up Heath's spine, and he could do no more than stare helplessly at the man who was his leader, his friend, and the love of his life, even though Checa refused to bond with him. Was this distance between them really what Heath wanted? Was this the way it would be now? Could he give up… what?

This one moment was about more than who would help him bathe. Heath wasn't well enough to continue the journey. Checa would have to find another to complete the Pledge—someone else he'd work with, perhaps bond with and live his life—without Heath. This was about stepping back from Checa so they could find their own paths from now on. If they couldn't bond, they couldn't continue as they were. His heart pounded slowly in his chest, a thudding dirge to his past.

Everything he was or had been up to this moment was linked to Checa. What would happen after the Warrior Pledge? Checa was involved reluctantly, and only in order to protect Heath. He'd made it clear over and over that there could never be anything more for them. Could Heath wrench himself away and turn in another direction? What would he really lose? "You're sure this is the way you want it?" Checa's voice was as calm and deep as always, but Heath imagined he could hear a world of hurt behind the words.

Was he abandoning Checa, just as Checa's wife, Xefra, had? No! He wouldn't believe that, wouldn't let it happen. Not ever.

But he had to accept that he and Checa were never going to be more than they were. Friends and lovers, never Bond-Mates. Not as Heath desperately wanted them to be.

The Princess came around to stand beside them. Heath turned to look at her liquid green eyes, staring wide-eyed at him. Those eyes were so like a Mafdeti's. She didn't realize it, but she needed him too—at least until this mission was over. A lump formed in his throat. Was he finally going to give up on his dreams? What would his future be without Checa?

He swallowed thickly and turned to the man who'd saved him from himself, who'd shown him what love was really like. Heath tried to put all his love and respect into that look, and he slowly nodded.

For long minutes nothing moved. Not even the air around them sighed, just the symphony of their hearts beating a lament. Then Checa reached a large hand toward him and gripped the back of his neck, moved in for a kiss.

It was deep and soulful and contained the whole of their past in just a few seconds of heated wanting. Then it softened, salty with tears of farewell, and lingered on a sweet promise. Tears burned Heath's eyes as he opened them to find his lover striding purposefully away from him.

Heath heaved a ragged sigh, and once the last Mafdeti had disappeared through the doorway, he pushed himself to his feet. Then he turned to the scowling Princess.

"You love him," she accused.

He felt her anger like a blow and pressed against the rock behind him. "Of course." Why would there be a problem with that? He looked more closely at her angrily set jaw and glowing green eyes.

A grin slipped out. He couldn't help it. She was spitting at him like a jealous mate, and damned if he didn't like it, even if it wasn't Checa. He would love Checa forever, but the Warrior Pledge called to him. If he made it to the Lake of the Damned, he doubted he would survive the ritual, so he should release Checa now.

The Princess stomped her foot like a spoiled child and spun to stride away. Heath flicked a look at the doorway to the pool, but Checa had long disappeared.

"Will you help me to the pool, Princess?" He hoped he'd done the right thing, letting Checa believe he had a thing for the Princess. All he really knew was that he couldn't hold on to Checa endlessly. Not without some sign that Checa wanted to bond with him. Especially with the Warrior Pledge looming.

Ardelle stopped, her small body quivering with the effort to remain still. He held his breath, not at all sure which way she would go.

"I can't do it without you," he whispered in the still air.

Relief flooded through him at the infinitesimal droop of her shoulders. She wouldn't abandon him yet. He still had a chance to win her over so they could work together for the Pledge. He wasn't sure why she was so important or how their roles would mesh, but he'd spent most of his life training as a Seer and he trusted those instincts completely.

Heath held his hand out to her as she returned to him, and he reminded himself to go slow. He might know they were destined to work together, but she didn't.

"Checa would have carried you," Ardelle panted as they lumbered into the wide man-made tunnel. The crystals in the rock gave off a soft glow, enough to see by. "Great lummox like you, and you pick me to help. By the great Thalazar, I barely reach your armpit." They stumbled over the uneven ground. "You fall, and you're on your own, you brute. You'll crush me if I try to stop you."

Heath dared a chuckle but fell silent quickly so he could use all his energy to remain upright. She was right. If he fell, that was where he would stay. Neither of them would have the strength to move him. He was a fool to have insisted she help him. It would have made much more sense for Checa to take him to bathe.

"Wait," he rasped, disgusted that he wasn't more recovered by now. Still, it had been a skin strike. If there'd been some fur left under the lash mark, Jun's herbs might have worked more quickly. "Take this one," he gestured to a low opening in the side of the tunnel. A soft golden glow spilled onto their feet from the small gap.

"Why?" Ardelle stopped, jerking him to a standstill.

Heath sighed. She was a princess. Like him, she was used to giving orders, not taking them. He nodded down the main tunnel. "Down that way is a large pool with Checa, Rim, and the rest of the Mafdeti." He gestured to the side tunnel. "This way is a small pond separated from the others. Totally private." He leaned down, placing his lips next to her ear, sucking in the warm scent of her. "No one to watch you bathe," he whispered.

She tilted her head away from him, exposing the soft skin of her neck, gasped, and abruptly moved away. "That's not going to happen, Heath. When this mission is over, I'll be taking up royal duties."

Heath staggered, reached for the wall, and sucked in cool air close to the rock. She was right. He had to stop playing with her to cover up his devastation that he and Checa were over. He knew it, but that didn't stop him still wanting Checa. "My apologies, Your Highness. My behavior has been untenable."

Ardelle glared at him, then tilted her head regally. Heath almost smiled at the expression of martyred duty on her face as she positioned her shoulder under his arm and shuffled him toward the opening. Thankfully it was a short walk. Frustration built like an expanding balloon in his chest. It was just a matter of sleep and food and more of Jun's herbs to rebuild his strength, but they didn't have time for any of that.

Heath had to duck his head to get through the low opening that revealed a cave rippling with wonder. Golden light washed over them as they straightened. He stopped just inside the entrance and watched her discover the cave. Ardelle tilted her head up; her smooth skin glowed like dark honey in the buttery light rippling around them. For the moment she was totally absorbed in the wonder of what she was seeing. It was the first time since they'd taken her that she wasn't tense, watching him or Checa.

The hair at the nape of Heath's neck rippled at the loss of his lover, and he forced himself to focus on the Princess and pushed everything else from his mind. He drank in her soft gasp as she took in the glistening globes of amber hanging above them. Some of the globes were a classic egg shape, dark shadows deep within them. Crystalline sand crunched softly underfoot as they moved closer to the still, bright pool. The amber ceiling, rich cream sand, and round yellow light wavering over the water gave the impression of being immersed in the sun.

"It's beautiful."

Heath breathed deeply in satisfaction. His gift often resulted in him being shunned, but sometimes, like just then, he would bring a look of wonder and pure pleasure to someone's face. It was worth it all, just to see the Princess look like that.

Ardelle left him swaying as she walked under the glistening globes of amber resin.

"It's absolutely stunning, Heath." She turned to him, her green eyes liquid bright. "However did you find it?"

Heath smiled at the scents of sand and sun wafting around him. He shrugged, no more able to explain to her how he could *see* the rock and the spaces between than he could to anyone else. "It's just a thing I do." He nodded to the pool nestled under an amber-bubbled overhang. "The water will be chilly, but you must want to get clean almost as much as I do."

She smiled and crouched to swish the tips of her fingers through the water. The light fractured, sending splinters of butter, gold, and ochre dancing over her smooth scalp. Heath's heart skipped a beat and his throat thickened, releasing a low purr of appreciation.

A sense of peace settled in him as Ardelle stilled while the guttural sound filled the cave, and he listened to the way the purr changed as it hit the bumpy ceiling. It bounced backward and around, distorting, changing tone, echoing deep inside his belly, and grew into something beautiful and bewitching before fading away. Slowly and deliberately she rose and turned to him, her eyes wide with wonder, her breathing as erratic as his.

Heath's chest expanded as he inhaled her scent. She wanted to know things as much as he did, regardless of the way she stood, still and contained. Heath lurched forward before regaining his balance and padded softly to her. Her features froze, her eyes wide in her face, and he reached a tentative hand to touch her soft skin. Could there be something between them? Could he *make* there be?

"So smooth," he murmured, a hint of purr still in his voice. He allowed his fingers to wander over her skin, following the path with his gaze, marveling at the smoothness of skin totally devoid of hair. He inhaled deeply of her scent, stronger now she was aware of him. Part of him couldn't believe he was this close to her, caressing her, when he'd never been this close to anyone but Checa. She wasn't just letting him touch her, she was participating. Slowly she leaned into him. Her eyelids drooped, her quick breath wafted warm over his wrist. He trembled as he slid his fingers across her cheek and around to the back of her ear.

So cool, so soft. His fingers tightened before he managed to release the tension coiling within him. He wasn't sure if he wanted this, or wanted to make himself want it. If he did this, he would lose Checa, that was for sure.

Regardless of what he'd thought before, Heath couldn't risk that. Up until now his life had been incomplete. He'd known it the whole time he and Checa had been together, and he had always believed that if they just bonded, the empty places inside him would cease to exist.

Checa was everything to him, but Checa was never going to bond with him. The sooner Heath made himself accept that and moved on, the sooner he'd be able to find something else.

Perhaps Ardelle could be the beginning of the answer. Her presence might fill all those holes he'd lived with for so long that he'd almost forgotten they existed, especially with Checa filling most of them even without the Bonding. What he had with Checa was changing, seeming to shift sideways with their search for the others to complete the Warrior Pledge. Without Checa, Heath's life would be a shell, a series of actions and reactions without meaning. That couldn't happen. He had to find the way to Checa's heart, to become as important to Checa as Checa was to him.

"Heath?" Ardelle took a small, hesitant step toward him and raised a hand to cover his wrist near her face.

Her touch was at once innocent and sure, and he slipped his hand around the back of her head, her soft skin cooling the heated pads of his fingers. Her mouth relaxed and opened slightly. He leaned down, looking deep into her soft green eyes. Another purr rumbled through him, enveloping them as it bounced around the cave. His lips touched hers, heat against cool, and one cell at a time, he lost himself in her.

His heart stuttered, stopped, and kicked back double time. His mind screamed *Not Checa! Not Checa!* Under his thumb her pulse echoed the frantic reaction of his own. His fingers tightened. His body wanted nothing more than to pull her into him, devour her in a mating frenzy, bond with her… but he couldn't. She wasn't the Bond-Mate he wanted, and they both deserved better than a frantic, clandestine coupling completed to hide the cracks in his relationship with the man he'd always wanted.

She tugged him down into the kiss. Heath slipped his tongue between her lips, sipping, absorbing the feel and taste of her, allowing it to sink into his veins, become part of him. His knees nearly buckled when her warm, moist tongue, as smooth as the rest of her, tangled with his, learning him, drawing him to her.

He couldn't breathe except through her and with her. His head spun, twisting his reality inside out. Her skin, still cool beneath his heated touch, set fire in his veins, almost the same as the way Checa lit him from within. His senses sank into her, following his breath, coursing through her body. A black so thick it absorbed all the light in the cave descended over him. He could see nothing, feel nothing, smell and taste nothing but Ardelle.

She could become the world in which he lived. It could be Ardelle who gave him reason and purpose, not Checa. If he let himself, he could do this. With only his mouth, he sank deeper into her, no longer able to feel where he touched her, knowing only that she was surrounded by him and he was consumed by her. He couldn't tell which breath was hers or which touch was his. Cell by cell they merged one into the other, the only points of consciousness where her fingers pressed at his wrist and his at her nape.

14.
THE SKY IS FALLING

A CRACK of thunder split them apart. Heath ducked instinctively, collapsing to the glistening sand. Fuck, he needed to rebuild his strength—and quickly. Jun had to have given him the wrong quantities of herbs.

Ardelle crouched over him, a mixture of concern and bewildered arousal on her face.

"I'm sorry, Princess. That was unforgivable. I was using you to cover my own inadequacies. I'm just weak after the norrgel-strike. All I need is a few days' sleep and I'll be fine."

"I know that," she scoffed. "Are you all right? You don't seem much better than two days ago, and we don't have any more time for you to heal. We need to find out what the Yeudan have planned for the Two Moons' Cross. If Checa's right and we can't leave you behind, you need to be healthy."

It was as if the kiss had never happened. Even when Heath and Checa were on patrol, Checa didn't dismiss him so coldly. Heath flopped back onto the sand and stared up at the golden ceiling. "Good luck with that." He waved a hand toward the water. "You go and bathe. I'll have a nap first." He closed his eyes to shut out everything that tugged at him to move, to do, to fix it all.

Ardelle tugged on his arm. "No, you're coming into the water with me."

Heath groaned. "Just leave me be, Ardelle. I want to rest awhile." He needed to. He needed time to understand, deep in his soul, that he and Checa would never bond, no matter how right it was or how much Heath wanted it. And no matter how attractive he might find the diminutive Princess, Ardelle wasn't for him either. Even the thought of being close enough to kiss her again wasn't enough to get him moving, although if Checa came in and wanted to kiss him, Heath would probably be on his feet in a second. When silence enveloped him, he assumed the Princess had let him be, so he allowed his breathing to slow and drag him toward sleep.

"Hold still."

The Princess's voice was so low and soft it washed over him like warm water. Heath cracked his eyes open and watched drowsily as she frowned and placed her hands on his chest. Her fingers were cool on the planes of his pecs, even through the light padding of his chest hair. The chill sank into him, cooling his overheated body.

Ardelle's fingers slid up, over his collarbones. "I'm going to try something my grandmother told me about once. I don't know if it'll work, but I think I know what to do now. You have to stay very still and relaxed. Breathe slowly and evenly." Her hands tunneled through his hair and brushed the skin beneath.

Heath sighed. He didn't care what she thought she was doing. He was too exhausted to move.

Ardelle began to hum, the sound low and smooth. His breathing slowed and deepened under the mesmeric sound, and as he sank further into sleep, the bone-deep weariness and weakness that had ruled his waking hours since the norrgel attack lessened. His muscles jumped under her hands. He could almost feel the oxygen surging through his blood, healing and strengthening him, but a lethargy surrounded him, keeping him calm and still.

Ardelle continued to hum, the sound low in her chest like a purr, only melodic. It rippled from her hand through Heath's skin and deep into his gut. It absorbed him, removed every vestige of consciousness or individuality from his mind, twisted each cell in his body until it aligned with Ardelle's hum. For a frozen second, his body seemed stretched tight, needing to expand, explode, something, *anything* to accommodate the new knowledge, the new energy inside it.

The sound of growth and knowledge and need grew and pulsed within and around him, roaring painfully in his head before it sank in synchronized pulses that reverberated through every atom in the cave.

Later—it could have been seconds, hours, or eons—Heath came to himself. What had just happened? He stared at the Princess, numb and confused. They'd been on the sand with Ardelle rubbing her hands on his chest. Now she sat in the shallows, silent, her pants and shirt in tatters, and he was sitting chest-deep in the middle of the pond like some pagan god arisen from the depths, his breath harsh in his chest. Shredded pieces of cloth floated around him. Ardelle's leather vest, singed around the edges, bobbed in the water between them.

Oddly, Heath felt newly arisen. His strength had returned. He flexed his fingers, moved his shoulders. No, not returned—he was stronger than he had been for days, but his muscles felt like they were made of jelly. Like they would hold firm for a while, but if he got too hot, they'd melt away. "What happened?"

Ardelle opened her mouth but all that came out was a squeak. She tried again. "Y-you said you needed rest. I gave you that." She looked around the cave, the bewilderment growing in her expression.

Heath swiped up the remnants of the Princess's clothing and made his way to shore. At least he was clean. "I've had more than rest, Princess." He squatted in front of her. "I'm almost healed." He lifted a hand and cupped her cheek, forcing her to look at him. "What did you do?"

She shook her head. "I… I don't know, Heath. Grandmamma told me a story once, and I thought I'd try it." She looked around the cave again. "I don't know what happened."

He stayed silent for a while. "If it was just a story, what made you try it? What was it about the kiss that made you think it would work?"

A smile bloomed on her lips. "Grandmamma told me if I thought I could do something, I should try it, just to see what happens." The smile stretched into a grin. "We tried a lot of things whenever we managed to evade Mother."

"And the kiss?"

She shrugged. "It was almost as if I could feel you, cell by cell. I knew which ones were injured and what had to happen to fix them." Pink tinged her cheeks. "I don't know. It just felt right." She frowned. "It stopped too early, though. I don't think you're really healed, Heath, no matter what you feel right now."

"Even if the way I feel now doesn't last, it's enough to get us moving again."

Heath had more questions, especially about how she felt things cell by cell, but before he could ask anything, thunder rumbled around them and they both looked around the cave. "We're too far underground to hear thunder here," he said.

They sat silent for a few moments, but no other sound came to them. Whatever the rumble was, it had stopped. Heath rocked forward. If kissing him made things clearer for Ardelle, perhaps he could use a kiss to learn more about her. He'd never tried it that way before, but it might work. He leaned over Ardelle slowly so he didn't frighten her. She stayed quiet, her wide green eyes, though still innocent, holding more knowledge than they did before. He lowered his head, intent on the lips that relaxed and parted as he drew closer. It was good before. If what he suspected was right and Ardelle was like him, it might be better now.

A crack of thunder split the air above, followed by splinters of amber showering around them. A large shard landed between Heath's arm and ribs. Ardelle cried out and he rolled them toward the cave opening, covering her with his body.

It wasn't thunder.

Double fuck and damn the wings, the roof was falling! One of the egg-shaped nodes of amber split and cracked, falling away and sending shards shooting at them. A soft grunt escaped him as his shoulder burned, then his neck. Each splinter whistled in the still air, some landing flat and some spiking down like spear tips. They had to get out of there or they'd die. If the shards didn't kill them, they'd be buried under the shattered amber.

Cautiously he raised his head. Around them the sand was clean, crystallized butter in the fractured golden light. His brain was sluggish, so recently focused on nothing but kissing the woman in his arms. He'd just identified which direction the doorway was when Ardelle raised her knee, gripped his hair, and rolled them both.

"Aargh!" he groaned as his back pressed into the sand, sending a sliver of amber deep into his flesh. Twice more they rolled and the small stone quickly fell away. By the time they stopped with Heath on top again, sweat and blood matted his hair and his breathing was as fractured as the amber. "Damn the wings, why did you do that?"

"We had to move."

She lay quietly beneath him, not breathing hard at all. She was dirty, a spot of blood high on her cheek from a sliver of amber, but her eyes were alight with the excitement of action in an emergency. Fuck, she was gorgeous. Maybe if he kissed her often enough, he could forget Checa and move on with his life. Heath lowered his head, intent on her lips, the need to kiss her in the joy of survival making the pain in his back no more than a burning nuisance.

Another deafening crack shuddered through the cave, followed by a soft thud in the sand near them. Then silence. Heath's lips had barely touched hers when a soft chirrup sounded to his left.

"What now?" Would he never get to taste her properly? Or was he just leading her on because he was curious? He was better than that. "I'm sorry," he whispered and released her.

He turned his head and froze.

Golden-faceted eyes rolled and twinkled at him. A fetid growl washed over them, making Ardelle cough.

"Hold still," he whispered, not willing to turn his head from the mesmerizing stare.

The creature squatted about three feet high and almost as broad, balanced on thick thighs, its long, clawed feet digging into the sand at the water's edge. Soft scales of liquid gold, butter, and cream shimmered in the light as it swayed closer. Its snout was long and narrow, and a forked tongue so pale pink it was almost ivory flickered toward them, tasting the air. The chirrup sounded again, a quick contraction in its long throat. The snout moved closer, elongating the neck nestled into the narrow shoulders.

Heath shifted, pushing Ardelle to one side, still beneath him but away from the animal. She twisted her head to peer under him. "What is it?"

He ran his gaze over the beast, taking in the thick thighs, short arms, bulbous belly, trident-tipped tail, claws… and spikes that seemed everywhere. "I…."

That was impossible. Those creatures had been extinct since just after the Descendants arrived, killed in the failed Wars of Independence. "It's a dragon. The amber exploding must have been its egg hatching." Disbelief and awe echoed in his voice, bouncing around the cave.

The dragon raised its head at the noise, revealing a long, tapered neck. A rumble began in its throat and rolled through Heath's body, triggering a growl deep in his gut. The dragon's rumble ceased abruptly. The nose dipped closer; razor-sharp claws dug into the sand.

Heath raised himself to his hands and knees, facing the creature head-on. He took a deep breath, then growled a warning at it. A whimpered chirrup returned. Heath crawled toward the beast, slowly and steadily, trying not to limp because of the wound in his back. The dragon waited, the facets in its golden eyes flickering at him patiently.

Fuck, Heath hoped the histories were right, because if they weren't, he'd end up this dragon's first meal, not its companion. He released a gentle purr, freezing when he caught movement out of the corner of his eye. "Don't move, Princess."

Ardelle slipped a knife into her hand; the glint had caught Heath's attention. "Move out of the way so I can get a clear shot."

"Stand down, Princess." He took another crawling step toward the dragon. "I know what I'm doing."

From the corner of his eye, he saw her grip on the knife change. She still held it ready to fly but less poised. She would still be able to respond in less than a second if something went wrong. Heath hoped he would be able to tame this little dragon before Ardelle forgot herself and killed it.

He kept his gaze locked on the dragon's eyes as she reclined on the soft sand, sucking on a fragment of amber, her tail twitching in the shallows. His heart beat with the fervent wish that all the legends were true and he wouldn't die a fiery dragon death.

Heath crouched low on one knee, his supplicating hand lifted toward the little dragon. "Hello, my beauty," he murmured, his voice barely above a whisper. The dragon stilled, its horned head tilted to one side, listening intently. Heath allowed a soft purr to escape. "Will you tell me your name?"

The glistening eyes flicked to Ardelle, then returned to Heath. "What need of my name have you, furred one?"

The dragon's whisper slithered through him. Heath had to fight against the overwhelming desire to either lie down and surrender or stand and fight. That wasn't a creature to be beaten or obeyed. If he chose either of those options, he'd lose it entirely. "I would honor it, beauty."

"And the power you claim?" The forked tongue flickered in and out, as if tasting the honesty of Heath's answers.

The legend of taming a dragon was hazy. Stories abounded of Mafdeti claiming absolute dominion over the dragons and of dragons betraying them, enslaving them. Heath didn't want either of those things. He didn't want to put the dragon in danger either and have her go the way of all the others after the arrival of the Descendants. Holding absolutely still, he fought the urge to turn to Ardelle. She didn't know him or his thoughts or desires, nor did she know the legends of the dragons.

What power could he claim? Visions of wealth and nobility flashed through his mind, but he dismissed them almost before the images formed. Those things weren't important to him.

The dragon waited patiently, head tilted, tongue flickering as if she could taste more than flavors and scents. As if she could even taste his *thoughts*. Something deep inside Heath settled, and suddenly he was sure it was female. She looked so adorable he had to smile, and with the smile came clarity.

He shook his head. "I claim no power of yours, beauty, that you don't willingly give. But if you would like a friend and companion, as well as an occasional adventure, I would be honored if you would choose me."

The silence hovered between them, thick and palpable. Eventually Heath had to release his breath, disappointment like an anvil in his stomach. The beauty didn't want him.

He sighed. So be it.

"Are you having an Adventure now?" The serpentine head tilted farther, then swung slowly to peer out of the low, narrow opening.

Heath's breath caught in his throat. Was she interested? Would she follow them? Destroy them? Or join them?

He answered slowly, all his attention focused on the golden dragon in front of him, his heart thumping beneath his breastbone. The response to his answer would change the course of his life. "We are fulfilling the Warrior Pledge, beauty. You would be most welcome to join us."

Again silence filled the cave. Even Ardelle held still and remained quiet, although Heath could practically feel her vibrate with the need to ask questions, to take control.

The dragon eased her head forward, her tongue sliding out to lick his shoulder. Heath hissed as the amber embedded there was slowly drawn out, disappearing into the dragon's mouth with a crunch.

"I think I will for a time," said the dragon, "but first I must bathe and eat." Her tongue flickered again, licking up more amber from his skin.

Agonized creaking filled the air and the dragon looked up before moving deeper into the water.

Heath looked up too. Nearly all the low-hanging bulbs of amber showed deep cracks. The one directly above him crazed, small splinters falling, just missing his face. "Fuck! The whole thing's going to come down."

He spun to the Princess, scooped her up, and half ran, half dragged her to the opening of the cave. He dove for the entrance, twisting to protect her, and slid through into the tunnel with the roar of shattering amber reverberating in his ears. As soon as they landed, they scrambled into a crouching run toward the large cavern, but the dust and debris dislodged by the fall of the ceiling soon overtook them. Heath tugged Ardelle into a small alcove and they huddled there, noses pressed against each other's bodies to filter the air enough to breathe.

When the worst of it was over, Heath raised his head. The entrance to their little bathing chamber was completely blocked. Not even a glimmer of golden light showed through. Beside him, Ardelle shivered. He sucked in a deep breath and dropped her vest into her lap, grabbed her hand, and tugged her to her feet. "Come on. We need to get to Checa before he thinks I'm dead and kills himself trying to find me."

If Checa was still talking to him.

15.
CHANGE DENIED

"CAVE-IN!"

The cry accompanied a low roar and the crashing of rocks, the sound a slow-building storm in the tunnel to the pools. Checa surged forward, already halfway to the entrance to investigate the last rumbling in the tunnel.

Heath.

He was almost across the huge cavern when dust billowed from the opening to the tunnel. He stopped short. Fuck. The Princess was with Heath. Orders fell from his lips almost before his mind caught up. "Check the other tunnel to make sure it's still intact. Don't go too far." His well-drilled men moved automatically in response to his command. "Rescue formation. Jun! Be ready with first aid."

Checa held his position in front of the angry bulge of dust as it swept toward him. At this second in time, it was a separate, living entity, pulsing in the entrance of the tunnel. There was no point going in until the dust settled enough for them to breathe. How bad would it be down there? That much dust wouldn't come from something small and manageable. His gut clenched at the thought of what he'd find.

Not Heath. Please, not Heath.

His throat worked against a lump. He was swallowing dust, that was all. His eyes burned and watered, but that was from the dust. Nothing else. The dust hid Heath from him as it flowed into the cavern and over him, his hands clenching and unclenching at his sides in an effort to keep still, to not go running into the debris to find his—

His stomach clenched at the word his voice wanted to scream.

Bond-Mate!

Checa frowned and pinched his nostrils almost closed to make breathing easier as the grit washed over him. A pinpoint of golden light shone eerily through the haze. The light caught the crystal particles in the air, reflecting and fracturing, shooting tiny rainbows into the cavern. Checa's frown deepened to a scowl as the pinpoint grew larger. His cats scrambled at the flick of his fingers.

Defensive positions.

What the fuck was it? Something was back there behind the dust. Coming closer. Checa growled a battle warning, then half turned toward Rim. The woman had been at his shoulder since their wild ride across the dunes. He was relieved to see her nod as she moved away, her body loose and ready in a fighter's stance. She knew what to do as well as his men did.

Checa stayed in the middle of the opening, his focus for whatever was coming. He hated fucking surprises. He needed to get down there and find Heath. Yet here he was, standing like some virgin sacrifice for a demon from the depths.

A low rumble reached him from behind the dust cloud. It shook and shuddered through him, twisting his stomach and threatening to push his last meal back out. Damn the wings, what the hell was coming? He flexed his fingers; the soft *snick* of his claws extending was comforting. Behind him six more soft snicks sounded beneath the rumble that now permeated the cavern and caused lime-rich water to tremble and drop before its time. Stalactites shivered and swayed in the onslaught, already streaked brown from the dust. If one of them broke and fell....

Another flick of Checa's fingers and his men moved again. Rim, noticing the rearrangement, moved closer to him.

The dust blanketed them, covering them in a thick, gritty coating, stinging their eyes and clogging their nostrils. Then it dispersed throughout the cavern. The light lost its halo, and bobbing closer began to look like…? The height of a man's head, but smaller. Almond-shaped, orange-gold.

Checa's heart thudded.

Breathe. In. Out.

There was nothing… he knew of nothing… fuck, what *was* it? A faint tremble inched up his spine, but he snapped his head up, suppressing it. Whatever the creature was, he would deal with it. He released a warning growl.

A response growl echoed from the tunnel. Checa huffed a relieved sigh before he could stop himself. *Heath was alive.* Checa's shoulders dropped and tears burned his eyes before he regained control. He retracted his claws and signaled his men.

Relax, but be aware.

Checa still didn't know what the light was coming from. That certainly wasn't Heath. He tried to move through the floating debris toward Heath, but he was still frantically trying to get air into his lungs, his body still frozen at the thought of losing the man who meant more to him than his own life. Finally he managed to haul in a deep breath and collapsed in a paroxysm of coughing.

Dust.

Can't breathe.

Checa was on his knees now, and on his hands, his chest heaving. He raised streaming eyes to Heath.

"We weren't gone *that* long, Checa." The laughter always present in Heath's voice bubbled into a chuckle. All around Checa, his men relaxed and stood down. "But if you really want to worship at my feet, I'll let you." Heath grabbed Checa by the arm and hauled him upright before tugging him into a quick hug, then bouncing on his toes in excitement.

The tightness in Checa's chest eased a bit. Heath was laughing. No harm had come to him from the cave-in. Checa steadied himself on his feet, his grip on Heath's biceps iron-hard. He couldn't bring himself to let Heath go now he was here, alive and whole.

What the…?

"You're well!" The exclamation burst from him. An hour before, Heath had barely been able to walk. Now he looked healthier and— Checa's gaze traveled over the compact form in front of him—fitter than he'd ever seen him. He cleared his throat. That was over now. Heath had chosen Ardelle to help him, had told him in that one action that he didn't need Checa. The emptiness inside Checa echoed in his mind, a cry of loss and loneliness, and he held still until the feeling passed and he was sure he could move without betraying himself.

Heath was grinning at him, eyes full of light and promise, a look Checa hadn't seen on his face for years. Not since… fuck. Before Xefra.

Don't think about her.

"Yeah," Heath said. "Ardelle has talents like you wouldn't believe. I don't think it's permanent, though," he added with a frown. "I felt better before."

Checa flicked a look at the Princess, who reddened and ducked her head. He didn't even have time to wonder what level of talent could heal a man *that* quickly, or what other talents they'd explored together back there, before Heath was off again. There was no shutting him up once he got excited.

"You'll never guess what we saw in the small cave," his lover cried.

No, not lover. Not anymore.

Ardelle's head snapped toward Heath, a fleeting look of astonishment immediately buried beneath the regal calm.

Heath waved a large chunk of amber in front of him.

Checa breathed a sigh of relief. That's what the "light" was. The amber had caught the light in the cavern and reflected it like a beacon. Checa's lips tugged, begging to share the joke, to share the joy, but he kept it under control. Heath's lips twisted, a sure sign he was just barely holding his story in long enough for Checa to ask. Checa didn't have the heart to make him wait. "What did you find in the cave?" he asked dutifully.

"There are dragons, Checa! They're not extinct."

"One dragon," said Ardelle quietly beside him.

Heath flicked a hand dismissively. "There's more than one. The whole ceiling came down. When only one nodule broke, a dragon fell, so with the whole ceiling, that cave will be full of dragons." He bounced on the balls of his feet again. "Do you know what that means?"

Checa's heart pounded. He knew the legends Heath was referring to, but he didn't believe them. If there were dragons, or creatures that looked enough like dragons to get Heath so excited, Checa needed to get a look at them. "Get the team ready to move out. We need to be able to move immediately if there's a threat."

Heath huffed at him. "There's no threat. The legends say the dragons are our warrior partners. They will fight with us when we need them. But we have to rescue them. They're stuck there."

"That's only one of the legends, Heath. These creatures, even if they are dragons, could just as easily destroy us all." Checa signaled to Rim to join him, then turned back to Heath. "Get the team mobilized. I'll check out this cave of yours."

Heath shook his head. "We need to clear the debris and get them out. We can't leave them there to die in that cave."

"The entrance of the cave is blocked." Ardelle's voice was quiet but firm. "No one will be getting in or out anytime soon."

Heath shrugged and shoved the chunk of amber at Checa. "Even more reason to dig them out. We have to help her."

Her? Fuck, he's imprinted on a damned dragon, just like the histories say.

"The mission comes first, Heath. You know that." Checa fixed his best "I'm the boss" glare at Heath, who glared right back. "The dragons will get themselves out if it's possible."

Heath snorted. "We have to get them out, Checa. They're only babies. We still have time."

"How much time do we really have?" Checa tilted his head, waiting for Heath to check.

Heath sighed in defeat and closed his eyes. Checa allowed a moment of true grief to wash through him as he witnessed Heath's disappointment and loss at what he sensed around them. Heath knew, as well as Checa did, that if they took the time to dig the dragons out, they'd be too late to perform the Warrior Pledge.

"Fuck." Heath glared at Checa. "If there's a way, I'll find it."

Heath shook himself as Checa had seen him do thousands of times. Shaking the bad off and focusing on the good. Heath grabbed Ardelle's hand and jogged toward the rest of the team, gesturing wildly with his free hand.

Leaving Checa holding the orange-gold rock.

Alone.

Again.

He couldn't breathe. His lungs simply stopped moving. He couldn't even turn to see where Heath finally settled.

Together. They were together. Heath and Ardelle. They hadn't bonded yet, but they would, he was sure. He had been expecting something like this. He'd told Heath often enough to find someone else. He didn't really think he'd go ahead with it, though. He had no right to… to… feel like this. This was the best thing for Heath. Unlike with him, Heath's mother would approve an alliance with the royal house of the Descendants.

A soft hand touched his arm. His senses jumped, but he forced himself not to react except to take a deep breath. "Come on, Checa. Let's check out this dragon of Heath's."

Slowly he turned to Rim. Her face was long and angular, her lips chiseled, masculine. Of course they would be. Her sun-browned skin was streaked with dust, a sparkling frame of tiny crystals caught in her feathery hair and on her eyebrows. Compassion glowed in her gaze and her warm scent wreathed around him.

He could curl into her, release his pain and loneliness, and she'd take it all. She could be everything to him, almost as much as Heath was. Checa knew it.

But he'd destroy her if he did that. It wasn't his destiny to be happy. How many times throughout his life had that been proven to him? His sire, his mother. The Bastard next door. Xefra. He refused to look at the couple on the far side of the cavern, knowing Heath was still bouncing as he and his Princess entertained the rest of the team with their story.

Heath.

Jaw clamped shut, Checa strode for the tunnel to the bathing caves, clambering over the debris left by the collapse. He ignored the soft patter of Rim's footsteps behind him.

IT WASN'T difficult to find the entrance to Heath's cave. Rough sandstone rocks lay piled against the wall of the tunnel. Checa and Rim shoved some of the larger pieces of rock away, revealing the entrance jammed with a wall of amber chunks that glowed eerily, backlit from the light inside the cave.

"Where's that light coming from?"

Checa shrugged. "There are vents throughout the rock in this desert. Our history says they were caused by escaping gases when the earth was formed." He stifled another shrug. "However they got there, they bring fresh air and light underground." He frowned at the light piercing the orange amber. "There must be a lot of skylight vents in that cave, unless the cave-in brought the whole roof with it and it's now exposed to the surface."

They tested the rubble at the entrance. Not even a shard moved.

"Nothing's going in or out of there without some effort," said Rim quietly.

Checa nodded. "I think it's safe to say whatever it was Heath and Ardelle saw is in there to stay. We don't have time to dig through and still be at the lake before Makai and Nayeli cross."

They stood quietly for a few minutes, and Checa thought he heard a soft chirrup followed by a rumbling purr.

"Would the collapse of this cave have weakened the area?" Rim asked.

"It's possible. I'll ask Heath when we return."

"Heath?"

Checa nodded. "He'll know." He continued to stare at the golden rubble, not willing to return to the large cavern yet. He needed time to accustom himself to the idea of Heath and Ardelle together, and him and Heath... not.

After a few more moments of silence, Rim moved. "We're both dirty again from the dust." She touched his elbow briefly. "Come down to the other cave and bathe."

Checa turned and followed her down the tunnel, conscious he was walking farther away from Heath with each step.

It was dark. They'd forgotten to grab a torch when they left the cavern. The only light in the bathing cave was a slight phosphorescent glow from the pools. It was eerie and... intimate.

Why was he here with her? With only her? Checa stopped suddenly, his fists clenched, his teeth grinding as her scent twirled around him in a seductive dance. He knew he could do it, but he wouldn't. If he bonded with anyone, it would be Heath. It didn't matter if he was attracted to anyone else or not. He'd tried that path with Xefra, and it had ended in disaster. Happiness wasn't part of his future. Neither was love. If he thought he could make Heath happy, he would have bonded with him years ago because Heath was perfect for him. Rim would be a poor substitute, just as Xefra had been.

Checa strode jerkily into the pool and swam, allowing the movement of the water over his body to wash away the dirt and grit of the cavern. Diving beneath the surface, he closed his eyes and wished it would wash away the wanting. All of it: the past and the future and the dark emptiness inside him.

His gasps for air when he broke the surface almost drowned out the sounds of Rim bathing at the other end of the pool. Almost. He dove again, stayed down longer. Finally he couldn't dive anymore. His breath rasping, he draped himself over a large rock at the back of the pool, his body aching as the sounds of Rim dragging clothes over damp skin reached him.

This was impossible. How was he supposed to do his job with Heath constantly there beside him, in front of him? Each time they went on patrol together, it got harder. With the most important legend of his race coming into play, it was impossible. He constantly worried about Heath, constantly checked on him. Checa didn't even need to look at him or smell his unique scent. Just to know Heath was there was enough to send his mind shooting in a million different directions and his body in one. They still had a long way to go on the mission and Checa couldn't guarantee success, even without Heath's distracting presence.

Fuck, every time Heath moved, Checa could smell him. His body hardened, one part in particular, as images of the way Heath's muscles rippled under his skin assaulted his imagination.

It was a good thing Heath was focusing on Ardelle. They suited each other: a prince and a princess. She'd be better for Heath than Checa could ever be. Checa would never be more than he was then.

The light shifted in the small cave; he refocused to see Rim stand straight after securing her boots. Their gazes locked, and Checa realized he'd been staring. He slammed his eyelids closed, but it was too late. His imagination conjured images of her sleek, warrior's body overlaid by Heath's.

It would be easier if Rim were a man. Checa froze.

She could be a man.

Surely then he could want her instead of Heath. He could focus on his job again, go back to the way it was. The wrongness of his life pinched at him, but he shoved it away. That was just how things were and he was used to it. He'd learned to accept it years ago, so why was he yearning for things he would never have? It was a pointless waste of time.

Finally he left the water, shaking droplets from his hair. His skin prickled as his body dried. Rim stood by the doorway, waiting for him. Watching. Subtle curves beckoning, begging his touch. There was nothing, no response. She wasn't for him and never would be. No. He had to stop thinking that. He needed to make it possible for Heath to move on. If Rim were a man, Checa could want her.

Checa stalked to her, grabbed her shoulders, and shoved her back into the wall of the cave. "Change back," he growled.

She frowned at him, her gaze shocked and wary.

"Change back to the male form." He shook her lightly, his fingers digging into the muscled flesh of her shoulders. "You don't need to be female anymore. We've taken you. You know we won't harm the Princess. We need you for the Pledge, so we'll keep you with her. So change back." He glared at her waiting gaze. "Change, damn you!"

Rim regarded him solemnly for a while, then nodded slightly and closed her eyes. Beneath his hands her skin shimmered. Her face wavered in front of him, rippling slightly between feminine softness and masculine angularity. Then it stopped, neither one nor the other, but something in-between. Creases formed between her brows, droplets of sweat beaded her forehead, her breathing deepened with the effort.

Time crept by but nothing changed. Then slowly, so slowly he wasn't sure at first it was happening, her features softened again, and finally she stood before him, brown eyes wide with fear, bottom lip trembling. Fully female.

"I… I can't," she stammered. "It won't work."

Her fear grew, a tangible thing, thick and oily between them, twisting around his heart and squeezing it. Damn the wings, what was he doing?

He dragged her to him and held her against his damp chest, his hands riffling through her short, silky hair, breathing in the warmth and strength of this warrior woman. "It's all right. Don't worry about it. When the time comes, it'll work again."

It was all nonsense, for he knew nothing of the sort, but he had to soothe her, had to calm her. He couldn't leave the fear in her to grow and fester. Stepping away, he grabbed her hand, avoiding her puzzled gaze. "Come on. We need to get moving again."

They were almost at the main cavern before Checa realized he still held her hand, warm and solid in his. He dropped it and curled his fingers into a fist. For a minute it was almost like holding Heath's hand. Checa shook his hand out and strode into the cavern. He looked around for Jun, found him entering the cavern from the opening they'd used to get in. The Mafdeti had been AWOL again. Only for a short time, but Checa didn't like his men unaccounted for when on a mission.

As he watched, Jun shivered and wrapped his hands around his stomach as if he was in pain. Even from that distance, Checa could see sweat beading on his face and chest. Checa knew of no sickness going through the ranks. Had Jun been injured and developed an infection? Checa dismissed that scenario. Jun was their medic. If he was ill, he'd treat himself.

Jun went directly to Talon and leaned in close, speaking quietly. Talon's frown also indicated something amiss, so Checa stepped toward them, intending to find out exactly what was going on with those two.

"Checa? Are we taking time to eat before we leave?" Rim asked beside him, distracting him from Jun. He turned and began issuing orders to rest and eat before they had to move out.

He would speak to Jun later.

JUN FROWNED as he gathered his gear ready to move out. The soldiers traveling with Rim and Ardelle had disappeared. The Exiles hadn't seen them, and Jun couldn't scent them. They weren't anywhere in the tunnels. He glared at Checa as his leader conferred with Heath. It was Checa's fault Jun had lost sight of Fan. If he'd waited just a few more minutes, Jun would have had time to let Fan know what direction they were heading. He scowled, a low growl escaping. Checa always stopped him from achieving what he wanted. He rubbed his stomach, the low ache a constant presence along with the nausea he'd felt since they'd taken the women.

He checked his gear was packed securely. Either the soldiers had returned to Hawkesby once they lost Rim and the Princess or they were on the surface in the middle of the breeding season. They could have done either. He knew if it was up to Fan, he would track the Princess and find a way to contact Jun. They'd travel at night and find shelter during the day.

Jun brushed the sweat from his forehead as he set his pack down and leaned against the cave wall, waiting for instructions. It wouldn't take Fan long to catch up to them, and then Jun would see his lover again.

16.
THE WORLD MOVES

DRAGONS.

Dragons weren't extinct, and Heath had discovered them. Well, one dragon.

Everyone sat around him, listening as he told his story, his arms large and mobile, describing the shape of his beautiful golden girl. At the other side of the cavern, Checa stared at him morosely. Heath needed to talk to him, let him know he'd tried with someone else, the way Checa often told him he should, but it wasn't going to work. Nothing and no one but Checa would ever be right for him.

He brushed the growing melancholy away and shot a playful grin in Ardelle's direction as she sat silently beside him, but he didn't really see her, absorbed in his tale of a future with dragons as partners in a war that didn't exist. And perhaps would never exist. The half-dozen Yeudan that had attacked Rim's valley didn't pose a serious threat. It was the Warrior Pledge that was important. That was the way to bring prosperity back to their valley, to regain the power they'd once had.

Beside Heath, Ardelle remained silent, her presence ignorable. Almost. She sat there like an extra throwing knife, not needed in the kit but kept handy just in case. He faltered in the telling of his tale when she shifted her back against the rippled cavern wall, wedging her shoulders between the ridges of rock. Behind his eyes a hum began, almost as if it came from her.

"And then the sky fell in!" he recounted dramatically. "Well, the ceiling of the cave, anyway. All the bulbous amber cracked and fell, and we had to get out of there before we were crushed. Who knows how many other dragons were born?"

Who knew how many of them survived the cave-in?

Heath fell silent at the reminder and shifted uncomfortably against the rock at his back, the itch of it vibrating through to his fingertips.

The deeper Ardelle pushed into the buttresses behind them, the louder the hum in Heath's head grew. In it was a note of waiting, of change. It wasn't comfortable.

Ardelle leaned forward, darting looks around the cavern as if she felt it too. Finally she brought her gaze to Heath. There'd been a fine tension to her as he wove his stories for his men, just something in a tilt of her head or her slight distraction. The way she moved, then stopped, little frowns on her face. As his men began to gather their equipment in preparation for leaving, Heath turned fully toward her. He'd had no idea he'd been paying such close attention to her, but now had to ask.

"Can you feel it?" he whispered.

Heath had always believed he was the only one who could feel the planet live, but perhaps others could too. It seemed unlikely, but what else would be causing Ardelle those slight pauses and frowns? They coincided with all the little jerks and rumbles in the humming that Heath could feel through the rock.

Time to take a chance on someone other than Checa and his men. "It's coming to a time of change, a compensation for difficult times," he said cryptically.

He wanted to find Checa and tell him he'd finally remembered not to tell everything at the first opportunity, but before he could shift his gaze to the other side of the cavern where Checa rested, Ardelle reacted.

She gasped and nodded. "Yes, you—" She looked around frantically, then slumped back. "No, there's nothing." She sighed and tucked her chin down.

Heath heaved a sigh and leaned back into the rocky alcove, sitting at an angle to fit. Fine crystals bounced out of the coarse surface and floated to rest on his knees. Small flecks of glittering stone stuck in the hair on his legs, making them shine in the dim light.

"What do you think?" he asked.

Ardelle glared at him. "So, now you want to know what I think, like I'm just another comrade to talk to? Well, fuck that."

Amused shock filled him. A princess of the realm didn't swear. Not aloud. He chuckled when Ardelle looked around to see who else had heard, and he laughed out loud when a gleeful snicker escaped her.

She waved her hand. "They aren't my men. It doesn't matter if I swear." She sat forward and murmured, as if to herself. "We need to move soon."

Heath placed his palm flat on the floor of the cave, a frown forming between his brows. Beneath his fingertips the rock grumbled and stuttered, a portent for a violent splitting. An earthquake was coming, a bad one. "Hmm," he said, "but we have time yet."

Ardelle closed her eyes. "Six hours and forty-three minutes," she said, then gasped as Heath grabbed her shoulders.

"You *can* feel it too?"

Am I really not the only one?

She stared at him, her mouth gaping open and closed. He could almost hear her mind ticking over as she decided what to say.

Dare she admit it?

"Feel what?" she asked, caution edging her voice.

"The rock. It doesn't want us here."

"The rock? What are you talking about?" She tried to move back, away from his fierceness, but she was already tightly wedged between the buttresses.

"How do you know it'll collapse in six hours and forty-two minutes?" Heath had adjusted the time automatically.

"I don't know about the rock! Only madmen can feel the planet."

His gaze sharpened.

Ardelle giggled and pointed at his face. "Your face." She laughed.

He relaxed and squatted down in front of her, making his body look smaller, less threatening.

She sighed in relief, probably thinking he was going to leave it be.

"Tell me what you feel. What do you hear that makes you sure of the time we have?"

She opened her mouth, then snapped it shut and shook her head. Sweat beaded on her forehead.

"Ardelle, tell me."

"The planet." The grumble came from deep inside her, as if involuntary and unstoppable.

Heath stared at Ardelle, his heart beating frantically. "You can feel the planet? The whole planet? Not just pieces of it?"

Her mouth flapped open and closed again. She took a deep breath, looked around the cavern, then nodded once.

"I can feel the pieces," Heath whispered to her, for the first time since he was twelve, explaining the detail of what he did to someone other than Checa. If she could feel it too…. His breath caught. There were more than just him. He'd never be completely alone again. His deep voice rumbled between them. "Every grain of sand, every droplet of water, each beat of every heart of all the living things… but it's all fragments. Nothing is whole."

"Zar, you believe me. You really believe I can do that." Her words came in frantic gasps, as if she'd never considered such a thing could happen, that it was the most wonderful thing that could *ever* happen.

She took another deep breath and committed herself to trust him. Or perhaps she thought she was heading to an insane asylum; Heath didn't know which.

"In the high reaches of the Seven Mountains," said Ardelle, "there's a snowstorm. The drought at Esolba will break within the next two days, and beneath us an earthquake is rumbling. It will hit in six hours and forty minutes, and this cavern will be destroyed."

Heath remained squatted in front of her, hands on her shoulders, staring blankly at her face. He could barely breathe. She could do it too. She was like him. A freak. But she could feel the whole planet, not just the pieces he could read. By the ancestors, she could really do it.

He dragged her forward, pressing his lips against hers, so quick and fleeting it might not have happened but for the force of it making his lips tingle. Then he sat back and grinned. "By the Elders, you're beautiful."

Then he left, striding purposefully across the cavern to the crumbled tunnel they'd come through earlier. Before he reached the entrance, he noticed Checa and Rim crouched over packs, obviously checking the contents, and he detoured to them.

"Checa! I'm not the only one." He couldn't hold the excitement in one more minute. As with every other time he'd had something wonderful or terrible happen, the first person he wanted to share it with was Checa. Always Checa.

"What in seven kinds of frozen hell were you just doing?" Checa demanded.

Heath froze. Nothing. He had no response at all in the face of Checa's sudden anger. Guilt flooded him, even though he and Ardelle did nothing more than kiss. The fact Checa often encouraged him to find someone else didn't ease that. "You know me, Checa."

He didn't want to say more about what he'd done with Ardelle until they had some time alone together. He flicked his gaze from Checa to Rim and back again. They were so close together over the pack, so comfortable. Without him. Had Checa ever been *that* comfortable with him?

He looked back at Ardelle sitting alone at the other side of the cavern; her expression told him clearly she'd just ripped herself raw exposing her deepest secret to him. And Heath had run away, at least, not so much run away from her but toward Checa. As he always did.

And all Checa could do was rebuke him.

As he watched, Ardelle lunged forward, gasping as the skin on her shoulders shredded on the tightly fitted rock enveloping her. Twisting and turning, she ignored the ripping cloth and scraped skin and scrambled from her hiding place, then stumbled a few steps before gaining her footing. By the time she'd wrestled her way to her feet and lurched two steps, Heath had left Checa with Rim and strode along an intercept path to her. He followed as she disappeared down the second tunnel.

He looked up and saw, fifteen feet above, a narrow slit in the rock. The sun was high but past the zenith, the raucous cries of the norrgel a howl on the wind. "That's our way out," he murmured. "But opening that up means there's no time now to dig the dragons out." His voice was quiet and accepting, but inside he was stiff with anger and loss.

Ardelle stared at him, then quickly turned away.

He scowled as he saw the blood dribbling down her arms. "Medic!" Heath grabbed her arm and twisted it to see the damage.

She brushed his hands away. "There's no time for that. They're just scrapes." She was panting, not from the run across the cave and down this tunnel, but from fear. "We have to get out of here. We have to get to the surface and away from this area. It's going to collapse."

"Calm down, Ardelle."

Her breath hitched, and Heath would bet his mother's favorite hat that it was because he'd used her name, not her title. She quieted immediately.

"It's all right." His fingers slid down her forearms and grasped her wrist.

"We have to leave." She sounded dazed and shook her head slightly.

Heath hummed deep in his chest. It would be a purr in his other forms. He smiled again at the knowledge he wasn't alone anymore. "We do, but we have time. We need to work out how to get up there"—he jerked his head above them—"and out." His hands ran in small circles over her back. "Rest while I call the others. Then we'll make plans and move out. We have time to be far enough away from here before the quake hits."

Ardelle nodded. Heath lifted her onto the ledge of a small alcove where a slight rise of the rock formed a chaise. By that time, Jun had arrived and begun treating her wounds. "It's just a scratch," she said.

Heath brushed his hand over her scalp and tucked her into his chest, letting another low hum roll through him. She nestled into him, released a long sigh, and slept.

"You'd be perfect for me, Princess," Heath whispered as she lay on the rock. "You'd be absolutely perfect, if only I could love you half as much as I love Checa."

But it was no use. Heath didn't know how much damage he'd done to his relationship with Checa, but he had to fix it. Even if Checa never agreed to bond with him, what they had was more than Heath could dream of having with anyone else. Thinking he could just attach himself to someone else had been foolish.

He stroked his hand over Ardelle's head again, then went to tell his lover about the earthquake.

17.
GETTING OUT

RIM HAD lost control. He trailed along behind Checa trying to work out exactly where it had gone so wrong. When they left Analee, Rim had known what he was doing. He'd been in charge, a warrior on a mission to save the world. He had given orders unhesitatingly and kept his men alive in the face of danger.

Now his men were gone and he'd somehow taken the role of submissive to the leader of a band of Mafdeti. He had contributed nothing to the mission for three days. Not since he'd discovered how little he knew.

It all seemed so clear before. Take the ruby to Hawkesby, invoke the Warrior Pledge, go to the Lake of the Damned, lead the charge against the invading Yeudan, save his valley, and become the hero of the ages. No problem. Instead, here he was, docile and subservient. Disgust churned in his stomach. Being female wasn't an excuse for weakness. Why was he behaving like this?

Rim had always grabbed control. Even more since his first Change from male to female. Yet here he was, in a situation of his choosing where his own ignorance meant he was little more than a hanger-on. It went against everything he'd strived for, everything he believed in.

He was a first-grade warrior, the leader of his community. Not a follower, not a person to meekly accept the decisions of others without question. If he didn't know enough, he'd find out. The Mafdeti seemed to have another agenda, and Rim needed to find out what that was. If he didn't, it was possible they would destroy any chance he had of saving his people from a hostile takeover.

Decision made, Rim lengthened his stride, half jogging to draw abreast of Checa.

The Mafdeti didn't even glance at him.

"Tell me about your Pledge," Rim demanded. "Everything you know."

Checa looked at him then and frowned, but he didn't pause. "I've told you the Pledge."

"Heath recited a poem, but that's all I know. You didn't tell me anything about it."

Every cell in Rim's body screamed at him to stop, that the Mafdeti didn't want to talk at all, and especially not about this. But he couldn't. He was a warrior and Protector. It wasn't in his nature to be a follower. Not for long, anyway. "The Pledge I know is a subclause in a peace treaty between Analee and the Imperials. Why are the Mafdeti involved at all? Why do you have the Pledge in the poetic form?"

The big Mafdeti's sigh shuddered through his entire body. "The Pledge is a prophecy from the time of invasion. It has been passed down for generations. It's what we know will happen when the time is right."

Checa was still only giving Rim part of the story. He needed more. "Passed down? Orally? Since settlement?" He scowled. "It's probably so different to what it was, it's unrecognizable from the original. Oral histories are never accurate."

The rust-colored hair in front of Checa's ears lifted and prickled, though there was no breeze. Rim half expected the cat-man to hiss at him.

"The stories are learned from the knee and passed on exactly as learned. There are no errors. The Seers also have a written record."

From Checa's offended tone, their stories must mean a lot to him. Rim took a breath to explain how errors could have been made, but he decided not to. If a society relied solely on oral history, they'd have to make sure it was accurate or they'd degenerate into a community of hearsay and superstition. Before he could say anything more, Checa continued.

"The rest of the Pledge talks about a golden birth releasing the waters of the damned and one of the warriors going home alone. That's obviously talking about the Lake of the Damned."

Before Rim could protest at one of them being singled out for survival and the others sacrificed, Checa said, "That fucking dragon of Heath's is going to kill us all!" Checa looked around. "Where the fuck is he?"

Rim hefted his pack over to the other shoulder, more questions hovering on his lips, but Checa strode away calling to Heath. Zar, the man was irritating. Like it would kill him to relax a little and explain things instead of tearing around as if the world would collapse without him in charge.

Rim stalked to where Ardelle sat on a ledge, a befuddled air surrounding her as she ate. He leaned on the rock beside the Princess, silently fuming as he watched the Mafdeti assemble beneath the skylight. Then he turned to the other woman, determined not to allow Checa's attitude make him rude to everyone else. "Did you get much rest, Highness?"

Rim only asked out of politeness. He didn't have the inclination to spar with the mouthy Princess at the moment.

"Yes, I did."

Rim looked more closely at her. Ardelle looked as surprised as she sounded. "You didn't expect to?"

It made sense she would be. Rim hadn't been able to stay still for more than a few minutes at a time; the need to escape from the caverns and complete his quest was almost overwhelming. The Mafdetis' indifference ate at his patience and his ability to stay calm.

"I hadn't expected to be able to settle at all."

"So, how did you?"

The Princess shrugged. "Heath purred." Bewilderment colored her voice.

"What? That wouldn't make any difference at all. What did he do? He must have done something." Rim sighed when Ardelle shrugged again and changed focus. "I don't think they have the same goals as us on this mission, and they don't tell us anything. I need to know more."

"*We* don't have the same goals, Rim." Ardelle waved her hand between them. "Why would the Mafdeti? What difference can they make, anyway?"

Rim raised an eyebrow at the Princess who glared back at him. Shit. If they were all working at cross-purposes, what hope was there of saving his valley? From anything. Anger bubbled deep inside and Rim fought against showing it.

Silence stretched between them. Rim's mind whirled, looking for a place he could wrest control from. This was his mission. His valley was under threat. He didn't need to be acknowledged as the leader in this group with the Mafdeti, but the threat to his people had to be addressed. He'd fight to the death for every one of the people he'd grown up with and had spent the last ten years protecting, but he couldn't do it alone. He needed the Princess on his side and the Mafdeti too. He had to make her realize that the Yeudan weren't just threatening his valley but the whole country. Without a complete translation of the papers they had with them, though, he couldn't prove it.

Rim needed to find something they could discuss that would return their relationship to the level of cooperation it had been at. Something, anything that would allow them to take control of their mission again, not just be ciphers for the Mafdeti in whatever they were doing. Before the Mafdeti had taken them, they were leaders of their own teams, colleagues and rivals. Now they were captives with no rights, no position, no responsibilities. He clenched his jaw—and the Mafdeti had no real idea what they were about. Finding common ground with Ardelle would at least get them back on the same side.

The safety of his people was Rim's primary objective. How did you build a rapport with a princess—someone you would never know in daily life? How did you get to know someone who was so totally different they were even a different gender? Rim coughed at the irony. Right now they were the same gender, but that didn't change things. He'd been a man all his life, and he was still that person. Fear gripped his insides, squeezing the breath from him. Would he ever completely be that Rim again?

He took a breath, preparing to jump into the unknown, to admit something so important and terrifying that simply voicing it might make it real.

"I can't change back." Rim didn't really expect a reply. The Princess probably wouldn't care. It didn't matter whether she was interested or not. Rim had needed to voice his fear so he could face it, rather than be crippled by it and then be unable to function as the leader he was.

Suddenly he had Ardelle's attention. The Princess was sitting on the edge of the ledge, leaning forward, her bright green eyes focused on him.

"You mean you'll always be female?"

"Zar, I hope not," Rim blurted before he realized how it would sound. "Sorry," he murmured. "I've been a man all my life. It's what I am, at least until four years ago."

"What happened four years ago?"

He eyed the Princess. And did he really have to think about his gender now? Ever? Rim sighed. He was the one who started the conversation.

"My wife died." His voice was flat and expressionless even though his palms were clammy and his stomach rolled as quickly as images of Beattie's death flew through his mind.

"I don't understand."

Rim shrugged. "It triggered the first Change." A tortured laugh erupted from his throat. "It would have been hilarious if I wasn't so terrified. I was crouching near the oily stain that was all that was left of Beattie after the norrgel had finished with her, wishing I was someone different, more like her. Then suddenly I was." He swallowed, forcing himself to finish telling the story for the first time since it happened. "It only lasted a few minutes, but I was hysterical for ages. Everyone thought I'd gone mad with grief."

They all still thought that, and Rim had never told them otherwise. Beattie was dead. The truth would change nothing.

"But you controlled it in the cave."

Rim nodded, still not able to face Ardelle's intense interest. He watched the Mafdeti tumble to the ground. They'd never be able to go straight up. They would have to collapse the far section of the cave and create a ramp. Without grappling hooks there was no other way. "That was only the fourth time I've been able to do that." He took a deep breath. "But when I tried to change back earlier, I couldn't." His fear caught in his throat, strangling his voice. "I got stuck halfway. Neither male nor female." He swallowed the bile threatening to rise and clenched his fists so the trembling wouldn't be too noticeable. "*Nothing*."

Rim would rather stay female than live in that world between.

Ardelle uttered a guttural curse, the words something no self-respecting Princess should ever have heard, let alone spoken. Rim's attention snapped to the girl in time to see her delicate features redden from the gently curved brow to the pointed chin. *Great.* Now they were both embarrassed.

In front of them, the Mafdeti tumbled again. "Oh, this is ridiculous," Rim exclaimed and stalked to the center of the cave.

He raised his voice. "Stop this at once and focus on that area." He pointed to the far corner of the cave where the ceiling near the hole seemed supported by a rocky buttress. He looked around for Heath, but he and Checa weren't in the cave.

The Mafdeti all stopped and stared at him. Rim nearly laughed, both at their comical surprise and at the various stages of living-pyramid construction. He put his hands on his hips and thrust his chin forward, looking as demanding and belligerent as he could. "Without grappling hooks, you're never going to get up to that hole. You need a ramp of some kind. Bringing that section down"—he pointed again—"will make one."

As one the Mafdeti stared at the section of arched rock Rim pointed to. *Well, that's working*, he thought. "Where's Heath?" he asked.

"He's with Checa," said the one called Jun.

When none of them moved, Rim huffed a sigh and turned to go and collect the Mafdeti.

Jun stepped in front of him. "They went off together," Jun said. "Alone," he added significantly.

Rim glared at the opening to the large cavern.

Well, shit.

18.
INTERLUDE

"HEATH!" CHECA jogged to catch up, grabbing Heath's arm as he marched down the tunnel that led to the destroyed cave. "You're not going down there. The cave's destroyed."

Heath wrenched himself out of Checa's hold and glared at him. "We have to try to save her. She's important."

"I don't know what you saw down there, Heath, but dragons are extinct. A legend. You were ill, barely alive after the norrgel-strike. You could have seen anything."

"Fuck you, Checa. Look at me. Do I look ill to you?" He stepped back a few paces, placing a yawning chasm between them. "You never doubted me before. You always believed I knew what I was talking about, even with the Warrior Pledge. What's different now, that suddenly I'm imagining things?"

"Heath…." Checa could hear the pleading in his voice and decided it was a good match for the hurt in Heath's.

"Don't *Heath* me. I'm not a child anymore, Checa. You don't need to coddle me." He gasped. "That's what you've been doing all along, isn't it? You've been humoring me to keep me sweet as if I were a child."

Heath raised his hands as if to ward off Checa and stumbled away, his face a mask of desolation. Then he turned and ran down the tunnel.

Checa followed, but he was too far behind to catch him when Heath stumbled blindly over fallen rocks outside the ruined cave and fell heavily on his hands and knees. "Heath!" That had to hurt. He reached down to help his lover to his feet and started checking for injuries, only to be batted away.

"Leave me alone, Checa." Heath kept his face averted.

His voice was thick with emotion and Checa's heart ached at the sound. He stepped in close and grabbed Heath's shoulders. Heath struggled, but Checa was larger and stronger and knew all Heath's weak points. Heath wasn't as strong as he looked either.

It wasn't long before Checa had Heath pressed up against the rock wall, immobile. "I can't," he said as he pressed his face against Heath's neck. He mouthed the soft skin there, tasting the lake water and dust and sweat that made up Heath that day. "Some days you smell like wildflowers," Checa mused. "And I know you've been lying in the south meadow and watching the clouds skid by."

"Checa?" Heath stopped trying to get out of Checa's hold. He flapped his hands by his sides but didn't move to touch Checa.

"Your eyes sparkle with joy when you run, no matter what form you're in, and afterwards you're so horny you climb me before I have time to brace myself." Checa breathed in again. Heath's skin was warmer, softer. "My day feels incomplete until I've seen you. Your smile makes me smile." He shook his head. "There's no reason for it. There's no explanation, but you make me happy."

Heath grabbed Checa's shoulders and pushed him back enough that they could look into each other's eyes. "But you won't bond with me."

"*I can't.*" For once, Checa didn't try to hide the anguish that caused. There was no explanation he could give Heath other than the one he'd given time and time again. He couldn't bond with Heath and tie him to a man like him.

Heath's palms cradled Checa's face. He brought him closer and pressed their lips together. "You're a fool," he whispered.

Checa nodded and deepened the kiss. He *was* a fool, the greatest fool ever to live, because he'd fallen in love with a man so good, so far out of his league, that he could never claim him. Checa pressed closer, his tongue delving deeper to taste the essence of the man who held his heart and soul in his palm. No matter how angry he was with him.

Within seconds, Heath moved, shoving Checa back. From long experience, Checa moved to brace himself. In the next second, Heath lifted his legs, climbing up Checa's body until he rested comfortably against his chest, legs wrapped securely around Checa's waist. He ground his hips down so their groins rubbed together almost painfully.

Checa lifted out of the kiss, gasping, thrusting, squeezing Heath closer to him. "I need you," he gasped, diving back into kissing the one man who could make him feel more alive than anything ever had or probably ever would.

Heath released his hold around Checa's shoulders and shoved his hands between them, tugging at their loincloths. Cool air brushed Checa's penis a second before Heath's hand engulfed the head.

"Lift me," Heath growled. "I want you in me."

"Heath—"

"It'll be fine. We've done it without lube before."

"I don't want you hurt."

"Then get inside me before I slam my head through a rock. I need you in me, Checa." Heath pressed back against the rock, panting with the exertion of trying to lift his legs higher and line up Checa's cock all at the same time.

Within seconds they collapsed on each other, giggling like fools. "We're like baby otters tumbling over themselves," said Checa.

"I still want you. Make it happen, Checa."

It was plea and a demand rolled into a whispered kiss against Checa's jaw, and Checa was powerless to resist. "Only you," he whispered. He swatted Heath's hands out of the way. "Flip your legs over my forearms."

Heath grinned such a sunny smile that Checa was helpless to do anything but return it. "You'll kill me yet," he grumbled as he stepped back from the wall and jostled Heath into the best position.

"Then we'll both go out doing something we love." The last word trailed off on a gasp when Checa's fingers found Heath's opening and pressed inside. "Oh yesss," he hissed.

"We need lube."

"We need you to get moving before the others wonder where we are and come looking," Heath teased.

"Bastard," Checa turned his head to check none of the others were nearby.

"You love it." Heath gasped again as Checa removed his hand and lined up his cock.

"Take your time," Checa ground out as he held as still as he could. Heath could lower himself at a pace that didn't hurt him so long as Checa remained in control and didn't slam inside him in one stroke the way he wanted to. "What we have is private."

"Says the man who's always fucking me in exposed places." Heath gasped as Checa's cock breached him, then lifted minutely before lowering farther. "Oh, yes, that's beautiful." He repeated the motion until he was groaning in pleasure with each lift or squirm. "I can't think of anything else that would make me feel this good. Just you."

"One day we'll be in a soft bed with the door closed, and there'll only be the two of us," Checa gasped. "Just us."

"Forever?"

Checa groaned. His heart screamed *Yes!* But he couldn't say that. The Matriarch would never approve a match between them, regardless of what she intimated before they left. "Do you ever shut up?" he asked instead.

"Make me," laughed Heath.

Checa grasped Heath's hips. "Hold on" was the only warning he gave before he slammed Heath down onto his cock at the same time as he thrust upward. Checa groaned into the sensation of being buried inside Heath. "You—" He gasped. "It's always you."

Heath tightened his hold around Checa and buried his face against his neck. A few more thrusts.

"Only you." Checa thought his skin would fly apart into a million raindrops and scatter to the winds so that all that would be left of him was his essence. He'd sink inside Heath so deep he'd become part of him. He'd tie himself indelibly to every cell of the only man he could ever love, and he would never release his hold. He could feel it happening now. Heath was absorbing him, cell by cell.

"Checa, Checa, Checa," Heath panted. "Take me."

For a second Heath's voice sounded inside Checa's head, and he jerked back to look at him. "Stop it, Heath," he said even as he continued to thrust and fly apart.

"Want you to—"

Checa knew what Heath wanted, but he couldn't give it to him. All he could give was this. He untangled one of his arms and cupped Heath's cheek. "Look at me, Heath. *Look at me.*"

Heath raised tearstained eyes to his. Checa's heart broke at the pain he was causing him because he wouldn't bond with him. "Stay with me, Heath. Stay—" No other words came because Checa's orgasm overtook him and his body froze and tingled and spasmed and jerked, and his life and his love flowed from him and into Heath.

Heath gasped as his own orgasm overtook him.

Checa held him as warmth flooded between them, sweet and sticky. "I'm sorry," he whispered as he disengaged and gently lowered Heath to the floor. "I—"

"You can't," Heath said harshly. "So you keep telling me." He stumbled a few steps, then straightened and tottered down the tunnel toward the large bathing pool. "Tell me something, Checa," he said, obviously expecting Checa to be right beside him.

He was.

"If we bonded spontaneously, with no decision from either one of us, what would you do?"

"Bonds don't happen spontaneously."

"They used to." Heath turned to grab Checa by his biceps. He shook him a little, but it didn't move Checa's bulk. "Bonds used to happen because people were destined to be together. They didn't control it or deny it. So, what would you do?"

"What happened—?"

"Checa! Answer the bloody question."

Checa sighed. He owed Heath that much at least. He grabbed Heath's hand and lifted it to kiss his knuckles. "If we bonded spontaneously, it would mean the fates agreed with me and we were meant to be, that there was no one better for us than each other. It would mean I'd be free to love you forever and be yours and only yours for the rest of my days and I would be the happiest man alive."

"Checa," Heath breathed.

Checa pressed a kiss to Heath's forehead. "But we haven't bonded spontaneously, so that means we either have a choice or there's someone better out there for you than me." He released Heath and turned away.

Heath slumped against the wall, silent. Then he asked in a small voice, "What about the dragon?"

Checa turned back to him, cupping his face, breathing in their combined scents. "Your dragons could mean the death of us." When he saw the anger building in Heath's face, he changed what he was going to say. "If the dragons are part of the Warrior Pledge, they'll be there when you need them."

Heath nodded dejectedly.

"Let's get cleaned up and out of here before we get caught in this earthquake you say is coming. How long do we have, and how far away do we need to get?"

19.
ON THE RUN

HEATH TRAILED into the cave after Checa. His body still buzzed from his orgasm and his ass ached, but it was becoming more and more difficult to let himself enjoy it. Every time they made love, Checa reminded him they'd never bond. The constant push and pull made Heath think he should break it off and try to love someone else, but that had turned out to be worse than Checa's constant rejection.

"Heath...." Checa said quietly.

Heath glared at Checa. "I don't want to hear anything else about how you won't bond with me, and I don't want you to tell me to forget the dragons either." He needed time to regain his equilibrium and didn't need Checa's guilt trips making it worse.

After a short pause, Checa continued. "I was going to tell you Rim wants to talk to you."

Heat flooded Heath's face. He located Rim and strode over to her.

Rim nodded at him. "Heath, we need to find a way up there." Heath dutifully looked where Rim pointed. "If we bring down that arch, the rubble could form a ramp of sorts. You know about rocks, so where does that rock need to be hit?"

Heath studied the arch. The rock hummed behind his eyes. There was a lot of instability, but he couldn't tell exactly where the weakest point was. "I'll need to feel the rock to find the weakest point."

Rim huffed. "Buttresses that shape always have a weak point near the base. This one isn't perfectly formed, so the weak point could be anywhere in the bottom third. Focus there. You might have to try a few different points to weaken it enough so it collapses under the weight of the rock above."

Heath stared at Rim. The woman might as well have turned purple for all Heath understood what she said.

"Basic engineering," Rim intoned drolly.

Engineering. He looked at the rock again.

Really? There's actually a name for it?

Heath shivered from his head to the base of his spine as though the new information needed to be physically assimilated as well as mentally. "I'll check," he murmured as he strode to the curved wall, mumbling to himself.

Why have I never heard of this engineering before? How will it fit with my reading of the rock?

Heath looked up to find Checa standing back with a small smile on his face. "What is there for you to find amusing?" Heath mumbled as he pressed his hand against the curve of rock. He slid his fingers upward, enjoying the change in textures from smooth to grainy and back to smooth, then lumpy. *There.* He retraced his touch. In his mind's eye, the rock changed, became more loosely packed, a little spongy. He looked up at Rim, purposely ignoring Checa.

"Tell us where to hit," Rim demanded.

Heath's hands ran over the stone just above his head as he closed his eyes and felt for the best path to shuffle the grains to weaken the rock. "Don't worry, I can do this myself. Stand back."

Heath *pushed* at the rock and felt the cascade of movement run down the curve. The floor beneath their feet trembled, grains of sand jumped with the slight vibration.

Ardelle jumped from the ledge and joined Rim. "It's not the earthquake. It can't be yet."

"Earthquake? What earthquake?" Rim looked to Heath and Checa for confirmation.

The small vibrations in the floor shivered up Heath's legs and through his body, and shuddered so deep inside he gasped. It wasn't quite pain, but he couldn't catch his breath.

"Heath?" Checa called.

"It's fine," he ground out as he dug his finger in against the rock. "Just get back."

They all stumbled backward, away from Heath and the trembling rock around him. Fine flakes of stone, glistening with points of crystal, rained down in a sheet in front of him, obscuring his view of half their group and glancing off the limbs and torsos of those who hadn't managed to move quickly enough. The flakes were so thin and light they didn't bruise, but if they fell lengthwise, they sheared off hair and skin. Heath pressed harder and the vibration increased in force, the sound of falling stone being drowned beneath a throbbing roar that seemed to come from deep inside the rock.

Through the curtain of shards, Heath saw Rim lose her footing, tumbling to the ground, half on top of the Princess in a tangle of arms and legs. Heath's lungs filled with crawling dust and he coughed, tucking his head against the rock beneath his hands, shoving his mouth and nose in a pocket of cleaner air where the rock was cracking.

Suddenly Heath's hand pressed against air, and a glancing blow from falling rock had him snatching it back to his side. In front of and around him, rocks tumbled down. After a fist-sized lump landed on his shoulder, Heath turned his focus to the debris now falling from above. He crouched against the wall, under the overhang. The rocks fell in a sheet in front of him, occasionally bouncing back and hitting him. He would have bruises, but as long as he didn't get hit on the head or buried, he was safe enough.

He lifted his head as sudden silence filled the cave, broken only by an occasional hacking cough as the Mafdeti recovered and rose up, apparitions in the cloud. His eyes tracked Checa's easy movements before looking to the rest. Almost as one they shook the dust from their bodies, the individual colors and patterns in their hair once again visible. Quickly they checked for injuries, then reassembled, waiting for orders from Checa.

Sunlight streaked around them, fingers of light seeking them out under the precarious overhang, the only thing left of the cave. Heath sighed with satisfaction. "Well, that worked."

He'd taken two steps up the gravel ramp that had just formed before Rim disentangled herself from Ardelle, surged to her feet, and chased after him.

"Wait!" She skidded to a halt beside him. "There are norrgel up there. We have to wait till dark."

"We can't wait any longer than we already have," said Heath. "There's only four hours left before the earthquake. We need to get away."

Ardelle came and stood beside Rim, green eyes shining brightly through her dust-caked skin.

Checa joined them. "We'll run as we did before," he said to Rim. "You'll be protected from wing-strike."

Rim rounded on Checa a split second before Heath did. "*We* might be protected, but what about you? Heath has just recovered from a wing-strike that nearly killed him. If others are hit, how long will it take them to recover? And your Warrior Pledge says we need four to complete it. Can you guarantee the safety of all four of us? And what about the rest of the team? Are you prepared to sacrifice everyone?" She turned back to look at the gaping hole above them. "There has to be a better way."

"Of course there is, Changeling."

Gasps echoed through the cavern. Heath released a cry of delight and rushed toward his golden dragon lounging in the arch to the larger cavern. Feet skittered over fallen rock and stones as Heath's companions scrambled away from the dragon's weaving head. Heath was sure Jun squeaked before he tripped over in his rush to put distance between him and the golden beast.

"Beauty!" A smile overtook Heath as he strode to her. "I'm so glad you're unharmed."

"It would have been quicker if you'd helped." The dragon blinked and puffed up her chest. The move tilted her body so far backward she staggered. Once she'd righted herself, she said, "I will protect you all."

Everyone stared at the portly dragon glowing in the dusty light. She was just a little more than a man's height, her thick thighs planted firmly on the ground, useless wings plastered to her spiny back.

Rim's mouth hung open. "You?" she sputtered. "How can you protect us?"

The golden scales rippled in a supremely indifferent shrug. "I'll think of something."

And then she waddled up the graveled slope, the weight of her body dislodging small rocks that slid back into the group of stunned people left behind.

Heath recovered first. "Well, come on, then." He ran lightly up the rocks behind the dragon and stopped at the top of the rise, waiting for everyone else. "It'll be safer if we stay with the dragon rather than straggling behind," he said to hurry them along.

Several moved automatically, then checked themselves and looked at Checa, who gestured for them to go ahead.

Checa stopped beside Rim at the base of the ramp. "I'll take the tail."

Checa's eyes, still silver after their lovemaking, searched Heath's face as if looking for clues to a puzzle.

Heath was still too angry and upset with Checa's rejection to give him even the smallest of smiles; although since Ardelle, Checa now knew exactly what Heath felt each time. He turned and walked out into the bright desert.

20.
EARTHQUAKE

CHECA STARED as Heath loped after the dragon. "High alert," he called belatedly as they climbed from the cave into the sunlight.

The afternoon was hot and bright. The heat of the desert shimmered knee-deep.

The altercation he'd had with Heath before they left the caves sat like a stone in Checa's stomach. He hadn't been able to get Heath to see anything from his point of view. Not the Bonding nor the danger the dragon could bring them.

Heath was convinced his dragon was the stuff of legends. Checa agreed, but the legends he remembered led to destruction of the Mafdeti people.

Heath was also convinced Checa and he were destined to be Bond-Mates. Checa wanted that too, but it wasn't going to happen. Every time Checa rejected him, Heath moved farther away. One day soon their connection would snap. Even as each day Checa began a new journey toward that day, believing it was the only thing he could do for Heath, he mourned it. It was the one path of action on which he agreed with Heath's mother.

Heath jogged indignantly toward Rim. Checa almost chuckled. Heath liked to joke and tease, but he was very possessive, and at that moment Rim was usurping his place in the team.

Checa should warn Rim about Heath. He lengthened his stride for a few steps before he noticed how the woman strode beside his friend, confidence blazing from her as she scoured the sky for wings. She wouldn't see as far as he and his team would with their Mafdeti eyes, but she'd handle anything Heath could throw at her. Checa slowed again, pulling back to enjoy the show.

He was surprised when Rim called out, "Wings westward!"

Even as Checa reacted, he wondered how he and his cats could have missed it. "Jun! Talon! Cover?" He raced toward Ardelle. He had to get close enough to protect her if the wings spotted them. Heath was still with Rim.

Jun yelled, "Nothing!"

Ahead of them, almost the same color as the sun-bleached sand, the dragon snapped out her wings. They were much longer and wider than Checa had anticipated given the way they lay smoothly along the sides of her body. He ducked under the translucent overhang of her wing and the solution hit him like a rock in the face.

"Everyone to me," Checa called. "Double time." The rest of the team quickly joined them under the dragon's wings and they ran in tight formation. Ardelle was three steps in front, close enough if she needed assistance. Heath and Rim were to his right and ahead. He picked up his pace as the rest of the team increased theirs.

Checa fell into step just behind Rim as she jogged along beside Ardelle, her easy lope fluid and unconscious. He wondered what Heath would think if he proposed a closer working treaty between them and the Descendants living in the valley. He could see Rim becoming a colleague, perhaps even a friend.

"Checa!"

Checa jumped at the sharp command. He hadn't realized Heath had dropped back and jogged next to him. He scowled at the smirk on his friend's face. It didn't seem quite real. Heath chuckled. That sounded forced as well.

"Is that what you want?" Heath asked. "I thought you decided women weren't for you after what Xefra did to you."

Checa's scowl deepened. Heath was still a teenager when Checa had married Xefra, and Heath had never liked her. With good cause. "I don't need a woman. Do you?" He had to ask since Heath and Ardelle had… he wasn't sure what they'd done. They didn't seem to be still interested in it now, whatever it was.

The words hid everything else churning inside him, like he couldn't imagine being genuinely attracted to anyone other than Heath, like he couldn't see himself sharing his life with anyone other than Heath. It was always and only Heath. Perhaps it always had been and Checa had kidded himself that he wasn't just waiting for Heath to grow up.

A harsh laugh burst from Heath and he slapped his thigh. "Checa, that's the biggest crock of shit I've ever heard. You haven't had anyone but me since that bitch died." He ignored Checa's question and turned his head to follow Rim's progress. "You don't want to bond with me, so you must want someone else."

"It's not that simple, Heath," Checa growled. Nothing would ever be that simple with the way he felt about Heath.

The way Heath was looking at him, face all serious, eyes piercing, made Checa feel Heath could look into his soul and know every thought he had. It was as if he were a rock that Heath could see right through and know what it was made of. Checa scowled at him, about to tell him to stop it, when Heath nodded and turned his head away.

"You're right," his lover said. "It's not."

Needing to change the subject, Checa said, "What if the dragon's attacked? If she really is the Golden Birth from the Pledge, we can't let the norrgel see her."

The dragon swung her head to the side, one baleful eye focusing on Checa before returning to the front as she continued her lurching jog across the hot sand. "I'm the same color as the sand." Checa could hear the word *fool* in the tone of her voice. "They won't see anything from above except the cloud of dust we're making."

"Could we ride you, beauty?" Heath reached a hand out to caress a smooth scale.

The dragon huffed a smoky warm breath into the sand, then swiveled her head to look at Heath. "If I allowed anyone to ride me, it would be you." She turned back to the expanse of sand around them and increased her pace. "You may call me Kimi. Now run."

They ran on, as silent as the sun sliding down the arc of sky.

Late-afternoon sunlight washed the rocks gold and rust and spiked through Kimi's outstretched wings as the norrgel retreated on the last breeze of the day. The dragon flapped her wings. Checa followed the rest of the team and ducked out from under their shelter. He covered his eyes against the stinging dust stirred up by the dragon's movement.

"What's she doing that for?" asked Checa.

"Her wings are stiff. She wants to stretch them out." Heath was beside him again. A few moments ago, he'd been at the front, five men away, but then, when Checa wanted a question answered, he was right there.

As always.

"Can't she flap somewhere else? That stings." Checa clamped his lips against anything else that might sound like a childish whine. He hadn't indulged in complaints when he was a child; he wasn't going to do so now. Especially not when life was good.

Heath chuckled, reached over, and squeezed Checa's hand. "I'm sure you'll be in control again soon enough."

They continued their relentless jog across the desert. Checa's feet fell one after the other, the black cast by his body undulating in time beside him, growing longer as the earth swallowed the bleeding sun. Soon the red faded and his shadow merged with the blackness of the ground. They ran on, allowing the night to blanket their silence with stars.

The band of warriors came to an abrupt halt when a startled cry sounded from above them. Checa looked up, his jaw dropping at the sight of the golden dragon in the air.

She's flying.

No sooner had the thought formed in his head than Kimi plummeted, slamming chest first into the rough ground, her hind legs flailing in the air as her tail flipped over her head.

Heath rushed forward, the cry of her name on his lips. Checa followed more slowly, arriving near the dragon's head in time to hear her speak.

"Oh, that was fun! I want to do it again."

And then she was gone, running into the distance and once again lifting from the ground.

A few hundred double strides ahead of them, she plummeted again, landing in an ungainly heap of flapping wings and flailing hind legs, her golden scales glistening in the low light. Checa winced as the ground shook from the impact. That had to hurt, but within seconds the dragon was giggling and up and running again. This time she stayed in the air.

Checa stopped and stared. She had been plump and ungainly on the ground, but in the air she was all sleek gracefulness, cold blue starlight glinting from her golden scales.

She was beautiful.

For the first time, Checa could understand why Heath was smitten with her.

Through the cool evening came a soft cry. "How do I turn around?"

Checa laughed and watched her until he couldn't tell her from the stars. Then he called his men to order.

"We need to find another passage before sunrise," he called softly. "We rest after the zenith." Time was getting short; they would have to run longer each day to be at the lake in time to unlock the door. If they didn't make it, the Mafdeti's opportunity for regaining their rightful place in the world would be lost.

"What about Kimi?" Heath kept twisting his head from side to side, searching for his dragon.

"She'll work out how to turn around eventually. She'll find us again." Checa shrugged. The Pledge didn't definitely refer to dragons. The Golden Birth could be anything. "Or not."

Checa reached out and took a grip of his lover's wrist, stopping Heath's words before they formed. It was enough to remind Heath of their mission. There was nothing they could do to help the dragon Heath had found and still get out of the area in time to save themselves. The growl Heath emitted told Checa he didn't like it, but he had to accept it; the Warrior Pledge was their priority.

They ran on.

The trembling began soon after. It couldn't be exhaustion. They'd only been running a few hours.

Checa gritted his teeth and kept going. Another hour before a quarter hour's break, and then they'd continue. They needed to put enough distance between them and the caverns to make sure they were safe. Checa was sure they'd make it—almost sure. Then the ground heaved beneath him and he sprawled on his face in the gritty sand. A low rumble vibrated through the earth and tingled through his arms and down his spine.

The earthquake.

Too soon.

Were they far enough away to escape injury? Checa shoved himself to his suddenly unsteady feet. "Spread out!" he yelled even though every instinct screamed at him to huddle together. If they separated, surely at least some of them would be safe. His gaze searched his team in the dim light, checking that Rim was safe and near Ardelle. Then he sought Heath's brown skin glowing in the evening light. Finding him, Checa lurched and grabbed him as another tremor rippled the ground beneath.

Around them grains of sand jumped like fleas and the rocks beneath them heaved. Checa stumbled. A gastrointestinal growl rumbled deep beneath his feet as he steadied himself, and he felt the echo of it in his stomach. The earth lurched again, tossing him into the air. He landed with a crunch; Heath thudded on top of him half a second later, his hot "*Oomph!*" blowing the hair from Checa's neck. He barely had time to register the sensation of Heath's chest pressed into his back before Heath rolled off him, legs still tangled in Checa's.

Groans and gasps of his men landing leapfrogged around them, broken by a piercing scream. Checa surged to his feet, heaving Heath up with him even as he ran toward the scream. The sound ended abruptly. Checa's skin prickled with foreboding and his heart thudded in his chest as he ran toward the dying echoes of the cry.

A solid arm slammed into his chest, flinging him backward onto the hard ground. *Heath.* Checa lay there wheezing, trying to make himself listen to Heath while his lungs fought for air and his tailbone stung.

"Crevasse," Heath rasped as he grabbed Checa's wrist and hauled him to his feet.

Checa winced as his back protested, then looked into a yawning blackness two feet in front of them. He gripped Heath's hand tighter. "Fuck." His whisper deepened the cold dread pooling in his stomach. He lifted his gaze to the barren, starlit landscape a few meters away. "Ardelle?" he asked, but he already knew the answer. Rim stood a few feet to his left.

After dropping to his stomach on the still-trembling ground, Checa inched his way to the edge of the drop and looked over. The Princess lay motionless, a charcoal shape on black, on a narrow ledge about ten feet below. One leg and hip dangled precariously over a hole so black Checa couldn't see where the bottom might be, if it even had one. The fur on the back of his neck bristled. If Ardelle woke and moved, she'd go over and be lost to them forever.

A whimper beside him broke the silence that had settled with the earth. Rim lay beside him, her fingers gripping the edge of the chasm as if to stop herself jumping over to get Ardelle.

On Checa's other side, Heath exhaled. "Fuck."

"I think I can reach her." Checa kept his voice calm, the voice of the leader to be obeyed. "Have Jun bring the ropes."

Heath didn't move, his gaze locked on the woman below. Checa grabbed Heath's chin and tugged it toward him. "We'll get her, Heath." He didn't know what was between Heath and Ardelle, but it wasn't what he'd assumed in the cavern. Heath was like a puppy with her, as if he'd found his best friend. Whatever it was, she'd given Heath a gift. For the first time since he discovered his talent with rock, he was truly comfortable in his own skin.

Shit, that was it. It had to be. Ardelle was like Heath. "She'll be all right," he said, trying to convey his acceptance and support, to promise Heath the world, all in one small sentence. Checa let go his bruising grip. "Now get Jun and the ropes."

He held Heath's gaze for long seconds before Heath scrambled back from the edge.

Checa inched closer to the edge himself, preparing to go over.

"I'll go."

Checa turned to the soft voice beside him. "Don't be stupid," he scoffed, then resumed his vigil over Ardelle.

Rim pushed to her knees beside him. "I'm lighter. I'll get down there more quickly, and you'll be able to pull both of us up together. If you or any of the others do it, you'll have to wait down there until Ardelle is safe."

Checa didn't take his eyes off Ardelle. He would have to tell her to freeze if she woke or she'd go over the edge. "So?"

The sigh Rim released made Checa feel like a difficult child. He glared at her before turning back to Ardelle.

"So there'll be aftershocks. If we don't get both people up as quickly as possible, we could lose one."

Checa didn't respond. She was right, but he didn't have to like it.

Heath skidded to a stop beside them, one end of the rope already trailing behind him to the group of Mafdeti waiting to provide counterweight. Checa grabbed the rope as Rim reached for it and expertly knotted it around her body, leaving a length free to tie around Ardelle. He touched her wrist before she could go over the side, and raised his eyes to hers.

"Be careful," he growled, and not just because they needed her to be the fourth in the Warrior Pledge. In the short time he'd known her, he knew he could call her friend.

Heath slipped into position behind Checa and used his body to hold him steady.

Rim nodded slowly and Checa released her, leaning his shoulders back into Heath as Rim slipped over the side into the yawning blackness.

21.
RESCUE AND ATTACK

CHECA'S BARKED orders washed over Heath as he leaned back, his arms firmly around Checa's chest, helping him maintain his resistance to Rim's weight. He didn't even know if Ardelle was breathing. He had to believe she was because they'd never complete the Warrior Pledge without her. He also needed another treatment of whatever she'd done in the cavern. He'd managed to keep up with everyone else, but he was exhausted. The earthquake happened at about the same time he was contemplating collapsing and begging to be left behind.

Guilt ate at him. What if he had bonded with her in the cave? Apart from making the biggest mistake of his life, the Bond would mean he would be mentally attached to her. He'd be a blithering mess by now, and all over someone who would make a better friend for him than a lover. For probably the billionth time, he wondered why Checa wouldn't bond with him.

The same answer came to him, just as it did every time. Heath might feel the Bond-Call for Checa, but Checa clearly didn't feel the same for Heath, regardless of the way he acted when they were together. If Checa didn't feel it by now, he probably never would. Waiting hadn't accomplished anything. Heath should abandon all hope and move on. If that was possible.

What was he without Checa? He'd still be a warrior and a Seer. He'd still have family and friends, but he'd never have another lover; there was no one he wanted like he wanted Checa. Making love to anyone else would feel shallow. Hollow. More lonely than being on his own.

"I've got this, Heath. Tell me what's happening down there," said Checa as he shifted. Heath moved to lie on his stomach to watch Rim rappel down to Ardelle.

Rim slid down the sheer rock while Checa, with the rope looped over his shoulders and around his back, fed line to her. Behind them the rest of their team was providing counterweight, waiting for the chance to haul the two women to the surface.

Heath kept his gaze focused on Ardelle.

"Watch her," Checa murmured behind him. "If she moves, get her to stop."

Heath felt a small bubble of annoyance grow. Checa had just told him to watch Rim. Now it was Ardelle. "Just hope Rim knows what she's doing. If not, I'll be going over and getting them out."

Rim oscillated between bewildered innocence and scary-assed competence, and Heath wasn't sure which one was true. Rim abseiled quickly and expertly down the rock face, and Heath drew his first deep breath since he realized Ardelle was gone.

A rumble, too deep to be felt, too far away to be heard, echoed in the back of Heath's brain.

Double drett and damn the wings.

"There's another coming!" he said to Checa.

"When? How bad?" Checa didn't move; he still held firm to the rope lowering Rim to Ardelle. The rope went slack and he adjusted automatically, pulling it taut, ready to haul the women up.

Heath kept his gaze locked on Rim.

Hurry up, woman. You have to hurry.

Sand began to dance around them and in the darkness beyond where the women balanced; he thought he could see the rock trembling.

"Bad." His voice shook from his effort not to jump over the edge, to finish tying Ardelle and get them out of there. He could see Rim was working quickly. "Come on. Hurry up."

Finally she looked up and raised a hand, indicating she was ready. Heath leaped to his feet, grabbed the rope Checa held, and took off. "Run!"

Checa reacted immediately, as did the rest of the team, and they hauled the women up the side of the chasm even as the ground beneath them jumped and shivered, groaning with the effort of movement never meant to be.

Heath kept pulling on the rope even after Rim's grunts indicated the women were out of the chasm. Checa shot him an inquiring look but didn't pause. A hundred paces away, Heath fell heavily to his knees, the sand beneath him heaving. He gripped the rope more tightly and pulled it hand over hand, bringing the women closer.

Rim had twisted herself so she was on the bottom, her back bumping over the rocky ground. She held Ardelle close, pressing the Princess's head to Rim's chest. Their legs flailed and bounced, and Heath winced at the thought of the bruises and grazes they'd both have. When the women were at his feet, he stopped pulling on the rope. After checking Ardelle was breathing steadily, he began tugging at the knots tying the Princess to Rim.

Heath watched, his fingers suddenly numb, as Checa helped Rim loosen her knots. Her hands were scraped and bloody, and dark smears stained her cheek and chin. Shreds of what remained of the back of her shirt hung dark and moist from her waist. Her back was probably a mangled mess.

Guilt rode him and finally released the frightened paralysis he'd been gripped in.

"Sorry," he murmured to Rim as he went back to work on the knots at Ardelle's waist. "We had to get you up."

He looked up when she didn't respond but ducked his head at the look on her face. She wasn't watching him. She was staring at Ardelle as if the Princess was all she needed to survive. And the damned Princess was unconscious.

Heath huffed as the last knot came free. Who was he to criticize? He probably looked at Checa the same way. Carefully he lifted the Princess into his arms, cringing when her head flopped back. After that rough haul out of the fissure, it was too late to worry if she had a serious injury, but he didn't want to cause more damage. He turned to Checa, who was helping Rim to her feet.

"We have to get out of here. The quakes are reaching farther than I thought they would. This whole area's going to go. You'll need to gallop." He started northward, hoping he hadn't misread the signals. He could really use Ardelle's overview right about now. He jogged on, knowing he wouldn't make it on two feet, hoping the others would at least get moving.

"If the area's going, you need to gallop too." Checa jogged beside him, rope in hand. Behind them, Rim limped along, not complaining but clearly not able to keep up. Heath was about to argue when Checa gestured and growled, the leader clearly in charge. Heath changed to were form, and Checa and Rim moved Ardelle until she straddled Heath's back; then Checa tied her on. "Go!" Checa shouted as the ground bucked and rippled, the earth groaning as if in pain.

Heath paused long enough to see Checa grab Rim and swing her onto his back even as his body folded underneath him and his ginger cat emerged. They took off. Several times, Heath stumbled, sliding on the heaving ground, but he recovered and kept going, always northward, dodging around falling rocks and bouncing ground.

Suddenly the ground heaved more strongly, knocking them all onto their faces. A creaking screech filled the air and dust swirled and flowed around them. Heath coughed the dust from his lungs and sent his senses out. The chasm was closed.

He dragged himself to his feet, shaking a little to ensure Ardelle was still tied on securely, and galloped north once more.

Aftershocks, large and small, kept them moving northward at the same frantic pace throughout the night. Their gait was clumsier now over the breathing earth that seemed to sap their strength. Heath was even less coordinated than the younger members of the team, who were less practiced, less able to hide their exhaustion, and he stumbled.

He moved automatically, breathing heavily with the strain of maintaining the fast pace while carrying the Princess, knowing he was dropping back with each step. He couldn't keep up the pace, any energy he'd got from Ardelle long since used up.

They stopped in the hour before dawn. Heath gingerly lowered himself to the ground, careful not to jar Ardelle even though every muscle in his body trembled with overuse. Carefully he changed to human form beneath her and loosened the knots that held her in place. She slid to the ground beside him. He flopped onto his back and forced his arms and legs into a long, painful stretch as the sky lightened to a dull gray.

"The aftershocks will continue all day, but the worst is over."

Heath snapped his head to the woman beside him. Her eyes were still closed and she hadn't moved, but she'd definitely spoken.

"My head hurts." A small frown wrinkled her forehead as Heath raised himself on one elbow and leaned over her. "What happened?"

Heath brushed a shaky finger down her pale cheek. "You fell, but you're going to be okay." He didn't know for sure that she would be okay, but she appeared lucid. That was a start.

Ardelle twisted, then groaned. "Zar, everything hurts. I think even my toenails ache. What did you do to me? Drag me over the ground or something?"

A laugh barked from deep in his chest. "Something like that. Just rest. Jun will bring you something for the pain."

Suddenly light-headed, Heath flopped onto his back and grinned at the sky. Ardelle could feel pain—everywhere. There couldn't be any major injury, surely. He sat and smoothed his hand over her scalp, finding the bump caused by her fall, just behind her ear. Drett, he'd seen people die from bumps behind the ears. His eyes burned. They were becoming friends, so she was important to him and he didn't want her harmed.

"Rest now." He stared at Checa a few feet away, tending to Rim, selfishly grateful his lover was unharmed. Even his jealousy of Rim was muted underneath the gratitude.

Within ten minutes, Jun had treated Rim's and Ardelle's injuries and given Heath a tonic for his exhaustion, and they were ready to move on. Ardelle still looked woozy. Heath still ached everywhere and was more tired than he should be after a run, but he had enough energy to continue.

"Do you need to be tied on again?" Heath had already stuffed the rope back in Jun's pack, anticipating her response.

"I'm fine," Ardelle snapped. "Let's get moving."

The band of worry clenched in his stomach most of the night eased. If she could scowl and snap at him, she was going to be fine.

Rays of golden light kissed the clouds, and a light fog that quickly burned off blanketed the ground when they began running again. The first norrgel screech echoed across the desert at the same time Jun found an entrance underground. Heath took human form and stood with Checa as the others dropped into the tunnels below, while the cries of the wings grew louder. They weren't close yet, but the sound made the welt across his back twitch. Checa placed a warm hand on his shoulder but said nothing.

Heath took a deep breath, nodded to Checa, then lowered himself to the tunnels below, his long legs making the drop easy. Once underground he relaxed his muscles. The screech of the birds faded behind the thick rock.

After Checa had joined them, they swung the women onto their backs again and the group ran on in were form. These tunnels were old, little-used thoroughfares, abandoned when the trade routes changed fifty years before. No one spoke. They knew as well as Heath did that they had to keep going no matter how tired they felt. They'd been running all night, but the earthquakes had cost them time they couldn't afford.

JUN JUMPED as Fisher stepped out in front of him. He'd known the Exile was close, had smelled him as soon as he entered this side tunnel, away from his team. But the man moved quietly, almost as quiet as a Mafdeti.

"Most of the tunnels in this section are blocked. There's only one way for you to go."

Fisher's voice betrayed no emotion. His face was still, lips barely moving as he spoke. Jun wondered again if he and Fan had done the right thing in trusting him.

"No one dies," Jun said quietly.

"I've told the men." Fisher nodded. "But we'll do whatever we need to do to take the Princess."

"That's not good enough, Fisher." Jun leaned forward in an attempt to intimidate the slender man. He straightened again when Fisher just stared at him, his black eyes as dead and expressionless as his face. "*No one dies,*" Jun emphasized, but the words sounded tentative even to his own ears.

"This tunnel will be sealed as well. You'd better get back to your team." Fisher turned and disappeared around the bend in the tunnel.

Jun stood still for several minutes, hands clenched, jaw tight, almost sure now that he and Fan had made a very big mistake. "Fuck, Fan, I wish you were here."

The absence of his mate was a physical emptiness Jun fought against every second of every day. He spun on his heel and jogged back to his team. No sooner had he cleared the secondary tunnel than a deep rumbling echoed from the opening. Now there was only one way for them to go. Jun took up his place at the end of the line of his men.

EVERY MUSCLE in Heath's body screamed. They'd long ago left their fast, easy pace behind, and now forced their sweat-soaked bodies across the ground to the sound of Checa's drill count. Their training was the only thing keeping them going.

Heath heaved a deep breath. He was already pushed to his limits after the norrgel-strike, and he considered passing Ardelle to Jun, but the thought of her riding the other cat caused a cold lump to form deep inside him. She was part of the Warrior Pledge, one of the four, just as he was. Only one of the four should carry her. That meant him or Checa.

Heath couldn't see Jun either up ahead or behind anyway, so the point was moot. He pushed the pain and tiredness away and kept going, knowing he would keep her with him until they could rest or he collapsed.

"I'm fine now. Let me down."

Heath ignored her imperious voice. They were too close to Exile territory to rest. They couldn't afford any delays.

His sense of the moons' movement wasn't as clear as Checa's seemed to be, but he could tell time was running out. Heath wasn't sure exactly how the ritual was going to help them regain their position in the world, but Seer Pretto was sure it had to be done, and that was enough for him. They had less than five days to get to the lake, and they'd have to run for most of them if they were to make it. If they remained in cat form throughout the day, they'd make good progress and leave the Exile territory behind.

Even there the earthquake had an impact. Several times during the morning, small tremors bounced sand and stones around their feet. Rockfalls rained on them twice before Checa called a break at zenith and the troop stopped in a tunnel narrowed by a rockslide. "Eat and rest for ten minutes."

Heath looked closely at Checa, who didn't appear any more comfortable stopping here than Heath was, but they needed to rest, if only for a few minutes. After Ardelle slid off his back, Heath changed to human form, stretched his arms and legs, then collapsed beside her, breathing heavily as he looked around. The tunnel was narrower there and the rockslide made it almost impossible to move through. They would have to go one at a time. He sniffed the air. It was full of the smell of dust, the scent of his own sweat, and Ardelle. He smelled Checa and Rim and the various scents of their men farther away. Underlying it all was a thickness, rancid and rotting: humans too long unwashed. But it was still, not too fresh.

"What do you think?" he asked Checa.

"It's either a day old or the Exiles have learned how to camouflage their scent. It's still too close." He looked again at the rockslide.

Heath examined the position of the rocks but couldn't see anything about it that looked like it had been deliberately laid. "Are we clearing first?"

Heath didn't suggest resting for longer. That wasn't the place for it. If they cleared the rocks, they could go through more than just one at a time. His breathing was almost back to normal, although his muscles still quivered from overuse, but the longer they sat there, the more uncomfortable he became with traces of Exiles surrounding them.

Checa regarded him closely. "What's on the other side? Is the tunnel clear?"

Heath placed his hands on the rocks, one high, one low, and closed his eyes. "It's clear for at least the next fifty meters, then it curves. I can't sense any obstruction to that point, but there's something blocking it past there. It doesn't feel like rock." His heart beat steadily as he realized what he'd just intimated. If it wasn't rock, what could it be? Did he feel the bodies of Exiles? Were they alive? And if they were, were they a threat? Even his ability to sense others' hearts didn't help him through rock. He huffed quietly. If the Exiles were alive, of course they were a threat.

"How close are we to their territory?" Checa asked. "Is there another way around?"

Heath shrugged. He was too tired for the concentration necessary to pinpoint exactly where they were. He closed his eyes and sent his senses out again.

"Close, I think, but we've been turned around a lot with the earthquake and the tunnels," he murmured, shaking his head. "I can't sense any other way. This road branches farther up, but until then this tunnel is the only one going in the right direction."

Checa nodded, the decision clear in his expression. "We can't take the time to clear the rocks. It would give them too much time to prepare. We'll have to go through one at a time."

He gestured to his men and they formed a line that kept the women in the middle of their group. Rim was limping, and Ardelle, while alert, squinted against an obvious killer headache. He and Checa couldn't carry them over the rocks. They'd take them up again once they got past the slide and continued their run.

"Be alert," Checa growled and searched the faces of each of his men.

Jun jogged up from the rear. Heath wouldn't want to be in Jun's place later. Checa wouldn't work with a man who kept disappearing. At the signal to move, Jun pushed to go through first, brushing past Heath. Jun's scent was strange, but it often was, like he'd rubbed up against one of the Descendants. Heath dismissed it from his mind as they waited tense minutes for Jun's all clear. He held his breath and Ardelle's arm to prevent her moving without him. On Jun's signal they began crawling through the narrow space.

Heath pushed Ardelle a little as she climbed over the fallen rocks, and she slid through the narrow opening to the tunnel. Jun was on the other side to help her through. Before the Princess's foot landed on the smooth surface of the road on the other side, Heath began to scramble through.

Halfway through the odor hit him like a rock to the back of his head. *Exiles.*

"Behind us!" he yelled, almost falling the last few feet. "Move!"

It wasn't necessary. The rest of them were already moving. Checa pushed Rim through the rockslide as the rest of his team turned for defense. It was perfect strategy. Separate them into two groups, then attack.

Heath joined the others on his side of the rocks, only now noticing the odor wasn't just behind them.

"In front too," he called, knowing Checa would know what he meant.

An odorous wall of humanity rushed toward them. Damn the wings, there were dozens of them. They'd never be able to get through. Heath reached forward to grab Ardelle and thrust her behind him before he noticed the practiced fighter stance she'd automatically dropped into. Then he grinned. The Princess could handle herself. Even covered in bruises and still recovering from a head injury, she'd be difficult to defeat, and she wouldn't thank him for trying to protect her.

The *snick* of seventy claws releasing joined the building roar of the Exiles as they continued to spill around the corner and fill the tunnel in front of them.

"Enhance!" The call came from Checa to go to full were form, including the large incisors. Hell, his situation must be dire too.

"Ardelle, get behind me!" Heath grabbed her, trying not to pierce her with his claws as the men in front of him dropped, their toenails releasing to claws, their legs articulating and their shoulders hunching as their hackles rose. Heath crouched in front of Rim and Ardelle, growling at the pain the large incisors caused as they were released from his gums.

A small rock sailed from behind his head and smashed into the grimy face of a man running toward him. He flicked a look around to see Rim and Ardelle arming themselves with more rocks. He loved resourceful warriors.

He roared the attack, and the five of them surged toward the wall of unwashed Exiles pouring down the tunnel.

22.
BETRAYAL

THE STENCH and noise rolled over Rim in a sickening wave. He picked up some stones and pegged one at the Exiles. It went wide. The second one lobbed high and fell short. Thalazar the Great, what was wrong with his aim? Then he realized.

Fucking female physiology.

Rim deliberately changed his stance, turning sideways and sliding the stone through a smooth arc. Bull's-eye. He quickly shot off the half-dozen stones he'd scooped up, his aim now true as it usually was. Six Exiles hit the ground and didn't rise again. Across the other side of the tunnel, Ardelle was just as successful. There wasn't time to gather more stones; the Exiles were too close. Rim's training suppressed the terror he should be feeling and he reacted automatically. He drew two of his long fighting knives, adjusting his grip when his slightly smaller hands felt awkward on the hilts, and waded into the seething morass, targeting the men who slipped through the Mafdeti defense.

The three Mafdeti fought so smoothly it could have been a dance if they hadn't left a pile of bloody dead bodies in their wake. Every kick, every slash, every bite counted. And those fangs? Rim nearly pissed his pants when the cats roared and he saw the huge teeth piercing their gums to sit over their bottom lips, the tips almost touching their chins.

Rim slashed the neck of an Exile who came too close, then twisted and kicked the one beside him under his chin. The clamor of the battle around them buried the *snap* of his neck as his head flipped back from the force of Rim's foot. He completed his turn, stumbling a little when his breasts swung with the momentum and his foot landed awkwardly. He groaned in irritation. If he didn't get used to this body soon, he'd get himself killed.

He flicked a look to the Mafdeti again. Most times it took only one slash of claws or teeth to kill a man. If the man was fast enough to evade the first, the second strike never missed.

The tunnel was wide enough for only eight men abreast, so that made their fight easier, but they were massively outnumbered. Rim kicked a foot at the Exile rushing at him, slamming his heel into his groin. During his arching return to a two-footed stance, he swung his arms around and sliced open the bellies of three more men coming from the side. The metallic scent of blood filled his lungs, along with the stench of intestines. And still more took their places, all looking alike as if the ones before had risen again to fight some more. They crowded him, leaving no room for more varied fighting, so Rim settled into his hand-combat rhythm, ignoring the jarring on finer wrist bones than he was used to. He wouldn't last long; after the earthquake his head throbbed with every movement and his back stung. His breathing was already heavy, his shoulders strained with every movement, and he barely kept his tight grip on his knives.

The Mafdeti disappeared under the bodies, although Rim could still hear their growls and the screams of those they sliced. Then the pack of Exiles toppled over and the Mafdeti rose again.

Rim stabbed and slashed, watching the movement around him, aware and ready for attack from the sides and back as well, his focus intense, his training removing every vestige of emotion. The repeated movements finally smoothed out, as he became used to the different weight and flexibility of this female form.

The growls grew, rising and falling in tandem with the screams of men.

"Rim!"

Ardelle's call reached him over the cacophony. He slashed and kicked his way to the Princess and they stood side by side and fought for their lives.

A feline scream rose above the noise of battle and cut off abruptly, but Rim saw Heath throw off two men. Ardelle was still fighting beside Rim, so his heart only thumped painfully once before he resumed his own fight. How many were there? Rim was fighting uphill now, over the mound of bodies in front of him, slipping on blood and arms and legs. His shoulders ached, the muscles in his shredded back were on fire, his thighs burned, and his thrusts became less precise and less forceful. He swallowed the bile that rose at the stench of death surrounding him. Beside him, Ardelle's movements were slowing as well. Yet still they were both unscathed.

Rim slipped, leaving himself open for a slash to the shoulder. One Exile came close but veered away at the last minute. They weren't trying to kill them then, or even injure them. Why would they want them unharmed?

A chill ran down his spine.

"Come on, you bastards, fight properly," Ardelle growled beside him.

Rocks scattered behind them. Men tumbled through the narrow opening, then surged forward, overwhelming the Mafdeti on that side. Zar, the Exiles were breaking through! What had happened to Checa and the others who were with him? The growls stopped, and soon the only sounds of battle were the ones Rim and Ardelle were causing. But they fought on.

Rim knew he was going to die. He slashed the neck of a man reaching for him, the strike so full of anger the Exile's head lolled to the side, nearly severed from his body before he fell. Warm blood settled in a crimson spray after he landed in a heap at Rim's feet.

"Clear!" came the cry from the back of the crowd and all the Exiles dropped like stones.

"Oh shit." The words were barely out of Rim's mouth before a rough net was thrown into the air. Surrounded by the dead and dying, Rim and Ardelle had nowhere to move and could do little more than wait for it to descend on them. Rim crouched and readied his knives for a quick slash through the netting, assuming he was quicker with his knives than the Exiles would be with the current. Beside him, Ardelle noted what he did, and shifted her grip on her knives.

The twisted links of rope thudded on top of Rim, the unexpected weight sending him to his knees.

"Contact!"

Too slow.

Pain pulsed through him, targeting his nerves. His muscles spasmed and his jaw clenched hard, slamming his teeth together with a snap. He couldn't even scream. Beside him, Ardelle twitched, a low groan vibrating from her. Thalazar the Great, this was worse than any the Imperials had. He fought to contain his own whimpers as the pain twitched and pulled at his limbs. His breath blew in harsh gasps; his heart raced and thudded painfully. Sweat slithered over Rim's skin, chilling him and stinging his eyes. The smell of urine thickened the air. Him or Ardelle? He didn't know, knew nothing other than the pain, and all around him the faces of the Exiles rose and wavered, their black-toothed grins mocking him.

"Clear." The voice seeped through the fog of Rim's mind. Then silence descended.

Tremors continued to wrack his body, muscles twitching spasmodically as the coarse netting drew away from him. He cried out as it dragged on his suddenly too-sensitive skin.

Rim's breath was harsh in his ears, panting, drowning any other sound. His life became immersed in the shooting arrows of pain running along his nerves. Calloused hands grabbed him by the front of his shirt and swung him over a broad shoulder. He screamed as the pain intensified with the movement and the air slammed from his lungs. His knives fell to the ground, his nerveless hands unable to form fists. There was only his breathing, his thudding heart, and the pain.

EVERYTHING WAS quiet. Rim's back was warm, much warmer than his face, and the hiss of flames eating coal was nearby. The air was thick with rancid coke smoke. He kept his eyes closed and his breathing regular, even though his throat burned, thick and sore from the fumes.

"You sure they were dead?"

The voice came from behind him, somewhere farther away than the warmth. It was a low-pitched baritone, but coarse and uneducated, Outer Reaches Hawkesby and something else Rim couldn't recognize. Not a local dialect.

After a few seconds, he realized what it was. Yeudan.

"They were cats, Fisher. Cats don' stop fightin' 'less they're dead." The second voice held the slow, seafaring accents of the Grewin Peninsula. He was a long way from home.

"Did you check?"

The second man took a long time to answer. Rim held himself still, waiting through the almost-guilty silence. Where were the others? Surely they couldn't all be dead. A small spark of hope, deep inside him, thought he would know if they were, even though it didn't work that way. His chest ached, and he opened his mouth to hide the sob rising in him. This was ridiculous. He'd barely become friends with Checa and Heath, for all that they were on a mission together. Rim hadn't reacted like this, not anywhere close to it, since his mother walked into the fields surrounding her home at the height of norrgel season.

"We checked all t' ones we c'd reach. There were couple buried under t' bodies 'v our men. Left 'em there." Bitterness colored the rough voice. "If'n they weren't dead then, they would've b'n soon after."

"Fisher, they're awake."

The new voice came from close by. The change in Rim's breathing must have given him away.

"Let the King know. Sit them up."

King?

"Daddy's here?" Ardelle asked beside him.

Broad hands with fat fingers flickered in front of Rim before grabbing him under his arms and lifting.

Rim gasped as pins and needles shot through his body. It was better than the pain from before, but he still couldn't move. Every muscle ticked and jerked, sending the painful tingles to his hands and feet. Surreptitiously he forced his toes to curl inside his boots. It hurt, but hopefully it would help get his muscles moving again. He couldn't escape if he couldn't move.

The man arranged him, doll-like, against the wall of a medium-sized cavern. Rim growled when his captor's hands slowed as they passed over his breasts. He gave Rim a rancid grin and pinched his nipple before moving away, giving Rim his first look at where they were.

Rim blinked to accustom his eyes to the light, but the bizarre sight remained. Where on Zar were they? A large, almost-round table dominated the cavern. Short stools surrounded the table, one of them still rocking slightly on uneven legs. The floor was covered in threadbare rugs, none of them quite square, their garish colors patchy against the soft sandstone floor. Boxes were lined up around the edges of the cavern, their contents spilling over. Silks and pearls competed for space with brass cups studded with glass or semiprecious beads. On top of one of the boxes balanced a child's wooden carriage, one of its wheels broken in half. Some distance behind the table, a huge throne-like chair leaned drunkenly to one side.

Lowering himself into it was a wizened old man cloaked in coarse linen and poorly tanned furs. His skin was so wrinkled it folded in on itself; his lips were nonexistent, sucked into the prune face. The only thing about him that commanded attention was his eyes. They were bulbous, electric blue with tiny pinpoints for pupils, and they stared unblinking at Rim.

What were the Yeudan doing so far south? Why would they infiltrate Imperial lands when they must know they'd be killed on sight?

Ardelle landed beside Rim with a thud. The same big, beefy hands arranged her limbs to mirror Rim's. Then the stocky man stood to the side. Near the table stood a tall, wiry man with pitch-black hair and blacker eyes. His skin was mottled, some parts dark chocolate, other parts ivory smooth, like glowing clouds in a night sky.

"Here they are, sire. The supreme sacrifices, just as you predicted," the thin man said. He was the man with the Yeudan accent, but he wasn't Yeudan. The man called Fisher.

"That's not Daddy," said Ardelle.

"No," replied Rim.

That tiny, wrinkled old man with the scary eyes wasn't their king. Sacrifices? For what? And who predicted it? Zar, had they fallen into another weird prophecy from history or was this just some delusional, crazy bastard?

The old man regarded them silently for several minutes. "They are the ones. Take them and prepare them. The norrgel will bless us for this." Rim's jaw dropped. The old man's voice was a surprising deep bass that reverberated around the chamber and sent tingles down Rim's spine. The King's narrow chest didn't look big enough to produce a sound like that.

Beefy Hands bent to sling Rim over a shoulder, but the King spoke again. "Ensure they're well bound."

Shit. Wildly, Rim looked at Ardelle, seeing the same apprehension in her face. Frantically he wriggled his toes again, hissing at the pain that shot up his legs. His head dangled, but he ignored the hard bone digging into his stomach and stared at his hands, willing them to make fists. The fingers twitched and tingled painfully, but they moved. He focused on each muscle in turn—his calves, thighs, buttocks—and made them clench and relax on command. It was getting easier to move, but it still hurt like a bitch.

Beside him, Ardelle, similarly upside down on a man's shoulder, was doing the same thing, her face screwed up against the pain, but she was otherwise silent.

They were carried into an adjoining chamber as oddly furnished as the main cavern. A large square dais dominated the space. The jewel tones of the handwoven rugs draping it glistened in the flickering light from fires positioned at the four corners. Rusty chains threaded through holes around the edges of the dais and crisscrossed the surface. Half a dozen skinny, filthy women stood sentinel along one wall in front of billowing tapestries. None of them wore more than a loincloth, and the youngest ones, appearing barely in their teens, were completely naked.

"His Majesty wants these prepared."

As Fisher spoke, Rim was tipped over Beefy Hands's shoulder and dropped onto the dais. The blood rushed from his head back into his body, causing an instant headache and more painful tingles in his fingers and toes. He still couldn't move enough to fight back. Zar, if they got him chained down, he'd never escape.

Rim stared into the black eyes of the spotty man. "Let us go." The effort to speak left him panting.

Fisher regarded him silently, his eyes glowing deep and mysterious in the firelight. Then he shook his head. "I don't have a choice."

"There's always a choice." Rim thought he'd yelled the words, but all that came out was a sibilant whisper.

Fisher's attention shifted, and Rim followed his gaze as well as he could with the limited movement of his body. His breath caught. Jun was standing at the entrance to the cave. He'd survived. If he was alive, perhaps the others were as well. Heart pounding, Rim renewed his struggle to make his body obey his orders to move. And then he stilled. Jun wasn't bound or constrained in any way. He was just standing there, as if he was comfortable in the presence of the Exiles and Yeudan. Puzzled, Rim turned his gaze back to Fisher, who scowled and strode away from him.

"What're you doing here?" Fisher's angry query carried easily to Rim.

Jun's fists clenched. "You said no one would be killed." He kept his voice low, but his anger resonated in his chest.

Thalazar the Great, he betrayed us.

If Rim could move, he'd kill the bastard. He clenched his fists, surprised when they responded immediately and without pain. Slowly he flexed each muscle, relieved that they all responded. The effects of the netting had worn off. He felt weak and sluggish, but at least he could move. Beside him, Ardelle shifted too, and Rim turned to look at her.

"Get him," Ardelle whispered.

"No time. We have to get out of here while we can."

Rim checked that Fisher and Jun were still deep in conversation. "While they're occupied," he whispered.

Ardelle nodded, then tapped his hand once, twice. Before the third tap landed, Rim surged off the dais and rushed toward the women lined along the wall. There was nowhere else to go. Zar, he hoped those women would let them escape.

All the women except one stared dully in front of them, but the oldest crone watched Rim and Ardelle stagger toward her. Before they could reach the tapestries to hide, Rim tripped and fell, his legs still weighty and uncoordinated. The old woman's gaze flickered to where Fisher and Jun argued. She grabbed one of the tapestries and pulled it aside. "Quickly."

Rim pushed his feet under him and lurched to the revealed opening.

"The left fork," the old woman whispered. "There are weapons at the first opening, then keep going." The heavy cloth settled into place as the woman dropped it, and Rim and Ardelle were alone in a silent corridor.

23.
SURVIVAL

FUCK, CHECA hurt. He scrunched his eyes closed to focus better on feeling. The Bastard was standing on his hand and had slammed a bloody pole across his back, and he couldn't breathe. Had he punctured a lung? Dammit, the Bastard had beaten him good this time. He must have fought again. The Bastard always hit him harder when he fought. His ass wasn't on fire, so that explained the pain. The beating was always worse when the Bastard couldn't get it up.

Checa flexed the hand that wasn't underneath the boot. It worked. He methodically tested his arms and legs, then finally tried to move his head and open his eyes. Ah, it wasn't his lung. His face had simply been pressed into someone's stomach.

A dead someone. Fuck, the Bastard had brought another one home. The scent of blood was strong, and as the air moved when Checa shifted, he felt the liquid slide and cool. Drett, he was lying in a puddle of blood, nearly drowning in it.

Memory flooded back—not the Bastard. He'd been dead since Checa was sixteen, his stomach sliced and his intestines flowing on the floor.

The Exiles.

Checa moved again and hissed as the pain sharpened. He'd bet the cook's best laying hen at least one finger was broken, and maybe a couple of ribs. The rest of it felt like bruising, though his right shoulder hurt like a bitch and his head throbbed. He'd be able to move if he could just get rid of whatever was on top of him. He shuffled a bit, but froze when the weight settled deeper into his back. It was pitch-black, no light at all, so even his enhanced eyesight picked up nothing. What was he under?

Suddenly the weight above him moved. A hard body part, possibly a knee, landed on his broken hand. Checa shouted at the pain slicing through him.

"Checa? Hang on. I'll get you out."

Heath's voice, harsh and nasal, and then the weight above him shifted again.

"Fuck," he shouted, but it gurgled as his face was once again thrust into the pool of blood.

"Keep calling," Heath commanded. "I'll find you."

The weight moved again. Checa realized what was on top of him. Bodies. Dozens of dead bodies. How the hell did he end up under a pile of corpses? Last he remembered he was fighting alongside Jun. He ran through his memories as Heath removed more bodies from above him.

Jun had been on the other side of the rockfall. Why did Jun come back on this side? An elbow nudged Checa's head and he saw stars. Drett, he'd been hit on the head so hard it would plague him for days.

Finally enough bodies were removed that Checa could push himself up on two hands. And collapse again with a shout of pain. His fucking shoulder must be dislocated. He lay panting through the pain and nausea. Once it settled, he carefully rolled himself over, holding his arm close to his body.

Heath knelt above him, sweating and pale, his face covered in blood and his right elbow cradled in his left hand. Heath's relieved grin broke something deep within Checa as he realized how close to death they'd both come.

"Broken collarbone, broken nose, clip to the head. The rest nicks and bruises. You?" asked Heath.

Checa grunted. "Broken finger, cracked ribs, possible dislocated shoulder, possible cracked head."

Heath ran his gaze over him. "Definite dislocated shoulder, two broken fingers." He looked closely at Checa's eyes. "Glad you're alive, Checa."

Checa nodded, wincing at the pain it caused. "You too."

"Your head will be okay. I assume most of that blood isn't yours?"

"Don't think so." He took a careful breath. "The others?"

"Can't find Ardelle, Rim, or Jun. The rest are dead."

Checa closed his eyes and took a breath. Lives cut short—good ones. He forced his thoughts back to his mission. He would grieve the loss of his men later. "So we find them."

Checa pushed his way out of the morass of bodies and stepped close to Heath. Heath was still alive. Checa could lose everything else and still go on as long as Heath was alive. He raised a hand and trailed the fingers down Heath's neck, closing his eyes against the relieved sting of tears as he felt his lover's pulse beat. He opened his eyes to a soft smile of devotion, and he was totally unable to do anything other than return it.

Checa stepped back and cleared his throat. "Help me set this shoulder, and then we'll make a sling for your arm and splint my hand."

Checa reached over with his left hand and lifted his right arm toward Heath, bracing his feet against tumbled rocks. Heath grabbed the wrist and tugged. Checa yelled as the shoulder joint scraped and pulled, then popped back into place. Runnels of sweat-thinned blood dripped from his face, and he swallowed the nausea caused from the reduction. Carefully he rolled and pushed himself to his feet, swaying and blinking the spots from in front of his eyes before he steadied. "Fuck. I feel like I've been on a five-day bender and brawl."

He'd suffered worse at the hands of the Bastard, so he knew he'd survive. He shoved the pain to the back of his mind and surveyed the carnage in the dim light. The Exiles had attacked from both sides of a rockslide at the narrowest point of the tunnel. "This was too well organized." His stomach churned with anger. He looked away from the bodies of his men, unable to acknowledge their loss. They'd deserved better than Checa had given them.

Heath nodded. "They knew we were coming."

Checa regarded him with narrowed eyes and nodded. Heath returned the gesture.

Checa didn't need to say more. Jun had been sneaking away for weeks. Checa had thought he had a lover, but now he saw a darker reason for Jun's distraction. If it was him, he would pay for his betrayal and the death of Checa's team.

They found the medi-pack and pulled out what they needed. Heath located Checa's broken rib. It poked outward, so a lung puncture was unlikely as long as he was careful. Checa held still as Heath rolled a couple of adhesive patches over it to hold it steady. A couple more around his hand secured his broken fingers.

Checa fashioned a sling for Heath out of the pack itself, keeping a pocket to hold as many items as possible on the inside. While they worked, Heath darted curious looks at him and finally spoke.

"Are you going to pursue Rim?"

"What are you talking about?" Checa stared at Heath, not knowing how to answer.

"You could bond with her," Heath persisted.

Checa scowled. "Why would I want to when I have you?"

"You don't want me."

"I don't want anyone else." There was more, and Checa should say it, but he didn't know how, so he continued to silently work the pack into a sling.

"She's perfect for you, you know." Heath's grin lit his battered face, but it was crooked, out of place. "She can be both man and woman. You were married to Xefra. You could have pussy again."

"Don't be crude. I want her as much as you want Ardelle." Checa tugged Heath's hand up to his opposite shoulder more roughly than he needed to, then winced when Heath hissed at the pain. "Sorry." He tied the pack straps around Heath's neck. "I have all I want with you."

"You don't really want me."

Checa glared at him. "Is that really what you think?"

Heath shrugged and looked away. "You use me, you say it's love, but you won't bond with me. What else am I supposed to think?"

"Are you trying to make me angry?"

Heath's voice softened. "No. I just want you to know it's okay if you want her. We both know we can't keep going the way we have been without a Bond."

Checa clamped his jaw tight against a howl of anguish. Heath had been the only good thing in his life for so long that he didn't know what he'd do without him—and he didn't want to learn.

"If there was a way to bond with you, to have only you for the rest of my life, to announce it to your mother and the whole world and live openly and honestly as your Bond-Mate, I'd bond with you right now. I'd merge myself into you and become one with you, and I'd never want anything else. But you know as well as I do that your mother would never approve of it. As Matriarch she can break Bonds, and she'd break ours without even considering the consequences."

"She's not that bad—"

"Don't lie to yourself, Heath. She'd break the Bond and one of us would die." Checa worked steadily on the makeshift sling, but at that point he was basically just smoothing the straps of the bag around Heath's neck so he could maintain contact. "I'm not going to bond with you and risk you dying."

After a long silence, Heath continued. "I always thought you and I would eventually… but you're really not going to let that happen, are you?" Heath's voice caught and he swallowed audibly. "Things between us are going to change."

Checa closed his eyes and forced himself to keep breathing evenly, as if his heart wasn't breaking. He pictured the way Heath had been with Ardelle, so kind and gentle. That was what Heath needed: time to face the future, whatever it might be. He opened his eyes and reached a hand to cradle his lover's face. "They already have."

Heath turned his head and kissed Checa's palm. "I will love you all my life, Checa."

But we're still ending it.

"Hold still while I set that nose." It didn't seem possible they could make it work anymore, perhaps not even the friendship they'd begun with so many years ago. Checa's throat thickened with grief and his eyes burned, so he said nothing more.

Put it aside. Get the job done.

Heath grunted at the crunch of pain, then stared at Checa pointedly as he held a cloth over Heath's nose to stem the bleeding.

"I'm fine." Checa tried for an unconcerned tone, but by the way Heath regarded him, he'd failed. He shoved himself to his feet to put distance between them.

Heath followed him, not allowing the distance Checa desperately needed. Heath slung his arm around Checa's back and hugged him close, careful not to squeeze his ribs. "You are worthy of love, Checa. You deserve it and every speck of happiness this life has to offer." He reached up and pressed a warm, soft kiss to Checa's lips. "Believe it. I do."

Yet you're still ending us.

The thought continued to loop through his mind. Checa riffled his fingers through the thick hair at the back of Heath's neck, enjoying the silky softness—perhaps for the last time, although he didn't want to believe that. Then he pulled away.

Heath and Checa worked together to arrange the bodies of their fallen comrades so that they could rest easily in the next life. They left the bodies of the Exiles and the Yeudan where they landed.

"So," Checa began, then cleared his throat. He didn't want to know, but he had to ask. "What about Ardelle?"

"She's great, isn't she?" Heath stopped what he was doing and grinned at Checa. "She understands me totally, Checa. She can read the planet too, so she knows what it's like for me. She knows what it's like to be considered a freak." He turned another slain warrior's face toward the east so that sunlight would be the first thing the man saw when his spirit woke again. "I always thought I was the only one," he said softly. "Have you seen the way her green eyes flash with temper?" He huffed at his own fancifulness.

Checa stood over the dead. He was supposed to wish them luck in their future lives, but all he could see in front of him were images of Heath and Ardelle, Ardelle and Heath. His stomach churned at the thought of them together. He couldn't do it.

He had to, for Heath's sake. He slung his good arm around Heath's back, looping his hand under his arm, away from his injured collarbone. "You'll get to spend all the time you need with your fiery Princess."

Heath shook his head and snuggled closer. "If you seriously think she's what I want, you're a delusional idiot."

Checa ignored the taunt, not understanding why Heath would say that but sure he'd find out later, and ran a mocking gaze over their bodies. "We're going to be slow with only three legs between us, but we'll find the women and bring them out."

Heath attempted to change to were form, but his injuries would make running too painful. They couldn't change to cat form without falling asleep to heal. "Won't work," he said. "It'll be too slow and way too painful for you." Their human form, with its strangely higher tolerance for pain, would have to do. "Let's track." They loped over the remnants of the battle and climbed through the rockfall to find the scent of the women and the Exiles who'd taken them.

"About forty all up. I'd have thought there were more." Heath surveyed the pile of dead Exiles.

Checa barely glanced around. "There were. We didn't get them all."

"Pity."

"There were only seven of us."

"Nine. Ardelle and Rim are warriors too."

Checa frowned. While all Mafdeti trained as warriors, only the males went on active duty. Their women were too rare to risk. He couldn't imagine Rim, the leader of her own valley, accepting such a passive role. Ardelle either. "Nine," he grumbled.

Heath strode at his side, only the careful cradling of his arm showing the pain he was in. This area of the tunnel, while stinking of Exiles, was empty. "I think we should move away. Where do you think would be a good place to live?"

"What?" They lived in the Aylmer Mountains, as they always had.

"The four of us should live close," Heath said patiently. "You and I love the mountains and Rim has her valley, but Ardelle will rule her people one day and might want to live in Hawkesby."

"You'd go underground?" How could Heath even consider such a thing? Hawkesby was a grim enough place to visit. He wouldn't want to live there, to never wake to the morning breeze and the rustle of rodents in the undergrowth. Checa shuddered, suddenly feeling claustrophobic in the tunnels.

Heath shrugged.

Checa frowned at the man beside him. Was he mad? "You do know the chances of us all surviving are slim?" Checa would die to protect Heath.

Heath looked at Checa as if he thought him slow-witted. "We'll survive." As if that was fact.

"You don't know that. That's why I'm here: to keep you safe."

Heath glared at him and strode ahead.

Within minutes he was back, never able to stay angry. Checa loped along, allowing his lover's casual chatter to wash over him.

"I'll bet they'd love the outcropping overlooking the wildflower meadow. I remember sitting quietly with you in the early mornings. And it's midway to everywhere."

Checa shot a disbelieving look at Heath but was ignored. Silence and Heath rarely occupied the same space for long.

"Remember how the sun hovers on the horizon, a glowing semicircle that kisses the velvet petals with gold. When the whole of it rises, the flowers wave pink and blue and mauve in the breeze, and you'd sigh." Heath slipped his arm through Checa's. "The first time I heard you sigh like that, I was eight. It was the saddest sound I'd ever heard. You crouched there, a mass of bruises and cuts. I thought you were going to hit me when I came close, but you let me clean up the worst of it." He dropped a casual kiss to Checa's shoulder. "You let me stay afterward too. And in all the years since, you never once told me you didn't want me around."

Checa snorted and Heath shot him a look from under his lashes.

"Well, if you did, I knew you didn't mean it."

They laughed then. The quiet, comfortable laugh of friends and lovers who've been through much and know their relationship will never be the same again. Checa hoped it would endure in whatever form it took. It had to. Heath was everything good in Checa's life.

"Thank you," Checa said quietly. The thanks was for more than this reminder of who they were. Heath had saved Checa back then. He saved him every day, even if he never realized it.

Heath grinned cheekily, but his eyes were soft and misty. He opened his mouth to reply, then paused and scented the air. Between one second and the next, he went from open, teasing lover to focused warrior.

In tandem they slipped down the tunnel to a wide intersection.

Checa shot a quick look around the corner. "Four guards, large cavern beyond." Heath's claws snicked out and Checa put a restraining hand on his arm. "We're outnumbered and injured. We have to find a different way in."

Heath nodded reluctantly and pressed his hand to the rock.

An angry cry echoed down the tunnel and Checa leaned around the rock to see the guards run into the cavern. "Something's happened," he whispered. "Come on. There'll never be a better chance."

Silently they ran down the tunnel and slipped into the cavern. Gaudy rugs and tapestries covered the floor and walls. Checa slipped sideways behind a dusty tapestry, Heath close behind him. Together they made their way around the cavern to the opening most of the men had disappeared through.

24.
THE ENEMIES

A TINY old man—Yeudan from his prominent eyes and the bright red beads threaded through his hair, swathed in stiff, odorous fur—stood in front of a line of cowering women. Spittle shot from his mouth as he yelled, "Fools! Where did they go?"

The oldest woman, hair matted, face scarred, bowed low. "Forgive us, Your Majesty. We weren't told to watch the women."

The old man backhanded her across her face, his rings tearing open the fragile skin. She fell to the ground. No one moved to help her. Heath surged forward but Checa held him back. Checa tightened his grip on Heath's arm, partly to hold him still, but also to remind himself that if he tore the old man's head off his shoulders then, their mission would be forfeit. If they were successful with the Warrior Pledge, they'd have a better opportunity of effecting real change for those women. Right then there was nothing they could do.

The rationalization didn't help much. The weaselly old man still got away with harming someone less powerful.

"Find them!" The old man pointed to the dais. "Prepare another sacrifice." As he stalked from the room, bouncing dust bunnies following his trailing robe, he spoke again. "I want to hear our glorious leaders feast. Only when they're appeased will they allow us to live in peace."

"Who are they feeding? Feast on what?" asked Heath in a low whisper.

Checa scanned the cavern, noting the black feathers displayed in earthen vases. "I think it's the norrgel."

"The norrgel are their leaders? They're birds."

"No one said it had to make sense." Movement near the main entrance caught Checa's eye. When Heath stiffened beside him, he tightened his hold on Heath's arm. They watched as Jun sauntered into the room. He sniffed and frowned, and Checa was sure he'd scented them, but then he focused on the group near the dais.

"Rim and Ardelle are more important," Checa said softly, "but I want him marked."

Heath growled his agreement, and he and Checa began sidling around the side of the room. They moved slowly so as not to disturb the tapestries, but stopped between each one to check the lay of the land.

A mottled man with black eyes spoke next. "There are only two entrances to this room." He stepped closer to the dais and pointed at groups of men. "You, go through the women's quarters and make sure they're not hiding there." Lecherous grins bloomed on several faces. "You have ten minutes, so all you're doing is searching."

The man's voice was hard, promising retribution. The grins faded and the group pushed aside one of the tapestries behind the women and disappeared down a tunnel.

Checa and Rim were about a quarter of the way around the room when Jun began backing away from the group of men around him. They paused, watching where he would go.

"You lot, go through the main chamber and check the tunnels through there." The black-eyed man strode over to the women and bent to help the injured one to her feet.

"You will recover, old mother." His voice was surprisingly gentle as he spoke to her. He handed her to the woman at her side.

The old woman shook her head. "He still wants a sacrifice." She gestured to the women around her. "I won't allow it to be one of them."

"No." The thin man's voice was so low, Checa couldn't tell if he was agreeing with the woman or protesting her decision.

She laid her hand on the man's arm. "The time to stop this is coming—" She flicked a look at the tapestry Checa and Heath were peering out from. "—but it isn't yet. Align yourself with them, and you'll defeat these animals and bring peace to our land." She turned to the women standing with her. Most of them had tears streaming down their faces, but none made a sound or moved to stop her. "Look after the wee ones," the woman said to them. "Keep them safe."

Two of the women nodded, and then one by one they kissed the old woman on her cheek and slipped behind the tapestries into the tunnels beyond.

The old woman walked toward the dais.

"They're not just feeding them. I think they're worshiping them too." Checa reached over and gripped Heath's forearm, preventing him from rushing to help. "I know you want to save her, but we have to put our mission first."

"You don't even believe in our mission."

Checa ducked his head so he spoke directly into Heath's ear. "I might not believe the same way you do, but I believe in you. You say the Warrior Pledge is the only way to move forward, to stop more people being sacrificed, so we'll finish the Pledge, and hopefully no one else will have to die like this."

"They're going to feed her to the norrgel." Heath pressed his forehead against Checa's chest and closed his eyes.

Every atom in Checa's body was straining to burst from their hiding place and save the woman, just as he knew Heath was, but he knew it wouldn't work. If they revealed themselves, they'd be killed. They were injured and outnumbered, and they couldn't fight every battle they came across. He hated it, but he knew it was the only thing to do. He had to stay focused on their goal.

He raised his gaze to Heath. "Let's get out of here and find Rim and Ardelle. I want this finished so we can come back and beat the shit out of that Yeudan bastard and those damned Exiles following him." He peeped around the edge of the tapestry to see if the others in the cavern were occupied. He and Heath would be exposed for a few seconds, and he wanted to get away cleanly. Checa met the deep black gaze of the tall, mottled man and froze.

The man didn't react but turned back to the remaining men and led them to the other side of the dais, their backs to Checa and Heath. Two men were chaining the old woman on the rock. Beyond the group, Jun stepped behind one of the tapestries. Checa watched the wavering fabric mark Jun's progress around the room until he slipped into the tunnel where the first group had gone.

Checa nodded to Heath and, after checking the small group at the dais was still turned away, he dashed silently after Jun. Checa and Heath slipped behind the tapestry in time to see him take the left fork.

Checa signaled "extreme caution" to Heath, then took the lead. The black-eyed man had sent men through here, but which direction were the women's quarters in? He'd shown kindness to the old woman, but he'd still allowed her to be a sacrifice. Checa and Heath padded silently along, checking each turn cautiously.

Jun had disappeared, but there was nowhere he could have turned off. His scent was strong but light—he was running. Checa picked up his pace but slowed again when Heath hissed in pain. Checa's own hand and shoulder ached and his head throbbed. Heath's injuries were as bad, and he still wasn't fully recovered from the norrgel-strike. If Checa thought they had the time, he'd insist they rest long enough for Heath's injuries to begin to heal, but they had to deal with Jun, then find Rim and Ardelle and get to the lake.

The tunnel stopped abruptly; a stone wall loomed ahead of them. Checa slowed to a walk and approached cautiously. There had been no branches, and he'd seen no other escape routes. He glanced at Heath, who shook his head. He hadn't seen any either. Less than an arm's length from the end wall, Checa realized there was a fissure at the corner, similar to the one they'd taken Rim and Ardelle through when they first found them.

They sidled through a dogleg to come out in a narrow tunnel that seemed to draw light from the surface through glistening crystals. The ceiling was lower and varied in height, and the walls were crudely cut rock. Water trickled in rivulets and tiny waterfalls down the walls. Over the noise of the water, Checa heard a small *snick*. Signaling to Heath, he moved forward, looking for the place where Jun was hiding, waiting for them.

Heath dropped back a few paces.

Jun pounced with a roar just as Checa passed a shallow niche. Jun landed on Checa's back, taking him to the ground. Checa landed heavily on his injured arm, grunting from the pain in his ribs and gagging against the nausea his agonized shoulder caused, then rolled to avoid the deadly accuracy of Jun's claws. Checa had trained with Jun from a teenager, so he knew exactly how good Jun was. Injured as Checa was, it would take all his skill to best him.

Suddenly Jun was lifted from him and flung into the wall. Heath followed through, pressing his body solidly onto Jun. Checa surged to his feet and joined him. Together, using their uninjured sides as much as possible, they pressed the traitor hard against the wall.

"Why?" Checa asked.

Jun sneered. "My family have been leaders and Elders for generations. You're nothing but trash, Checa, yet they made you Commander, simply because your eyes turn silver. You know nothing of the Pledge and are too much of a coward to fight the Imperials for our rights. The command and the Pledge are mine by birthright, and I'll do whatever I have to do to get them. I will save our people and return them to their former glory."

Jun had always been snarky and entitled, but he was one of Checa's best men. Then he'd begun sneaking away, coming back relaxed, almost as if he'd been well fucked, but also tense and secretive. The last few days, Jun had been edgy and temperamental. Now he was pale and sweating. Fine tremors ran through his body.

Had he been planning this all along? And now he was caught, he didn't want to die? "I wish we had time to kill you slowly, Jun." Checa snicked out one claw and gouged a thick horizontal line across Jun's left cheek. Jun howled and tried to tug his head away, but Heath held him steady and pinned Jun's hands above his head.

"You've caused the deaths of good men and you've put the entire mission in jeopardy." Checa began a diagonal cut under the line he'd just drawn. "Now everyone will know you for the traitor you are." He deliberately kept his voice steady and conversational because he knew it would unnerve Jun.

Sounds of pursuit echoed down the tunnel. Jun's eyes flicked to the source of his salvation, and the sneer returned. Checa pressed heavily against Jun's throat, cutting off his air.

"You know all those stories about me slicing people open and leaving them for dead?" Jun turned terrified eyes to Checa. "I killed the first one when I was sixteen. I was tried and convicted, then made Captain of the Guard. You've seen me do it. What do you think your chances are right now?"

Except in battle, Checa had killed only two men, but he'd never disabused his team of the notion that he'd kill anyone if he thought they deserved it.

He stepped back, his handiwork on Jun's face complete. Heath moved away too. Blood ran from the cuts and dripped off Jun's jaw. Jun's mouth twisted into a sneer, a sure tell he was going to jump them in anger. Checa slashed his arm horizontally across Jun's stomach. At the last minute, he'd retracted his claws, so the only damage done was a thin, shallow slice, but for a second, Jun didn't realize it. He screamed and clutched his stomach.

Checa stepped back as the man who'd betrayed them slumped to the ground and vomited. Checa grabbed the hair at the back of Jun's neck and pulled his head back. "You'd better run a long way, *traitor*, because if I see you again, you'll be added to that list."

Checa dropped Jun's hair, then turned and ran down the corridor. After a pause, Heath joined him.

"It was that bastard you killed, wasn't it?" Heath's voice was an odd combination of anger and acceptance.

"What was?" Checa hoped Heath would drop it. He didn't want to talk about the Bastard. Ever. It was his past and best left there.

Of course, Heath wouldn't let it go. For a while he mumbled to himself as if suggesting people and dismissing them. Then he said, "The old man next door." Checa ran faster, holding his ribs, trying to shut Heath down, but Heath continued. "*He* was the bastard who did those awful things to you."

Checa stopped; Heath barreled into him from behind. "What things?"

Heath shrugged. "Whatever it was that put such pain in your soul, that made you believe you'd never have anything but violence. That you'd never find love." Heath began jogging, taking the lead.

The breath caught in Checa's throat. He followed Heath. Once he was identified as the Silver, the details of his case had been erased. No one knew what the Bastard had done to him. He'd never told anyone any of it, except what he'd done to Warden and the others. But Heath knew. Even though Checa had thought it was in the past, that no one would ever find out, Heath had known all along.

And he'd stayed with him.

Checa came to a stumbling stop, gasping as he tried to breathe through the tightness in his chest.

Heath knew him, all of him.

"Checa?" Heath stopped when he realized Checa wasn't moving. "What's wrong?"

Checa couldn't speak. He ducked his head and ran on, with Heath running silently beside him.

25.
THE SEARCH

HEATH RAN down the tunnel in a loping lurch that was supposed to protect his injuries, but he thought nothing would. The fight with Jun hadn't helped. His collarbone shifted with every step, shooting fiery tendrils of pain through his torso. Beside him, Checa developed his own fumbling gait, accompanied by a grunt every second step.

They kept their pace as fast as they could, but every hundred paces or so, Heath paused to listen.

"No sign of pursuit yet." That worried him. The Exiles weren't known for allowing strangers into their stronghold. Heath had only known two people who'd come out alive, and neither of them walked again. "They're working with the Yeudan."

"There was only that one old man and half a dozen soldiers," responded Checa.

"And all the ones that died in the ambush. A lot of them had red hair and big eyes, but I didn't make the connection before now. Face it, Checa. For some reason the Yeudan have come down from the mountains and the Exiles have allied themselves with them."

"I'm surprised they haven't formed an alliance before now. They both hate the Descendants with a passion."

"It's not an alliance. The Yeudan were clearly in charge."

"One crazy old man screaming. It doesn't mean he's in charge." Checa was arguing for the sake of arguing. He agreed with Heath, but he needed to explore all possibilities so he could work out exactly what was going on and how he and his soldiers could respond to it. Heath grinned at him. They'd played this game before, many times. Checa grinned. "What about the black-eyed man?"

"You noticed what color his eyes are?" Heath grinned again. "Usually it's only the people from the Lonely Isles who have eyes that dark. Matches their skin. But he's not from there. He's not an Exile either. He doesn't carry himself like anyone I've ever known before. Where do you think he's from?"

"So he's not an Exile. Definitely not a Yeudan with that black hair and narrow-set eyes. He knew we were there. He let us escape."

"So, a possible ally?" Heath hoped so. The further into this journey they went, the more obvious it became that they needed all the allies they could get.

"Possibly."

Heath pressed a hand against the rock wall beside him and read the grains of sand along the tunnel, toward the Exile caverns. "Still no one behind us."

"They're probably still searching the main caverns."

Heath didn't believe for a minute he wasn't concerned about the lack of pursuit. There was nothing they could do about it except remain vigilant. Another half-dozen fumbling steps, and Heath couldn't take the silence any longer.

"Are we sure Rim and Ardelle went this way? What if they went the other way and are trapped or captured again?" After a few more stumbling steps, he continued. "Shouldn't we check?"

"If they went down the other way, the Exiles will find them. If that's the case, we have to go on without them."

"Without them? Checa, we can't! It's the Warrior Pledge. We need the four of us to complete it."

"I know the Pledge is between four people, and the goal seems to be to bind our races together, but there's nothing concrete. It's little more than a myth. Let's not forget that what we actually have here is some sort of rot destroying the land and Yeudan invaders who've begun working with the Exiles. That's what we have to deal with, and we have to do that with or without Rim or the Princess."

"No! You've read the prophecies. You know it's more than that. All the signs are there: Makai and Nayeli making another attempt to choose the victor, the rot in the land, the threat to our way of life… my vision. It has to be done now, or we'll lose everything."

It was the same argument again, over and over. Heath ground his teeth, half-sure that Checa did it just to irritate him.

They reached the end of the tunnel. In unspoken accord they fell silent and crept to the opening, allowing enough time for their eyes to adjust to the change in light. Checa signaled Heath to wait while he did the basic recon; then Heath joined him.

The area outside smelled fresh and clean, like a light rain had washed through not long before. In the bushes that surrounded the small clearing and tipped over the edge of the escarpment into the valley below, birds twittered. The sky was dotted with cotton wool clouds but otherwise empty. Checa flicked his fingers toward a scrappy path. "No norrgel or Exiles." He crouched to inspect a broken blade of grass.

"That's odd," said Heath. "We're not that far north or west."

"Two distinct footsteps." Checa stood. "One small. This is them." Checa looked at the empty sky, a worried scowl marring his features. "Let's move while we can."

He set out at a double-paced trot, but quickly slowed and gripped his shoulder.

Heath jogged along beside him, his gaze alternating between the track they were following, the bushes around them, and the sky above the Hawkesby Plains. "I don't like that there are no norrgel, Checa. It's another sign."

"Heath, you're being ridiculous." Checa looked at the sky. "It's close to sunset. They've probably all gone to roost."

"Checa—" Checa never dismissed him. Never.

A waft of dead animal and the crunch of leaves in the bushes to their right were the only warnings they had before four Exiles landed on them. Heath managed to twist so he landed on his good shoulder, but the pain that flashed through him stole his breath and brought spots to his vision. For several seconds all he could do was try to breathe again and allow instinct to take over. His claws snicked out, and while he couldn't think clearly enough through the pain to formulate a reasonable response, he still managed to dig two claws deep into the belly of the Exile trying to throttle him. The man screamed and his grip loosened enough for Heath to roll away and kick out at him. The crunch of bone as Heath's heel connected with the man's jaw was loud in the sudden silence. Heath panted, staying as still as he could until the burn in his collarbone reduced.

If Heath had even an hour's grace, he could change to full cat form and sleep while his bone knitted and the bruises healed. Without the Change it would take days to heal, and it would only happen that quickly if bastards didn't keep jumping him.

"You still alive?" asked Checa.

Heath turned his head to find Checa lying propped against a tree, his elbow cradled in his palm. He was pale with pain. "How's your shoulder?"

"Still in place." Checa groaned as he pushed himself to his feet and stood swaying, eyes closed, face even paler than before.

"Don't vomit on me. I already smell bad enough." Heath struggled to his feet, trying not to use his arm, which would jar his collarbone. "Have none of them ever heard of bathing?"

"It didn't look like hygiene was high on their list of priorities."

Checa came over to inspect Heath's injuries. Heath toed the Exile he'd kicked, but the man was either out cold or dead. Heath didn't have the energy to check and couldn't bring himself to care much either way—particularly not after losing so many friends a few hours before. He hissed and pushed Checa away when the bloody man prodded his collarbone. "You know I could check you over as well." He grunted. "Do you want me to see how your shoulder is holding up?"

"Sorry." Checa dropped his hand and looked away. "Rim and Ardelle definitely came this way." He returned to the problem at hand.

"We'd catch them easily if we could change to cat form."

Checa didn't respond, and Heath lapsed into silence. There was no point lamenting what couldn't be. If they changed to cat form, they'd sleep so they could heal. Without the time to allow healing, they'd be worse off trying to run on three legs in were form, and as they were beginning with broken bones, the Change would be extremely slow and painful.

"Are you sure you're okay to continue?" Checa asked.

Heath nearly snapped at him, told him he was a big boy now and could look after himself, but there was something in Checa's voice that stopped him. It always came down to the same thing. Checa didn't want to bond with him, but he still cared about him more than anyone else did... possibly even Heath's parents. Heath resisted walking into Checa's warmth and wrapping his arms around his lover. He contented himself with a finger-light touch to the back of his hand. "I'm fine, Checa." He nodded into the undergrowth. "Let's go before more Exiles come."

Checa took the lead, stopping every dozen steps to check the trail they were following. Heath grabbed a fallen branch that still held leaves and used it to fluff up the grasses they walked through.

When they reached the edge of the escarpment and could see the way to the mountains, he threw the branch away and they broke into an ungainly jog.

26.
WATERFALL

LIGHT GLINTED gold and silver off the swirling waters of the river as Checa and Heath neared the waterfall at the base of the mountains. Rainbows hung in the mist that drifted droplet by droplet onto Checa's body, refreshing him after the long run. The thunder of the water pounding down the cliff and gouging out the rocks below enveloped him, reverberating through his body. Water ran in runnels down his face and plastered his loincloth to his body. Heath was drenched as well, his skin glistening, each muscle catching the light as he moved.

They'd rested for a few hours, not risking changing to cat form to heal. Checa needn't have worried because he was almost completely healed. Only his ribs ached after running for so long.

Heath wasn't moving anywhere near as smoothly as Checa thought he should be. Compared to their usual swift healing, he didn't appear to be healing at all. His skin was pale, his nose still bruised, although the swelling had reduced. His eyes were stained dark from the bruising and showed a tension Checa recognized as pain. He still favored his left arm and shoulder, but the small bump on his collarbone told Checa it had begun to knit. Checa knew Heath needed to be cat, and for far longer than he'd originally thought, but they had to find Rim and Ardelle. They had less than three days to the moons' eclipse.

They were close, though. The prints Checa was tracking were fresh, made less than an hour ago, possibly only a few minutes. Every time he rounded a tree, he expected to see either Rim or Ardelle trudging through the forest.

Giving directions by voice was impossible; they'd long since reverted to touch and hand signals if they were more than an arm's length apart. The forest was still dense, so they couldn't see the falls yet. The noise and spray carried a long way. The mist was heavy with meaning; they were close to the falls.

Heath paused and shoved his hand into the undergrowth. Checa drew nearer, curious to see what he'd found this time. When Heath brought out his hand, he was holding a large stick insect, its exoskeleton dark gray and rough like the bark of the tree it had been sitting on. After grinning at Checa, Heath returned the insect to its home, and Checa watched as it bounced a few times before stilling, once again becoming almost invisible.

When Heath moved to continue on their way, Checa held him back. This might be the only opportunity he'd have to make sure Heath knew how he felt. He drew him close. Heath came easily, as he always did, resting in Checa's arms as if there was nowhere else he'd rather be.

"You know I love you, don't you?" Checa asked against Heath's ear. It suddenly seemed like the most important thing for Heath to understand about him, about them. "We're not just fuck buddies," he insisted. "We never have been. You've always been the most important person in my life. If I could, I'd grow old with you."

"I love you too." Heath tightened his hold around Checa's waist. "I always have. As I grew, my love for you grew too, until it became something that was strong and true and will last a lifetime. I don't want to be with anyone else, Checa. Only you."

Checa breathed a sigh of relief, then inhaled deeply of Heath's scent. No wildflowers today, only sweat and blood, with a touch of fear and anger. It was still his Heath. He raised his head and cupped Heath's cheeks. "Love me," he whispered. Heath might not hear the words but he would read them on Checa's lips and in the frantic beating of his heart. "Love me now, as purely as you've always loved me and as surely as I'll always love you."

Heath smiled and reached for him, just as Checa knew he would, had dreamed he would. Checa lowered his head and pressed his lips to Heath's.

As always happened when Checa touched Heath, everything bad that had happened to him disappeared. There was no more Bastard, no more Exiles or Yeudan. There wasn't even the Warrior Pledge and the danger and responsibility that came with that. All there was, all there would ever be, was Heath. Heath's smooth, warm skin pressed against him. Heath's breath fanned across his cheek and neck. Heath's fingers alternately trailed delicately across Checa's shoulders and dug into the taut muscles of his back.

They were so close to the waterfall that a cooling mist washed over them, taking with it the dirt and detritus of the day, leaving them clean and fresh. Heath dropped to his knees, his nimble fingers untying Checa's loincloth and allowing it to drop onto the wet ferns beneath them. He licked his lips and leaned forward, intent on Checa's rigid cock, but Checa held him back.

"I want you to love me," he said again.

Heath looked up, his eyes sparkling with mischief. "I'm trying to, but you stopped me."

Checa riffled his fingers through Heath's hair but kept him at a distance. Between them his rigid cock bobbed, so hard and needy Checa swore it was steaming in the cool air. He swallowed heavily, knowing Heath needed it to be said. "I've never said this to anyone, Heath…."

Heath stopped trying to reach Checa's cock, his face suddenly serious. "Are you ending us?"

"What?" Checa stepped back, then dropped to the ground in front of Heath. "What about this scene here could possibly give you the idea I want to end us?"

Heath slumped to the ground and lowered his head. "You won't bond with me." He looked up. "And that's fine—well, not fine, but I sort of understand why. But now you won't let me touch you either."

Checa settled himself into the soft ferns and dragged Heath onto his lap. "You're an idiot, you know that, don't you?" He gripped Heath's head and pulled it to his shoulder. "But you're my idiot. Now shut up and listen, and then you can decide if I want to end it."

"Checa—"

"Shh. I love you, Heath. I just told you that. I also said I wanted you to love me. Did you get that part? That I want *you* to love *me*?"

Heath's body stilled. He was so still Checa couldn't feel him breathing. After so long that Checa was sure he'd passed out, Heath gasped.

"Are you serious? You've never wanted me to do you before. Are you sure you want to? It's a big thing and we're out here in the middle of nowhere and it's your first time." Heath stopped babbling and straddled Checa. "Are you sure?"

"I'm sure." When Heath would have dived into a kiss, Checa held him back, his heart pounding. He'd be sweating too, if water from the mist wasn't already dripping off him. His throat was thick. He wanted to run but knew he couldn't. This was Heath, and it was important. "But it's not my first time."

Checa's lap emptied faster than the spray from the waterfall could wet his hair. Heath scrambled backward, his mouth moving. He was yelling. Checa could tell because of the small frown between Heath's brows and the tension in his neck, but he couldn't hear the words over the roar of the waterfall. He didn't need to hear what Heath was saying, though. He could imagine it.

What do you mean it's not your first time? Who else have you been with? I thought we were together, and now you tell me you cheated on me? When? When did this happen? You haven't had time to do anything with anyone else, so when did you do it? Who was it?

Heath's mouth froze wide open and he stopped flailing his hands around.

Checa remained where he was and waited. It wouldn't take long. Heath was the smartest person he knew, and as soon as Heath got over his jealousy, he'd realize exactly what Checa meant. The roar of the waterfall faded away and the mist seemed to clear around Heath's face. Checa saw exactly when realization came to Heath.

Heath's mouth snapped closed, his bottom lip trembled, and his eyes filled with tears.

"That's why I didn't tell you before now." It wasn't quite true, but Checa didn't need Heath's pity. He didn't want anyone's pity. It had happened. Nothing could change that. The Bastard was dead and would never hurt another child. Checa was fine.

As suddenly as Heath had left Checa's lap, he was back in it, so fast that Checa's head cracked against the trunk of a tree fern. His gasp of pain was swallowed in Heath's kiss. It was savage, bordering on painful, and just as Checa would have pulled away, Heath gentled it. His lips teased and nipped at Checa's, his tongue darted out to tickle against Checa's. Heath trailed kisses over Checa's face and along his jaw, whispering between each one. As he neared Checa's ear, the words became audible.

"I'm sorry. I'm so sorry you had to go through that. I wish I'd known. I'm glad I didn't know because I would have killed the bastard, but I was such a skinny runt he'd have killed me first and you'd have been all alone. I'm glad you let me be your friend. I don't want you to be alone. I'm so sorry I didn't help you."

"Heath."

Heath continued, his apologies becoming more scrambled and incomprehensible.

Checa pushed him back and held him in place when Heath would have kissed him again. "Stop it, Heath. I was sixteen when we met. I killed the Bastard just a few months later. There was nothing you could have done about anything because you didn't know me then. You were just a kid. And you did help me. So much."

He didn't think what he was saying made any more sense than what Heath had said, but it calmed Heath enough that they sat quietly, draped over each other, breathing each other in until every breath was once again soft and even.

"I still want you to make love to me," said Checa into a silence that once again contained the sound of the waterfall and the mist.

From his place, face buried against Checa's neck, Heath nodded. "I want that too, but not here, not now."

"Why not? I told you I want it."

"I know you did, and you never say anything you don't mean, but this isn't just about you. It's me too, and I want to do it properly. I don't want a rough coupling in the woods. We've done that sort of thing before. I want a soft bed and low lights and fragrant oils." He sat back enough to look Checa in the eye. "I want to spoil you and seduce you. I want to make it as different from what that bastard did to you as I can, so you never, ever think I could be him."

"You're nothing like him, Heath. You are a good, kind man."

"Then let me do this right. Okay?" Heath smiled his soft teasing smile, the smile that meant he expected to get his own way. It always worked.

"Does that mean I don't get a blow job either?" Checa grinned at Heath, knowing he'd take the bait and the situation would lighten.

Heath punched him in the shoulder, just hard enough that he felt it, but Checa howled and toppled to the side, clutching his deltoid. When Heath, predictably, leaned over to make sure he wasn't injured, Checa grabbed him by his shoulders and tipped him over until Heath slid onto the ground beside him. Checa kept a hand under Heath's shoulder to ease him down so his collarbone stayed steady. He ran his thumb softly over the break and frowned. It should have healed by now.

"Don't start getting protective, Checa. You want a blow job and I want to give you one, so work out how to make that happen, or I will." Heath's soft smile belied his teasing words.

Checa lowered himself onto Heath's body, aligning their cocks. He reached between them and tugged Heath's loincloth out of the way. They both groaned as their cool, wet skin met and warmed.

"Checa."

"Shh," said Checa. "No more talking. I want to love you." As he spoke he gently thrust his hips, rubbing their cocks against each other.

Heath lifted his legs to wrap around Checa's hips, increasing the pressure. Heath groaned, his upward thrusts increasing. "Oh, you're going to be the death of me."

Checa stopped moving and looked deeply into his eyes. "Never. I'll die before I see you harmed."

Heath pulled Checa's head down to kiss him, and Checa sank into it. Their bodies, perfectly aligned after years of practice, moved together, the cool moisture adding to the building sweat so that they slipped and slid against each other, building heat and pressure. The kiss continued, a gentle tangling of tongues and nipping teeth. Checa wrapped his arms around Heath, drawing him closer all over, needing him like he'd never needed anyone.

"You are my life, Heath," he whispered. "Give it to me."

Heath didn't answer. His breath rasped, his hands moved frantically, and his thrusts became hard and fast. "Close," he said.

Checa shifted lower so the tip of his cock bumped against the lip of the head of Heath's cock at every thrust. His heart pounded, his throat raw with harsh breaths. His blood sang as Heath released a long, low groan and froze, straining against him. Against his cock, Checa felt the first pulse of Heath's orgasm and his own rhythm faltered, then became as frantic as Heath's grip on Checa's back. His balls drew up tight and the tingle began at the base of his spine, the harbinger of his own orgasm.

By the time Checa's breathing had evened out, Heath was gently running his hands up and down Checa's back. "I love the strength of your muscles. I can feel all of them, trace the edges and the way they move and dip into your spine."

Checa lifted up onto his elbows, favoring his newly healed shoulder, and regarded Heath. He wanted to say more, to give Heath everything he wanted—Checa's life and future—but he couldn't. He'd told Heath he loved him, but nothing had changed. He'd loved him before, and he loved him still, but the Matriarch wouldn't approve a Bonding, no matter what Seer Pretto intimated. "Let's clean up and then find Rim and Ardelle. They'll have to stop at the waterfall because they don't know the way in. It'll take them time to find it."

The dreamy expression on Heath's face disappeared, and he wriggled out from under Checa. "This way." His voice was flat and emotionless.

Checa regretted spoiling their moment but knew it was for the best. He grabbed his loincloth and Heath's, and followed the nearly invisible trail to the river.

Heath was already in the water by the time he reached the bank. The spray was thicker there, a needling, swirling rain that pricked at Checa's skin.

"Stay in the shallows. The falls are close and the current's fast," Heath yelled over the drumming. He reached for his loincloth and quickly washed himself and it. He was dressed and waiting on the bank by the time Checa had cleaned up and tied his own loincloth in place.

Without warning, Heath crouched behind a tree. Checa closed the distance and crouched behind him, leaning forward so he could speak directly to Heath. "What's wrong?"

"We're close."

"And?" They needed to reconnect with Rim and Ardelle and get this mission back on track.

"There's someone there."

Checa made to stand up but Heath grabbed his arm and pulled him back down.

"It'll be Rim and Ardelle," Checa said.

"It's not."

"How do you know?" He peered around the tree but could see only more trees. "You can't see anything."

"Heartbeats."

Checa stared at him. That was new. Heath had never been able to feel heartbeats like that before. Heath counted water droplets and grains of sand, not the sound of hearts.

Heath shrugged. "Since Ardelle healed me—"

"Not very well."

Heath glared at him. "I can sense more now." He gestured toward the waterfall. "Two of the heartbeats feel familiar, so I've felt them before. They must be Rim and Ardelle."

"Do you think the others might be Exiles or Yeudan?"

"I don't know. One of them is different."

"What do you mean?"

How different can a heartbeat be?

Heath shrugged, opened his mouth to speak, looked away, then back again. "I think it's Kimi."

"Kimi?" *Who? Oh.* "Your dragon?"

Heath's smile was instant and full of light. "My dragon." He nodded. "Yes, I'm sure it's Kimi." He stood and pointed in a different direction. "We'll go down this way and come along the river from a different angle. That way we can see exactly who's with Rim and Ardelle before we're on top of them."

Before they moved away, Checa noticed wide ripples had formed in the pool they'd bathed in. He turned to find a dark head before it sank below again. It was Rim. She moved toward them, a dark blur under the water, before bobbing to the surface again, this time with another person clutched close, the bald-headed body limp. Checa strode into the water, diving under as soon as it was deep enough. The strong current immediately tugged him sideways, away from the small bank where he'd left Heath. He fought his way to the surface, momentarily disoriented before locating Rim and Ardelle. He surged forward as the water washed Rim and Ardelle closer to him.

Checa swung a hand out, grasping a fistful of Rim's shirt before she could be washed away. Then the river grabbed his legs and they were dragged under the water.

The quiet was immediate. It wasn't silence, but the thunder of the waterfall was muted. Checa tumbled over, tightening his grip in Rim's shirt but unable to tell if he still held Rim, just her shirt, or nothing at all. With his other hand, he flailed against the force of the water, looking for something to grab on to and stop the river washing them away.

The arm that held Rim's shirt was wrenched behind him so hard he almost gasped. He pushed the impulse down and struggled to hold his breath as the river tumbled and tossed them. Something slammed into his lower back, a cold breeze blew across his forehead, and he lifted his chin to suck air into his aching lungs before the roiling water dragged him under again.

Before Checa was sucked down too far, his hair snagged on something. He fought, but it didn't release, buffeted by the angry water before he began to rise. The cold kissed his face between the spatters of river; then his nose and chin were clear and the tugging on his hair disappeared, replaced by hands looped under his armpits.

Heath.

Checa sucked in greedy breaths as coarse sand scraped across his back. A weight tugged his arm, tugged again, but he didn't let go. There was something there he had to hold on to. It was important even though he couldn't remember why. Checa's head was above water, then his shoulders; the pressure around his chest eased.

Checa's sluggish brain realized Heath was there, pulling him out of the water. Heath tugged on his arm and he groaned.

"You can let go, Checa. I've got them." Checa scrunched his eyes tight. He'd thought he would never hear Heath's voice again. Checa had probably inhaled more water than he thought.

He landed on the sand, gritty and warm against his cold cheek, and relaxed, panting and coughing under the muted roar of the waterfall. It wasn't bad. He hadn't been in the water long. As soon as he could breathe properly and had warmed up a bit, he'd be fine. He pushed himself up onto his elbows, coughing. "How are they?"

"Both breathing. We need to get to shelter before nightfall."

Checa pushed himself to his feet, then dragged Heath up from where he was kneeling beside Rim and Ardelle. Both lay in recovery position. Checa buried his hands in Heath's hair and laid his face in the juncture of Heath's neck and shoulder; he breathed in his clean water-and-fern scent. "Thank you." His whisper was hoarse.

Heath hugged him back but stayed silent. After a few minutes, Checa drew back and smiled at him. Heath returned the smile. Then, as one, they returned to the two women and went back to work.

If it wasn't for the warmth lingering in Checa's heart, their interlude might never have happened.

Checa lifted Rim across his back. He grabbed her flapping hands and settled them around his neck. "We'll go slowly, Rim. Just stay still and you won't fall off."

Rim coughed in response, then went limp, only the occasional cough interrupting her rest.

Heath loaded Ardelle onto his back in a similar way, and they set off for the waterfall.

They rounded a bend in the path. Checa stopped short at the sight that greeted him.

Glistening cream and gold scales glinted in the low light on a bulging tummy supporting short arms that held a stick of orange amber to the long snout. A wet pink tongue rippled out, slurping at the amber. Ridged horns ran in a line from the front of the head and disappeared over the back. A thick tail twitched between the heavy hind legs that waved in the air as the animal reclined on a pile of rocks at the base of the waterfall, washed by and surrounded by roiling water.

Checa stood and stared, openmouthed. Another dragon. Until the one Heath had found, dragons had been extinct, and then, on one mission, he'd seen *two*. He looked closer. If this dragon wasn't so big, it could almost be Heath's. But that one was barely half the size of this one.

Heath sidled up and peeped around Checa's shoulder.

"Kimi!" Heath yelled and ran toward the dragon, who swung her head toward the faint call.

Golden eyes swirled. Kimi's eyes. It *was* Heath's dragon, but she was huge. How could she grow so fast?

Heath stopped at the water's edge, beaming at the dragon. Kimi lumbered to her feet, lodging the amber node securely between two horns on her tail. Several more pieces of the fossilized resin dotted the gaps between the horns along her tail.

Then she spread her wings.

Tons of water thundering down the cliff hit them, and bounced in great arcs. The wall of water slammed into Heath, knocking him off his feet and washing him down the slight slope toward the mad waters of the river. Checa jumped forward and grabbed Heath's hand before he could be washed away.

Heath cried out to Kimi again, but the dragon was looking at the darkening sky. Overhead came a mournful cry from a lone norrgel, flying late toward the nests.

"Dinner!" Kimi flapped her wings, washing water over them again; then she lifted and was gone.

Checa tracked her progress until she was obscured by the trees, then turned to Heath.

"Are you all right?" he asked, leaning close so that Heath could hear him above the roar of the water.

"I hope she comes back. What did she mean 'dinner'?" asked Heath as he watched the spot where Kimi had disappeared.

"I don't know." Checa ran his hands over Heath, checking for further injuries.

Heath batted him away. "I'm fine. Stop that!" He glared at Checa, then turned to where they'd left Rim and Ardelle. In accord they scooped the women onto their backs and began the trek away from the waterfall. Heath tugged his makeshift backpack sling into position as he walked.

"Where are we going?" Rim coughed after speaking those few words.

"We need to find shelter," Checa said.

They used the old trails even though the waterfall was less than a third of the size it had once been. The trails were damp, but not as slippery as they'd been when the land was at its best. The higher they climbed, the quieter the falls became. The sheer drop provided no resistance to the water, so it sounded little louder than a dancing stream. Only the force of the water hitting the pool below made noise.

Checa enjoyed the spray cooling his face. "Heath and I used to come here during the summer," he told Rim. "It didn't matter how hot it was in the village, the dappled sunlight and the water kept everything here cool. It's a good place to block out everything you need to forget." He looked up to find Heath poised on the rocky entrance to the cave behind the waterfall, glaring at him. Checa had no idea where he and Heath would go from here; the only thing he was sure of was that no matter how their relationship changed, he would always need Heath in his life, the same way Heath would always be in his heart. Checa needed to tell him that soon.

He settled Rim more securely on his back and continued the climb automatically.

About two-thirds of the way up, Heath reached out through the water and tugged them sideways. Checa had been so focused on moving upward, he hadn't noticed the opening to the cave.

He crab-walked through the water, falling onto the damp floor of the cave shortly after lowering Rim to the floor. They were wet and too cold, but at least they'd be safe from the cougars. Those cats preferred still water and never climbed there.

The cave behind the waterfall went back a long way. Checa knew which tunnels were dead ends, so it shouldn't be difficult to find the one leading to the lake. Heath and Ardelle had moved to a dry and quieter area at the back. Ardelle was awake and breathing easier. Checa checked Rim was comfortable and not too cold, then stood and shook the water from his hair before crouching beside Heath.

"Which way?" he asked, nudging closer so he could feel Heath's cool skin against his.

Heath snuggled in, then settled with his head resting against Checa's arm as he motioned to a narrow opening. "All the openings lead to the Lake of the Damned, but this one connects with all the others as well. We'll have options if there's a rockfall or someone is waiting for us."

Checa closed his eyes. "Twenty minutes to dawn," he said to Heath. "Then we have to move again."

Checa's internal clock roused him after the twenty minutes. He and Heath still leaned against each other, their backs to the rock wall.

"Checa." Rim sat in an untidy heap just inside the entrance. A jutting rock provided some protection from the water, but she was wet and shivering again. Checa had turned to look at her before he realized there was no way he should have been able to hear her from that distance and so close to the roaring water.

"I'll bet that's part of the Warrior Pledge," said Heath. "I can feel you inside my head, and sometimes I think I can hear Rim and Ardelle talking, even when it couldn't be possible." Heath rubbed his cheek against Checa's shoulder. "I think this is going to change us."

Checa could feel Heath inside his head too, but he didn't mention he'd been able to do that for a couple of years, since Heath had finished his Seer studies. The sensation had only grown stronger while they searched to complete the Warrior Pledge. Checa knew it was one of the signs of Bonding, but he kept telling himself it wouldn't happen unless he did it deliberately. Bonding only happened spontaneously in fairy tales.

Perhaps Heath was right and there really was no way to fight it, but Checa had to try. It was bad enough he'd drawn Heath into his violent existence. Heath had so much he could accomplish in his life. Checa couldn't tie the younger man to him and prevent him from reaching his potential. The words were an echo of the ones the Matriarch had said to him two years ago, but Checa still agreed with them. Mostly.

There were some days that Checa wanted to forget about his past and what everyone thought of him moving through the ranks so quickly. He wanted to bond with Heath, be with him forever. Checa looked over at him as he settled Ardelle, and he thought he could do it. He could bond with Heath, regardless of what anyone else thought.

Then he thought of what would happen if he did, to Heath's position as a Seer and his relationship with his family, and Checa knew he couldn't do that to him.

He went over to Rim and lifted her into his arms, inwardly shaking his head at his actions and ignoring the hurt in Heath's eyes. After just a few steps, he stopped when Rim pushed against his shoulder. His fucking sore shoulder. "What?" he growled.

Rim lifted her head. "Put me down. I can walk."

Checa lowered her to her feet and followed her. Rim walked ahead, soon reaching Ardelle; then she reclined beside her and leaned close so they could talk.

Heath waited for Checa a small distance away. Checa settled silently beside him, closed his eyes, and dozed for the remaining time before dawn.

27.
INSIDE THE MOUNTAINS

LESS THAN a man's length into the tunnel they took to the lake, Heath wrinkled his nose. At first he thought the smell was him. They'd spent a lot of time wet, and until their rinse-off in the river, had been unable to bathe lately. After the Exile caves, they probably had all manner of things he didn't want to think about absorbed into their skin. But the odor got stronger the deeper they went into the mountain. Whenever he could, Heath put his hand over his nose and mouth. The stench built until it became so thick it coated his throat and filled his lungs.

The crystal-encrusted walls twinkled softly. There was enough light getting in from somewhere to reflect off the crystals, so they could see where they were going. This tunnel was natural. There were few places where they could walk upright. Most of the time they clambered over boulders and squeezed through narrow spaces, and the ceiling got lower and heavier the farther they went. Heath took a deep breath and ignored both the odor and the panicked sweat breaking out on his body. Ahead of him, Rim and Ardelle slithered and slid, their slimmer forms moving through the tight spaces easily and quickly. They soon drew away. Behind him, Checa moved methodically and steadily, still calm and focused.

Heath gripped the edge of another boulder and hauled himself over and through the opening to a wider section of the tunneled caves. All he could see in the dim light was more boulders with gaping holes around them.

Checa moved in beside him. "How close are we to the headwaters?"

"Take the right." Heath nudged Checa's hip as he spoke, indicating Checa should take the lead. "Another few turns." He looked up at his lover and huffed in annoyance. "I wish I'd remembered that earlier." Then he closed his nostrils to narrow slits the way Checa had.

A few seconds passed before Checa responded, and then he ducked his head almost shyly. "I got used to doing it automatically when I was a kid."

Heath nodded. He knew more of the details of Checa's childhood than most people, but even that wasn't much until the revelation last night. He'd learned to accept each small comment Checa made with equanimity, and fume about the abuse he'd suffered later. Heath learned a long time ago that there was nothing he could do about it. The bastard was dead, and Checa rarely saw his mother anymore.

They wriggled around another boulder, and the tunnel widened enough so they could walk upright. Heath tried not to gag as the stench intensified. "This must be what's causing the rot in the Analee Valley." A few steps later. "If the Yeudans invade, there's no way Rim's people would be able to use these caves as a stronghold in the way she anticipates."

"We don't know what's here for sure," grunted Checa. "We'll know soon, though."

"At least we can move more easily in these tunnels, especially since we can't change yet."

All at once it struck Heath that this might be the last time he'd be able to speak about himself and Checa as *us* or *we*. It had become second nature to think of them as a couple, two parts of a lasting relationship, but he was coming to accept that Checa meant it when he said they'd never bond. Sometime soon he would lose Checa and every hope he'd ever had of being happy. Heath's vision narrowed and his chest became so tight he couldn't breathe.

"Heath?" Checa's warm body moved behind Heath and draped around him. His thick fingertips riffled through Heath's hair.

Heath leaned back into the broad chest that signified *home*.

Heath's harsh breathing filled the rancid air, thickening it further. Sweat dribbled from his temple down his face and dripped from his jaw. He was in the middle of a fucking panic attack over nothing more than thinking of losing Checa. He forced himself to breathe evenly, closing his eyes so all he was aware of was Checa's body pressed against his, Checa's fingers warm and gentle as they rubbed circles over his chest. Heath leaned back into the larger man, squirming a little to rub against the solid muscle and warm support. Checa's deep voice rumbled through Heath, talking about the end of the tunnel, reminding him it wasn't getting smaller and there was always enough air.

By the Elders, the man thought he'd panicked because of the space. Heath opened his mouth to set Checa straight, but stopped. Should he tell him?

"Heath?"

Internally, Heath shrugged. What was he risking? No more than he risked every day. "I don't want to lose you," he whispered.

Checa's arms came firmly around him. "You won't. I'll always be there for you."

"But you won't bond with me."

A long pause, and Heath was sure Checa would tell him no—again. Checa had always been implacable. "I don't know what's going to happen with the Pledge. I might not survive."

Slivers of Heath's heart sheared off and floated away in the thick, moist air. He didn't think he'd ever feel whole again.

"I'm tired of fighting it, Heath. I know it might not mean much to you now, and I don't know how we'll stop your mother breaking the Bond, but I want to bond with you."

Heath gasped. Checa couldn't be serious. He remained still so as not to stop Checa talking.

"I won't do it now, no matter how much I want to, because if I die, you'll never be the same again. But if we survive this, the first thing we're going to do is bond. I want to live the rest of my life with you, and I don't want it to be this half existence we've fallen into without the Bond. I want to give all of myself to you."

Heath slumped in Checa's arms. Now he'd been given what he wanted, he didn't know how he felt. "You're only saying that because you think you'll die."

"The Warrior Pledge says there'll be death, and I always thought it would be me. As the Farseeing, you're in danger. I will die to protect you. But maybe things will fall out in a different way. There might be a way we can both survive. I want to make sure you know how much I want you. I want you to know I'll be yours forever, before we go into whatever is at the other end of this tunnel."

"Are you sure?" Heath turned his head to look for any hesitation in him. "You don't have to promise this to make me fight harder. If you do, there's no way I'm going to let you out of it later. It's a done deal. You have to be sure this is what you want."

"The only thing I've ever wanted in my life is you. Bonding with you will make me the happiest man alive." Checa leaned forward.

Heath knew the signs of a gentle, teasing kiss coming, and he circumvented Checa's actions. He dove in, tangling his tongue with Checa's and pulling him close, every inch of their bodies touching. As always, Checa responded, but it was different this time. This time, Heath could feel the promise in the kiss. He could feel forever in Checa's fingertips as they traced down Heath's spine. Heath breathed Checa in, almost immediately recognizing the beginnings of the Bond thread forming. Reluctantly he drew back. Heath didn't want to force him into it, even now that Checa had said he'd bond with him. When they bonded it was going to be glorious and mutual. "You promise?"

"We'll be Bonded and grow old together," Checa promised. "It's all I want."

Once their breathing evened out again, they moved on, Checa touching Heath often in silent need or reassurance. Heath wasn't sure which one it was, but it didn't matter. He needed both.

There was the Warrior Pledge to complete and the Yeudan invaders to vanquish. He was a warrior and would deal with whatever came his way. His future with Checa would come later.

The tunnels seemed to go on forever. Climbing over rocks and between them became rhythmic, the motions themselves soothing. As long as Heath kept moving, he could stay calm. He wouldn't need to think at all.

The air grew heavier. Dust wasn't a problem, but moss and lichen sprouted on the walls, and algae grew in the puddles. Heath's feet slipped on the green mounds, and he had to dig his fingers into thick sludge before he could find a grip on the rocks. Moisture ran down his face, gathering in his eyebrows before dripping into his eyes and off the end of his nose and chin. His loincloth stuck to him and tugged against his thighs and buttocks with every move.

The attention he needed to maintain to prevent painful slips and falls had Heath once again focused solely on his mission. It had begun in blind faith, but as all the signs came together, he realized there was more to it than a prophecy. There was real need in his land. The Descendants were battling a rot that Heath was sure came from the Lake of the Damned. There were Yeudan intent on enslaving them all and sacrificing them to the norrgel, and the Exiles were working with the Yeudan. Heath wondered if the Warrior Pledge was the answer, a culmination of actions that would solve all the problems.

Or was he on a fool's errand? Had he been so insistent that the signs were all there for the Warrior Pledge because it had been a sure way of spending more time with Checa? Was he that selfish?

By degrees the light changed. The soft, filtered glow that bounced through and off the embedded crystals in the walls of the tunnels gradually became sharper. The muted gold strengthened to a sharp white that spilled into the tunnel. Heath squinted against the strong light, slowing and blinking so his eyes could adjust. He was looking directly into a glare like midday sunlight reflecting off a pond.

The air cooled as the light grew; the moisture condensed and formed fog that slunk into the tunnel behind the brightness. Where the cold air hit the warm, moist air of the tunnels, droplets formed and fell to the floor, creating a wall of fine mist that formed puddles and runnels beneath their feet.

Heath slowed further. Whatever was beyond the fog was in bright light, and he knew there would be a few seconds where he'd be effectively blind. He blinked and focused through the fog to the other side of the tunnel, making sure he could see in the light. Then he moved forward a few steps into the fog before stopping and allowing his eyes to adjust again. There was nothing to see once inside the wall of fog. It was so dense Heath could barely see his feet.

No sound carried through the cloud, and he raised a brow at Checa, little more than a shadow at his shoulder, wondering if he had any ideas. Checa had slowed at the same time as Heath, their movements coordinated by years of practice, and held up a hand for him to wait. Checa's claws snicked out; Heath followed suit. Together they crouched. Checa seemed barely more than a ginger-brown lump on the muddy ground.

Checa moved forward, disappearing into the white blanket. Heath followed slowly, careful to place his feet in secure positions and to keep to the side of the tunnel as much as possible. Their shadows played out behind them, but Checa and Heath would still appear as dark masses to anything on the other side of that fog.

The stench seemed stronger here but somehow subdued, blanketed in the fog the same way sound was. Water dripped somewhere and dribbled everywhere. The muffled sounds could have been right beside Heath's ear or a hundred feet away. He couldn't tell. His sense of being closed in resurfaced as he waded resolutely through the thick cloud.

Something soft brushed his leg and he jumped. He nearly cried out but managed to stifle the yell into a whimper. The warmth rose up his body and eventually formed into Checa, standing so close that Heath could smell him.

"It's a large cavern. Rim and Ardelle are there, but so are others." Checa's breath fanned the hair around Heath's ear, making him shiver.

"Possibly the other heartbeats I sensed at the waterfall. Rim said her men had orders to assemble here." Heath asked.

"I recognized some scents from around the waterfall, but there're more than that there. Some are Exiles, but not all. I think Yeudan."

"Another ambush?"

"Likely. How do you want to play it?"

Heath grinned, loving that Checa always asked his opinion before making a decision. He shrugged carelessly. "There's not much we can do other than go out there and find out what the situation is. Either the others are already captured or the Exiles are waiting for us before they attack. Either way they'll be expecting us. You go left, I'll go right. We'll meet in the middle on the other side." Separating would minimize their chances of being taken at the same time. One of them might escape or at least last long enough to find the others.

Checa nodded. "Together."

Yes. Together. Like always.

Checa began to move before Heath had time to nod. They moved swiftly through the fog toward the light. The mist folded back, revealing a jagged opening, the left side comprised of fallen boulders and crushed rocks that spilled halfway across the opening.

Checa clambered over the rocks, melting into the fog at the same time Heath slipped through and stepped right. The fog thinned a few feet outside the tunnel entrance but still provided them with coverage while they found the most secure vantage points.

Heath moved slowly, his claws out. A rumbling growl sent a shiver down his spine. Checa's canines had dropped. Heath's collarbone was finally beginning to heal, so he also changed into full were form, ready for whatever came his way.

Suddenly the cavern erupted in sound and light, flames arcing through the air. Fuck, they had some sort of flamethrower. When the flame extinguished, cries of men who'd been hit punctuated the sudden darkness. Heath had to find a way to neutralize that weapon or they were all dead. He dropped to an awkward crouch and ran. He only just made it behind a large broken column as another line of flame hit the rock behind him. The shots had come from the same position. Heath hoped there was only the one weapon. He had to find a way around behind it to stage his attack.

In the fog, Checa snarled. Heath's heart beat in time with the almost-rhythmic ring of steel on steel beyond the fog. Had Checa engaged the enemy or been hit? Another column of flame lit the cavern. The fog breathed with Heath, undulating around him, sometimes enshrouding the cavern, other times parting to reveal snatches of movement or stillness. Dead bodies lay around him, both Yeudan and Descendants, some stabbed or sliced, some burned.

The fog rippled again, almost in time with the battle echoing around the cavern, and Heath could still see soldiers hiding. He had no idea where Rim and Ardelle were. They might be captured or dead. He moved stealthily around boulders, making his way toward the center of the fighting, careful not to slip on the icy ground.

As he peered around a large boulder, he saw the backs of five men winding a large brass reel. A pulley system attached it to a wide pipe. One of the men poured oil into a funnel, another lit a wick. Two men braced themselves against the trestle the pipe rested on. The last man, left to hold the reel while the others took their positions, stepped back, hands raised. The reel spun, releasing the pulley, and burning oil shot from the mouth of the pipe. Heath scrambled to the top of the boulder and jumped.

Two men fell before Heath hit the ground, their throats spurting blood from the slashing of his claws. He dispatched the other three just as swiftly, then stood amid the carnage, dizzy and swaying.

Eventually the sounds of battle intruded. Heath looked around the rocks he was behind to find Yeudan soldiers drawing knives and moving in formation, following the path of the last burst of flame. A voice called out, that same guttural language he'd heard before. The Yeudan with a demand for surrender or an instruction to someone, from the tone of it. Heath sidled around more rocks, knowing he'd done all he could to even the playing field. He still wasn't fully healed after the norrgel-strike, so continuing to fight alone was foolhardy. He had to find Checa. Fighting beside him would give them their best chance of surviving. If not, at least he'd die with his mate by his side.

A scream rent the air. Heath's breath hitched and he shuffled sideways into thinner air, trying to see despite the pressure in his chest. It was a high-pitched, feline cry.

Not Checa.

There were no other Mafdeti. All Heath's team were dead except for Jun. Was the bloody traitor there too? With the echo off the rocks, there was no way he could tell which direction the noise came from. Another scream, different pitch. *That* was Checa. Heath's scalp prickled and he inched farther away from the shrouded entrance.

Another scream. This one human, but Heath couldn't tell who it was, although he thought male. A low grumbling filled the air and Heath grinned.

Checa wasn't hurt. He was attacking. Heath surged forward, moving toward him.

And trusting only his own
Hold to reason's hard edge
Man must await the Pledge
To find the way home alone

—extract from the Warrior Pledge, prophecy of the Mafdeti, natural inhabitants of Thalazar.

28.
THE BATTLE

As HEATH moved farther away from the entrance, more of the cavern became clear. It was oval, the walls curving in, then upward to form a round funnel above him. Sunlight streamed in, harshly bright in the middle of the cavern, dim and shadowed at the walls. One side of the oval shone dully, a solid wall of ice. The middle teemed with people, groups surging over boulders and attacking. Around the edges of the conflict, bodies lay draped over and in front of scorched boulders and broken columns. As Heath watched, more fell.

Heath dodged around a large boulder to find a better fighting position. He crept forward, hugging the shape and shadows of tumbled rocks. He ran his hand across the surface of the rocks, dimly noting they were carved. The Seers would love to study them. He'd never been in this part of the mountains before, and these carvings represented a part of Thalazar's history Heath didn't know. He wondered if it was Descendant or Mafdeti history.

Another scream blasted through the air, followed by a victorious roar, the ring of steel, and shouting. Checa and someone armed with swords or knives had engaged the enemy. Heath used a foot to push himself off the flat rocks, gaining speed from the leverage. He charged into the light, zigzagging between mounds of fallen rocks, jumping over obstacles, and eventually dropping behind a pillar that had broken and now rested awkwardly, one end buried under a small mound of rubble. He sidled along the long, carved post toward the dim edge of the cavern. The air there was thick with smoke and the metallic smell of blood. Heath slowed his breathing and listened, closer now, and needing to work out where everyone was so he could insert himself at the best place.

Nothing. No one came to kill him, and the sounds of battle stopped. He peeped over the rock. Where had all the red-haired Yeudan gone? They'd been lying in wait a few minutes before, but now there was no sign of them. No sign of Checa either. Or Rim and Ardelle.

Heath's breathing was still too quick, too harsh after the rush of adrenaline to properly hear if there was anyone hiding beyond the next pile of boulders and rubble. The harsh sunlight in the center of the cavern made it impossible to see across, and Heath avoided looking directly into the center so he could still see shapes and hopefully movement, at the edges. He scanned as much of the cavern as he could see, his searches becoming less methodical at every pass.

After the third sweep, Heath stopped, his fists clenched and eyes closed. With all his creeping around in the shadows, he'd taken too long inspecting the carvings on the columns and all the fun was over. He'd left Checa to fight on his own. For the first time in his life, Heath allowed his intellect to jeopardize the mission. If Checa died…. Heath heaved a sigh through the sudden tightness in his chest.

A clash of steel on rock rang through the cavern and Heath ducked, edging under the pillar and creeping toward the sudden sounds of battle. The Yeudan hadn't won yet. He clambered over the outcropping of fallen pillars and rubble and stopped short at the scene that met him. The dull green of the military uniform of the Analee Valley was everywhere, surging toward the far edges of the cavern where the enemy must be. Heath sighed in relief, confident now he hadn't missed it all.

Closer to his right, Checa, Rim, and Ardelle formed a tight triangle, using knives and claws to fight a smaller pocket of the enemy on that side of the cavern. The sight of them eased the tension in his jaw. Blood striped Ardelle's neck in a wide smear, but the cut under her chin seemed shallow enough. Rim had a few small cuts on her forearms but nothing serious. Checa showed no injuries.

Heath climbed over the rocks, working his way to a position closest to Checa and his new friends so that he could join them and form a fourth side of their defense. Once he was high enough and ready to jump, he lifted his gaze and froze; the reason for this new battle suddenly became clear.

Storming out of the fog, led by Jun and the Exile who'd helped the old woman, were dozens of Exiles, raggedly dressed, poorly armed, but obviously trained. They immediately engaged the Yeudan. Not allowing himself to think about the implications of either the Exiles' training or their appearance there, and particularly not about Jun's presence, Heath launched himself into the fray, landing heavily on top of two Yeudan, his claws slashing and killing them before they landed.

A large hand clasped Heath's bicep and hauled him to his feet.

"About time you got here," growled Checa. "We could use some help."

Heath spun his back to Rim and Ardelle and slashed the forearm of a charging soldier. "You're the one who started without me." He flexed his knees and blocked a downward strike.

Checa huffed and turned to focus on his own sector. Heath grinned as he slashed and stabbed and kicked, feeling almost invincible with the others at his back.

"Rim's team have engaged," he puffed out as his claws dug deeply into the stomach of another Yeudan. "Exiles just arrived, also fighting the Yeudan."

"So that's what started this panic," said Rim behind him.

"Jun's with them."

Checa slashed his claws forcefully through two soldiers before calming again to a steady, maintainable rhythm of attack and response.

"If they don't kill him, I will," he ground out.

"Not if I get to him first," Heath returned.

"Shut up and fight," Ardelle said, "or none of us will get to kill the bastard."

Heath's grin grew. By the ancestors, he loved his bloodthirsty team.

He stumbled, caught himself, and continued slashing automatically, years of intensive training saving him from a grave error of judgment. With Rim's soldiers arriving in force with the Exiles, they now outnumbered the Yeudan, but the battle wasn't over yet. He twisted a little, just enough to feel Ardelle and Checa at his shoulders, then focused solely on staying alive.

They were all tiring. Heath could feel the strain in his shoulders and thighs, more than there should be. Beside him, Ardelle's responses were slowing. Heath widened his swinging arc so he took on more of their attackers.

They came in waves. The sounds of battle continued over the other side of the cavern, but here it seemed like they lined up and waited their turn. The four of them could easily have been overrun, but they were holding their own.

"This is like the rockslide," Checa said.

"Yeah, but who's trying to kidnap them this time?" Heath asked as he thrust his claws into a brown-clad Yeudan's stomach. No sooner had he pulled free and kicked the man away than another took his place. "This is getting ridiculous. They're timing it to tire us."

"And wasting a lot of lives to do it," grunted Checa as he sliced across the neck of another attacking soldier. "And wasting time. Why are they stalling?"

"They couldn't be waiting for the moons, could they? It's getting close." The attack pattern became predictable and Heath fell into the rhythm. Every third or fourth time, he shifted his feet and changed his angle so that he wouldn't become so used to the rhythm that he wouldn't notice if it changed.

At first the low rumble at the base of Heath's brain felt like another rhythm change, but then he realized what it was.

Another earthquake. Not an aftershock!

This was just as large as the previous one, and closer. Heath was just about to call out when Ardelle yelled.

"There's another quake coming!"

The earth rumbled through his head again. Fuck, it was strong enough to bring half the place down. "Work toward the ice," he yelled.

Without even a pause, Checa surged forward a step; Heath stepped sideways at the same time. A heartbeat later, Rim and Ardelle stepped with them. It couldn't have been more coordinated if they'd rehearsed it. Heath grinned as he slashed another soldier's knee.

Within minutes they were at the base of the overturned pillars near the ice wall, rearranging themselves so their backs were to the rocks as they fought. It was at once a strong position and a vulnerable one, with their backs to the wall and nowhere to go if they were overrun. The earthquake was nearly upon them, and the solid rock wall abutting the ice would give them the best protection.

Heath thrust and slashed as a Yeudan swiped at him, and then Heath shot a look at a small group working their way toward them.

It was Jun. And the Exile, Fisher, with him.

"Why is he heading to us?" Heath asked.

Checa swung around at Heath's question, glimpsed Jun and Fisher, swung back, and sliced open another enemy's belly. "Stay focused," he growled as he slashed at an arm swinging a blade toward Heath's head.

"I would if you didn't keep stepping in and taking my targets," Heath groused as he crouched to stab a claw into the side of a knee, twisted his hand, and sliced through the tendons holding the lower leg to the kneecap. The brown-clad man screamed and dropped, forming a convenient barrier between them and the soldiers pressing forward.

Ardelle, on Heath's other side, chuckled at him as she dug a short knife behind a brown-clad soldier's eyeball and popped it out. A hoarse yell accompanied the soldier's grubby hand, slapping over the empty, bleeding socket.

Rim, on the other side of Checa, muttered loudly at Heath. "If this earthquake doesn't hit soon, I'll be fighting ankle-deep in blood."

Heath blocked another slashing stroke from a soldier, his claws sliding along the soldier's upper arm firmly enough to give him a close shave. Beside him another soldier's sword sparked against Ardelle's crossed knives and drove her to her knees. Heath swung his hand sideways, slicing through the soldier's throat, spraying Ardelle with blood, but at least she could regain her feet and keep fighting.

Blood welled from a stinging slice across Heath's forearm, and dread settled in him.

We might die.

The vibration rumbled at the base of his scalp again. *Soon.*

A black-furred hand slashed through the arm of a soldier coming at them, followed by another arcing spray of blood. Black fur? Jun! The bastard. He was in were form. Heath moved, hoping to get a clear strike at the traitor, but the low roar of moving rock filled the cavern at the same time the ground beneath them began trembling. Heath's slashing arc went wide as his feet skittered over the heaving ground. Checa dropped to his knees, reaching out as he went down. Braced against the rock at his back, Heath grabbed Checa and pulled him to safety. Rock screeched against rock and the ice groaned. No one could fight against the jumping sand and gravel, the rocks tumbling randomly around them. Ardelle and Rim struggled to sheath their knives before they dropped them.

All around them soldiers fell to the floor. Heath pressed back against the pillar behind him, Checa warm against his side. On his other side, Ardelle bumped against him as Checa turned and tugged Rim in close. Heath turned toward Checa, and together they bowed their heads, forming a living cocoon around the two women, all huddled in a corner formed by rock and ice and large pillars that seemed to be stable. Heath raised his head and watched in horror as the curved wall of rock reaching over the middle of the cavern undulated under the onslaught of the earthquake. Huge plates of rock sheared off and crashed to the ground, shooting splinters in every direction. From the screams many of the shards—most larger than a man's arm—found a mark. Left behind, the ceiling became a lumpy, glistening expanse of amber.

It was over before Heath had time to rub his hand over Checa's warm chest as it pressed against him. The silence was so absolute Heath's ears rang. For long moments no one moved. Then a low burble began, and Heath realized it was dozens of people groaning and clutching their injuries. Heath pushed at the bodies hemming him in, a little claustrophobic and vulnerable without swinging room, and with Yeudan and Exiles mere feet away. He had to push hard at Checa to get him to move enough so Heath could see more of the cavern.

People lay among boulders. The upper reaches of the cavern were free of stalactites, and most of the pillars that had stood in the large oval space were gone, tumbled into rubble, burying anyone they landed on. Most of the people he could see lay still, with bloody rocks near their staved-in skulls, but some were writhing and groaning in pain. As he watched, he saw more, a wider field. Green-clad soldiers, the Analee battalion, held Yeudan prisoners, tying them with homespun ropes. A few Yeudan called out a guttural word, and those who looked like they might fight again stopped. The invaders had surrendered.

To Heath's right a man climbed to his feet and leaned back against a straight section of the cavern wall, shoulders slumped. The tall, thin man from the Exile caverns—Fisher, Rim called him—lifted a shaky hand and wiped at the blood trailing from his left ear. In front of him, another man staggered upright. Jun. Fisher reached out a hand to the traitor, holding his elbow until Jun steadied.

Checa said something, but it sounded like water tumbling over rocks. Heath swiped at his ears, then looked at his fingers. No blood, so his eardrums were still intact. He looked carefully at his team. Checa, Rim, and Ardelle all seemed unharmed.

As his heartbeat calmed and his hearing returned, Heath was finally able to take note of the numbers of Yeudan. "This is more than an advance scouting. Not quite an invasion, but a formidable force," he said as Checa came to stand beside him.

"What does your Warrior Pledge say about this?" asked Rim from behind Checa.

"It talks about calming evil, a battle, and shattered peace. This could be it." Heath looked around. "This isn't a full force, so it's probably only the beginning. What do you know about the Yeudan?"

Rim moved over until she stood beside Heath. "The Yeudan all but disappeared decades ago. We haven't been able to find out much. There's a problem with the language."

"They're using an old Imperial dialect. The Yeudan first contacted us five years ago and have been trying to negotiate what they call a *treaty* ever since, but there's nothing to gain for us," Ardelle said quietly as she turned a body and checked the shoulders. "Our last contact with them was one year ago. Now I know why they stopped negotiations."

Heath glared at her as she moved on, oblivious. "This is my home. I have a right to know if an invasion is imminent," he said, but Ardelle ignored him. He turned to Checa. "We need to prepare to defend ourselves, not live on oblivious while some snot-nosed royal decides our livelihoods weren't worth the bother. They don't have that right!"

Checa patted his back. Heath shrugged the condescending touch off, but Checa replaced his hand.

"So we get ready," he said quietly. "We do what we need to do."

Together traitor and thin man
Bring a sorrow true
Course found, the four break through
Dead man and kin unplanned

      —extract from the Warrior Pledge, prophecy of the Mafdeti, natural inhabitants of Thalazar.

29.
THE TRAITOR AND THE THIN MAN

CHECA AND Rim circumnavigated the cavern, with Rim giving orders to her own soldiers and Checa interrupting every other sentence. Rim knew what she was doing, but all the men Checa had with him were dead. He needed to give orders to someone.

After a second terse comment from Rim, Checa walked away. He looked over to where Heath was scrambling toward him over bodies, sliding in blood and entrails and melting ice. As Heath came closer, Checa could see his muscles trembling like jelly after hours of fighting, but he moved quickly. The day had been wave after wave of fighting and retreating, but it seemed unbelievable that the battle with the Yeudan was already over. It wouldn't be if it weren't for the earthquake.

He flicked a look at the cavern walls, and the layer of ice shining wetly in the golden light. Huge shards lay at its base, probably casualties of the earthquake. The sweat dripping from his body was cooling fast. If this was where they needed to be for the Warrior Pledge, they had to finish quickly or find a place to keep warm.

The light in the cavern was changing, an indication that the sun had set and the moons risen. Checa closed his eyes briefly, gauging the time they had before the eclipse. Less than an hour. The night Makai and Nayeli would cross paths and appear as one in the sky.

The deadline for the Warrior Pledge.

As he moved, Checa looked around at the signs of occupation. The piles of bodies around him and the makeshift living quarters were obvious around the cavern and indicated the Yeudan had been hiding there, and for quite some time. Checa and his group had seen no sign of them on their regular patrols. He would have to ask Rim and Ardelle what they knew about it.

The Crystal River had been dry for months. The wall of ice beside him gave a reason for that, although he didn't know how it could have formed.

Checa stopped Fisher from his headstrong rush toward the ice with a punishing grip above his elbow. "You should stay with your men." He trusted the Exiles about as much as he trusted the Yeudan.

Fisher paused, but Checa had the impression it was only because he wanted to, not because Checa held him in an iron-hard grip.

Fisher said, "The Yeudan society is a deeply religious one. They believe the norrgel will protect them from a threat from the skies. They offer sacrifices to the norrgel at each full moon and each dark moon to keep their people safe from the increasingly active birds. The Yeudan believe a time is coming when the norrgel will rise up and defeat all their enemies. That time is the time of the eclipse, where the moons cross orbits and look like just one moon in the sky. To appease the norrgel at such an auspicious time, and to gain their continued protection, the Yeudan have planned a major sacrifice." He looked steadily at Checa. "They've been blocking the Lake of the Damned so the Descendants in the valley have to venture farther and farther for water. They've captured people and are holding them, ready for the sacrifice at dawn on the morning after the eclipse. The Exiles have been taken with a similar goal in mind.

"There are numerous stations throughout the valley and in the desert surrounding Hawkesby. The Exiles have been moving into position for weeks. I need to find them and free them—if they've survived the earthquake. There are plans to burn every dwelling the Yeudan and their allies locate over the next year, so that every day the people are left without shelter when the norrgel arise. Once they finish with the valley, they'll move south through the mountains and into the desert and beyond, burning everything as they go." He tugged his arm free from Checa's shocked hold. "The Yeudan believe if they do this, the norrgel will not only spare them, but they'll protect them from the fire coming from the sky." He shrugged. "Whatever that is."

Fisher's gaze locked on the ice wall, peering at it as if he could see through it. "They've been guarding the ice. I want to see what's behind there so I can put a stop to the massacre they have planned."

Checa stared at the Exile. No, he was more than that, but Checa didn't know exactly what. Fisher knew a hell of a lot about the Yeudan and their plans. If what he said was true, Checa's homelands would be burned and everyone killed in a superstitious frenzy. The valley would die, and his people would be reduced to living in caves, fighting a guerrilla war. Panic rumbled low in his stomach, and he suppressed it ruthlessly. The survival of his people was paramount. He looked around wildly. The Mafdeti and the Descendants couldn't ignore the threat; they'd have to fight together. Allies. Surely once they knew the threat, even the Lonely

Isles would join in the fight. It would be enough. It would have to be. "We'll fight them. No one will take us."

Fisher paused, a grim smile pulling at his thin face. "The Yeudan have grown strong since they retreated to their northern strongholds. They've brought other tribes into the fold and they're experts in stealth. You need to locate secure underground positions that are easily defensible." He turned to survey the wall again. "What's on the other side of this?"

Ardelle came up beside them and watched Fisher serenely.

Shit. She'd known all along the Yeudan were coming. Anger bubbled in Checa, but it had nowhere to go. Even as he realized her complicity, he knew she'd had no real control. Her father was still King, and her mother was a formidable force. Ardelle was just a girl—Checa tilted his head speculatively—but perhaps she wasn't playing at soldier anymore. Perhaps now she really was one.

Checa leaned close to Heath; their hair tangled together in a riot of earthy oranges and creams mixed with browns, russets, and grays. "What do you think?"

"It's time."

Checa jumped, not expecting Heath's voice to be so resonant. He'd lost track of the moons while listening to Fisher.

"Apparently we're about to be invaded by the Yeudan. I think that's a more important factor than what the time is," said Rim snippily as she came up beside them.

Checa stared at her. "The invasion will unfold as it will, Rim, but we must complete the Warrior Pledge to be ready for it."

Ardelle moved almost trancelike toward Fisher. "The thin man brings sorrow true."

"You know the Pledge," Heath exclaimed, shock battling a joyous grin on his face as he separated from Checa and strode to Ardelle.

"It was in a fairy tale."

Everyone stopped and stared. Checa recovered first, grabbing hold of the anger bubbling inside him. "A fairy tale!" He glared at Ardelle.

"The Pledge is a treaty," exclaimed Rim indignantly.

They still didn't know what they were doing. "It's more than a treaty, Rim," said Checa, lamenting his assumption they knew the same Pledge he did. "And more than a thousand years old. Legend tells the tale of it coming from the dragons." Checa snapped his mouth closed.

Heath would leap on his admission that the dragons were more than just an extinct animal come to life.

"*Where are you?*" The cry, filled with anger and anguish, interrupted them.

Checa turned with the others and stared at the far end of the cavern piled high with rubble. He strode forward, a scowl on his face, claws snicking out as he moved through the crowd of injured people beginning to recover and the dead who never would. Heath and the others followed, automatically fanning out in a monitor-and-protect formation.

A howl echoed through the chamber, and Jun, still in were form, clambered over more rubble, turning over bodies as he went. Jun's fur was matted with blood and sweat, and even from this distance, Checa could see his eyes were wild and frantic in a desperate face. "Where are you?" he cried again.

Jun spun in a circle, blood dripping from his fingers, stopping suddenly as he saw Ardelle.

He ran to her, stumbling over bodies, knocking aside those recovering as he pushed through, but never taking his eyes from her. "Where is he?" he cried. "He was traveling with you." He grasped Ardelle by the upper arms, his claws digging through the thick cloth of her shirt.

Checa saw her wince and moved toward her at the same time as Heath and Rim.

"*Where is he?*" Jun shook Ardelle until her head flopped back and forth.

Checa reached him and hauled the hysterical Mafdeti away from the Princess. "Who the hell are you looking for?"

Jun seemed not to notice as Heath came up behind him and pinned Jun's arms behind him. Jun's head swung back and forth as he searched the crowded cavern. "I can't find him. He must be here."

"Who?" Checa put so much force behind the word that the sound echoed through the chamber and shattered Jun's hysteria.

"Fan!" Jun's voice wobbled as he stared at Checa. "I can't find him. Haven't felt him for days." He looked around again before turning back to Checa. "Weeks. Not since Hawkesby. Where's Fan?"

Fuck, Jun was Bonded.

Checa's throat seized as he remembered a man's screams just before they first found Rim and Ardelle outside Hawkesby.

To his right, Ardelle whimpered. "He's gone," she whispered.

Jun's head swung in her direction. His canines dropped and his elliptical pupils dilated until they were almost round. He wrenched away from Checa, out of Heath's hold, and strode to Ardelle. Rim intercepted him, standing in front of the Princess, giving Checa and Heath enough time to each grasp one of Jun's arms, holding him back.

"Fan?" His voice was soft. Bewildered.

Beside him, Heath groaned. Checa shivered at the compassion in his usually cheerful features. Checa opened his mouth to speak, but no sound came out.

"It was a norrgel-strike." Rim's soft contralto filled the painful silence. "He was protecting his Princess." Rim moved closer to Jun, forcing the Mafdeti to focus on her face. "You know the man he was. He could have done nothing else."

A growl, low and wrenching, filled the chill air of the cavern. Jun struggled against the hands that held him, howling his pain. His canines dripped saliva and his clawed hands slashed impotently at the air. The muscles in his chest and arms bulged with the strain.

Checa and Heath stumbled against the power of his grief.

"Let him go," Checa said quietly.

Heath stared at him. "What? You can't be serious. He's a traitor. Men died because of him."

Checa kept his gaze on the black Mafdeti in front of him. "This is punishment enough."

Checa looked at Heath, seeing the same grief in his eyes. Together they released their hold on Jun and stepped back.

Jun shifted to full cat form, threw back his head and roared, the sound high and haunting. Then he tore into the fog still blanketing the tunnel entrance to the cavern. Within seconds he was gone.

"What will happen to him?" Ardelle's voice was hesitant.

She couldn't know exactly what happened any more than anyone who wasn't Mafdeti could, but Jun's grief was a palpable shroud over them all, chilling Checa and twisting him up inside.

"They were Bonded," Heath murmured, wonder and sadness rounding his vowels as a shiver ran through him. He reached a hand out to Checa and pulled him close.

"He's gone feral." Checa grasped the back of Heath's neck and drew him close to his body. "It happens sometimes with a really deep Bond."

Heath rested his head on Checa's shoulder, and Checa held him tight. He didn't know what was going to happen between them, but he needed Heath close to him right at that moment. The cold, lonely emptiness that was Jun-without-Fan swelled inside his chest, wrenching a low, keening cry from him.

Joined in peace and battle they merge
Linking ever hearts and minds
Four become one; two moons rebind
And as one will lead the purge

    —extract from the Warrior Pledge, prophecy of the Mafdeti, natural inhabitants of Thalazar.

30.
TWO MOONS BECOME ONE

AFTER A few minutes, Heath realized they were still clinging to each other as if Jun's grief were contagious. He separated himself from Checa and stood tall.

"I can give you a fighting chance," Fisher said.

"Exactly how do you plan to do that, Exile? What's so special about you?" demanded Ardelle.

She stepped away from her companions and tilted her head. Heath had seen that exact expression on the Queen.

Damn, she's going to be good once she grows a bit more. So regal and sure of herself. So determined. And that passion. Her people will follow her anywhere.

Heath relaxed and grinned as Fisher matched her haughtiness with a condescending glare. "I've lived with the Yeudan. I know their strengths and weaknesses and can share those with you if—" He waved a hand toward the defeated Yeudan behind him. "Give me those soldiers and I'll use them to defeat the others."

"You said they're deeply religious. They plan to kill thousands of people in the name of their religion. You can't change that depth of faith just by saying you will." The Princess was indignant.

Heath's lips twitched as the girl took a deep breath and settled the mantle of royalty over herself again. He leaned toward Checa to share his thoughts, but Checa beat him to it.

"She isn't just going to be good. She'll be magnificent." Checa frowned. "If she lives long enough."

Rim stepped forward. "You working with one group of fanatics isn't going to change anything." Her eyes narrowed. "We need more than that. What is the threat from the sky they're so afraid of?"

Fisher shrugged. "I don't know. They say it's a deadly fire that burns the Yeudan and eats norrgel for breakfast."

"There's nothing like that. It's not just the threads on their wings that are poisonous. The whole norrgel body is deadly. Nothing can eat it." Heath's voice was quiet and confident.

"And yet your Pledge says something will defeat them," Fisher stated.

"Then *we'll* defeat them." Checa crossed his arms over his chest. Fisher turned to him and they began arguing, although Checa would probably call it a negotiation.

Heath took the opportunity to escape. They had a ritual to prepare for. He grabbed Ardelle's hand and dragged her to the wall of ice and rock dissecting the cavern, then bent his head to hers.

"There's a verse in the Warrior Pledge that talks about melted walls and fire in the sky." He nodded to the partially obscured sculptures encased in ice. "We need to melt this ice wall," he whispered. "You know, with our *abilities*."

"What?" the Princess exclaimed before shooting a frightened glance at Fisher, then turning back to Heath, arguing heatedly. "I can't do that."

"If I can, you can. You have a wider view than I do. I only see the details." He pulled her farther away from the others so their voices wouldn't carry so far.

"Heath—" Ardelle began, but he cut her off, not wanting to listen to any argument.

"Have you ever warmed your bathwater when it got too cold?"

Ardelle took a step back, indignant. Heath had to stop the laugh that wanted to burst forth. Was she thinking about him imagining her in the bath? He looked over her head to Checa. He was the only person Heath wanted to bathe with.

Ardelle noted the look and deflated. She narrowed her eyes at him, took a deep breath, then nodded. "Fine. Tell me what to do."

Heath examined the section of ice closest to them. "Can you feel where it's thinnest? Can you feel any cracks inside it?" He closed his eyes, then pointed. When he opened his eyes, he'd pointed to a thick, milky white section of the ice wall. "There."

Ardelle turned to look, then gasped. "It's already breaking down. The earthquake must have done that."

"So it won't be difficult for us to move a few ice crystals around and help it along."

Ardelle's pale eyes were large. "But it'll come down on top of us."

"If we can crack an ice wall, I'm sure we can deal with the blocks that fall from it. It'll be as easy as finding a pathway through rock." Heath saw, in the way Ardelle stood taller and lifted her chin, that she was going to agree. He grinned at her and rubbed his hands together. "Okay, let's do it."

Before they could do more than push one tiny crack wider than it had been, Checa called them back to the group.

"So… are you going to give me the Yeudan?" asked Fisher when they'd joined the rest of them. "I know I can get them to interpret their prophecies differently."

"You're not going anywhere," exclaimed Rim. "You'll be coming to Analee to answer some questions and then incarcerated for espionage, insurrection, and anything else we can lay at your door."

Beside Heath, Checa remained silent. Eventually Checa looked up at Heath. "What do you think of him?"

Heath moved closer, partly so they could talk and not be overheard. He ducked his head so the others wouldn't see his smile. He didn't really need to stand so close to Checa to speak to him, but he liked it, so he did it anyway. "Rim said Fisher helped them escape the Exiles, and he did get the Exiles to fight with us. The battle is coming anyway. What difference could it make that he goes back and joins them?"

"He could take with him all the information he's gathered."

"He's probably already passed all that on to them." Heath leaned his shoulder against Checa's, gratified when Checa shifted so Heath's shoulder settled more comfortably against his chest.

"He's cunning enough to remain undetected here for months. Don't you think he'll use that cunning when leading the invasion?" Checa's arm settled around Heath's back.

"We'll have the Yeudan here. Fisher doesn't need them. We can question them about his methods."

Checa returned to regarding Fisher. After a few seconds, he released Heath and stepped forward. "How long do you need?"

"Checa! He's an enemy invader," exclaimed Ardelle.

"And possibly an ally," said Heath. "We're beginning from a position of weakness because we haven't had any indication before now what the Yeudan had planned." He stepped forward when Ardelle opened her mouth to retort. "You've known about them for ages but haven't done a thing to counter any offensive. You thought they were religious nutcases spouting nothing but hot air. We can handle skirmishes with the Exiles. They're sporadic and always in small numbers. This invasion from the Yeudan won't be anything like that. We don't have a single regiment mobilized and are woefully unprepared for any kind of battle. Guerrilla warfare presents its own special needs. We need every advantage we can get."

Fisher smiled. "And that's what I can offer you. Let me leave and you'll have time to prepare and train. You keep me here and the attacks will begin immediately, and you won't have a chance."

"We only have your word that an attack is imminent," countered Rim.

"Look around you. Does this look like an advance scout group?" Fisher stepped forward aggressively.

Heath moved between them. "I don't think we can take a chance that a full-on stealth invasion isn't coming. Fisher's right. This number of soldiers isn't an advance scout. These guys are serious about whatever they're here for."

"If I fail to get through to them, you'll only have a month to prepare, longer if I can keep communications open. All they'll know is what I report to them."

"Okay," Heath said, rubbing his hands together, anticipation of working toward a common goal making his skin buzz with excitement. "Let's get ready for the ritual and then we can do all our soldiering."

"What ritual?" asked Rim. "We fought against the invaders. The Warrior Pledge has been enacted."

"Oh no, that's not the Pledge. We have a whole ritual to perform at the peak of the eclipse."

"Why do we need to do that? What will it achieve?"

Heath stopped and stared at Rim in consternation. All the histories said the ritual had to be performed, but he couldn't recall one that gave a reason other than the usual morbid portent of widespread death and destruction.

"Checa?" Heath asked. *Please support me on this*, he wanted to say. *Please blindly trust me.*

"Our Seers all believe this will give us an advantage in the coming wars," Checa said. "I've seen what Heath can do as a Seer. If he says enacting the Warrior Pledge is still necessary, I believe him."

Heath couldn't help it: he jumped forward and into his love's arms. "Thank you," he whispered to Checa, then turned to the others. "And what do we have to lose, right? Makai and Nayeli's fight is swift. They'll only be in position for a few minutes. That's all it will take. If the ritual does nothing, fine. But if it's important, we'll have done everything we need to."

"What about the Yeudan?" Fisher asked.

"The ritual is too close now. We'll talk more about the Yeudan once we're done." Heath strode to the ice wall.

CHECA FLICKED a look up through the funnel. They could clearly see Makai and Nayeli above, one nearly covering the other. The light in the cavern dimmed as the eclipse progressed. His skin crawled, calling him to action, but he wasn't sure yet what that action should be. It seemed everything was happening at once.

The Yeudan invasion had been ordered for when the moons crossed. The Princess's Warrior Pledge had to be completed by then too. The Mafdeti's own Warrior Pledge also had the same deadline. Every aspect had converged to this one point when the moons became one. But which ritual had to be first? And what did it all mean?

"Checa," Heath called. "Come and look at this."

Checa entertained a second of frustration. They had a cavern of dead Descendants, Exiles, and Yeudan, and many more in need of urgent medical attention. Their home and their lives were under threat, and as well as that, several legends and treaties had the same deadline—the crossing of the lunar orbits—and Heath wanted him to look at something?

Then Checa's brain recognized the tone in Heath's voice. It wasn't anything life-threatening, but whatever it was, Checa had to be there. He turned toward the man who had made the difference in his life, turning it from something to be endured to a thing of joy.

Heath stood with Ardelle near the ice wall, beckoning Checa over. Ardelle had pressed herself against the ice, hands bracketing her face as she attempted to peer through the frozen window.

"You have to see this, Checa. It's better than we thought." Heath bounced on his toes as he spoke.

Better? Checa hadn't thought anything was good to start with, except for Heath himself. He lengthened his stride, reaching out a hand to grab Rim's arm and tug her along with him. "This is more your area than ours, Rim. What's he found?"

Rim shook her head. "I've never been this deep in the mountains before. I didn't know of any large cave past the headwaters of the Lake of the Damned."

Checa huffed. "There isn't one. We're *in* the lake now." He turned toward Heath. "So what am I looking at?" If he looked at Rim's shocked face any longer, he'd laugh. He never laughed.

Heath grabbed his hand and dragged him to the ice. Checa left his fingers wrapped loosely around Heath's as he peered through to the other side.

"Fuck," he breathed and pressed closer, needing to see more details. Ardelle shifted sideways so he could move across for a better angle. On the other side of the ice stood four stone pillars, the face of each pillar engraved with a life-sized image of a person. Two Descendants and two Mafdeti.

Checa tilted his head as if that could help him work it out. "What the fuck are they doing?"

"It's the ritual of the Pledge," Heath said from behind him. Checa turned to see Heath and Rim rolling broken pillars away from the center of the cavern in the cool moonlight, dimmer still. Soon it would be too dark to see much; even the reflection of light off the ice and crystals wouldn't make it better.

Checa flicked a look at Ardelle, but she seemed as confused. Together they moved to where the others were rocking a boulder to move it away from the lighted center. "That doesn't explain what you're doing," said Checa, putting his hands on his hips.

Heath grunted as the boulder rolled back toward him, and he shoved it away again. His muscles felt like wilted grass, but they needed to clear the area. Rim bent to take over the task as Heath stood to speak to Checa. "This whole thing has been about the Warrior Pledge. Rim invoked the Pledge when she went to Hawkesby, requesting assistance against the Yeudan. We are the four who will carry out the ritual in order to ensure Thalazar survives the invasion. I'm the Great Heart Farseeing, Rim is the Changeling, Ardelle is the Pure, and you are the Silver Shining from Rock."

Ardelle pointed to another broken pillar that needed to be moved, then glared at Fisher, who'd come to see what they were doing. He grinned and bent to move the rock. Some of Rim's soldiers noticed and left their supervision of prisoners to come over to help.

Heath grinned, then turned back to Checa, hands on his hips in imitation of him. "Did you notice the symbols around the figures carved into those rocks, or did you get distracted by the fact they were naked?"

Checa's face heated. It wasn't so much the fact that the drawings were of naked people that had distracted him, but that they so closely resembled the four of them. Now he couldn't get the image of them naked and touching out of his mind. Especially Heath. He growled, the sound coming deep from his chest. "So, why are you clearing here?"

"Every race has some version of the Warrior Pledge. This part seems to be only from the Mafdeti."

Finally, Ardelle stood in the center of the cavern; the moonlight streamed down on her bare head, casting long shadows over her face and a flat-topped rock at her feet. "I'm not sure exactly what this bit is about, but all the fairy tales have this ritual in them, and then suddenly we win the war. I think it's our response to and preparation for the invasion." She glanced at Checa and shrugged. "I'm going to take those diagrams on the pillars literally and see what happens. What else do we have to lose at this point, apart from a few more minutes?"

Beside Checa, Heath laughed, the full-bodied belly laugh that he hadn't heard in a long time. Something tight in Checa's chest eased, and he moved toward the diminutive Princess. "Okay, Princess Ardelle, what exactly do we do?"

Ardelle looked around the cavern. Most of it was in deep shadow at that point, the only illumination coming from the moonlight above. It was still possible to see the Exiles and Rim's soldiers treating the wounded or guarding the surviving Yeudan. Standing in the only light, the four of them, with Fisher, would be easy to see. "I don't care what the drawings show," she muttered. "I'm a princess and I'm not getting naked in front of anyone." She looked up at Heath. "The way we stood in the bathing cave. My skin burned where you touched."

Checa didn't like the thought of Heath touching Ardelle at all, but he nodded at her to continue. Calm authority settled around her like a shroud.

"Rim, get the Ruby of Authority and place it in the indentation in this rock." Ardelle pointed to the rock at their feet. The indentation she mentioned was little more than a pinhead hole.

Rim fished a tiny red stone from her boot and balanced the bottom carefully on the rock. "It doesn't fit. It's too small." The little ruby tipped over, unable to remain upright.

"Here." Checa handed her the matching ruby he'd carried from the Matriarch.

Rim bent again and jostled the two rubies side by side. First one tipped, then the other. Finally they clicked softly into place. Everyone sighed in relief. As soon as Rim moved her hand away, the moonlight caught at the facets, and the rubies began to glow.

Ardelle nodded, then continued, "You'll need to take your shirt off if we're going to mimic the stance on those stones."

Her voice held more power now she was giving orders, something they hadn't seen before on this mission. She was young, not yet twenty, but Checa would bet his claws that she'd be even more formidable than her mother when she grew a little more. And a lot more compassionate than the Queen.

Rim removed her shirt and Checa's mind blanked, just as it had that time they'd bathed and he'd glimpsed those magnificent breasts.

"Checa, you stand over here."

Heath thumped Checa on his chest. Checa jerked, recovering his senses slowly; he gave Heath a sheepish glance and moved in behind Rim as Ardelle instructed. She tugged his left hand and placed his fingers just below Rim's left breast. "Keep it there," she intoned. "Rim, when the moons cross, you need to Change, but don't go all the way to male. Hold it in the middle as long as you can."

Rim gasped, but Ardelle ignored her. She pulled Rim's left hand up so the fingers pressed into the soft skin below Checa's left ear.

Ardelle stepped under Checa's right arm, snuggling close to his side and pressing against Rim, keeping the rock at their feet in the middle and exposed to the light from above. She giggled a little. "I feel like I'm arranging dolls."

She pushed the collar of her shirt down so that Checa's skin pressed against the curve of her neck and right shoulder. She pressed her left hand against Rim's bare shoulder blade. Heath stepped into their group, his left hand slipping behind Ardelle's neck to rest the fingers at the base of her occipital bone. Checa's right hand landed on Heath's shoulder just as Heath's right arm slipped in front of Rim pressing against the lower curve of her ribs, before his hand grasped Checa's upper arm.

"Okay," Checa said. "We're all arranged like mannequins. Now what?"

"Shh," said Heath. "Feel it."

No sooner had he spoken than Nayeli hid Makai completely and the light diminished further. Only one moon showed in the sky, directly above them, the beam of light narrowing until it shone only on them and the rubies at their feet. The light turned red and the rubies hummed, pulsing in the bloodred glow.

Checa's skin tingled where it touched the others, the sensation radiating outward until it was a soft buzzing throughout his body, but nothing more happened. "Nothing's happening."

Were they the wrong people for the ritual? Would it only work if they were worthy?

It was him—he was the one stopping anything from happening.

"Now, Rim, do it now!" yelled Ardelle.

Rim's face changed as it had in the cavern. The soft edges hardened, not quite enough to be male again, but something in-between. Her features contorted as if it hurt her to maintain the asexual state. As Checa watched, Rim's features changed again, still asexual but sharper, feline. Suddenly she looked half Descendant and half Mafdeti.

Checa looked at the others. Ardelle looked the same as ever, her regal features bathed in pink light as if it flowed through her and anchored them to reality. Pressed against Checa, Heath howled, but the howl turned to a scream as his eyes opened and he looked at Checa. Heath's eyes weren't the usual soft brown, but glowed green, the exact color Checa's usually were. As Checa watched, his own body burned and he knew that he, too, was changing, but he didn't know how.

Heat, as cold as the icy waste and as painful as a sharpened steel blade, knifed down Checa's spine, spun through his gut, and landed in the places the others touched and where he touched them. Every muscle spasmed, clenching in a rigor of pain so intense he couldn't suck air into his lungs. The red light seeped in and it burned too, deep in his lungs, and pounded through his heart.

He flung his head back and opened his burning eyes. Silver light streamed from him, sucking up all the moonlight and flaring raggedly around the cavern, cracking against rock and ice in a cacophony of screeching pain.

Checa screamed.

Silver brings them all again
In loyalty comes trials unknown
Four blended, a choice to own
Silver Bonds under ice and rain

—extract from the Warrior Pledge, prophecy of the Mafdeti, natural inhabitants of Thalazar.

31.
THE RITUAL OF THE PLEDGE

"SHIT, THAT burns."
  "Can't let go."
  "Can't move."
  "Hot, burning."
  "Need to hold on."
  "It stings where we touch."
  "If I let go, I'll lose them all."

Rim's skin twitched and stung all over, but where he touched someone else, or was touched by them, was a deep, burning ache. So deep he couldn't breathe through it, so deep his mind shied away from the pain of it, pretended it wasn't there. Rim gasped and groaned against the pain and tensed against the pressure building so far deep inside him he was sure he'd feel it for the rest of his life.

The words continued to whisper through his mind, but he knew they weren't his own thoughts. At least not *all* him. He recognized Checa's deep baritone and Heath's lighter tenor as Ardelle's soft cries mixed with his own groans, until it mashed together as if they were one voice, sharing the thoughts and building the sentences together.

A deep shiver wracked his body, straining against the touch of the others, but the burn dragged him back, leaning in against them, soaking up the heat and the thoughts of the other three with him. As if he were becoming them and they were becoming him.

It came to Rim then, like the icy waters of early spring, slipping into his consciousness, burrowing into his mind so far he thought he'd always known it. Or one of them had. He'd read about it often enough, had witnessed the ceremony, but nothing had prepared him for what was happening now. This wasn't the same; this was more than anything he'd thought possible. Nothing he'd ever known could have led him to believe that the thing that held him in thrall now could be possible.

Zar, people didn't pledge spontaneously. There hadn't been a true Pledge among the Imperials for decades. And they certainly didn't pledge with more than one person. Rim tried to break free but couldn't tug his hand away from Checa's neck. His fingers had fused to the warm skin below Checa's ear. He couldn't let go of the hold he had on Heath's upper arm either, and his shoulder blade burned under Ardelle's small hand.

He couldn't stop it. A shudder rippled through him, his stomach roiled, and his muscles cramped as he held his Change halfway to nothing.

"Hold it now."

"Don't change completely."

"Why not?"

Sweat ran down Rim's face as he forced the elements of his body into stasis so that it couldn't slide toward either male or female. His body hovered, bursting, burgeoning and shrinking at the same time. His muscles trembled and he swayed; the only thing holding him upright was his connection to the others. His face ached, his cheeks snapped, and his gums broke under the force of his teeth growing and lowering. Blood poured from his mouth and dripped off his jaw.

Checa's scream still echoed through the chamber, and his rough panting mirrored Rim's pained breathing. Behind Rim, Ardelle whimpered and pushed her scalding hand deeper into his shoulder blade, searing the skin. Rim hauled in a frantic breath, surprised he couldn't smell his skin scorching under the hands of the others. At the base of his throat, where no one touched, another burn began. He grunted with that pain as well, barely noticing Heath's groan beside him.

Inside his head he yelled, drowning out the cries of the others, yet at the same time absorbing them into himself. Around him the pulsing light from the moons-lit rubies washed over him like too-hot water. He flung his head back and opened his mouth to scream out loud, but silver light rushed in, gagging him. His lungs burned as much as his skin, red-raw air peeling away the layers of his body from the inside out. Before he could even think he'd die from it, a soothing salve rushed in before the tide ebbed again and the pain renewed. He reached in his mind for Checa, Heath, and Ardelle, and they were there, deep inside, the same ebb and flow pulsing in their bodies, and he joined them in the ride.

Rim tried to force the Change, first to male, then to female, but it didn't work. It was different from before, but he couldn't change completely now any more than he could in the cave.

The tendons in his neck strained until finally the edge of the second moon became visible. As the light increased, his body shifted, finally, back into his male form. Even though it got brighter, it felt less intense, and the burning from the others' touches reduced.

"My legs are about to give out."

"Zar, that hurt."

"Is it over?"

"What the hell just happened?"

When a quarter of the far moon showed, the pressure holding Rim connected to the others released. The muscles in his arms burned as he dropped them to his sides, and he groaned, sinking to his knees, panting, sweat dripping from him. Around him he felt the others stagger and fall too, and he turned and reached out to touch them.

Even before the touch became real, the places where the others had held him throbbed and the emptiness inside him reduced.

"What the hell just happened?" Checa's raw baritone rumbled across the air between them and echoed in his head.

Beside Checa, Heath shook his head like a dog trying to dislodge a flea, and Ardelle jumped, her eyes wide.

"Say something again."

"Drett," Checa swore, pressing his hand against his head. "What the hell is going on?"

Ardelle laughed, the high, breathy sound showing exhaustion that matched Rim's own. "It's an Imperial Pledge."

Rim sucked in a breath. He'd been thinking the same thing, but she couldn't be right. Pledging rarely happened anymore, and even when it was attempted, it rarely took. No one had reported the melding of minds that was supposed to happen. It couldn't be possible he'd pledged with all three of them.

Even as Rim thought that, the rightness of it settled within him. He was Pledged.

"What's that?" growled Checa.

"It's a melding of minds and bodies, a union between two Imperials. It's a Life-Link, unbreakable. They're life partners."

"We're not Imperials. We can't pledge," exclaimed Heath. His voice echoed in Rim's head as well as around the cavern. "And there's four of us!"

Rim chuckled, unable to hold the seriousness of the situation at the expression on Heath's face. "I don't think that's a consideration." He grinned at the lowered tenor of his voice and the shocked faces before him. He ran a hand down his flat chest to rest comfortably on his groin for a second. A sigh of relief escaped. Male again. *"Thank the Protectors for that."*

"Christ, you're even gorgeous as a man."

Rim grinned up at Checa as he pushed to his feet. Rim's gaze followed the motion, zeroing in on a mark on Checa's neck, clearly visible under the sweep of russet, cream, and ginger hair. "What's that?"

Checa frowned at Rim, raising his hand to the spot Rim pointed at. "There's another one."

The skin at Checa's wrist looked burned with what looked like a tattoo. Both marks Rim saw were similar: three cat's whiskers, but the one on Checa's neck was enclosed in an ellipse, like an eye.

"You're Bonded." Heath's voice was both shocked and dismayed.

Rim looked at Heath, noticing a similar burned patch on his shoulder. "So are you."

They all looked. Heath's mark was different from either of Checa's.

"They should be the same," Checa said. "You're my mate."

Heath started, then a shy, sweet smile, so different from his usual playful grin, teased his lips as he looked at Checa adoringly.

"What do you mean?" Ardelle was turning Heath around, checking his whole body. "He has four, and they're all different."

"Four? But the Bonding is only between life partners." Heath pulled Checa closer. "There's another one on your arm where I was holding you."

"So I've bonded with you." Checa's gaze was intent, heated, and even though it was directed at Heath, Rim felt his cheeks heat. "A spontaneous Bond. No one can break it." Checa smiled at Heath as if there was nothing more in the world he wanted.

Heath grinned at Checa and reached for him. "About time."

"But where are the other marks from? We aren't Mafdeti." Ardelle turned her attention to Rim, pushing his body around, then back again. "Rim has four too. We're Imperials. We can't bond."

They matched Bonding marks. Every one of them had a mark that matched the others. All the marks but one were positioned where one of the others had been touching them. The other mark was in the traditional position for a Bonding mark: the base of the throat, just above the clavicle.

"We've pledged *and* bonded with each other," said Rim, finally expressing in words what they'd all noticed.

"But how?" Heath touched the cat's whiskers on Checa's arm, his Bonding mark.

Rim shivered at the awe and love that shone from the russet Mafdeti's eyes.

"I'm more interested in why," said Checa, making Heath gasp and move away. He didn't get far before Checa grabbed him and dragged him back in. "Stop it, Heath. You and I are Bonded the way we've always been meant to, but we never intended to bond with anyone else. Four people can't all be Bonded." He looked at all of them in turn.

Rim said, "Perhaps only you two are really Bonded and we've just tagged along for the ride. Our marks will probably fade soon." Rim hoped so.

Fisher's voice broke into their private reverie. "I don't know what kind of weird shit you all just did, and I don't want to. What I do know is that it's time to get moving." He reminded them that they weren't alone and the Pledging-Bonding thing wasn't their only problem. "The Yeudan aren't going to change their plans to feed all of you to the norrgel just because you decided to get married."

Rim turned to the thin man and gasped. Fisher stood in front of the ice wall, milky now in the dim moonlight as the moons traveled slowly apart across the sky. And Rim could *feel* the ice melting. He knew, down to the droplet, how much water was contained in the wall and exactly where the first shard of ice would break away and begin a rush of water that would wash away the rest of the ice and refill the lake.

He reached a hand out to grab Checa's arm. "I can feel—"

"…the ice melting," finished Checa.

"You can feel it too?" asked Heath.

"I thought it was just me." Ardelle shot a look at Heath. "And him."

"We need to…"

"…get to…"

"…high ground…"

"…right now."

As one they turned and scanned the area. Several boulders and broken pillars lay around the cavern. Groups of soldiers, Exiles, and Yeudan, some treating the injured, gathered around.

His heart pounding, Rim yelled, "Get to high ground!" and rushed toward them. He grabbed the arm of an Exile. "The ice is melting. Grab as many as you can and get them up high." He shoved the man toward a group of the injured.

Thankfully the Exile was used to taking orders and passing them on, so Rim only had to point and shove to get the next one moving. By the time Rim turned around, Checa, Heath, Ardelle, and Fisher had done the same with other groups and everyone was moving, climbing on top of boulders and broken pillars, shoving toward the tunnels with shouted instructions to run and climb. Victor or prisoner, it suddenly didn't matter. What mattered was saving as many lives as possible.

At the other side of the cavern, Rim saw others assisting the injured to higher ground. Nearby, Ardelle conferred briefly with one of her guard who had survived the trek, before moving on again. An echo of Ardelle's relief that her friend was safe coursed through Rim. She turned and smiled at him, her awareness of his own relief for his men clear in her mind.

A CRACK rent the ice, louder than any thunderclap Checa had ever heard, no matter how close. He flinched and looked around them before yelling to more people to move. The low-lying areas were almost clear of the living, and Rim pushed Ardelle on top of a large boulder near the wall where they'd entered the cavern.

From the other side, Heath ran toward them. "The water's going to rise higher than this," he yelled over more cracking ice.

Behind Checa, Ardelle scrambled down and ran toward the ice wall, crying, "Over here!"

"No!" Rim ran after her.

Checa's instinct was to help Rim stop Ardelle, to drag her away from the ice and to safety, but then the voices in his head whispered again.

"There's a crack here, a way through."

"Trust her...."

"Get to her...."

"Keep her safe."

Shit. Checa raced with the others after Ardelle, who'd come to mean as much to him as... as... not Heath, but close. So had Rim. Shit. Shit. He couldn't think about this now. The ice at the edge where Ardelle was heading was beginning to crack. They'd been safer on the rock. She was going to get them all killed.

Checa turned to find Heath and go to him, but Heath was close. Checa grabbed his arm and dragged him along on their mad rush to find a safe haven.

The fissures were almost visible… almost. They weren't there yet, but Checa knew without doubt that they would soon be. In his head he could see the way the ice would fall, could see where the water would swell and where it would run. And Ardelle and the others were crowding into an area that simply wasn't safe.

"You have to get out of there," Checa called. "We'll all get washed away."

Ardelle grinned at him.

Grinned! Damned arrogant Princess.

He rushed to her and grabbed her arm.

"No, Checa, wait. We can do this." She was laughing, enjoying the drama and the danger.

Checa's heart pounded and fearful sweat trickled down his neck. "We can do what?"

Beside him, Heath was smiling too and Rim was quiet. Checa sucked in a calming breath and decided to take his cue from Heath. Heath would never let him down, and he wouldn't let them do anything that would get them killed.

"You can feel the world, can't you?" Ardelle's joy was a tangible thing, making her bounce on her toes.

Checa narrowed his eyes at her. "Is that what it is?"

She laughed again. "We can all feel it."

"And if we can all feel it, we can all move it," said Heath.

"Move it?" Checa asked.

Ardelle bounced again and Heath laughed, and suddenly Checa understood. Two weeks ago they each thought they were the only one who could feel the world and all its pieces. Then they found each other, and with the Bonding, all four of them had the same abilities. Not just the same abilities, but the abilities multiplied by the four of them. Four times as strong. Blended and shared and strengthened. For the first time in their lives, they had found the one place where they truly belonged.

But what did that mean for Checa? His only special ability was his silver eyes. Did that mean that they all had eyes that would glow when they killed someone?

"You're not alone." The words in his head resonated with the personalities of the other three.

Rim came up behind Checa and drew him closer to where Heath and Ardelle waited impatiently. Heath gestured urgently to Fisher and he joined them as well.

"Fisher, you get behind us, up against the rocks." Heath looked steadily at Checa before giving Rim and Ardelle a nod. "We need to concentrate together for this to work."

"*If* it works," said Ardelle.

Heath glared at her, and Checa couldn't help but smile at the two of them. They were like squabbling siblings. Then they both turned and grinned at him before Heath's face settled once more into serious lines. "We need to push the water away from us when the ice cracks."

Checa scowled. "How do you think we'll do that, Heath?"

Heath sniffed, and Rim chuckled at him and said, "You're so cute when you do that."

"I am not cute." Heath glared at Rim, and Rim and Ardelle burst out laughing.

By the ancestors, they were about to be washed to their deaths and they were laughing! This Pledging-Bonding thing had sent Checa mad. He'd never be the same again. "Just tell us what to do, Heath. We'll admire your cuteness later," he growled. "You'd better hurry. The ice is going to crack." Checa shifted to make more room for Rim in the small alcove of rock and ice they'd pushed themselves into.

"Okay." Heath sighed, closed his eyes, and took several deep, calming breaths. "Close your eyes and feel where the water is behind the ice. Don't think about the ice or where the fissures are that are going to crack. Just think about the water. Feel it swirling and pushing against the ice. We're not going to move all that water, but we need to feel the weight of it."

He became silent, and Checa reluctantly closed his eyes too, trying to push away the sure knowledge that the water was going to tumble over them and they'd drown. He sucked in another breath, jamming his rising panic under the calm assurance he felt from Heath.

"Now go deeper," Heath said. "Separate the water into droplets. We're just going to move the droplets. One at a time. Droplets of water aren't heavy at all, so it won't tire us."

Checa huffed a laugh. In a bizarre way, that actually made sense.

"Thanks so much," Heath intoned. "Keep your eyes closed and concentrate. We don't have much time."

Just as Heath said that, the ice cracked again, dislodging several monumental shards that crashed to the ground and shot slivers through the cavern. Checa's eyes jerked open. The moonlight, now dim and slanted high up the walls, caught the frozen water and melting droplets and reflected off them in pastel rainbows. He took a scant second to admire the subtle colors, then slammed his eyes closed again, frantically imagining the water behind the ice.

"What if I can't do it?"

"Of course you can do it."

"I can do it, so can you."

"We're Pledged now."

"And Bonded."

"And Bonded—so we can share our abilities."

"Anyone want to be a girl?"

"Don't be flippant, Rim."

"Being a girl isn't bad, idiot."

"I don't want to die."

"None of us do."

"We won't if we can do this."

By the time they finished their internal conversation, Checa could see, in the shadows inside his eyelids, every droplet of water waiting behind the ice wall, pressing on it, eager to get out.

The ice cracked again, making him jump. And then again. Even though he expected it, the whiplike thunder was still shocking. The tremors within the ice wall echoed in his body. Before he could take another breath, it all tumbled down, roaring and clanging like cymbals, making him gasp, shattering his concentration. And from behind the ice, came the water.

"Keep focused. Let it all go. Just the droplets. We only have to push the droplets away."

Heath's encouragement sounded deep inside Checa's consciousness and he lifted his hands palm-out in front of him, eyes still tightly closed. Cold water sprayed over him and swirled around his ankles, but the maelstrom came no higher than his calves and was no more violent than a small creek with late-spring runoff.

"It's working."

"Of course it is."
"Don't lose focus."
"Just push the droplets away."

It was easy at first. Heath was right; the droplets of water weighed nothing. But it didn't stop. The water kept coming and there seemed no end to it. Checa's skin heated as his muscles strained against the constant effort of pushing water away. He sweated, the warm salt of it mixing with the chilled spray from the lake water. His arms began to burn, then tremble. His shoulders followed suit, and eventually every muscle in his body shuddered with the effort of pushing droplet after droplet after droplet of water away from himself.

Finally the weight of water lifted, although the roar of it continued. Checa opened eyes that felt as if they weighed more than the largest boulders behind him. The light had changed again. The fight between Makai and Nayeli was over for another thousand years. The moons had set. The cavern was awash with the pale pink light of the rising sun. It bounced off turbulent wavelets as the lake rushed toward Rim's valley, desperate to fill the rivers and wash away the rot. Around the cavern outlet, the water was lumpy and dark, the bodies of the dead queuing to pour through the opening and out into the river beyond.

Checa staggered. The exhaustion from the ritual and the work of diverting the water drained him of the strength he needed to keep upright. A wet arm clamped around him and he found himself pulled back against Heath's broad chest. *Safe.*

Beside him, Ardelle panted, her chin resting on her chest, her hands braced against her knees. Rim flung one arm around her to hold her up and the other around Checa's shoulders.

"We did it," said Heath.

Checa swung to glare at him. "You sound surprised. I thought it was an easy thing?"

Heath grinned unrepentantly. "I've never done anything like that with water before." He shrugged. "And the stuff I've done with rocks has always been an instant push for destruction."

Rim rolled his eyes and groaned. Ardelle gasped, then laughed.

"What?" yelled Checa. "You're telling me you had no idea what you—*we*—were doing? You could have got us all killed."

Heath's grin widened and he swung himself up to sit on a boulder while the water swirled and tumbled over itself at their feet. "It worked, didn't it?"

32.
A Real Relationship

CHECA GLARED at Heath for a few moments but eventually just hauled in a deep breath and looked away. He could feel Heath's mind as clearly as he could the others, and Heath was right. It worked. They were still alive, and being angry about not having done it before would be stupid. If everyone only ever did what they'd done before, no one would learn anything. And Checa knew he should always ask more questions before he agreed to anything Heath wanted to do.

Heath chuckled, then patted him on his shoulder.

Checa shook him off but chuckled too. *"Condescending prick, even if you are gorgeous and funny."*

"That's better than cute," Heath murmured inside Checa's mind. *"But don't forget talented too."*

Checa shook his head and looked around. Water still rushed by them, but the area of the lake was clearly visible. Once the ice wall had broken up, the cavern looked completely different. It was no longer a neat oval but had an elongated bay jutting deep into the mountain under a low, bubbled amber ceiling, and another bay threading its way toward the Analee Valley. The lake water flowed swiftly, only slowing as it threaded the bodies of the dead through the opening.

Chunks of ice, ranging in size from a fist to half his hunting cottage, danced drunkenly on the swirling water, crashing into submerged rocks and breaking down further. Mist formed on the water as the cold air around the ice floes met the slightly warmer air of the cavern. The mist played with the little wavelets, tapping and prodding like a playful child.

Checa shivered, sweat cooling his heated skin almost as much as the icy water around his calves. Peripherally he was aware they were still idly pushing the droplets away from them, causing an area around them to be a shallow, slow-moving whirlpool. As more ice melted, the depth increased. They were still standing in swirling current, but all around them rose a shallow funnel. "I'm not tiring anymore."

"That's because we aren't pushing as much water and we aren't trying to push it as far away. It isn't taking as much effort so we won't tire," said Heath.

Checa rolled his eyes. *"Thanks for the lesson, Heath, but I could have worked that out for myself."*

Heath leaned over and pinched the back of Checa's arm. He spun and glared at his… Bond-Mate… and scowled at the grin that was returned.

"Shit. Aren't you going to be a joy to live with," said Heath. He gushed with warmth and love, but beneath that was exhaustion.

"Enough," growled Checa as he checked the others were still with him.

Rim and Ardelle stood a few feet away, talking quietly. Fisher was nowhere to be seen. "Where the hell did the Exile go now?" Checa looked around. "I thought one of you were watching him."

"I'm usually in charge, Checa. Someone else does the watching for me," Rim reminded him.

"That's lazy. And careless."

"We're all leaders of our people," responded Ardelle, "but we're Pledged now and have to learn to work together."

Ardelle was more the focused warrior than Checa had ever heard her before, the spoiled young Princess burned from her by battle.

"There he is." Heath pointed to the middle of the lake.

Checa waded through the water and around a large boulder so he could see where Heath gestured.

Fisher waded through chest-deep water, his arms butterflying, hands cupped to push the water behind him. Every two or three steps, he stumbled and went under, surfaced and swam a little before finding his feet again.

Whether Fisher fell over unseen rocks or because of the gradually settling current, Checa couldn't tell. "Where's he going?" he asked, even as he saw what must be the thin man's destination.

"Zar, what's that?" Rim asked as he turned to look.

Halfway back down the lake, under a low ceiling of bulbous, egg-shaped amber, Fisher began climbing a dark, smooth slope.

"Where's he finding handholds?" asked Heath as he began moving toward Fisher.

Checa followed. "It must be something the Yeudan hid here and somehow froze the lake to hide it. Fisher would know all about it."

They waded through the water, always in the shallows as they continued to push each droplet away with the current.

"It's cold." Ardelle shivered.

Checa shrugged. "It was ice half an hour ago."

"There's no fish." Rim frowned. "The Crystal River had the best fishing when I was a boy."

Checa placed a hand on the back of Rim's warm neck, snatching it away as Heath growled at him.

"Give it time," he murmured to Rim. "It'll all come back now."

"Fisher!" Heath's cry dragged Checa's attention back to the charcoal monolith just in time to see Fisher lower himself over the far side.

"What the fuck does he think he's doing?" Checa pushed himself past the others and through the swirling water.

They moved faster, losing their concentration on the droplets, and the depth rose past Checa's thighs. He gasped as the chill saturated his loincloth, raising goose bumps on his bare skin. He tried to grasp for control of the water again, to visualize them all doing the same thing. The image faltered and morphed into something totally unexpected. Perched inside his head, like an owl surveying its domain, he saw the four of them, lounging before a winter fire, with Heath's dragon warming her tail at the hearth. At the center of them all was Heath, his skin warm and comforting. Where Checa's body touched Heath's, sensation soared, and Checa's breath caught in his throat.

He snapped a glance at Heath to find him smirking. "Bastard."

"We're Bonded now, Checa. We get to share everything." Heath chortled as Checa flashed an image of Heath over Checa's knees. "Oh, are you planning to spank me now?"

"Enough," interrupted Rim. "You two do realize we're both linked to you too?"

"What? Still?" exclaimed Heath.

Rim shrugged. "I don't think it's as strong as it was when it first happened, but yes, we're still there too."

"Do you think it will fade?" Heath darted a panicked look at Checa and Checa laughed.

"Worry about that later, Heath. We have work to do first," he said.

By then the others had caught up to Checa, and with them striding beside him, pushing at the water together, they moved more quickly.

None of them spoke, but Checa could hear their conversations inside his head. It wasn't just Fisher they were focused on. Ardelle assessed the strength of the Exiles and Rim's soldiers still perched on top of the boulders around the lake. Rim worried what the flooding river from the sudden purging of the lake was doing to his land and the people in his valley. Heath was still fretting about Kimi, and Checa worried that the Yeudan would escape. Behind all that, all of them wondered how bad the threat from the Yeudan would be.

Heath came up beside him and slipped his hand into Checa's.

Checa didn't deserve the comfort or the understanding, but he held on anyway, needing it more now than he ever had.

"You're so hard on yourself, Checa. You think you have to solve all the world's problems and have to fix everything for everyone. And if you don't, that means you're a failure."

Checa clenched his jaw and tried to stop his agreement, or his shame, flooding his mind. He could feel Heath poking around at the edges of his thoughts, prodding Checa to let him in, but he couldn't. There was too much darkness in there, and Heath didn't belong in the dark. He was laughter and light.

"You're a dick, you know that, don't you?" There was laughter in Heath's voice, just as there usually was, but there was also frustration and hurt. "We're Bonded, Checa. You know as well as I do that Bonding doesn't happen spontaneously, yet with us, it did. Think about that. With all the years you've spent resisting the slightest commitment to me, as soon as conditions were right, it happened anyway. Immediately, without a conscious thought from either of us. What does that tell you?"

Checa stopped, the icy water swirling with the sudden cessation of his movement. "It tells me you're mine and I'm yours, exactly the way we've always been meant to be, but Rim and Ardelle were dragged along too. You can't think we're all four meant to be Bonded for life? All *four* of us?" He reached out and touched his Bonding mark on Heath's clavicle. The brand was dark and vibrant against Heath's golden skin and sent a warm rush of pleasure through Checa. He'd dreamed of seeing his mark on Heath for half the time he'd known him—ever since he'd looked up from the sunrise over the valley one morning and seen Heath, all grown up. A man who knew him better than anyone else ever could. A man he could love.

"Our marks aren't that dark," said Rim as he inspected the blurred blue blush of Checa's mark on Ardelle's shoulder. "I think they're fading."

"See?" Heath bounced, the cold water slapping around his thighs. "Theirs are fading but ours aren't. I think yours is even darker than it was," he said as he pressed his fingers into the mark on Checa's arm. "You're mine, Checa. You know it, and I don't know why you're still resisting."

"I'm not resisting." Checa groaned. "You don't know what I've—"

"I'm in your head, you idiot. Just like you're in mine. Is there any part of my life you don't know about now?" Heath grabbed Checa by the arms and attempted to shake him. "Just look, you stubborn man. Look at me and you'll see."

Heath's deep brown eyes regarded him imploringly. Checa sighed in defeat and looked. He'd always loved Heath's eyes, a deep, rich brown with no other colors in them, but they weren't like that now. Now there was a thin ring of green, the same color as Checa's own eyes. Marring the brown were striations of silver: narrow, wobbly lines that made the brown deeper and richer than ever. At first Checa thought Heath's eyes were ruined, but he looked deeper, unable to deny him, and saw he was wrong. Heath's eyes weren't ruined at all. They'd matured, become what they were destined to be: more than a Seer's eyes, more than a warrior's eyes. They were the eyes of a man whose purpose was clear; a Bonded man with a mission in life.

And he was Bonded to Checa.

"Your eyes aren't pure silver anymore," whispered Heath. He feathered his hand over Checa's cheek, just under his eye. "They're warmer now, with a green rim and streaks of dark brown through them. You can't keep denying it, Checa. We're meant to be Bonded, and that's what's happened."

"There's trouble coming, Heath." Anguish colored his words. If they were Bonded, then Heath would be drawn into any battle Checa had to fight.

Heath grinned at him. "What do you think the Warrior Pledge is, Checa?" Checa frowned at his mate. What did the Pledge have to do with anything? "Did you think we came here and performed a ritual like that just because the records told us to and the world would be magically saved?" Heath laughed and swung an arm around Checa as he got them all moving toward the exit. "The Pledge is a portent of great change. It's the beginning, Checa, not the main goal. We had to perform the ritual so that we'd be ready for whatever comes next. Without the Pledge, we'd fail. I don't know exactly what the Pledge has done for us, except bond us and link us with the two major forces in our land, but I know that's only the beginning."

"Do you think the Yeudan invasion is part of the Pledge?" asked Ardelle, coming up beside Heath.

Heath bounced a little with every third step, his excitement barely contained. "*Everything* is part of the Pledge. It's the trigger for the renewal of the Mafdeti. It's our time now to become again the people we once were, and more."

Checa had seen him like this before, and as with every other time, he gave in. "What are we going to become, sweet?" He looped his arm around Heath and drew him close, ignoring the way it became more difficult for them to push through the water.

Heath laughed, a surge of pure joy. "I don't know, Checa, but I know it's going to be marvelous."

"We're heading for war!" exclaimed Rim. "How is *that* marvelous?"

Heath flapped a dismissive hand. "I never said *war* was marvelous—"

"*We* are," finished Checa.

Myths alive, legends return
Raining gold upon the land
Hundreds follow adventures grand
Dragons clasp amber's dark burn

—extract from the Warrior Pledge, prophecy of the Mafdeti, natural inhabitants of Thalazar.

33.
FLIGHT

THE WATERS sloshed at him, rising above Checa's groin, climbing to his waist. The cold slithered across his abdomen before trickling beneath his loincloth. He was sure it wasn't any colder than the water that had already seeped through the fabric, but it made him gasp.

"Zar, look at the ceiling!" They all looked up at Ardelle's cry.

"That's what's making all the noises," Heath said.

All the glimmering amber nodules that hung bulbously from the ceiling had darkened. One above and in front of them showed a large crack down the center. As they watched, a shard separated from the bulb and speared into the now-roiling waters below. Checa jumped, floundering as his foothold was lost and the water pushed him backward.

"We need to get out of here. The ceiling is going to come down."

They turned, but the water was rising farther. Ardelle was already floundering, her teeth chattering. Rim reached for her, and for a few seconds, their fingers clung before the wake from the tumbling ice floes swamped the Princess and swept them all off their feet.

"Double drett and damn the wings," said Heath. "Make for the rocks."

"Which rocks?" asked Rim. "Ardelle can't swim."

"I can. You taught me," Ardelle called back before she was swamped and went under.

When she surfaced, gasping, Rim yelled, "I taught you how to float, so do that. We'll come and get you."

Checa caught a glimpse of Ardelle's pale face as she was swept along in the current. Rim picked up his pace, trying to get to her before she went under again. Checa and Heath joined the chase. They were swimming toward the head of the Crystal River, where the last few dead bodies floated out on the current. There was no sign of Fisher near any boulders or in the water. Checa spluttered, spitting out water washed up as Heath powered past him, pursuing Ardelle.

"Come on," Heath called. "They're both going to need rescuing soon."

Checa huffed a laugh and continued swimming with the current. A loud *crack* rent the air, startling him. Something large splashed down to his left, sending cold water arcing over him.

Another splash sounded behind him; then a smooth object sliced down the back of his left arm. Shit, the ceiling was falling.

"Checa! Here!" came Heath's cry.

Checa put his head down and started swimming toward the cry, not bothering to look where he was going, trusting Heath to have found some kind of shelter. It crossed his mind that by lying in the water to swim, he was presenting a larger surface area for attack, but he couldn't move quickly enough if he stayed upright. He had to keep moving and hope nothing landed on him.

Even diving below the surface wouldn't help. The shards of amber that speared into the water went deep. At least the water was deep enough now so that he didn't scrape over any rocks or amber shards as he swam.

Cries echoed across the lake. Checa had almost forgotten all the soldiers, Exiles, and Yeudan trapped on the other side, clinging to boulders. He hoped they could find shelter somewhere.

The rain of shattering amber became heavier and Checa's back and shoulders stung from being hit by debris. He pulled through the water faster, his lungs straining with the effort. A warm hand grabbed his arm as he powered through and pulled him sideways into shallows formed by tumbled rocks. He wedged himself under a rocky overhang, soaking up the warmth created by the other three bodies already there.

"You're developing a habit of pulling me out of dangerous currents," he said to Heath, with a quick kiss to his forehead. Heath grinned at him.

The semicircular pool of comparatively calm water gave Checa a chance to catch his breath and check on the others. They were all there, cold, wet, and panting as he was, but alive, and except for a few shallow slices and scrapes from falling amber, unhurt. The relief hit Checa like a blow to the head and he gasped; the water sloshed over his head before Heath reached out to steady him.

He pressed closer, soaking up the warmth Heath offered, and slung his arm around Heath's shoulders, offering the same. Heath looked at him, his gaze serious before he smiled and climbed up Checa's body. Checa automatically adjusted his stance to take Heath's weight.

Heath curled around Checa, still looking him in the eyes. "We can protect each other now."

Checa pulled Heath to him and planted a kiss on his lips. Weighted heat pooled in his groin and he felt a similar response in Heath. He leaned forward, tasting the soft skin at Heath's neck.

"Fuck," Checa groaned. "We don't have time for this."

Heath huffed a laugh even as his chest heaved. "But it's fantastic."

"Is it like that all the time?" Ardelle's voice was high and thin.

Checa turned to find her avid gaze on them.

Beside her, Rim shook his head. "I've never felt the need to kiss anyone else while under threat of being drowned or impaled by amber or killed by floodwater, so no, it isn't usually like that."

Ardelle grinned at him, shy innocence blending with newfound power.

"Fuck," Checa said again.

Heath slid his legs down, still leaning on Checa. He lifted a hand and drew Checa's face to his, gently pressing their lips together. "It's still us, Checa. We're still us." He swung an amused and heated look at Ardelle and then Rim. "It's just that right now, we have Rim and Ardelle riding with us."

Checa's tattoos throbbed. "We might all be family now, but *you're* my Bond-Mate."

Heath laughed, still leaning on him. "And you're mine." He settled back on his feet. "You know what this means, don't you?" He chortled, looking around them with a huge grin on his face. "We're the new generation of warriors, and together with our dragon allies, we're going to save the world and rebuild the Mafdeti race." He bounced on his toes. "The Warrior Pledge was right. We're going to be heroes."

"You don't know that for sure," Checa growled, gently cuffing Heath across the head. "So far all we've got is this Bonding-Pledging thing between us and a war on our hands that we might not win. Where are your precious dragons?"

Rim looked around with interest. "Is this like it was at the bathing pools?" All over the lake, amber still rained down, splashing into the water. As they watched, a large ball-shaped object tumbled from the ceiling and splashed heavily into the lake, spuming water in a high arc. For several long minutes, the water where the lump landed was calm. Then a long, horned head popped up and bobbed on the surface. Remaining in position, under the only part of the ceiling not raining amber, golden eyes blinked at them from a russet face.

Rim gasped. "She's gorgeous."

Checa growled. "Fuck, more dragons." He nudged Rim. "We still don't know if they're friend or foe."

Another baby dragon dropped into the water. This seemed some kind of signal, as suddenly the ceiling opened up and instead of amber, it was raining dragons.

"I hope they're on our side," Checa whispered.

"Or no side at all," agreed Rim, even as he smiled at the little dragon who'd dropped first.

Abruptly the cavern was quiet except for the soft plopping sound of baby dragons, ice, and lightweight amber bobbing to the surface. Rim's dragon—with the way they were making eyes at each other, Checa could think of her no other way—floated serenely toward their group, snagging shards of amber from the water as she slid past them. Once one piece was wedged between two horns along her neck, back, or tail, she reached for another. When she was close enough for Checa to see the swirling apricots and golds in her eyes, she stopped and tilted her head to the side.

"Is this an Adventure?" she asked, her bell-like tones carrying easily across the water.

Heath burst out laughing as Rim grinned and replied, "Yes, my beautiful one, it is. Would you and your friends like to join us?"

"Fuck this," exclaimed Checa. "Not you too."

Before Rim could respond, Heath rested his hand on Checa's shoulder. Checa closed his eyes, feeling with the Pledge-Bond how deep their commitment was to each other.

"Checa," Heath said softly. "I know you don't trust what you can't see, but in this you have to." He kept talking, and with a quick shake of his head, stopped Checa from responding. "The dragons belong here as much as we do. They're native to Thalazar, just as we are." Heath's hand rubbed soothingly up and down Checa's arm, the touch firm but so gentle that Checa could swear it was silk. "The dragons will help us," Heath said. "They'll join us on our *adventure* against the Yeudan, and they'll help us win."

"Adventure," Checa scoffed.

Heath grinned and drew him closer still. His lips twitched. "I wonder what talents they have."

Checa turned to Heath and looked deep into his eyes. "So this is your grand adventure."

Heath threw his head back and laughed, and Checa's breath locked in his lungs. Damn the wings, the man was beautiful when he laughed.

"Okay," Checa huffed when Heath regained control. "We'll assume the best legends will work and the dragons can be our allies. We'll probably need all the help we can get. Hopefully we'll have until summer to convince these dragons that war is a grand adventure."

"You already have a plan, don't you." It was a statement, an expectation borne of experience. Heath clapped his hands. "Let's get started then." They all grinned at each other.

"Tomorrow," growled Checa as he pushed himself out into the water. He stretched his hand to Heath and watched as Rim helped Ardelle back into the current. "I've just bonded with the love of my life." Checa smiled at the gentle warmth that suffused Heath's face. He lowered his voice, so just Heath could hear him. "I want to get out of this damned cavern and into a comfortable bed so we can make love like we never have before. After that we'll run off and be soldiers again." He tugged Heath into a tangle of limbs and laughter as they floated through the tunnel opening and out into the early-morning light.

The Crystal River was flowing again, the water clear and cool. They rounded a bend, made their way to shore, and stood shivering in the crisp breeze as they looked over the landscape. There was evidence of a recent flash flood, with debris dangling halfway up the battered trees. Everywhere Checa looked the ground was puddled and littered with a stomach-clenching combination of dead bodies and melting ice washed from the lake, and glistening amber shards in cream, gold, orange, and pale green. The air was clear and crisp, and sweeter than anything Checa had smelled for a long time. He soaked it in, knowing that as the sun rose and heated the land around them, it wouldn't stay that way.

Checa noticed Rim's and Ardelle's men, along with other survivors, already hauling bodies from the water. As soon as they spotted Rim, two broke away and ran toward them.

"Thank Thalazar you're all right, Princess," one with a ruined voice rasped through the air.

"That was some ride, huh, Rim?" asked another. "You're you again." The soldier's gaze slid to Rim's bare chest. "That's almost disappointing."

Rim reached out to cuff his friend upside the head as he grinned at them.

"Just wait till you hear the rest of it." Heath laughed, shivering damply in the cool breeze.

Checa linked arms with Heath, and Rim and Ardelle did the same. He breathed in their combined scent, long days since the last bath, and chuckled.

"Definitely," said Heath. "I want a bath before anything else." Then he gasped and reached a hand for Checa.

Checa barely had time to shift his hold on Heath to catch him before he fell. "Heath, what's wrong?"

Heath shook his head. "Nothing. I'm fine." He struggled to stand but stumbled. Checa swept him up into his arms and laid him gently on the ground. "It's all right, love. I'm just tired."

"You haven't healed properly since the norrgel-strike. You should be well by now."

Heath shrugged. "I think Jun did something to retard my recovery. It'll take longer, but I'll be fine. I know I will."

Checa regarded him silently. Heath's face was pale and beaded with sweat. The area surrounding his broken collarbone was red and inflamed. This was more than retarded recovery—Heath wasn't healing at all. Checa pressed his forehead against Heath's and mentally traced their Bond-Link.

"No, Checa. Don't do that."

Checa kissed Heath's forehead, then repositioned so their foreheads were connected again. "You're my Bond-Mate now, and I choose to give you my life force." He closed his eyes and willed some of his energy to flow into Heath. In his mind he saw their energies mingle and even out until Heath was healthier than he'd been since the norrgel-strike. Checa felt weak but not unwell. "I call that a win," he whispered.

"*Checa*," groaned Heath.

Checa shook his head. "You're my home, Heath. My everything. You would do the same for me." He watched acceptance flow over Heath's face; then he pulled him to his feet and they turned to the group of people around them.

Ardelle had her head tilted in the way that always preceded a million questions. Rim pursed his lips, and Checa knew he would be getting a lecture on consequences soon. The others ranging around them showed varying expressions of shock.

Suddenly the stance of Rim's men changed. They stiffened to battle readiness, their gazes no longer on Checa or Heath but angled behind them. Before Checa could ask or turn to see what the problem was, a low, melodious voice spoke from behind him.

"There you are."

He spun around at the words, staring at the huge cream-gold dragon lounging under the trees at the top of the riverbank and sucking on a shard of amber. The leaves on the trees around her trembled.

"It's Kimi! I know it's her," Heath exclaimed, his face lighting with pleasure.

"Are we starting an Adventure now?"

34.
HEADING HOME

"WHAT ARE you doing?" Kimi leaned her head on Checa's shoulder.

She'd been doing it to both Checa and Heath since the first call of "Wings up!" and Checa had to grit his teeth against an angry retort. "We need to move the bodies out of the river and then burn them," he said for the eleventh time.

It was probably the twentieth time, but he only began counting after Kimi returned from chasing the norrgel at midmorning. He dragged the pale, bloated body he'd retrieved away from the water and toward the sad pile they'd created a few hundred feet away.

They moved their way downstream as they cleared each section of the river, and would soon have to make a second pile of bodies. Across the river, Rim had already moved his team farther down the bank. By sunset the sky would be full of smoke and the horizon dotted with the orange glow of funeral fires. The sickly sweet smell of burning flesh filled the air.

"This isn't an Adventure," said Kimi.

"No, it isn't," said Heath. "We need to do this first so that no one gets sick."

"Why would they get sick?"

"When people die, their bodies slowly disintegrate and go back into the land. We can get sick if we're near the bodies as they do that or if the bodies are in the water."

"Why don't you let the norrgel eat them? It would be quicker."

"The more the norrgel eat, the more norrgel there are," said Heath.

Checa moved into the water again and grabbed another body snagged on a broken tree trunk, happy to leave Heath to explain things to Kimi.

"Yes, I know," said Kimi with a hum. "That's a good thing."

Checa groaned. How did Heath expect them to work with dragons when the creatures didn't have even a basic understanding of how things worked? "If norrgel came here now, they wouldn't just eat the bodies we've pulled out of the river. They'd attack us as well."

Kimi nudged his shoulder again—*Why is she always touching me?*—and followed him to where he dropped the body with the others. "I'll protect you," she said. "I'll keep you both safe until your dragon arrives."

"My dragon?" Checa glared at Kimi. "I don't have a dragon."

Kimi hummed again. "Many dragons have hatched. We won't fly until yours arrives."

"You've been flying every day." Checa looked over the landscape dotted with hundreds of dragons in jeweled colors.

A number of them followed one person they'd chosen as their own; the rest said they would find their partners soon. Kimi was the only one who split her attention between two people: Heath and Checa. Ardelle's dragon, whose name was Dawn, was a brilliant green. Rim had a russet dragon called Bran following him around.

"That's practice." Kimi looked to the east. "And for food."

Checa returned to the river. While he'd been distracted by Kimi, others had cleared that section of water of both bodies and debris, and the water now flowed freely down the river to the next blockage. As he walked toward it, he thought about what Kimi said about allowing the norrgel to feast on the dead. In a macabre way, it made sense, except for the inevitable increase in the birds' population. There were too many norrgel to comfortably coexist as it was. In fact, Checa had thought they'd be quickly overrun by norrgel, with so much food around, but they hadn't seen any except in the distance.

"Why is more norrgel a good thing?" he asked.

Before Kimi responded, a cry went up. "Wings up!"

Fluttering filled the air as all the dragons stirred and flexed their wings.

Checa added, "Where do you go in the mornings? You always fly away when the call goes up."

Kimi shuffled on her broad flat feet, obviously eager to take to the air. She raised her snout and sniffed. "Lunch."

She took a few fumbling steps and leaped into the air, her body immediately streamlining and becoming graceful. One after the other, the rest of the dragons lifted off. They all headed to the west, directly toward the norrgel making their way back to their nests in the mountains to the east.

"She said 'breakfast' this morning before she flew away," said Heath. "What are they eating?"

Checa smiled, everything suddenly clicking into place. "I think they may be eating the norrgel."

"They're poisonous."

"How many norrgel have we seen today?"

"I've heard a lot, but none have come close."

Checa took a moment to survey the area around them. "We need to get all the bodies and other debris out of the river, but I think we can leave the rest to the norrgel. Do you think the dragons will leave the norrgel alone long enough for them to clean this up?"

"Checa!" Heath protested, but then went silent.

"We have to do something. We can't take the time to do a proper cleanup here when we know the full force of the Yeudan are on their way. We need to prepare for battle."

Heath flapped his hands at Checa. "I'm thinking," he said as he stared over the littered landscape. His eyes glazed as they always did when he sank into a vision. "Deep in the Pass of Nines, in dark of night, hand on right, against all odds feeling might, silver strength and black arise."

After a few seconds' silence, Heath turned to Checa. "Some of Rim's soldiers can finish here if we're leaving it to the norrgel. We need to go to the Pass of Nines." He strode to the river, calling for Kimi. By the time he'd finished washing, Kimi had landed on the bank.

"Kimi, will some of the dragons stay here and protect some soldiers from the norrgel?"

Kimi's eyes swirled as she regarded Heath. "Can they eat them afterward?"

"They can't eat the soldiers."

Kimi darted back a few fumbling steps. "They wouldn't eat their own!" she said indignantly. She raised her snout and trumpeted, then looked back at Heath. "They'll help clean the river. After their feast they'll find us."

"They're going to eat the norrgel, right? Not the soldiers or dead people?"

"They're dead. What do they know?" Kimi's golden eyes glowed orange for a second before she trumpeted again.

Within seconds all the other dragons joined in.

"I think they're laughing," said Checa. "I bet that was a joke."

Heath scowled, but Checa wasn't sure if it was because he thought the joke was in poor taste or because he didn't think of it first.

They left at midnight after getting some rest and ensuring those staying behind knew what to do. Checa was glad to be leaving the area with its increasing stench of death. He'd expected Rim to remain to lead his people with the cleanup and their own preparations for the expected Yeudan invasion, since his people were closest to the Yeudan lands and would bear the brunt of the invasion, but Rim marched with them. None of them had questioned it when Rim ran to catch up to Checa and Heath. Ardelle joined them about ten minutes later after having a heated discussion with the last of her personal guard. She appeared pleased with the outcome, and she was alone when she joined them.

Above them three dragons circled lazily in the still air, and Checa tried not to resent the fact that the others all had their own dragon and he didn't.

"Kimi said it won't be long and your dragon will come," said Heath as they jogged side by side. They'd remained in human form because Heath still wasn't well enough to change to cat form without a lengthy recovery period, and it was the only form Rim and Ardelle had. That luxury of a healing shift had to wait until they reported to the Matriarch.

"I don't see how. There's only one underground section between here and the Pass of Nines, and there's no amber there."

"There's no amber through the Pass of Nines to the village either, but I know that's where we need to go."

Checa shrugged, forcing a nonchalance he didn't feel. Inside him was a child who wanted what the other kids had. He'd never had that, and had ridiculously thought that now he was the Silver and a hero of the ages, he'd be just like everyone else. "Ridiculous," he muttered.

"What is?" asked Heath.

Checa didn't want to tell Heath, but they were Bonded now. Heath would know what was bothering him as soon as he let his guard down. Bonding with Heath was everything Checa had ever wanted; he wasn't going to start the rest of his life keeping secrets from him, especially a secret like this. The only reason he didn't want to share was because it made him look like a jealous child.

"I wanted a dragon of my own." He clamped his jaw tight. Now he definitely sounded like a sullen child.

Heath chuckled and patted Checa's shoulder. "Kimi said your dragon was coming. You just have to be patient."

Checa shook his head. "The dragons are hatched, and the ones who could have partners have already paired with someone. If one of the unpaired ones wanted me, he'd be here with me now." He ran his fingers through the tail of Heath's hair, needing the slight contact to ground him. "It's okay. I have everything I never thought I'd have. I don't need a dragon as well."

"Do you need a hug, Checa?" Ardelle teased from behind them.

Checa ran through all the rude gestures he could make and dismissed each one. Regardless of what else Ardelle was or what they'd gone through together, she was still a princess, and he couldn't be that rude to a princess.

"We bonded with them at the same time," said Rim to Ardelle. "I know it's fading, but it's still obvious that Checa isn't the hugging type."

Heath winked at Checa as Ardelle and Rim passed them, arguing over whether or not Checa liked to be hugged.

"Yeah, I know. Get over myself."

"You'll get your dragon, Checa."

They jogged in silence until the sky lightened. As the breeze lifted, Kimi landed in front of them in a flurry of dust and stinging pebbles. Ahead of them the other dragons landed to confer with Rim and Ardelle.

"It's sunrise," said Kimi.

"Do you really eat the norrgel, Kimi?" Heath leaned against her portly belly and scratched under her chin. Kimi purred and moved her head until Heath scratched her jaw.

"Yummy."

Bran trumpeted as the edge of the sun cleared the mountaintop and the norrgel took flight.

"Breakfast." Kimi flapped her wings, stirring up dust and gravel, then leaped into the sky.

The other dragons followed.

THEY REACHED the foothills to the Pass of Nines in midafternoon. The dragons had spent the day circling overhead. The norrgel hunted somewhere else.

"What's it to be?" asked Checa as he surveyed the sky. "It'll be twilight before we reach the entrance, but there's no real cover here to camp unless we trust the dragons."

"We should keep moving," said Heath. "The quicker we get through the pass, the quicker we can make our report to Mother and start preparing for the Yeudan."

"Agreed," said Rim.

Beside him, Ardelle nodded. "I don't think we should split up yet. The same reasons we had for coming here together hold. We'll all need to go to Hawkesby, as well as to Rim's stronghold."

Checa scowled but stayed silent. He wasn't sure exactly how a significant separation would manifest, but the discomfort he'd felt when Rim and Ardelle had first crossed the river to work from the other side still ached in his joints. The Bond he shared with Heath was strong, but the connection to Rim and Ardelle had weakened through the day. At the beginning the Bonds between the four had been thick blankets wrapped around them. Now only the Bond with Heath was that encompassing, bright and warm. Checa's link to Rim and Ardelle was a thin tensile rope, securely fastened. Until it became more elastic or even broke, they'd have to stay together.

They climbed steadily through the scrubby brush and over haphazard rock structures. The vegetation thickened as they climbed higher, the area having resisted any attempts at farming. As they clambered over rocks and pushed their way between and beneath trunks and branches, the sun swung low to their right and a breeze sprung up. The sharp pine scents swept over them as the breeze curled around the bushes and swirled its way along the hillside. Halfway up, the direction of the wind changed again and brought with it a rancid odor Checa recognized from the Exile caverns.

"Alert!" Heath called just as a group of Yeudan bounded from behind the rocks and attacked.

A low growl punctuated the clash of steel against rocks as the Yeudan slashed with swords and knives. Checa swung toward the sound and ducked as Jun, in cat form, sailed through the air. As Checa turned to the new threat, he changed, his body popping and stretching into his cat form. The speed of his change made him dizzy for only an instant, but it was long enough for Jun to pounce.

They landed heavily on the rocky ground and rolled, slipping downhill as they went. Checa sank his teeth into Jun's shoulder and wrapped his arms and legs firmly around the black cat's body, digging his claws in to hold Jun close. Jun's claws sank into Checa's back, too, digging so deep Checa groaned with the pain. They continued to roll.

Jun's head hit a rock and bobbed just enough for Checa to move and bite down on Jun's throat. Checa shook his head, tearing through muscle and tendon and artery. His mouth filled with hot blood and he shook his head again. Beneath him, Jun went limp. Checa held on, waiting for the pulse of blood into his mouth to slow and stop, and then he stepped back.

Jun's lifeless paws fell from his back, the claws retracted in death. Checa's back hurt, each puncture stung. His legs ached; his head ached. He staggered a few paces and shook his head, spraying blood around.

Sounds of battle punctuated Checa's harsh breaths and he looked uphill to see a Yeudan warrior sail through the air, arms reaching for a handhold that wasn't there. He landed across a rock and didn't move. Checa shook himself again, then loped up the hill to join the others. As he climbed, he leaped over the inert bodies of Yeudan; he counted ten before he found Heath.

Checa's change from cat to human was just as swift as it had been the other way, and he staggered to where Heath lay, still and barely breathing. "What happened?"

Heath opened his eyes and smiled. "I'm fine, Checa. Just need to sleep for a—"

"Heath!" Checa landed on his knees and reached for him. Checa's heart pounded; his eyes burned. Heath couldn't die now. Not now. Not ever. He couldn't.

Rim tugged on Checa's shoulder, but Checa shrugged him off. "Let Ardelle in, Checa. She can help him."

"Where's he injured?" Checa patted his hands all over Heath, looking for a wound. "Where is it?"

"I don't think he's injured at all," said Ardelle beside him. "He was fine, just fighting slower. Then, when all the Yeudan were gone, he just… collapsed." She insinuated herself under Checa's arm so she was kneeling between him and Heath. "Move back a bit so I can work." She lay her hands on Heath's chest and began to hum.

Rim's hand slipped around Checa's bicep and drew him to his feet. "Let Ardelle see what she can do, Checa. She's our best hope."

"He hasn't been healing," said Checa. At any other time, he'd be embarrassed at the tremble in his voice, but… this was Heath. "I think Jun did something."

"I don't know how you usually recover from norrgel attacks," said Rim. "We don't." He looked into the distance. "Not ever."

"It's not working," said Ardelle, her voice strained. Sweat dribbled down her neck.

"What do you mean it's not working?" Checa wanted to scream. He wanted to drag her away from Heath and cover him with his body, protect him from anything that could hurt him, but it was too late. Heath was already hurt. He was dying. Checa could feel it in their Bond.

"Checa, come and help. You're Bonded. Use the Bond to heal him." Ardelle leaned over Heath, the strain carving deep lines on her forehead and beside her mouth.

Checa dropped to his knees on the other side of Heath. He lowered his head until their foreheads touched. "Don't leave me, Heath," he whispered. "Be well again." He traced the lines of the Bond and prepared to give Heath his life force. All of it. He'd rather die himself than have Heath die.

"Wait!" Rim knelt behind Ardelle. "Let me try something." Checa looked up, ready to dismiss Rim, to deny him the right to help. "He has time. I think this will work."

Checa sat back.

"Keep working, Ardelle," said Rim as he put his hands on her shoulders.

"What are you going to do?" she asked, but she kept her focus on Heath.

"When we were…. During the Warrior Pledge, I felt like I was part of you all, as if I could change, not just to a woman but to anything. That I could change others too." Rim leaned forward, pressing his forehead against the back of Ardelle's head.

Checa growled, "Heath doesn't need to change. He's perfect as he is."

Rim closed his eyes. "He's ill. That needs to change. If I can replicate the Change I did before, I can tap into Ardelle's healing and magnify it."

Checa watched as Rim's features changed as they had when he changed from female to male during the Warrior Pledge. As Rim had then, he again morphed through a stage where he looked almost Mafdeti as well as human. This time he stayed in the Mafdeti form but without the fangs. Checa's breath caught. Ardelle's features were changing too, becoming more Mafdeti than Descendant. When she hummed, it became a purr.

Beside him, Heath stirred. Checa looked down to see Heath's beautiful brown eyes, streaked with silver, looking up at him. "Stay with me, Heath," he whispered as he leaned down and pressed a kiss to his forehead. "Don't leave me."

Heath smiled and closed his eyes again, but Checa could see his chest rising and falling in an even pattern. He could feel Heath growing stronger through their Bond. Tears slid down Checa's cheeks, the first tears he'd shed since his first time with the Bastard.

Deep in the Pass of Nines
In dark of night, hand on right
Against all odds feeling might
Silver strength and black arise

—extract from the Warrior Pledge, prophecy of the Mafdeti, natural inhabitants of the planet Thalazar.

35.
THE BLACK RISES

THEY FOUND a shallow cave to sleep in that night, halfway up to the entrance to the Pass of Nines.

Checa carried Heath and laid him on a sandy patch that Rim had cleared of pebbles and debris. The three dragons crammed inside after them and curled up on top of each other in a pile that blocked most of the entrance and kept the warmth inside. Bran and Dawn watched as Rim and Ardelle settled for sleep, then closed their eyes. Kimi stretched her neck so that her snout pressed up against Heath's knee. Her golden eyes spun with worried whirls of gray.

"Change now," Checa told Heath once he'd made him as comfortable as he could. "You'll recover quicker in cat form."

"We have to report to the Matriarch."

Heath rested his head against Checa's chest, an exhausted but welcome weight.

"She can wait an extra day or two. You're more important." Checa shifted so Heath could lean against him more comfortably.

"You're only saying that because we're Bonded." Heath's voice was full of wistfulness and uncertainty.

"That's right," replied Checa. Heath's expression changed, becoming wary and sad. "Don't forget why we Bonded, Heath," Checa whispered.

"We Bonded because of the Warrior Pledge."

Checa cupped Heath's cheek and turned his head to make sure his lover looked directly at him. "The Warrior Pledge was the catalyst for a spontaneous Bond. That never happens." He ran his fingers through Heath's hair, untangling the knots. "We Bonded because we love each other." He pressed his lips to Heath's, a kiss of promise, of forever. "I love you and can't imagine living my life without you." He lifted back to see Heath's beatific smile. "Now change so you can heal the rest of the way. I'll be right here when you wake up."

By the time the sound of Heath's sigh had faded, Checa held a large, heavy, sleeping cat with tortoiseshell fur. He gently lowered Heath to the ground and curled around him. His hand pressed against Heath's chest so he could feel Heath's heartbeat, steady and strong. He rested his head behind Heath's and listened to his Bond-Mate breathe.

Checa's stomach rumbled, but he ignored it. He would eat in the morning, after Heath woke.

Heath slept the whole of the next day. Checa shifted so he leaned against a large black rock, his leg pressed reassuringly against Heath's back. From that position he could watch over Heath and see the cave entrance.

Rim and Ardelle hunted for food, then cooked while Checa watched Heath sleep. Checa ran his hand through Heath's fur over and over again. The light entering the cave gradually changed from bright white to slanted yellow. The evening breeze brought with it a change in Heath's condition. His exhales became purrs. Checa rested more comfortably against the warm rock at his back and closed his eyes, finally able to sleep.

"I'M HUNGRY."

Checa opened his eyes to find Heath in human form, grinning at him. Checa returned the smile before checking on Rim and Ardelle. They were on the other side of a small fire, asleep. Next to the fire, keeping warm on flat stones, was a haunch of meat. Beyond the entrance the sky was a bluish purple. Sunset. The dragons were gone.

Norrgel screeched, the sound cut off abruptly. Checa eyed the meat by the fire warily.

"They wouldn't give us norrgel to eat," said Heath. "Now feed me." He eyed the meat hungrily.

The sound of their voices woke Rim. When he moved, Ardelle also stirred. The four of them ate while they discussed the best time to leave. Checa wanted to stay another day.

"There's no point in staying another day. I'm fine," said Heath. "Whatever you did to heal me worked."

Ardelle blushed, and Rim ran a hand through his fine hair. "I'm not sure exactly what we did," said Rim, "but it worked."

"It looked like you turned into a Mafdeti, just like you changed into a woman, and then you sort of... merged... with Ardelle." Checa had been thinking about it, trying to work out exactly what happened. He'd been so distressed over Heath he hadn't paid much attention, but there was one image stuck in his head. He was sure he hadn't imagined it. "For a split second, you sort of sank into Ardelle, and you both sort of became a different person. Then Heath's breathing changed. When I looked up, you were you again."

Both Rim and Ardelle grew pale as Checa described what they'd done.

"So the Warrior Pledge changed you both." Checa looked at Heath. "You can still feel the sand and water?"

Heath nodded. "I can feel the whole planet too. It began when Ardelle tried to heal me in the cavern where Kimi hatched, but it's sharper now, like it belongs. I've been having strange dreams that make me think I can see the past as well." He frowned. "And maybe the future."

Checa shifted uncomfortably. The rock at his back seemed warmer, almost hot. "So you all have extra abilities after the Warrior Pledge. I don't. I thought I would at least protect you—" He glared at Heath "—but I didn't even do that well. Frankly I don't know why I was needed at all."

"Because silver goes with black," said Kimi from the entrance to the cave. "We won't fly until you do."

Checa waved a dismissive hand. "You've said that before, yet you fly all the time. And what does it matter that silver and black go together? We're not dressing for a ball."

A new, dark voice rumbled from behind Checa. "What's a ball?"

They all jumped to their feet. Checa's claws snicked out. A second later so did Heath's. Checa's rock moved. As it moved, the firelight cast shadows to show that Checa's rock was actually just a small portion of an animal curled up in the back of a cave that was significantly larger than they'd thought. The large black dragon turned ponderously until his head slipped under a wing. Ruby-red eyes swirled at Checa. "Is a ball an Adventure?"

Checa's jaw dropped. Beside him, Heath laughed so hard he fell over.

"Why didn't you let us know you were here?" asked Checa.

The black dragon, Staton, told them he had been waiting in the cave for them since the first earthquake. Checa shivered as Staton's red eyes brushed by him and landed on Heath.

"You were sick." There was a sulky tone to his voice.

Heath sat down beside the fire and reached for the remaining meat being kept warm on stones. "I was unconscious. You're his, right? Not mine? You could have spoken to Checa at any time."

"You're the Silver's Bond-Mate, so you come first. I had to wait." Staton stretched his neck out so he could sniff Heath's food. He drew back sharply. "That's not norrgel."

"We don't eat norrgel," said Checa. "Their meat is poisonous for us."

Staton huffed and his browridges lowered. After a few seconds, his face cleared. "More for us," he said. Outside, Kimi trumpeted. "I'm hungry." Staton moved around the edge of the small cave, avoiding the fire in the middle, and slipped outside. His body filled the cave entrance as he passed through.

"He's huge," exclaimed Heath.

Checa went to the cave entrance and watched the four dragons take off. Staton was easily twice the size of Kimi, who was larger than Bran and Dawn. "He said he hatched when the earthquake happened—the same time as Kimi. How did he get so big so quickly?"

"There's no amber in here," said Rim. "Mostly granite and peridotite. There are scratches in the rock, like teeth marks."

Checa joined Rim at the back of the cave. "He's been eating *granite*?"

Heath joined them. "He might have eaten all the amber and still been hungry."

"He's been hunting norrgel," said Ardelle. "There are bones outside. I think they use the rocks like dessert, or perhaps to clean their teeth, or neutralize the poison."

The cave darkened as the dragons returned. Staton eased his way into the cave. "You could ask me, young one."

Kimi followed him and sidled up beside Heath. "Are they going to argue?"

Heath scratched Kimi's jaw where she liked it. "Why would you think they'd argue?"

"Yours argues about everything," she said.

Checa glared at her. Heath huffed a laugh but tried to suppress it when Checa turned his glare to him.

"You're obviously feeling better, so we can leave now. We'll travel until dawn, then rest while the dragons hunt." Checa strode to the entrance and peered out at the navy sky. "We should be home by the evening of the day after tomorrow."

Staton's glossy black head came to rest on Checa's shoulder, making him jump.

"Why don't we fly?" the dragon asked.

"*You* could fly if you know where you're going. *We* have to walk." Checa climbed over a rock outside the entrance and began climbing up to the Pass of Nines.

"Don't you want to fly with me?"

Checa turned at the dejected tone. "What do you mean 'fly with you'? Heath tried riding Kimi at the river, but she wouldn't let him."

"Of course not," Staton answered indignantly. "*I* wasn't there."

"Are you the only one who can fly with people?"

"No." Checa could hear the word *idiot* echo through that reply. "*You're* the only one who can fly me. If you're in the air, the others will fly too."

"What?" Checa was flabbergasted. "Me?"

Heath laughed. "You wanted to know what your purpose was, Checa. Apparently you're the dragons' king."

"Nonsense," said Staton. "*I'm* the King." He curled the tip of his tail around Checa's waist and lifted him to his back. "*He's* my rider."

Checa gasped as he landed on Staton's back between two large spines at the base of his neck. He adjusted his loincloth, leaving his hands protectively over his dick, as it brushed down the spine in front of him. Staton was huge, much higher off the ground than Checa had thought. He clamped his eyes closed and grasped onto the spine so he didn't fall off. He opened his mouth to protest, but the only sound that came out was a terrified squeak.

Heath cried out in surprise. Checa turned to find Heath sitting atop Kimi, clinging to the spine in front of him and bathed in a silvery light. Heath settled quickly, then grinned.

"Checa! Your eyes," cried Ardelle.

Checa turned to look at her. The light came with him. "Fuck! I'm the light." Beneath him, Staton moved, bunching his hind legs ready to launch himself into the air, and Checa tightened his grip. "Wait! I can't fly. I don't know how."

"Show me the way, Rider." Staton jumped.

The world fell away, within seconds becoming nothing more than a dark shadow beneath them. Checa looked down to see how high they were. Staton dove, following the light. Checa's ass left his seat and his legs flailed behind him, only his grip on Staton's spine kept him on the dragon.

"Fuck!" His heart pounded. His legs bumped along the dragon's flank. His fingers began to slip. He couldn't grip any tighter.

Heath, Rim, and Ardelle screamed as their dragons followed. "*Checa!*"

Checa raised his gaze again, sucking in a deep breath when Staton evened out and flew steadily again. Checa dropped onto Staton's back. He clamped his legs between smaller spines along the sides of the dragon's neck. When he shifted in his seat, he hardly moved. "Show him the way, he said. He'll fucking get us all killed." Checa held his neck stiff, unwilling to risk another dive.

"Which way, Rider?" Staton asked.

"You just keep flying the way you are. Don't veer off course when I look away."

"You only had to tell me," replied Staton sullenly.

Checa moved his head slowly as he surveyed the landscape far ahead. He searched for the landmarks for the Mafdeti stronghold east of the Pass of Nines. Once he'd located the landmarks, he held his head steady. "There." Staton changed course, flying along the line of silver light from Checa's eyes.

Behind them, Checa heard the trumpets of dragons.

"Checa!" Heath called. "They've all joined us!" He laughed. "How amazing is this?"

"Amazing, he says," grumbled Checa. "All he has to do is hold on. I'm the one they're all following. If I look sideways, they'll all fall off and die."

"It will become easier, Rider. We'll grow together." Staton sounded perfectly calm and at peace with himself. "A good leader always cares for those he leads."

After a time, Checa began to relax. As long as he didn't make any sudden moves, this flying thing was okay. He kept his legs tightly gripped around Staton's neck, supporting spines or not, and never once released his tight grip on the spine in front of him.

Anguished grief defeats entire
Crumbling tablet forms of stone
Amidst melted walls of bone
In the sky fly reborn fire

　　　　—extract from the Warrior Pledge, prophecy of the Mafdeti, natural inhabitants of Thalazar.

36.
THE MATRIARCH

THE MEADOW below Checa's lookout looked eerie bathed in silver light. The thick grass was gray and any wildflowers still open without the sun were a wash of pale pastels.

"Take it slowly, Staton. I don't want anyone falling off at this point." *Least of all me.* "I need to check the area, so I'm going to look around. Don't follow the light, okay?"

"But it's dark without your light."

"There's nothing up here, so just fly slowly and in the same direction. I'll be quick."

"I don't like this."

"You'll have to get used to it. I can't go places if I don't check them out first. That's the first rule of warrior safety."

"I'm not a warrior."

"I am, and I'm responsible for keeping everyone safe. If you want me to fly with you, you'll have to become one too. Otherwise, once we're on the ground, you can go your own way, and I'll go mine." Part of Checa hoped Staton would agree to that, but a bigger part hoped he wouldn't. There was no way Heath would let Kimi fly without him now that he'd tried it. Heath's exhilarated laughter had followed him the whole time they'd been in the air.

"I can't leave you! You're the Silver."

"I don't really know what that means, but it doesn't change anything. I need to complete reconnaissance of every area, and I can't do that if you change course every time I look away."

"Are you sure it's necessary?"

"Very sure."

"You won't let me fly into anything and get hurt?"

"I just told you I keep everyone with me safe. That includes you and all the other dragons." Checa had no idea how he was going to keep that promise, but he didn't question that was the way it would be. Before they'd left home, he'd been in charge of the guard. Now he was in charge of over two hundred dragons as well.

Staton huffed.

Okay, Checa was in charge of one dragon who was in charge of the other two hundred dragons. Same thing.

"Okay," said Staton. "I'll keep flying, but don't let me run into anything."

"I'll be quick." Checa did a quick sweep of the meadow and surrounding lands. Movement at the edge of the meadow caught his attention. "Is there any way I can turn this bloody light off?" he asked. "There's something down there, and I don't want them to know exactly where we are." It was too late for that, but he could still change course if he could get the damned light in his eyes to turn off.

"You want to turn the light off? But it's dark."

A laugh burst from Checa, but he hastily swallowed it. Surely the king of the dragons wasn't scared of the dark. A flash of bright yellow on the ground caught his eye. "It's okay," he said. "I know who that is."

He watched as the warriors behind the Matriarch fanned out. An image of her having a quiet word with Jun while Checa spoke to Seer Pretto flashed in his mind. It might have meant nothing, but Checa would never take chances with Heath's life. "Stay alert," he called to Heath, Rim, and Ardelle.

"Checa?" Heath urged Kimi to fly closer to Staton. "That's my mother."

"I know."

Heath regarded Checa solemnly for a few seconds before nodding. "You're wrong," he said. "But I'll stay alert."

"Staton, did you see where all the warriors on the ground went?"

"Of course. With your light, I can see everything."

"Can you get some of the other dragons to land behind those warriors and make sure they don't attack us."

"Are they the enemy? Do you want me to fry them? I can do that."

Staton's body trembled beneath Checa, but he couldn't tell if it was in excitement or trepidation. "No, just watch them. Knock them over if they try anything."

"How will I tell if they're trying anything? What does 'anything' look like?"

Checa sighed. He was expecting too much. "Never mind. Can you let me know if they move from their positions? Just do that." Checa narrowed his field of focus, picking out the best landing place. "Let's land down there."

Staton banked sharply and dove for the ground. Checa tried to tighten his grip even though his hands were already clasped around the spine as tightly as they could be.

Staton landed on the ground at a run, his thick hind legs whirling. Checa felt the back end of the dragon bounce a couple of times and had visions of him tipping over the way Kimi had done when she first learned to fly. He leaned back, which brought Staton's head up. He slowed immediately. Finally they were still, the dragon's sides concertinaing as his breath billowed from him. Checa panted too. Sweat ran down his back and chest and a fine tremble began throughout his body. He'd survived. They'd landed and he wasn't dead. He stayed where he was on the dragon's back while he caught his breath and calmed down enough that he would be able to stand without falling over. Around them the other dragons came in to land, with varying degrees of success.

"We're going to have to work on that," said Checa as he observed a few of Rim's soldiers come unseated and fly over their dragons' necks.

"What is the meaning of this?" The Matriarch's voice was as strident as Checa had ever heard it. He had to give Heath's mother credit. She had balls. It was the middle of the night and she'd come into a field to confront a large band of dragons and riders, and instead of hiding or setting up an ambush, she confronted them directly. He might not like her a whole lot, but he respected every yellow-clothed inch of her.

"How do I get down, Staton?" he asked as he pulled his legs from their secure hold and pried his fingers off the spine he'd had a death grip on. Staton didn't answer but instead twirled his tail around Checa's waist and lifted him down.

Checa stumbled a step when his feet finally found the ground, but he didn't fall over, regardless of how his knees shook with reaction. As soon as Staton's tail retreated, the light died. Checa blinked against the burn that remained in his eyes but didn't feel any other effects.

In front of him, the Matriarch blinked in the sudden darkness; the blue feathers on the brim of her bowler hat quivered. Checa grinned. He could see clearly, not affected at all by the sudden change in light. Behind him came the sound of people landing suddenly on the ground. Cries of "Hey!" and "You dropped me!" and pained grunts filled the air as the dragons divested themselves of their burdens.

So Kimi was right.

They'd only ride when Checa did. If he was off his dragon, they all were.

He waited a few moments until Heath's mother stopped blinking so rapidly and the scowl returned to her face.

"Matriarch," he said, projecting his voice so those closest would also hear. "The Warrior Pledge is complete. The dragons have arisen, and we return victorious." The last bit wasn't quite truthful, but it sounded good.

"What are you talking about?" The Matriarch stood stiffly in front of Checa. "You were supposed to die during the Pledge." Her gaze slipped around him, her eyes widening as she took in the large dragons all around them.

"What are you talking about, Mother?" Heath came up beside Checa and slipped his hand around Checa's elbow. "Thanks to a traitor, I nearly died. Checa saved me."

It was Rim and Ardelle who'd saved Heath, not Checa. They would have to have a serious talk about the way Heath accredited Checa with things he didn't do.

"They only did the physical part. You did the rest," whispered Heath.

"Bloody Bond," groused Checa.

"*Bond*?" screeched the Matriarch. "You can't be Bonded. I won't allow it."

She raised her hand, an action Checa had seen regularly for years when the Matriarch was about to bring judgment down on a criminal.

Heath stepped in front of Checa. "You can't break the Bond, Mother. It was a spontaneous Bond during the Warrior Pledge. It's fated. Unbreakable."

Checa's chest ached at the pride in Heath's voice. He stepped up beside him and threaded his fingers between Heath's, holding his mate's hand. "We'll face this together, Heath. Just like everything else from now on."

Heath beamed at him.

"Why don't you give us a brief report," said Seer Pretto as he stepped up beside the Matriarch. "You can give us a more detailed report tomorrow after you've eaten and rested."

"We began our journey with the search for the Changeling and the Pure," began Checa.

"And we found Rim and Princess Ardelle," interrupted Heath. "They're Descendants, but you wouldn't believe what they can do. Jun tried to get the Exiles and Yeudan to kill us, but Checa marked him and then killed him when Jun tried to kill me."

Checa closed his mouth and let Heath tell his story. It wasn't going to be brief. It wasn't going to be in chronological order either, but apparently the whole tale was going to be told right now.

"You forgot the earthquake," said Ardelle behind him. Heath turned to glare at her, then went on with his telling, weaving in the events of the earthquake.

Checa grinned and stepped back, gesturing at Rim. "Can you get someone to build a few fires here? We're going to be a while."

Rim regarded Heath and Ardelle silently, then nodded. "I'll organize some food too. Everyone's hungry."

Checa lifted a hand toward a warrior in his guard. After a few brief instructions, the man left, taking half a dozen others with him. "They'll bring something back."

Meanwhile, Heath was still talking. The Matriarch's eyes seemed glazed, but Seer Pretto appeared fascinated, often interrupting with questions. Ardelle had joined in, inserting her own observances with Heath's.

In short order chairs were brought for the Matriarch and her entourage, as well as Heath and Ardelle. Checa refused a chair, preferring to oversee the actions of his guard. Several sought him out and apologized, insisting they arrived in numbers because they'd thought someone had gone rogue. Checa dismissed them without reprimand. The Matriarch was their supreme commander. They would do as she said. He regarded his Bond-Mate and mother-in-law again. She wouldn't be saying much for a while, not with the speed Heath was still talking, but Checa would need to find out if she still wanted him dead.

The sky was lightening by the time Heath wound down. Between bites of strawberry cheesecake, he completed his tale with the way he and Checa had bonded spontaneously and could hear each other's thoughts.

After an interminable amount of time in silence, the Matriarch stood and walked to Checa. Behind her, Heath gasped but subsided when Checa held his hand up.

"I don't approve of this Bonding," she said. "You're nothing but a gutter rat. What makes you think you're worthy of my son?"

Checa bowed to the Matriarch, then stood tall. He had nothing to be ashamed of. Not anymore. "I am unworthy, Matriarch, a lowborn warrior." She smirked and opened her mouth to speak. Checa spoke quickly, raising his voice so her personal guard also heard. "However, unworthy or not, Heath and I are fated mates." Heath slipped around his mother to stand beside Checa. His arm brushed Checa's and Checa drew warmth and courage from it. "If we hadn't bonded during the Warrior Pledge, we would be bonding now. I'll never deny him." He wrapped his hand in Heath's. "It was our Bond that brought the dragons back to us." He straightened his spine. "I am Silver Shining from Rock, Rider of the Dragon King."

Around them two hundred dragons trumpeted their agreement.

Checa, still holding Heath's hand, turned to Rim and Ardelle. "Let's ride."

They strode to their dragons, Heath separating from Checa as they approached Staton. Kimi wound her tail around Heath's waist at the same time as Staton lifted Checa. When Checa landed in his place on Staton's back, silver light blazed from his eyes. Staton jumped into the air as soon as Checa looked at the sky. Checa fumbled his hold but finally clamped his legs in place and settled into his seat. Around him all the other dragons lifted off and followed, automatically fanning out in formation behind Staton.

Ally, enemy, colleague, friend
Charged protection overhead
Loss and laughter make your bed
Support and help always lend

      —extract from the Warrior Pledge, prophecy of the Mafdeti, natural inhabitants of Thalazar.

37.
THE NEW REALITY

THE VIEW from Checa's favorite spot remained unchanged. He leaned against the flat rock and looked out on his land. The breeze dropped as the sun peeped between the mountain peaks. A shiver ran across Checa's shoulders. To the north the line of trees that followed the river were little more than stalks, the tips of every branch brushed with verdant growth. Even this high up, he could see the blush of green that flowed over the valley from the Crystal River, outward in every direction. Within a couple of years, the valley would once again flourish.

Checa looked away from the valley and into the gradually lightening skies. He wanted to forget the Yeudan had plans to enslave them all, forget the demands for surrender Ardelle's family had received. He wanted life to go back the way it was, where all they had to worry about were the cougars and the occasional Exile raiding their winter stores.

In the ravine below, a flock of birds took flight, just as they did the morning his quest began. Heath still couldn't move anywhere quietly when he was excited. Okay, he didn't want *everything* to go back to the way it had been. Checa shook his head and huffed. Heath would never change, and he was perfect the way he was.

"Checa!"

His name carried in the still air and an involuntary smile overtook him at the joy he could hear in Heath's voice. Checa's muscles twitched, wanting to move, to go down and meet his Bond-Mate, see the morning light grow as it reached his features. Just that one sight would be enough to make his day complete, even if it hadn't yet begun.

That had always been the case, but it was more so now. Checa left the valley to its own future for the time being. The invasion would happen when it did, whether they were ready or not. Meanwhile he had Heath barreling up the mountain. He could feel Heath's excitement through the Bond but deliberately muted it. If Heath wanted him to know what the dragons had accomplished, through the Bond, he'd have told him as soon as it happened. He would let Heath tell him in his own way and in his own time.

Checa counted his breaths to ensure he remained in his place, sitting cross-legged on the platform. What had once been a test of his control had become a pleasure-filled anticipation.

"Checa!"

Heath was closer now, the sound of him crashing through the brush a rhythmic counterpoint to his rapid footfalls on the leaf-strewn ground. Checa allowed his posture to relax and straightened his legs. He shifted forward so his balance would be stronger, allowed the new smile on his face to widen, and waited.

Heath burst into the clearing like a new spring bloom, ran to the platform, and launched himself at Checa. Checa braced his legs against the edge of the platform, opened his arms, and caught the younger man as he flew to him. They landed flat on the platform, the bare skin of their chests fusing, Heath's sweat soaking into Checa's chest hair and becoming his own. Checa *oomph*ed as his head hit the stone and Heath's landing knocked the air from his lungs, but he didn't release his hold.

Once, this was all he had of Heath. Now, it was everything.

"Didn't you hear me coming?" asked Heath with a laugh.

"The Imperials in Hawkesby could have heard you. If you expect to be a warrior, you'll need to do better than that."

"Pfft," scoffed Heath. "I can move quietly if I want to." He wriggled on top of Checa, entangling their legs. "And I *am* a warrior."

In the back of Checa's mind, Heath's thoughts rumbled quietly. Over the last several weeks, the Bonds with Rim and Ardelle had weakened. They could still call to them whenever they wanted, but the effort had to be conscious. His Bond with Heath, though, was something entirely different. With every day they spent together, their Mate-Bond strengthened. It truly was one of the spontaneous Bondings the records told were destined for true and perfect loves. Heath had been right all along.

"Of course I was. I'm a Seer." Heath bounced up to sit squarely over Checa's groin. Checa groaned at the change in pressure and punched his hips up. Their loincloths prevented direct contact, but Heath's every ridge and bulge pressed against Checa and raised his interest.

Heath grinned at him. "Oh yes, that… but you've got to hear this. It's happening, Checa! It's finally happening." Heath bounced in his excitement.

Checa grabbed Heath's hips and lifted him off, ignoring the pouting scowl he got in return. Once they were both seated on the platform, dawn washing its gentle light over them, the soft breeze returned, he raised an eyebrow and waited.

"I can't even get angry at you for that anymore." Heath pouted. "Irritating man."

"Tell me what's happening this time, and how it's going to impact on the coming invasion."

"It's Kimi! She's done it."

Heath had taken over the training of the dragons, with Staton's help, while Checa continued to train the men and women. Kimi was the only golden one. Heath was convinced she would be Queen once she was full-grown.

"You'll have to be more specific than that, sweet one." Heath melted over Checa again, like he did every time Checa used an endearment, pushing them down so they could lie tangled together. "Last time you were trying to get her to do five different things at once."

"And she can do it! Just now she managed to move a rock with her mind, and she tipped a glass of water over, and disrupted the electrical circuits, and blew fire. All at once!"

Checa grinned at Heath's excitement. Staton had been able to do all that, and more, from the first day. "What about the sonic roar?"

Heath shook his head. "Not so close to people or settlements. I'll take her out into the desert to test that. Did you know they prefer to eat the norrgel roasted?"

The swift change of topic didn't faze Checa. "When did you find that out?"

"When Kimi blew her fire! Three norrgel got caught in the flame and the dragons went crazy. I thought we were going to have a riot."

"Hmph. No wonder norrgel numbers are so large. The dragons are their natural predator. Without them there was nothing to keep their numbers in check."

"Exactly. So with the dragons here now, the land will gradually become balanced again."

"Except for the fact the Yeudan are invading."

"We'll win. We have the dragons with us now, and Rim and Ardelle. It'll work, Checa. We'll train with them and keep our land safe so we can all live in harmony, you'll see."

Checa drew him close, burying his face into the soft tortoiseshell hair and breathing in the wild mint and sage scent of him. "I love you," he whispered. "I love that you always see the good in everything. I love that you don't give up. I love that you love me and trust me to love you back."

"Silly," said Heath, finally not squirming in excitement. "You're all I ever wanted, Checa. You're the best of me."

Checa didn't argue or deny it. He'd learned over the last few weeks that doing so would get him pushed into a blackberry bush—or a blow job, depending on Heath's mood. He was tempted to see which it would be this morning but decided there were pleasanter ways to get a blow job than hurting Heath. He trailed his fingertips over his Bonding mark on Heath's arm. Heath shivered every time Checa touched the brand.

"I want you," Checa whispered. "I want you to take me here, in the place we met. Right here where I first realized I loved you with every piece of me."

Heath squirmed and groaned. "Stop talking and roll over, before you find out how many blackberry bushes there are on this mountain."

Checa laughed, a full-bellied laugh that rang out over the valley. It was the sound that made his men stop their training and stare at him until he scowled at them again. It was the sound that made Heath's mother scowl until she smiled. He rolled Heath over until they were pressed together from chest to knee. He cradled Heath's face and kissed his forehead, smiling as Heath huffed and squirmed in an effort to bring Checa's kiss to his lips.

"You are everything to me, Heath." Checa lifted back so he could gaze into Heath's earth-colored eyes. Seeing those wonderful eyes, forever marked with Checa's colors, gave him the courage to say what he knew Heath needed to hear. It didn't stop his heart pounding or his hands trembling, but he could say the words. "I would die if I lost you, and not just because of our Bonding. You say I'm the best of you, but you are the best of me. You're everything that makes me the man I am. I never want to find out what I'd become without you."

"You won't have to," whispered Heath, his eyes suspiciously bright in the growing light.

"There's a war coming, and we aren't going to be ready."

"We'll be ready, Rider." After his last growth spurt, Staton's voice had deepened to a soul-rumbling baritone. He now stood taller than three houses from Rim's valley. He'd cleared a section of the forest adjacent to Checa's clearing so that he, too, could enjoy the sunrises.

"Listen to your dragon, Checa. We're more ready than you think we are, especially now Kimi and some others have learned to spit fire. And the war doesn't matter, not like you do. It took me most of my life to convince you that you belong with me. There's no way you're getting out of it now. You're stuck with me until we're both so ancient we totter instead of walk and I have to climb on top of you and yell in your ear to make you hear what I'm saying—not that I don't have to do that sometimes now."

Checa's throat tightened and his eyes stung. Instead of replying, he lowered his head and took Heath's mouth in a scorching kiss, letting him know without words how much he wanted just that. He could almost see them in his mind, sitting in front of a warm fire with a woven rug over their legs, as close as they could get, holding on to each other. Forever.

"That's what I want too, Checa. That's what we'll have."

Heath spoke through their Bond-Link as he flung his arms around Checa's neck and wriggled to open his legs, giving Checa room to settle on top and rub their groins together.

Checa wanted to lift up and strip them both. He wanted to sink deeply onto Heath's body and feel the way Heath burned as he took Checa and consumed him.

"We will, Checa. But right now, stay with me," Heath whispered through his mind, and it was enough.

They continued to kiss, giving and taking. Their hips undulated in the same rhythm and their cocks pressed hard and urgent against each other, the thin loincloths easily moved out of the way. In the kiss, Checa tasted joy and future, and some wild mint that Heath must have picked and eaten on his way up the mountain. He lifted his head, his breath harsh in his ears, his eyes blurred with rising passion, and below him was Heath. His Heath, with his head thrown back, ecstasy on his face, and Checa's name on his lips as he came.

Warmth skittered over Checa's skin as his orgasm peaked and exploded through him. He lowered his head and breathed in the heady scent of his Bond-Mate. Mint, sage, sex, and love all rolled together inside him and came back out with a word. "Mine," he whispered.

"Mine," Heath returned.

E E MONTGOMERY wants the world to be a better place, with equality and acceptance for all. Her philosophy is: We can't change the world but we can change our small part of it and, in that way, influence the whole. Writing stories that show people finding their own "better place" is part of E E Montgomery's own small contribution.

Thankfully, there's never a shortage of inspiration for stories that show people growing in their acceptance and love of themselves and others. A dedicated people-watcher, E E finds stories everywhere. In a cafe, a cemetery, a book on space exploration, or on the news, there'll be a story of personal growth, love, and unconditional acceptance there somewhere.

E-mail: eemontgomery11@gmail.com
Blog: eemontgomery.blogspot.com
Twitter: @EEMontgomery1
Website: www.eemontgomery.com

Ordinary People

E E Montgomery

When Queensland Police Force Constable James Laramee raids a hotel room, he finds Vinnie Canterbury on top of a naked, dead man, covered in blood. Vinnie promptly vomits all over James's shoes.

Thanks to a cocktail of horse sedatives and Hendra vaccine, Vinnie's memories of his ordeal are fractured. Finding the culprits and the reasons behind his abduction will be a challenge. With his apartment trashed, his building set on fire, and his clothes, phone and wallet gone, Vinnie needs a place to stay. To his surprise, James not only takes him in, but also lets him cry on his shoulder. It must be true love. Vinnie has plans for his future with James all mapped out, and he hopes he can get James on the same page.

THE PLANET WHISPERER

E E MONTGOMERY

Jonah Starovski, a Planet Whisperer, harnesses the energy surrounding dead planets and redirects it into new growth. Abandoned by the man who bought him from a brothel sixteen years ago, Jonah flounders in a world he's ill equipped to deal with. He must accept the help of a stranger in order to rebuild his life.

First Lieutenant Marcus Davis volunteers as Jonah's assistant without realizing the terraforming process requires Jonah's sexual release. Balanced on the knife-edge of fear and ambition, Marcus is faced with his mother's machinations and threats to his career. Marcus's parents bring their illegal scientific experiments to the planets Jonah is terraforming just as Marcus learns to accept himself and his feelings for Jonah. At the same time, Jonah's past catches up to him, putting them both in danger.

Jonah and Marcus must trust in each other to put a stop to the illegal activities, rescue an endangered animal, and create the future they both want—a future they can share.

www.dreamspinnerpress.com

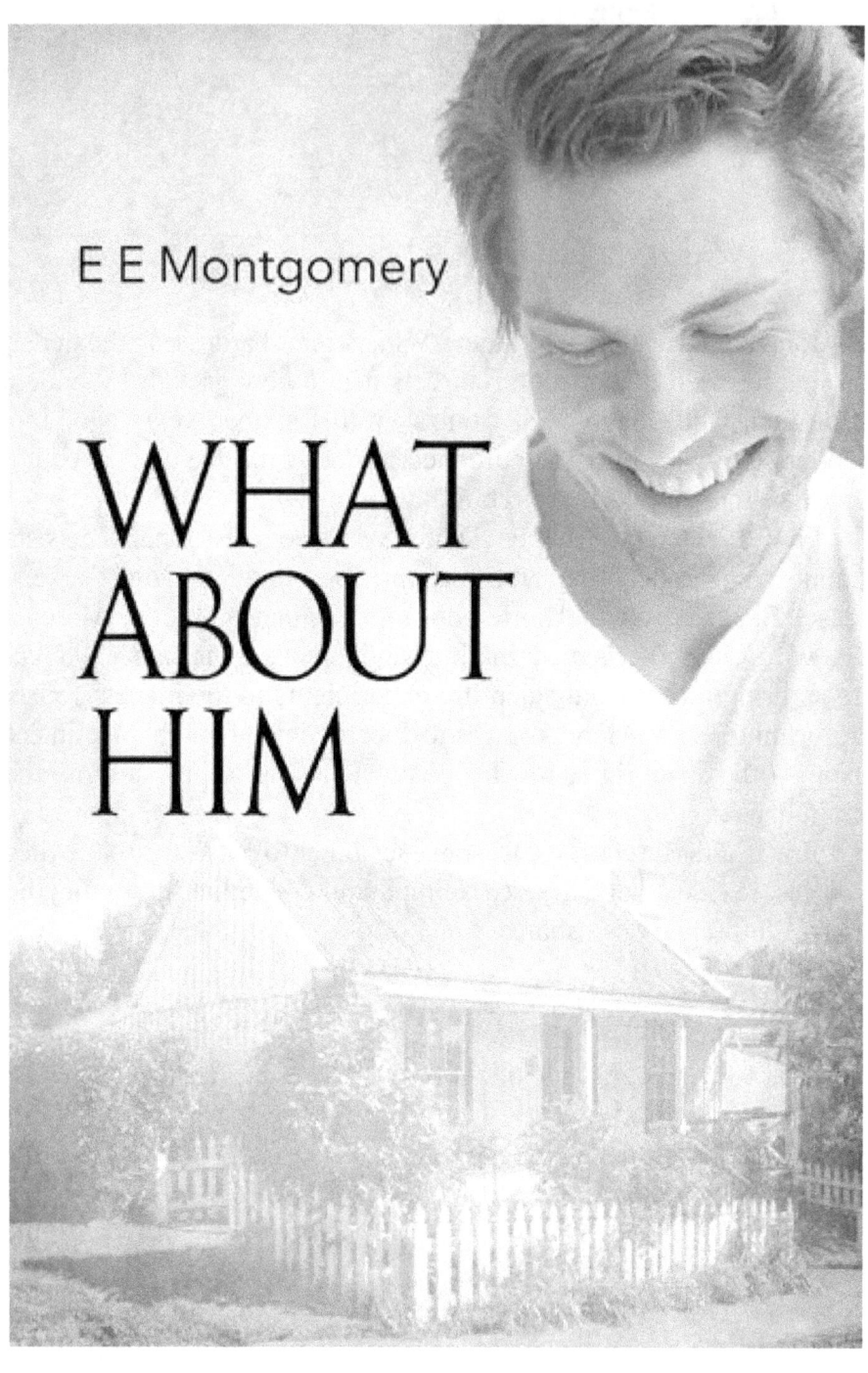

E E Montgomery

WHAT ABOUT HIM

There's a snake in Aidan's bed, but it's not the kind he wants. A nest of snakes under his house heralds the kind of disruption that Aidan has been trying to avoid all his life and turns him into a hysterical mess. First he sleeps with his best friend, Baxter. Until their one-night-stand, Aidan was happy with his life and their friendship. Now he's lonely and craves a relationship Baxter doesn't want.

Then Aidan meets Detective Sam Walters while consulting on a murder investigation and his dreams are suddenly invaded by a man who makes Aidan want to strip faster than an attack by green ants. Too bad Sam is straight.

When snakes take over Aidan's home and a gorgeous snake catcher comes to his rescue, Aidan's confusion is complete. To add to the mess Aidan's life has become, a man ends up dead on his living room floor, Baxter confesses to his murder, and calm, cheerful Sam yells at Aidan. It's enough to make a quiet professor of sociology prefer the snakes.

www.dreamspinnerpress.com

www.ingramcontent.com/pod-product-compliance
Lightning Source LLC
Chambersburg PA
CBHW051528260626
47170CB00003B/831